Lisa Marie Rice

ELLORA'S CAVE
ROMANTICA PUBLISHING

What the critics are saying...

&

A Winner "Maybe I'm prejudiced because "the beauty and the beast" is my favourite plot - but I just loved this book. The love scenes are masterly written and burning hot. The suspense keeps everything fluid without suffocating the love story. The book is not a page turner; it is a breathless-no-eat-no-drink-until-finished-page-turner. Lisa Marie Rice doesn't have to hide behind S. Brockmann or L. Howard. This is, by far, the best e-book I've read in a long time." ~ *Cupid's Library Reviews*

"Gripping, sensual and engaging, *Midnight Angel* is one of those books that you won't be able to put down until you're done." ~ *Fallen Angels Reviews*

"This book was so great I couldn't put it down! I loved the first two in this series, but they seem to get better and better with each and every book. If you have not read this book or the other two in this series, then run and get them now, you will not be sorry." ~ *Enchanted Romance Reviews*

"Midnight Angel...Lisa Marie Rice's mega-hot Midnight series. The plot moves quickly...as to the sex, it was explosive, as we have come to expect from Lisa Marie Rice's pen. Midnight Angel is a must read for those of you following the series, and if you have not tried it yet, what are you waiting for? Ms. Rice is in my author auto-buy list for a reason, and I am gladly adding her latest offering to my keeper shelf." ~ *Just Erotic Romance Reviews*

An Ellora's Cave Romantica Publication

www.ellorascave.com

Midnight Angel

ISBN 1419953842, 9781419953842
ALL RIGHTS RESERVED.
Midnight Angel Copyright © 2005 Lisa Marie Rice
Edited by Kelli Kwiatkowski
Cover art by Syneca

This book printed in the U.S.A. by Jasmine-Jade Enterprises, LLC.

Electronic book Publication August 2005
Trade paperback Publication December 2006

Excerpt from *Midnight Man* Copyright © Lisa Marie Rice 2003

Content Advisory:

S – ENSUOUS
E – ROTIC
X – TREME

Ellora's Cave Publishing offers three levels of Romantica™ reading entertainment: S (S-ensuous), E (E-rotic), and X (X-treme).

The following material contains graphic sexual content meant for mature readers. This story has been rated S-ensuous.

S-*ensuous* love scenes are explicit and leave nothing to the imagination.

E-*rotic* love scenes are explicit, leave nothing to the imagination, and are high in volume per the overall word count. E-rated titles might contain material that some readers find objectionable—in other words, almost anything goes, sexually. E-rated titles are the most graphic titles we carry in terms of both sexual language and descriptiveness in these works of literature.

X-*treme* titles differ from E-rated titles only in plot premise and storyline execution. Stories designated with the letter X tend to contain difficult or controversial subject matter not for the faint of heart.

Also by Lisa Marie Rice

&

Christmas Angel
Midnight Man
Midnight Run
Port of Paradise
Woman on the Run

About the Author

&

Lisa Marie Rice is eternally 30 years old and will never age. She is tall and willowy and beautiful. Men drop at her feet like ripe pears. She has won every major book prize in the world. She is a black belt with advanced degrees in archaeology, nuclear physics, and Tibetan literature. She is a concert pianist. Did I mention the Nobel?

Of course, Lisa Marie Rice is a virtual woman and exists only at the keyboard when writing erotic romance. She disappears when the monitor winks off.

Lisa welcomes comments from readers. You can find her website and email address on her author bio page at www.ellorascave.com.

Tell Us What You Think

We appreciate hearing reader opinions about our books. You can email us at Comments@EllorasCave.com.

MIDNIGHT ANGEL

ഔ

Trademarks Acknowledgement

Chapter One
Portland, Oregon
Saturday, January 15th
Parks Foundation
Opening ceremony of the "Jewels of the Czars" show

∞

"Fucking monkey suit," John Huntington muttered darkly, pulling at the black tie of his tuxedo.

Senior Chief Douglas Kowalski, USN (Ret.), watched his former commanding officer and current business partner shift his shoulders uneasily. Kowalski wasn't a smiler, hadn't smiled in years, but he was tempted. He and John, aka Midnight Man, had spent damn near twenty years together under the most intensely dangerous, life-threatening conditions on the face of the planet. They'd swum underwater close to the Arctic Circle, they'd spent four months under the Afghani desert sun without shelter, they'd once been trapped under fire behind enemy lines without food and with a gallon of water between them for a week.

On the scale of discomfort, a too-tight tuxedo just didn't register. And here big bad Midnight Man was growling with disgust over some cloth.

"Fucking tuxedo. Why the fuck I—" Midnight cut himself off suddenly, silenced by the sharp little elbow of his wife jabbing him in the side.

John's chest was as heavily ribbed with rock-hard muscle as Kowalski's own. There was absolutely nothing his beautiful wife Suzanne could do to hurt him. Midnight probably hadn't even really felt her dig. Still, Kowalski had learned in the two weeks in which he'd been John's business partner that Suzanne could hurt Midnight in ways that weren't physical.

For some reason known only to Midnight himself, he'd given his new bride enormous power over his life. What she wanted, she got. She wanted him to shut up so he did, pressing his lips together.

"Hush, John!" she hissed, looking around, a bright fake smile on her lovely face. She could have spared herself the worry. There wasn't anyone around to hear John bitch. Everyone was too busy oohing and aahing over the gazillion-carat Russian jewelry exhibit. Suzanne had designed the display cases, and Kowalski had to admit they were stunning. This evening was a professional triumph for her. Pleasing Suzanne was the only thing on this Earth that would make John squeeze himself into a tux.

Kowalski turned to look at the glittering assembly gathered in the magnificent turn of the century mansion housing the Parks Foundation. He moved easily in his own tux. He could never have found a rented tux to fit him. He had two of them, made to measure for his tall, big-shouldered frame by a tailor in Singapore. Both of them were beautifully tailored, with extra room under the left armpit for his sidearm.

The one he'd had to leave at home.

The only discomfort Kowalski felt was the lack of a weapon, something Suzanne had insisted on. John had blown up at that, but Suzanne had put her pretty little size six foot down and to Kowalski's amazement, John had caved in. The first time ever he'd seen Midnight back down on *anything*.

An unarmed Midnight was bad enough, but then Kowalski had nearly had a cow when Suzanne insisted that *he* go unarmed to the jewelry show opening, as well. She'd been specific about it, too, which meant she was learning fast from being married to John.

No weapons. None. No guns, pistols, rifles, machine guns, automatic pistols. No K-Bar. No Emerson CQC6 folder. No other kind of knife. No garrotte, no taser. Nothing. Zip. Nada. Both of them.

Kowalski had looked in shock at Midnight. *John* was the shackled one, the one who had to please his wife. Why the fuck was Kowalski supposed to disarm? Why couldn't he carry, like he always did? Kowalski hated being unarmed. It made him feel naked. He wasn't the one in love with Suzanne, so why did *he* have to put with this crap?

Kowalski had opened his mouth to say "sorry no, absolutely not, no fucking way," when he'd caught a glimpse of Midnight's pleading eyes.

John had saved his life three times and had taken a bullet for him in '98. Kowalski had saved *his* hide, too. The ties between them ran too strong and too deep for Kowalski to say no.

So with a silent sigh, he'd turned to Suzanne Huntington to say, through clenched jaws, that of course he'd be happy to come to the opening of the Russian jewelry show. Unarmed. He'd rather have had all his teeth pulled out without benefit of anesthesia.

Still, John looked grateful. This classified as a lifesaving IOU. Kowalski would collect, eventually.

Suzanne looked up at him. "Are you having a good time, Douglas?"

Kowalski almost didn't answer until he realized she'd addressed him. Douglas. Nobody on this earth called him Douglas, except Suzanne. He'd been Kowalski, or Senior Chief, so long he'd almost forgotten his first name.

"Absolutely," he lied. "Fascinating show. Wonderful jewels. Great jewel cases."

"Well, I'm so happy you're enjoying yourself. Now please tell my husband to have a good time."

Kowalski turned to John. "Have a good time, Midnight. That's an order."

John scowled.

Suzanne beamed at Kowalski, pleased. He nearly looked around to see who she was smiling at.

Beautiful women didn't smile at Kowalski. They barely managed to look at his face without flinching. He couldn't blame them—he knew what he looked like. He looked like a thug. A hard, dangerous and mean thug. Probably because he *was* hard, dangerous and mean.

It was unusual for a woman to smile at him. It was a credit to Suzanne that she managed to pretend he looked like everyone else.

He didn't. He'd been born big, with rough, irregular features and his life hadn't softened them any. His nose had been broken four times. Ten years ago, a tango had gone for him with a knife. The fucker had managed to slice his jaw open before Kowalski took him down. That had been seven hundred miles from the nearest hospital and he'd had to sew the gaping slash himself using his knife blade as a mirror. The Navy had offered to pay for plastic surgery to repair the damage, but he'd refused.

Kowalski didn't give a shit about the scar—the tougher he looked, the better—and, anyway, he'd had enough of blades.

Kowalski had spent his entire adult life being a hard man training other hard men to face death. You don't do that by smiling gently with a twinkle in your eye. He'd schooled his face to harshness until it was second nature.

It felt strange to smile, so he never did.

"Suzanne! There you are! What a triumph, my dear!" Two willowy men in white tuxes drifted up in a cloud of scent and kissed the air around Suzanne's cheeks. They were supremely elegant and overly thin. They gave Midnight an approving up and down glance, looked at Kowalski, shuddered, and turned back to Suzanne.

"Darling," one of the men said, as he took Suzanne's arm. "What brilliant design solutions you came up with. I tell you Nomura is insanely jealous." He pursed his lips. "Serves the old bitch right, he wanted to use glass and brass. Wouldn't have been the same at all. Let's have lunch with him next week and gloat. Come to think of it, let's make the rounds right now and gloat. So delicious."

John's scowl deepened. Not even he could be jealous of the two men. It was clear that neither man had ever fucked a woman, nor had they ever wanted to. Kowalski figured John frowned on principle, at the thought of not having Suzanne within touching range.

"My dear Suzanne," the other man said, "I just saw Marvin Lipinsky walk in. You must come with us right now and meet him. Do you know he's thinking of exhibiting his pre-Columbian collection next year? I'll bet you'd do a brilliant job on the displays. Come, darling. Let's go."

John moved forward. "No," he said. "I don't—"

Suzanne put her hand on his arm. She stretched up on her toes and kissed him softly on the cheek. "Be right back," she said, while her blue-gray eyes clearly flashed, *you stay put now. And behave.*

Her look at Kowalski was clear, too. *And you—you make sure he stays here and doesn't embarrass me.*

With a last, smiling glance back at her husband, Suzanne was led away.

John watched her, grim-faced.

A waiter in formal evening wear came to a halt in front of them. He was holding a solid silver salver with crystal flutes of champagne. John grabbed one and downed it in a gulp.

The waiter hesitated a moment before offering it to Kowalski. Kowalski clenched his back teeth. He knew he looked like a rough laborer, someone more comfortable on a construction crew or on a loading dock than in an elegant setting. But shit, he was clearly a guest, all suited up nicely for the occasion in a tux and everything.

Kowalski lifted a glass from the tray and sipped. The champagne was superb, dry and crisp. He looked over at John, who was watching his wife making the rounds, and took another sip. Might as well take your pleasures where you can find them. John sure as hell wasn't going to be entertaining company.

"Must be hard being married," Kowalski said finally.

"Nah," John replied, never taking his eyes off his wife. "Being married's fucking easy. Shit, I had no idea or maybe I would have gotten married sooner. I live in a gorgeous house. My wife designed a fantastic office for me. I get regular, delicious meals. Regular sex. Clothes washed and ironed. No, it's not being married that's hard." John swung his head around to look at Kowalski. Kowalski saw something in John's face he never ever thought he'd see. Fear. Vulnerability. "It's being in love that's really hard. It sucks."

This was a completely new John Huntington and it scared the shit out of Kowalski.

"Almost lost her, Senior Chief," John whispered, and his face looked haggard.

Kowalski answered sharply. "*Almost* don't cut it, Midnight. You know that." Their mantra in the Teams. *Almost* never cut it. You can't *almost* hit your target. You can't *almost* catch your tango. Nobody cares that you *almost* died when you make it back to base under fire—you go right back out into the field. *Almost* didn't exist.

John's jaw muscles jumped.

Kowalski had arrived in Portland a little over two weeks ago as John's new business partner. He was just in time to take over Midnight's business, when John went AWOL. The woman Midnight had fallen in love with had been under threat of death by Paul Carson, a businessman with organized crime connections. She had witnessed Carson murdering his wife. Carson had been gunning for her before she could testify at the arraignment.

When Midnight disappeared, Kowalski had filled in for him, getting a crash course in running a fast-growing security company.

16

Midnight reappeared four days later, when the FBI released Suzanne from protective custody. The danger was over. Paul Carson had had a fatal accident. His forehead had accidentally run into a .50 caliber sniper rifle bullet.

The next day, John married Suzanne. Kowalski still found it so weird that his friend was married. Warriors don't marry. They have sex, sure, to blow off steam. Soldiers fuck a lot—as often as they can, actually, because they are under a lot of stress and sometimes they have to go for months without. Sex is a guaranteed muscle relaxant. But love? Marriage? Not in the handbook.

He shook his head and sipped some more.

Suzanne made her way back to them, swaying gracefully over the marble tiles. John straightened, watching her every step of the way.

Dispassionately, Kowalski had to admit that Suzanne Huntington was a truly extraordinarily beautiful woman.

She smiled up at her husband. "There John, you see? That wasn't so bad, was it? I went away, spoke with some people about business, made some contacts and came back." She shook her head, dark blonde hair belling about her face. "Nothing to it."

John's scowl deepened and Suzanne laughed. Another beautiful woman came up behind her. Dark-haired, slender, dressed in a strapless red gown.

Kowalski knew who she was. Claire Parks, heiress to the Parks fortune and tonight's hostess. Very rich. Stinking rich, in fact. She was also the woman who'd been heavily messing with the mind of John's friend in Portland, Police Lieutenant Bud Morrison.

She'd broken off her engagement to Bud a few days after Kowalski arrived, and Bud had been a walking corpse ever since.

Kowalski finished his flute and plucked another off a passing waiter's tray. *Women.* He'd seen strong men, men not even the most highly trained enemy could take down, come completely undone for a woman. Simply go up in smoke. To a very real degree, women, particularly beautiful women, scared the shit out of him. He'd never been brought low by one, though. Thank God he was immune.

Claire Parks put her hands on Suzanne's shoulders. "Hi," she murmured, pressing her cheek to Suzanne's. "Congratulations on the display cases. They're gorgeous. Almost as beautiful as the jewels themselves."

"Thanks, sweetie." Suzanne smiled and swirled a lock of dark blonde hair behind an ear. "I worked hard on them. It was a pleasure and a privilege. The jewels are truly exquisite."

Smiling, Claire Parks looked around then froze when she saw Kowalski. She stared at him with a mixture of curiosity and horror, then looked away. Suzanne saw her glance and sighed. "Claire," she said with a forced smile, "I'd like to introduce you to Senior Chief Douglas Kowalski. He's John's new partner."

Claire Parks' thoughts might as well have been broadcast in flashing lights for all to see. *He* was John's new partner? This huge, fearsome bruiser, who looked like a contract killer in a tux? Kowalski could easily read what Claire Parks was thinking—Suzanne had to live where she'd see *him* all the time? Poor, poor Suzanne.

John's company, Alpha Security International, was based in one half of a restored factory in a bad part of town. Suzanne had done a fabulous job restoring the building, and being in a rough part of town suited the nature of his—their—business. The hitch was that she and John lived in the other half of the factory.

Pretty Miss Parks did her duty. She didn't shiver and she didn't recoil. She'd been taught her manners. She held her hand out, looked up at his face, made eye contact for a nanosecond, then her gaze skittered to a point somewhere past his right shoulder.

"Senior Chief Kowalski." Her lips turned up at the corners. It couldn't be called a smile, just a slight baring of teeth. "N-nice to m-meet you."

Shit. He made her stammer and she couldn't even bring herself to look him full in the face. She held her hand out gingerly. It trembled slightly. What the fuck did she think? That he ate female human hands for dinner?

Kowalski *hated* this. He hated being made to feel like a freakin' animal in a zoo. It had happened all his life, and was why he steered clear of civilians.

Coming here tonight had been a mistake, one he wouldn't make again. He'd had enough. He was going to shake hands with Claire Parks, make his excuses to John and his wife, get into his SUV and go home.

Maybe he needed to get laid. Maybe he could call that woman he'd picked up in Pearl last week and fucked. Charlene something.

Shit, no. She'd freaked him out. She kept asking for rougher sex, until he was sure he was hurting her. He'd pulled out at the end without coming. That was when she hinted that she'd like to be tied up and fucked even harder. He outweighed the woman by at least one-hundred and twenty pounds. He knew he looked scary, and in many ways he was, but he could never hurt a woman, not in any way. It was only when he saw the feverish, bright gleam in her eyes that he realized maybe Charlene *wanted* to be hurt. She got off on having sex with someone she considered violent. Like a drug, she was hooked on dangerous sex.

No, no sex tonight. Besides Suzanne—who was, of course, off limits—Ms. Freaky was the only woman he knew in Portland, anyway. He'd just go home and listen to that new Norah Jones album. That was it—settle down on his couch with the whiskey bottle close, listen to that smoky voice curl around him and get drunk. It was the closest he'd ever get in this lifetime to a beautiful woman.

But first he had to get through the next couple of minutes.

"Ma'am," he said. He took Claire Parks' hand in his for just four seconds. Kowalski had big, strong hands. He'd learned long ago how not to hurt with them. He squeezed gently, carefully. He chose his words, one by one, to be as unthreatening as possible. "My pleasure. This is a very beautiful building. My compliments on the show."

He had an unusually deep voice and he saw her eyes widen at the sound of it. Claire Parks' hand trembled in his, and he refrained from sighing and rolling his eyes as he let go. For the millionth time, Kowalski was glad he never dated ladies. The women he fucked didn't mind what he looked like. They just wanted their sex, hard and long. Exactly what he could give them. It worked out fine, just as long as neither party expected anything more.

It was then he heard The Voice. An angel's voice, beamed straight down from heaven.

Chapter Two
Portland, Oregon
Saturday, January 15th
Spring Harbor Psychiatric Institute and Correctional
Facility

෩

They were playing that song, *her* song, somewhere in the building. Someone in the place was playing *that song*. Corey Sanderson couldn't stand it.

That summer, we loved...

So trite, so old-fashioned, no backbeat, just the melody. That trilling voice, like something out of the nineteenth century.

Ack. Total shit.

No wonder the bitch's sales plummeted. Why hadn't she listened to him? He'd been positioning her for the big-time. It had all been in place—first the *Today* show and then the spread in *Vanity Fair*, with artistic nude photographs taken by Richard North, the celebrity photographer, no less. That had been a real coup. It had taken him weeks to set it up. And when he announced it to her, the little cunt refused. Flat-out refused. Refused *him!* No one said no to Corey Sanderson, no one.

She'd done it cool as you please, too, just before she'd cancelled the concert in San Diego. The one where he'd hired the backup hip-hop band. He'd invested a lot in the bitch, pulled in a lot of favors. Favors that hadn't been easy to call in, either, because it had been...a while since he'd been at the top of his game. Nothing serious, just a few little setbacks, but the music business moved fast, and was unforgiving. People were starting to speak of him in the past tense and that was intolerable. Corey Sanderson was The Man. Always had been. Always would be. And no Irish bitch would ever change that.

He'd chosen her as his comeback vehicle and instead of being grateful, she'd simply…refused. It was amazing to him, still. He could just picture her that evening, in his penthouse with the sky-high mortgage her disastrous tour should have lifted. When she'd asked for an appointment, he'd been sure it was to apologize. To promise to do better, to offer a blowjob in atonement. He'd accept them all. She was a pretty thing and he'd been trying to get her in his bed for a year. So he was fully prepared to forgive her and fuck her. And then she'd shown up with her father—her father!—to break her contract.

Was it any wonder he'd lost control?

She'd deserved everything she got, the bitch. A broken jaw and being blinded were just punishments, especially since he'd had to sell the penthouse to pay his lawyer.

Still, it was worth selling the penthouse, the condo in Aspen and the Mercedes to pay Edwin Gossett, attorney-at-law—the man who'd kept him out of jail. Sanderson had spent all of two weeks in the penitentiary before Gossett had managed to convince the judge and jury he needed psychiatric care. He shuddered violently. He could never go back to jail. His skin crawled at the thought.

No, he could stand it here for the next few years. He was Dr. Serena Childers' pet patient, and was allowed his music and his books and his special food. Serena was the director of the institute, and she was half in love with him. Here he'd stay—unless the Irish bitch recovered her memory, and then he was in deep shit.

That summer…

His head throbbed when he heard her voice. Allegra Ennis, the woman he'd planned to turn into the most famous singer in America and who'd turned her back on him. And who was responsible for his fall from grace.

The music drifted in from somewhere down the hall. Maybe one of the guards had turned on a radio. Tuned into one of those shitty local stations, the kind that played old singles sandwiched between dog food commercials. What other kind of station would be playing her?

That summer, so long ago...

Shaking with rage, Sanderson looked around for something to make noise with. Sanderson picked up his slippers and flung them against the door. They hit with a dull thud.

That summer, winter was far away...

Books! Two heavy paperbacks and a hardback. Sanderson threw them at the door. They made satisfactory sounds. The hardback's spine cracked and it landed on the floor like a wounded bird.

How could we know summer would never come again...

That bitch! Warbling away, like some little lowlife Irish nightingale. He'd done everything in his power to make her voice modern, but nothing had worked. She'd been so hard to train. Resisting, always resisting. Little cunt never knew what was good for her.

The door opened and Alvin looked in.

"Mr. Sanderson? Do you need anything?" Alvin walked in, voice and demeanor respectful.

Fuck yes, he should be respectful. Alvin knew who he was, what he could do for him.

Alvin was too tall with too-red hair, a lanky Howdy Doody-like figure with no voice, no musical sense at all. But he wanted to become a star, and Sanderson had promised him that he'd make it happen.

In return, Sanderson wanted Allegra Ennis dead.

"Alvin, get me a tape recorder." Sanderson smiled up at Alvin, finding his height ridiculous, hating his stupid freckled face. "We're starting tomorrow. When it's done, I'm contacting some people I know in California. We'll start with a demo tape you'll make."

Alvin's ugly face lit up as he ran to get a tape recorder. Sanderson knew exactly what was going through Alvin's head. He had visions of fancy cars and fancy women—fuckable women, vying to jump into his bed—his photograph in all the gossip magazines, the mansion with the pool. He was going to be a *star*.

Alvin was breathless when he came back, putting a cheap recorder in Sanderson's hands. Sanderson turned it over, considering. It was crap, but it could certainly record a voice accurately. It was enough.

"That's fine, Alvin, you can go now." He needed to concentrate for the next bit. "In half an hour bring Dr. Childers in here. And don't be surprised by what you see."

"Yes, sir." Alvin disappeared. He'd get Serena and it would start. All Alvin had to do was drive Allegra Ennis insane and then kill her, making it look like suicide. Sanderson knew it would never be traced to him.

Allegra was a dead woman walking.

Kowalski was taller than anyone else, so he got a clear view.

A redheaded woman on a raised dais. A beautiful redhead in a gauzy, green formal gown, playing a harp. With a voice like an angel.

He'd never heard anything like it. The voice vied with the harp for purity. He'd never heard the song before, but the melody, the rhythm of it, settled into his brain as if he'd been primed for it all his life. As if there was a place in his head waiting just for that one song.

Something about a summer. A lost summer and a lost love. The melody was haunting, sinking into the bones through skin and muscle. His entire being vibrated with the notes. In a lifetime of listening to music, Kowalski had never heard anything half as beautiful.

The singer was beautiful, too. Not in the way Suzanne or Claire Parks were. In a different way. Better way. She shimmered on the stage, as if she were half of this world and half not. Her pale skin glowed as if lit from within, like a pearl underwater.

He would have believed it if someone had said she really was an angel. It wouldn't take much persuading, with that voice soaring majestically. But she was a flesh and blood woman. The long auburn hair rippled glossily down her back, shifting as she played, fingers floating gracefully over the strings. Her eyes were closed as she finished the song, leaning close into the harp as if it were a lover. Her voice died to a whisper, one last silvery glissando of notes from the harp rising in the air. She leaned for a moment with her forehead against the rim of the harp, then lifted her head and opened her eyes at the spontaneous applause.

She didn't look at the audience at all. It was as if she were playing for herself as she started a new song, smiling gently, seemingly deep in thought. First a long instrumental introduction, then she started singing. Again it was a song Kowalski had never heard, but it became instantly recognizable, as if it was part of a long-ago memory he'd forgotten until now.

"Cruel Sun." A delicate ballad, a fusion of Celtic music and jazz. The cruelty of the sun, shining down after the death of a loved one. Longing, pain, helpless grief—they were all there, together with the final wry acknowledgement that the sun didn't care. It just kept on cruelly shining.

Kowalski vaguely heard an angry man behind him, arguing. He recognized the voice of John's friend Bud, fighting with Claire. He wanted to tell them to shut the fuck up, but to do that he'd have to turn around. He didn't want to miss a second of the music coming from this extraordinary woman.

The songs continued, one after another. He couldn't believe he'd never heard them before, never heard of the singer. He hadn't the faintest idea who she was, but he knew that he was in the presence of a world-class talent. He'd heard Pavarotti live, and this was an experience just as incredible as that had been. Like touching divinity.

Kowalski drifted closer to the stage, annoyed at the people around him. To hell with them all, with their sharp clothes and sharp voices, sometimes drowning the singer out. They'd started again with their stupid chatter, as if what they were hearing was background music, white noise. Muzak for jewelry exhibits. They were listening to pure magic and were too fucking stupid to realize it.

The singer didn't care. She didn't even seem to notice. She was singing to and for herself. She never looked around at the audience, trying to make eye contact. Half the time, her eyes were closed as she concentrated on the song, fingers flying over the chords of the harp, voice true and pure.

Kowalski hated the crowd, wishing they would all just *go away* so he could enjoy her all by himself. He bumped against the edge of the stage, as close as he could get to her.

Christ she was lovely. It wasn't just the voice, though it would still be exquisite even if she had seven chins and hairs on every one.

She didn't have seven chins though, she just had the one chin. A very pretty one, too, with nary a hair. Everything about her was pure magic, perfect and delicate. She had the true coloring of a redhead, without the freckles. The emerald-green floor-length gown was elegant but modest. The skin that showed was pale and creamy, the perfect features of the face almost devoid of makeup, accented by her dark auburn eyebrows. Even seated he could tell she wasn't very tall, but she was long-limbed, with a long, slender neck. When she turned her head slightly toward him, he almost gasped. Her up-tilted eyes were a stunning shade of dark green—the green of stormy oceans, of late spring meadows.

Kowalski couldn't drag his eyes away from her.

After seven songs, the singer leaned back in the pretty little gilt chair she'd been perched on, dropping her hands in her lap. The set was over. The listeners clapped politely and immediately headed for the buffet, which had been set up in the back of the hall on long trestle tables while she'd been singing. They streamed toward the food in chattering groups of threes and fours.

Assholes, Kowalski thought. They were in the presence of musical genius and all they could think about was free chow.

For the first time, Kowalski noticed Suzanne and John standing by the dais. Suzanne walked up the four steps of the dais and glided over the stage to the singer, putting a hand on her shoulder. The singer put her hand over Suzanne's and smiled.

Kowalski held his breath for a second, then let it out.

She hadn't smiled until now. She'd been too concentrated on the songs. Her smile was as magical as the music, lighting up her face. Suzanne had her arm around the woman's narrow waist and the two women were walking across the wooden stage. Suzanne whispered something in her ear and the singer nodded. They walked down the stairs together, moving toward Kowalski and John.

Suzanne said something and the woman laughed, the sound light and graceful, a continuation of her music. God, the sound sank straight into Kowalski's bones.

This was, in every way, a woman touched by magic. She and Suzanne were walking toward him and Midnight. Suzanne was a beautiful woman, no doubt about that, but Kowalski didn't even look at her as the two women approached. He couldn't keep his eyes off the singer. Her beauty was more than regular features, good skin, shiny hair. There was a luminosity about her, as if there were a halo around her. An angel.

27

Kowalski nearly snorted at the thoughts going through his head. He needed to get laid soon, with a normal woman this time. Not some S&M freak who wanted bondage and pain.

Halos. Angels. Maybe civilian life was driving him crazy.

Still, there was no doubt about the singer's talent. Kowalski loved music. Every kind. Rock, jazz, classical, opera. Vocal, instrumental. You name it, he'd listen to it. It was going to be a pleasure to compliment this woman on her voice and harp playing.

Suzanne hesitated slightly. She had to pass by him to get to John. She couldn't avoid introducing him to the singer.

"Allegra," Suzanne said, "I'd like to introduce you to John's new partner, Senior Chief Douglas Kowalski. Douglas, meet my friend Allegra. Allegra Ennis."

"Senior Chief Kowalski," she murmured, holding her hand out.

Fuck fuck fuck! The bright, glowing pleasure of her music drained right out of him, leaving his chest feeling empty, hollow. Allegra Ennis was looking straight at his tie. She couldn't even manage to do what Claire Parks had done—a brief meeting of the eyes—before pretending he didn't have a face.

To hell with this. To *hell* with it.

For the first time, Kowalski wondered if he'd manage in the world of civilians. He could never go back. He was retired now. No one in the Navy or any of the armed forces had ever had trouble looking at his face. So okay, he wasn't pretty, but he was fucking good at his job and that was what counted.

He'd been in the Navy all his life, but he wasn't anymore. Was this what was waiting for him out here? Spending the rest of his life with people politely refusing to look at him? Fuck that.

The intense pleasure of Allegra Ennis' music was gone, vanished with the polite, blank look on her face. *O-kay,* he thought. *Compliment her and get the hell out of here.* Maybe tonight he'd polish off the whole fucking bottle of Jim Beam.

"Ms. Ennis," he rumbled as he took her hand. If he had held Claire Parks' hand for four seconds, he'd have to shave it down to three with Allegra Ennis. "You have a lovely voice and the songs were beautiful. Truly exquisite. Please accept my compliments."

Allegra Ennis did something odd. Her head shot back and wobbled briefly as she looked up, trying to focus on him, like a sniper setting up a shot. There was something about her gaze —

And then it hit Kowalski like a body blow.

Allegra Ennis was blind.

Chapter Three

ℰ

"You little bitch, you're finally going to pay for what you did to me."

Smiling, Corey Sanderson switched the recorder off. That was the last of the recordings. So, that was that, it was all in place, the only thing missing was Allegra Ennis' dead body. The only way he could be safe was when she was dead. While she was alive, he could still be put back in prison. If it weren't for Gossett, Sanderson would still be there, in that nightmare of a cesspool.

He could never go back, of course. He wouldn't allow it. He had the brains and the will to make sure life arranged itself around him and his needs. It was no accident that he was the most successful music producer in history—four platinums, seventeen golds, whole music industries springing up around his tastes… Oh, yes, he was a mover and a shaker. A creator, an artist. Penning him up in a prison was obscene. This place— for all its cream walls, Mozart on the loudspeakers and pretty nurses—was bad enough.

He placed the miniature recorder Alvin had procured on his bedside table, an elegant art deco table replacing the ugly plastic…*thing* he'd found upon arriving. Serena was very understanding that a man of his tastes and sensibilities required a better décor than what was normally provided patients, and so Sanderson had his favorite armchair, his own porcelain flatware and silverware, crystal glasses and cashmere robes. No plastic plates and dreary hospital gowns for him. Serena was very good at allowing him what he wanted—no, needed.

Sanderson had always had two great seduction lines in life. One was, "Let's make beautiful music together." Sanderson's evening concerts were buying him very special treatment. Serena was extremely partial to Bach.

He rang the bell by his bed stand and two minutes later, Alvin Mitchell stuck his red head in the door. "Mr. Sanderson?"

"Go get Dr. Childers. It's time."

The other line was, "*Baby, I'll make you a star.*"

Allegra Ennis smiled up at him. A warm, genuine smile. "Senior Chief Kowalski. I'll turn your compliment right back around. You have a magnificent voice yourself." The smile broadened. "A true *basso profondo*. That's very rare. You should be singing Falstaff."

He searched her face. There was nothing there but friendliness and devastating beauty.

"Falstaff is a good role for a bass," he replied. "Or Boris Godunov. I loved Falchinetti as Boris. I heard him last year in New York."

The lovely face brightened. "Yes, indeed. Such a powerful voice. What a privilege it must have been to hear him live." She cocked her head to one side, sightless eyes riveted to his face. He understood that she was listening to his voice as intently as any art expert looked at a painting. "You would have the perfect voice for Hagen. I have Schumacher's recording of the role. And I'll bet you could sing 'Ol' Man River' just like Paul Robeson."

Her hand was like warm silk. He could feel the delicate structure beneath the skin, that magical combination of bones and sinews in the long slender fingers that let her coax such beautiful music from the harp strings. She hadn't withdrawn her hand, so he held it for just a little longer.

"I have Schumacher's CD, too, but I don't sing along." He snorted at the thought of him singing. "I'd love to belt out 'Ol'

Man River', if I could sing, which I can't. You wouldn't want to hear me when I do. I croak in the shower and it's a lucky thing the shower walls aren't glass, otherwise I'd shatter them."

She giggled, the sound liquid silver. "Now, now, Senior Chief Kowalski. That's for high C. You couldn't reach high C, ever." She gently withdrew her hand, sliding it out from his like a long caress. "And anyway, the idea of a note shattering glass is an old wives' tale. Nothing ever shatters when I go up to high C."

"Douglas," he surprised himself by saying. No one on this planet called him Douglas, except Suzanne. But he couldn't let Allegra call him Senior Chief or Mister or even Kowalski. In her mouth it would sound…odd. He was Kowalski or Senior Chief to everyone he knew except Suzanne…and now this woman. "Please call me Douglas."

"Okay, Douglas. And I'm Allegra. So rest easy and take your showers in peace. No matter how badly you sing, you're not going to shatter anything."

Kowalski was vaguely aware of John staring at him in astonishment. Either because he had used his first name or because he knew his opera. John had no idea he loved opera. No one did.

John opened his mouth, no doubt to rib him—Kowalski would never live this down—when a chattering, laughing group of people came up to Suzanne, surrounded her and bore her away. John stiffened and followed right on her heels.

Kowalski was alone with Allegra.

She was smiling up at him, waiting.

He could look at her all he wanted, he realized. It was something he was never able to do with anyone, let alone with beautiful women. If someone like him stared, it was considered harassment or worse. He'd come across as creepy, sick.

Instead, now, he could look his fill. Study her features, expressive of every emotion she was feeling. She had such exquisite coloring, skin the palest ivory, framed by soft, shiny, deep-red hair, undoubtedly natural. God, he could look at her forever, but he didn't dare. Better stick to the music.

"Those songs were truly beautiful. Who wrote them?"

A delightful little blush pinked her cheeks. "Thank you. Actually...um, I did. Most of them, anyway."

"You?" Kowalski stared. Already having that voice and brilliance with a harp was an abundance of musical talent. To be able to compose that kind of music, too... "Do you record? Go on tour?"

"I used to," she said softly, the smile gone. "But after...this," she fluttered her fingers next to her eyes, "I don't any more. I'm only here tonight because Suzanne and Claire insisted. It's the first time I've sung in public since the...accident."

Oh, God. Something tightened in his chest. She'd gone blind as an adult. "When did you lose your sight?" he asked bluntly.

"About five months ago." A veil of sadness passed over her face as she dropped her gaze, the amusement, the liveliness, the vivacity gone. It was as if someone had switched her off. She looked away for a moment.

It took all his self-discipline not to touch her, comfort her. "I'm so very sorry," he said. "It must be terrible to lose your sight."

Allegra turned her head back toward him. She was silent for a long time, lovely face solemn and intent. "Do you know, Douglas," she said softly, "the one good thing being...blind has done, is that it's forced me to concentrate on people's voices. Really, really listen. I've learned how to distinguish when people are telling the truth and when they're spinning their wheels, being polite. I think you really *are* sorry. Thank you very much."

Jesus. What could he say to that? A waiter walked by. "Do you—" he cleared his throat. "Would you like something to drink? Can you drink champagne while performing?"

"Sure an' alcohol never stopped a girl from singing," she replied, an impish gleam in her eyes, pure shamrock in her voice.

"Connemara," Kowalski said. "Eastern part of the county." He'd gone on stealth-training missions in Northern Ireland with the SAS for five years in a row. Whenever he had a free day, he'd gone down into Ireland. "But you haven't lived there for a long time. There's a heavy overlay of American."

Kowalski signaled the passing waiter to bring two flutes of champagne for them. That made three glasses, but it was okay. The flutes were long, narrow and only one-third full. And anyway, he had every intention of sticking around until Allegra Ennis, like Elvis, had left the building. By that time he'd have burned off the alcohol.

"You have a wonderful ear, Douglas. And you're bang on. When my mother died, my father and I moved to Portland. I was ten. When I go back to visit my cousins, though, I slip right into it. You'd think I'd never been away."

"I guess it's the early years that imprint a person. Give me your hand." The waiter was approaching.

Utterly trusting, she held it out to him. He took it just as some fuckhead behind her jostled her. She stumbled forward, startled. Kowalski put an arm around her waist to steady her. He glared fiercely at the man who'd bumped her. The man flinched, raised his hands—*sorry*—and fled.

"You okay?" he asked Allegra. He'd brought their joined hands up to rest against his chest. With his arm around her, they were in an embrace.

"Yes, of course. So sorry," she said breathlessly. "That was clumsy of me."

"No, it wasn't," he answered grimly. "That fu—that idiot pushed you."

She was so soft and warm in his arms. Slender, yet so richly woman. That lustrous spill of auburn hair spread over his arm, catching on his jacket and tickling his hand. Some fragrance, something light and spring-like, rose to his nostrils and he had to stop himself from sniffing deeply, like a dog.

He wanted to just stand there forever, with this woman in his arms. Gritting his teeth against the temptation, he made sure she was steady on her feet, then lifted his arm from her waist. He couldn't just stand there, groping her. Much as he'd like to.

Not to mention the fact that he'd developed a hard-on—a real *hard* hard-on. And if she moved just half an inch closer, she'd feel it.

Kowalski had a great deal of control over his body. He'd spent a lifetime developing it. He could go without water, food, sunlight, sleep or sex for just about as long as he wanted. He *never* had unwanted woodies, especially not in public.

But there it was, total boner, in a room full of at least two hundred people. He could no more have stopped his body's reaction to touching this woman than he could command his heart to stop beating.

He was still holding her hand. With the other he smoothed the tux jacket over his groin, and picked up a flute of champagne from the tray being held patiently by a waiter, whose eyes were studying the ceiling. Kowalski gently placed the glass in her hand, folded Allegra's fingers around the stem and let her hand go. He picked up a flute of champagne for himself, giving the waiter the narrow-eyed stare he gave new recruits. The waiter backed away immediately.

Man, just holding her hand had made the boner swell to painful proportions.

"Do you have your own glass?" she asked, face turned up to his.

"Yeah." Jesus, even her voice turned him on. Light, with that faint note of Ireland in it. It would turn a dead man on, and he wasn't dead. He carefully touched her glass with his. The crystal rang true. "Cheers."

"*Slaintè.*"

"*Fad saol agat.*"

The smile broadened. "Ye've spent some time in Ireland yerself, then."

"Well, of course. Kowalski's a famous Irish name, don't you know?"

"I guess that would be the County Cork Kowalskis, then?"

"The very same." Kowalski had a good ear, and he had the Cork accent down pat.

Allegra laughed and sipped. When she'd finished the glass, she sighed. "I guess I should get back on the stage. I promised Claire a couple more songs. Do you see Claire or Suzanne?"

"I think Claire went off to have a fight with Bud, and Suzanne..." Kowalski looked over the heads of the people in the room. "Suzanne's near the buffet table on the other side of the room talking to some old geezer in a cummerbund."

"Oh." The sound was hollow with disappointment.

"What's the matter? Do you need Suzanne for something? I can always go and—"

"No." She shook her head, frowning. "No, please don't. This is her evening. She needs to mingle. She's the talk of the show, it's going to be great for her design business. She worked so hard on the displays, she deserves to reap the reward."

Allegra was radiating distress. Kowalski couldn't pick up on the reason, but the air around her quivered with unhappiness.

"Allegra? Is there something wrong? You want me to go hunt Claire up?"

"No, no please. Don't bother her. I hope she's making up with Bud. Claire's been so unhappy since they broke up."

Yeah, maybe so, but it was Bud who was walking around with a week-old beard and red-rimmed eyes. Claire looked positively glowing.

"Okay, so you don't want Claire or Suzanne. Tell me what you need. Maybe I can help."

"Douglas..." She reached out, groping until she found his arm and clutched it. Without a word, Kowalski covered her hand with his, waiting for her to speak.

"Tell me, Allegra," he said gently, when she didn't speak.

"I hate this." Her voice was a sudden fierce whisper. Her fingers dug into his forearm. "I *hate* it." She bit her lip, eyes bright with the sheen of tears. Her fingers flexed open under his, then tightened again on his jacket sleeve. He felt her touch in every cell of his body.

"You hate what?" He kept his voice low.

"I'm afraid I—I need your help." She drew in a deep breath. "I can't make it up on the stage by myself. Could you — could you please accompany me?" She averted her face, deeply ashamed.

She was ashamed that she couldn't see. Jesus. His throat tightened.

If she'd only been blind a few months, she couldn't possibly have developed that extra sense blind people seem to develop as compensation for their lost sight. She'd trip over something or fall off the stairs. Hurt herself. God, he couldn't bear even the thought of it.

"Of course I'll accompany you." Kowalski put a finger under her chin and turned her face around. He smoothed the wrinkle between her brows with his thumb. He couldn't stand seeing her pain and frustration for another second. "It would be a pleasure. And that means I can get a front-row seat."

"Silly." She sniffled and gave a half laugh. "There aren't any seats."

"Front-row stand, then. I'll be right here when you finish. That way you don't have to worry about coming back down the stairs again."

Allegra let out a long breath of relief. "Thanks so much. I won't be long. Just a few more songs."

"It doesn't make any difference at all how long you take," he said quietly. "I'm a patient man and I don't have anywhere to go. I'll be here. I'll wait for you. For as long as it takes."

She stopped, face turned up to his. He could feel the intensity with which she listened to him, to his words. To what he meant behind the words. She couldn't see him, but she could sense him.

There was something happening here. He could feel it and so could she. She didn't even pretend she couldn't.

Her hand was still on his sleeve. She nodded, once. "Okay," she whispered.

Okay.

Jesus, yeah. Okay.

Feeling a sudden sunburst of joy in his chest, Kowalski kept her hand on his arm and led her to the stairs. He gave his patented death glare to anyone within twenty feet of them. They took one look at his face and scattered. The crowd parted for them like the Red Sea for Moses. He would have thrown a grenade in front of them to clear her path. They made it to the stairs without incident and he stopped. Obediently, Allegra stopped, too.

"We're at the stairs," Kowalski said quietly. "If you lift your right foot, you'll be on the first stair. There are four of them."

She nodded and he took her up them and walked her to the harp. With a gentle hand to her back, he seated her. She reached out to stroke the smooth curved wood, smiling faintly at the familiar feel of the instrument. "Thanks," she whispered.

"When the set is over, I'll come up on the stage to get you. So don't move, I'll be here. You can count on it."

Allegra slowly turned her head toward him at that, clearly understanding more than just the words. She nodded then turned back to her harp, leaning into it like a child leans into its mother. Kowalski walked back down off the dais to the glittering silvery sound of a glissando at his back. A salute to him.

His cheek muscles moved. It took him a full minute to realize he was smiling.

Alvin had his orders, and they were clear. He could follow orders, yes he could. Of course he could. Anything for Mr. Sanderson, anything.

Mr. Sanderson was going to help him start his music career. Being an orderly, wiping the shit from people's asses and swabbing their vomit off the floor was not for him. Not for long.

Mr. Sanderson had seen that right away. Oh, yeah.

Mr. Sanderson was a legend. *He* could tell Alvin was meant for better things. He already had a plan mapped out to make Alvin a star, but he couldn't do that if he was sent back to prison. No, Mr. Sanderson had to stay at Spring Harbor until he was released in a few years. No way could he help Alvin from jail. The only person who could send Mr. Sanderson back to jail was Allegra Ennis, and Alvin was going to take care of her.

Allegra Ennis was just a little speed bump on the road to his music career—and to stardom.

Alvin loped down the long, antiseptic corridor until he came to Dr. Childers' office. He knocked softly.

"Yes?" Dr. Childers sounded annoyed.

"Dr. Childers...Mr. Sanderson needs...help."

She put down her pen, looking alarmed, and rose. "Help?"

Alvin turned and walked back down the corridor. He could hear Dr. Childers' heels clicking on the slate floor. And he could hear something else, the sounds of destruction, becoming louder as he approached Corey Sanderson's room. Dr. Childers heard too, and made for the room at a trot. Alvin followed behind. He knew what she'd find.

Even knowing, though, he was shocked when Dr. Childers opened the door. In ten minutes, the room had been trashed, the expensive stereo equipment lying smashed on the floor, Mr. Sanderson's china in a thousand shards, CDs lying in broken bits. And Mr. Sanderson...

He was keening, an unholy wail, as he continued his destructive spree. A hospital-issue chair flew against the bulletproof glass of the windows, accompanied by a scream that had Alvin's hair standing on edge.

Dr. Childers closed the door just in time. The sound of another chair smashing against the closed door could be heard in the hallway. "Nurse!" Dr. Childers screamed. It was the first time Alvin had ever heard her express real emotion. "Nurse!"

It was terrifying. But just as Dr. Childers moved to slam the door shut, Alvin caught a glimpse of Mr. Sanderson. Their eyes met and he could see the light of reason in Mr. Sanderson's blue eyes. He even winked.

Alvin struggled to get himself under control. Mr. Sanderson was a genius. He knew what he was doing. He was setting the stage.

Tomorrow it would start.

Allegra stroked her beloved harp, Dagda, named after the fierce King of Eire. When his harp was stolen by a rival tribe, it flew back to his hand, slaying nine of his enemies.

Her Dagda wasn't a fierce warrior. Not at all. Her Dagda was gentle. He was her friend, her confidante, her child, her lover and — over the past five months — her consolation. Dagda had kept her alive and sane when she thought she'd go mad. She'd lost her father, her health, her career, her memory and her sight in one night. If she'd lost her music she'd have thrown herself out the hospital window.

Suzanne and Claire had fought fiercely with the doctors and nurses to let her have Dagda in the hospital room. They'd pulled strings and cajoled and threatened. Claire's father had gently reminded the Executive Board that the Parks Foundation had donated $12.3 million for the new Oncology wing last year.

And so Dagda had been with her the day she'd finally been able to sit up in bed. The harp had been placed right by her bedside where she could touch it. The nurses just cleaned around it every morning and every evening. In the way of humans everywhere, the unusual became the norm very quickly. And when Allegra had finally been able to get out of bed, she'd pulled herself upright on Dagda's column.

The second she'd been able to sit in a chair, Suzanne had positioned Dagda next to her knees and Allegra had been able to strum the strings for the first time in what felt like forever. She didn't need sight to play Dagda. Her hands knew what to do, all on their own.

Just those first sounds, a few tentative chords, had been enough for her to know that she'd made it, after all. She'd survived. Dagda had been her constant companion ever since.

Maybe she had another companion now, besides the darkness.

No, God, that was crazy thinking. Something that came straight out of her pain and loneliness.

She knew absolutely nothing about him, except his name. Douglas Kowalski. Good Irish name. Oh, and his rank in the Navy. Senior Chief. She had no idea what that meant.

She knew he was Suzanne's husband's friend. And partner. So presumably he was morally upstanding, or at least he wasn't going to embezzle the company funds. Allegra had only met Suzanne's new husband a few times, but he didn't strike her as the innocent, trusting type. Anyone he chose would be honest and smart. Suzanne's husband would never choose someone dishonorable or dull-witted as a partner.

What else did she know?

He was single. How had he put it? *I don't have anywhere to go.*

He liked music. He'd been to Ireland. He had a sense of humor.

He had the most incredibly delicious voice. The deepest she'd ever heard, the low bass tones making her diaphragm vibrate. It wasn't just the timbre, it was the steadiness of his voice. The kind of voice you instantly, instinctively believed. The kind of voice that if it told you the moon was made of green cheese, then you wondered what a slice would taste like.

He was tall. Very tall. She remembered that instant of disbelief when she'd first heard his voice way above her head. For a moment, she'd wondered if he were on steps, or even somehow on another floor.

He was strong. The second she'd touched him on the arm, she'd felt the muscles beneath the jacket sleeve, like warm, moving steel. She'd been held in his arms, for just a moment, but it had been enough to feel shielded and protected by something immensely powerful.

She knew he was standing just off the stage, listening to her, waiting for her. Allegra had absolutely no doubt about that. He was exactly where he said he'd be. She knew that like she knew the words to "Amazing Grace."

She felt connected to him. It was insane, but there it was. How on Earth could she feel connected to someone she'd just met? Who she'd exchanged just a few words with?

She struck an experimental chord. The playlist had been decided last week and she should be singing "Flying," but another song came out. An old Celtic air her father and his brothers used to sing when she was a child. They mostly sang it when they'd had a few beers too many, which they often did.

"Break of Dawn." It was always connected in her mind with happiness, unfettered joy. The baritones and tenors of the Ennis men had made it a rousing ballad, a male chorus of uncomplicated jubilation, but she played it slow, in a minor key. For someone who was tentative, unsure about happiness and joy.

Someone who thought all joy had fled from this world. Uncertain at the thought that it still existed. But still hoping.

Douglas would never have heard the song. He wouldn't know that she was changing it for him, that it came from the heart.

Maybe he would.

She was halfway through the song, lingering over the notes when she heard exclamations from the surrounding crowd. A cry, an angry mutter. A woman's voice rising in complaint. Steps moving sharply across the marble floor.

And then an explosion rocked her world.

Chapter Four

ह०

Kowalski was standing by the stage, watching her. There was a little island of space all around him. He'd shot such filthy looks at those near the stage who weren't listening that they'd just moved away.

Damned straight. Anyone not capable of listening to this wonderful music didn't deserve it anyway.

This song was beautiful, too, though not one she'd composed. "Break of Dawn." He'd heard it once in a pub near the Dublin docks. He remembered that pub fondly. It had been a real dive, the ancient wooden floorboards stained from uncounted gallons of spilled beer suds and thousands of cigarette stubs and probably a couple pints of blood from all the fights down the years.

The Shanty. Kowalski wondered if it had survived the smoking ban in Ireland.

Some drunken laborers had sung a rousing chorus of "Break of Dawn," surprisingly in tune considering how pie-eyed they'd been. Kowalski had been utterly charmed. The Irish workingmen hadn't been able to stand straight, but they'd sure been able to sing true.

Allegra's version was much more beautiful, a slow bluesy rendering, the same song but with a different meaning.

He understood very well what she was doing with the song. It became a lament for lost happiness, yet tinged with a blush of hope, like the first flush of dawn.

She was halfway through when the lights went out. The main hall was completely black.

This was bad news.

44

The exhibit catalog had helpfully explained that the value of the "Jewels of the Czars" was worth, at a conservative estimate, 520-million dollars. "Not counting," the catalog had cheerily added, "their value as antiques and historical artifacts. From that point of view, the jewels are literally priceless."

Coming into the turn of the century Parks Mansion, which served as headquarters for the Parks Foundation, he and Midnight had counted five security guards ringing the exhibit. Which meant at least ten on the grounds. And not the flabby, rent-a-cop kind with bunions, either. They were young and fit and vigilant, armed with MP5s.

Part of the security system was based on laser beams and infrared cells running off the electricity mains. No security system worth spit would be without a backup electrical system. If that hadn't come on automatically when the mains went, it meant the entire system had been taken down. Together with the security guards.

Very bad news.

Kowalski automatically reached for his weapon before he remembered he didn't have one.

Very, very bad news. The worst.

He could hear disgruntled male voices, a sharp woman's cry, a man's steps crossing the marble floor. The notes from Allegra's harp.

Jesus fucking Christ!!

Allegra couldn't know the lights had gone out. Something bad was coming down and she was exposed, helplessly vulnerable. All alone and blind on a raised stage. Kowalski was already up the steps and running across the stage when the first of the flashbangs went off.

Flashbangs are concussion grenades set to detonate in an explosion of mind-shattering light and noise—two million lumens and one-hundred-eighty decibels, plus a shock wave of air. Enough to shut down the central nervous system. Enough to guarantee instantaneous deafening and blinding lasting minutes. A flashbang victim drops on his ass and sits, stunned, totally unable to operate or even think.

Kowalski was saved by the fact that as he ran across the stage he had his back to the entrance, where the flashbangs came from, and by the fact that he'd had thousands of training sessions making dynamic entries with flashbangs. He'd trained himself to get past the initial daze fast. He was already planning his moves as he ran, and when the noise and light exploded, he carried on out of instinct, even though his mind was no longer capable of logical thought.

It was instinct that had him picking Allegra up and leaping off the back end of the stage, twisting in midair so she'd land on him. While the room was still lit by the explosion, he was rolling them under the stage platform.

He brought them to a stop under the center of the stage — more or less under where Allegra had been playing. When the lights went back on, they would illuminate the edges of the stage but wouldn't penetrate to the center, which would remain in darkness.

She was fighting desperately underneath him, trying to hit him with her fists, trying to knee him in the groin. Kowalski easily held her arms with one fist and opened his legs to encase hers between his knees, pinning her down with the full weight of his body. She was completely subdued, unable to move.

She was trembling wildly, violent shakes of her body. He leaned down to her ear, pushing away the soft hair. "Allegra, stop fighting, it's me, Douglas." She stilled immediately, breath coming in harsh little pants.

He kept his voice to a soundless whisper which he knew couldn't carry. Not that it made any difference. Nobody could have heard them over the screams and gunfire, which were now coming from the main hall.

AK-47s, Kowalski thought grimly. These guys were pros.

The lights came back on and Kowalski turned his head, giving himself a sitrep in his head.

Five heavily armed bad guys in ski masks in the room, which probably meant at least four, maybe five, outside, running perimeter. All the security guards ringing the exhibit area were dead, and the other guards outside must already be dead, as well.

The thieves were men who'd already killed, had blood in their nostrils. They weren't going to be averse to killing again. Where the hell was Midnight—

Kowalski's blood ran cold. These smart motherfuckers had rounded up about ten women in a little group as hostages, screaming for everyone to throw down their cell phones and sit down with their hands on their heads.

Everyone dropped. Cell phones landed on the floor like jacks in a child's room.

One of the thieves was standing watch over the women, doing the one thing in this world that could stop John Huntington. The masked man had figured out the situation in a flash. He figured the threat to the women would hold the men at bay, and had chosen the most attractive one as the best deterrent.

The man standing guard over the women was holding the muzzle of his submachine gun directly against Suzanne Huntington's beautiful head, her blonde hair curling around the muzzle. John was sitting against a wall, hands on his head, eyes riveted on the man threatening his wife. The thief couldn't know that he was holding a gun to the head of the wife of one of the most dangerous men on the planet.

But John was unarmed, damn it.

Bud and Claire were nowhere to be seen.

"Douglas." Allegra's whisper was shaky. She was trembling with shock. "What's going on? What happened?"

He looked down at her. The situation would be frightening enough for a sighted person. For Allegra, it must be terrifying. She'd heard two massive explosions, gunfire and screams. She could have no sense of the situation. Any other woman would be yelling her head off, as were many of the women in the room. But she was holding it together. The instant she'd heard his voice, she'd quieted. Her only reaction was a violent trembling.

He put his mouth next to her ear. "Jewel thieves. Armed. They've got everyone hostage." She opened her mouth and he knew what she wanted to ask. "Bud and Claire aren't in the room. They might even have left. John and Suzanne are sitting down. They're safe." She'd have to forgive him for the lie. He didn't want her worrying about Suzanne—the situation was terrifying enough for her.

A masked, armed man ran full speed toward the stage and Kowalski tensed, covering as much of Allegra as he could. He drew her arms close together under her. "Huddle under me, honey. I have a lot of body mass. I might be able to stop a bullet."

Obediently, she drew her limbs together. Kowalski figured he was covering over ninety-five percent of her body. Any bullet that reached them had to be a ricochet, most of its force spent by the time it hit him. He'd probably be able to stop a bullet from entering her.

The thief veered off to the right, combat boots pounding.

A silver-haired man stood suddenly, arguing in the loud, arrogant voice of the very rich. One of the thieves simply lifted his machine gun and blew him away with a burst of fire. Great gouts of blood erupted from the elderly man's chest and his head exploded in a cloud of pink mist.

The mangled body landed fifteen feet away, skidding bonelessly until it hit the wall, leaving a blood-soaked trail that was shockingly vivid against the white marble floor. The man lay crumpled in a bloody heap, like a shattered doll. There was complete silence in the room. A woman sobbed briefly, then cut herself off.

Allegra jerked. "Did they — "

"Yeah." Kowalski's voice was grim. He curled a hand over her head. With his other hand, he pulled his cell phone out of the tux jacket. He had exactly the right number on speed dial. Larry Morton, former jarhead, good drinking buddy. All-around straight-up guy.

Currently head of the Portland SWAT Team.

He clicked the number. "Hey Kowalski," a genial voice answered. "Howzzit hangin'? I'll bet — "

"Parks Foundation," Kowalski said in a low voice. "Hostage situation."

"Sitrep," Larry barked back immediately. There was no hesitation, not even a second to absorb the shock of what Kowalski had said. Kowalski could hear clanking noises in the background. Larry was suiting up. Fast response times and an ability to shift gears instantaneously were all part of a SWAT team member's mental makeup.

"Five bad guys inside the main hall. There must be more on the perimeter. Armed with AK-47s, two mags each. They killed all the security guards."

"Hostages?" Larry's voice was muffled. He'd be donning his body armor.

"At least two hundred. One guy's holding a gun on a group of ten women in the center of the room. The jewels are on the east side of the building, where the thieves are. I'm under the stage with the singer."

"Don't try anything, we're on our way. Fifteen minutes, max." Larry disconnected.

Kowalski didn't have to be told not to try anything, even if he had his weapon with him, it would be suicide. And he was not about to leave Allegra unprotected. Not for one friggin' second.

Let them steal the jewels. He didn't give a fuck. What were they — pretty rocks, that's all. What worried him was that the thieves might spray the room with bullets before leaving, to stop people from following them.

It would be the smart tactic. Leave behind scores of desperately wounded people who would be the focus of attention. Get away clean with over a half-billion dollars.

Kowalski curled his forearms around Allegra's head. She turned slightly into him. "What's happening now?" she asked.

They were smashing and grabbing. Suzanne had designed the display cases with strong safety features, with a lot of input from John. It took time to get into the cases and grab the jewels. At the rate they were going, they'd still be here when the SWAT guys arrived.

The fucker with the gun at Suzanne's head hadn't moved.

"Situation static," he whispered back. "Help is on the way. All we have to do is wait it out."

Allegra gave a small nod. She inched her hand up until it lay bunched against his neck. A gesture of reassurance for him or for her, he didn't know.

Kowalski didn't lift his head. His mouth was close to her ear, his head cushioned in the soft mass of her hair. The acrid smoke of the flashbangs and the cordite from the machine guns still lingered in the air of the room, but where he was, on top of Allegra, nose an inch from her temple, all he could smell was spring.

The situation was dangerous. Nine, maybe ten bad guys with AK-47s, still almost fully loaded. There hadn't been that many shots, the flashbangs had taken care of the crowd. Each bad guy had two extra magazines hanging from a lanyard attached to his belt. Each magazine held thirty rounds. Near as dammit to nine hundred rounds in the building, in the hands of men who'd already shown an extreme willingness to shoot to kill.

Even more dangerous was what was happening to his body. He was lying fully on top of Allegra, and he could feel almost every inch of the front of her body. Every delicious inch.

He was developing a hard-on. Belay that, he *had* a hard-on. In five seconds flat he went from warrior, coldly assessing the situation with all his blood in his head, to horny guy, with his nose stuck in a beauty's ear and every ounce of blood in his body streaming in hot liquid pulses straight to his cock.

She had to feel it. He was big and his hard-on fit right between her legs. There was nothing he could do about it. There was nothing he *would* do about it. Until he had a damned good reason for doing so, or until he knew Allegra was perfectly safe, he had no intention of getting off her.

Every tiny movement Allegra made only served to inflame his hard-on. Her breathing—God, that brought him into even closer contact with her breasts. Her breath came in little pants against his neck and his cock pulsed with every pant. Though she tried to remain still, he knew he was heavy and crushing her. She was making tiny adjustments to her position to find a more comfortable fit. She shifted her hips and his cock surged even more heavily against her.

It was impossible for her to ignore it any more.

"Sorry," Kowalski whispered.

To his astonishment, she smiled faintly. "It's an…unusual reaction."

No, actually, it wasn't. Lots of men's cocks went straight up when their blood was up. Kowalski knew men who went into battle with hard-ons, though he wasn't one of them. A medic once told him field surgeons often got boners while operating.

Allegra didn't need to know that.

"Stress," he whispered, though it wasn't that. It was having the most desirable woman he'd ever seen within kissing distance.

It was a thought. Hell, why not? If it weren't for their clothes, in their position, his dick would be in her. He moved his head forward, slowly. He wanted her to have plenty of time to let him know to back off.

But she did nothing. She could feel him coming closer, could feel his breath on her neck, she could feel his cock. Surely she knew what was coming. But she didn't turn her head away, or stiffen, or whisper "Stop."

The hand lying against his neck opened like a blossom unfurling in the sun and those long, slender fingers stroked him. Jeez, just that soft touch nearly set him off, like an electric wire between his neck and his balls. He brought his mouth against her neck, not in a kiss, but in a touch of his lips to her. His mouth lingered there a moment. She exhaled and her eyes closed.

He licked her, right where a vein was pumping, strong and fast. Her heart was beating fast, too. He could feel it under the lightweight, frothy material of her dress. Fear? Desire?

He shifted his hand until it covered her breast, letting the heavy, warm weight of his hand shape it. He could feel a hard little nipple. She was aroused, too. No doubt about it. Her nipple was stiff and hard. Every time his cock pulsed, her hips surged up slightly against his. She might not even be aware of it, but he was. Christ, was he. He could feel every movement of her body.

He kissed her neck, and she sighed. This was the welcome he wanted, the one he'd been waiting for. He trailed his lips up her neck, over her jawline, and finally settled on her mouth.

She opened immediately for him, mouth soft and warm, tongue rubbing against his in welcome. It was the most electrifying kiss he'd ever had. He slanted his mouth for a better fit, tongue deep in her mouth, moving, tasting her.

All he could do was kiss her but it was better than fucking anyone else. Kissing was great. Why had he ignored kissing all those years? It wasn't always high on the agenda in bed. A kiss was for the beginning, to establish that sex was going to take place. He rarely kissed while fucking and women rarely asked for it.

Yet it was so delicious. Every nerve ending he had that wasn't in his cock was in his mouth. He could feel everything about her, about her response, with his lips and tongue. They fit perfectly. When he slanted his lips, she eagerly met his until it felt as if he were sinking into her mouth. It was as intimate as sex, and as his tongue moved with hers, feeling the warm welcome, his cock became even harder, dying to be in her.

His tongue rubbed against hers and her hips rose up and rubbed against him. Jesus, he was hard as a rock.

Kowalski briefly broke the kiss. He needed to breathe and he needed to check the situation before his mind turned to mush. He shifted his head and tried to focus to something that wasn't Allegra's perfect skin and the taste of her. And froze.

Shit! Oh fuck, fuck, fuck!!

While he'd been busy with Allegra's mouth, the situation had changed drastically. For the worse.

Claire Parks had appeared against the opposite wall, the one Midnight was sitting against. Her bright red dress was like a flag to anyone who cared to see. She was sitting with her back against the wall, just like Midnight, and you had to watch carefully to see that she was sliding closer and closer to him.

Luckily, the bad guys were intent on smashing and looting, stuffing the jewels in canvas gym bags. The fucker with the muzzle to Suzanne's head kept shifting his attention from her to his comrades. He wasn't looking toward the back wall, toward where Claire Parks had suddenly appeared. Greed had blinded them all.

He'd seen this before, particularly in Africa. The hint of conflict diamonds could turn battle-hardened, mission-focused warriors into mindless animals. You never, ever took your attention away from the mission. Greed, lust, vengeance—they were all emotions you gave in to after the mission was over.

These assholes were already blinded by the fog of greed. They were seeing hundreds of millions of dollars in their hands and didn't—*couldn't*—see Claire inching closer to Midnight.

Kowalski was used to thinking three moves ahead and he could see it all in his mind, as if he were reading a novel, skipping ahead to what would happen next.

"Fuck," he breathed.

Claire was edging closer to John. Kowalski had to admit she was doing a good job. If you didn't know she hadn't been there before, you couldn't have realized she was moving. But she was. Claire stopped about a foot from Midnight and Kowalski could see her arm moving.

She was sliding something over to him.

Bud was alive. If he weren't, Claire wouldn't be here. And if Bud was alive, he was coming through. Kowalski had only met Bud a few times but he knew that about him. Bud and now Midnight were going to face the jewel thieves on their own. Kowalski didn't know what Claire was sliding over to John, whether it was a gun she'd somehow found or a knife, but there was no doubt John would instantly grab the distraction Bud was going to create to waste the guy holding a gun to Suzanne's head.

Leaving himself wide open.

"Douglas?" Allegra was clutching his arms. She'd picked up on his tension. He looked down briefly at her. She was pale, like a stricken unicorn, beautiful mouth wet from his, tight with tension. Her eyes were trying to follow him, failing, and he realized with a lurch how horrible it must be to be blind.

"Shh," he whispered, and bent to kiss her briefly. A touch of lips and then away because the temptation to linger, to stay at her mouth, was almost overwhelming.

"What's happening?" Allegra touched his cheek with her hand. "What's going on?"

She needed to know. Kowalski bent to her ear, keeping his eyes on what was happening in the room. There was tension in Midnight's shoulders. It was coming down soon.

"I think John and Bud are going to make a move," he said in a low voice. "I have to help them."

"No, God—are you crazy? What's the matter with you? Don't go out there! Those men have guns and you don't!" She gasped and tightened her grip. "Stay here," she pleaded in a hoarse whisper.

Stay here. Nothing he'd like better.

"I can't, honey." There was real regret in his voice, as he gently peeled her hands away from his satin jacket lapels. "I can't let them do it alone."

"But you called the police! I heard the man's voice, he said he was coming soon." Her whisper was fierce as she clutched at his biceps.

Kowalski nearly sighed. "Yeah, but John doesn't know that. I have to go. I can't let him and Bud face these guys alone." He studied Allegra's lovely face, committing it to memory. He wanted that image in his head if he died.

Professional warriors have no illusions about battle. No matter how smart you are, how hard you've trained, shit happens. And more often than not, it happens when you least want it. He'd seen guys get wasted two days before retirement, the day their first son was born, a week before their wedding.

Kowalski had been prepared to die, if necessary, each time he went into battle. All warriors were, otherwise they couldn't do what they did.

Murphy's Law was the one certainty in battle. The fact that now he had just met the most desirable woman on the face of the planet, and that she seemed to feel the spark too, only made it more probable that he'd be wasted, as if going up unarmed against five AK-47s, maybe more, wasn't bad enough.

He'd give his right nut to be able to stay right here, on top of Allegra, kissing her, until the good guys arrived and saved the day. But he wasn't being given that option.

Life is tough. Suck it up. The Warriors' Creed.

"Listen to me carefully, honey." She stilled, sightless eyes trying to track him as he moved. He lifted himself up, shrugging off his tuxedo jacket. He placed it over her, opened up lengthwise. It almost completely covered her. "Don't move until I come for you. If I…don't come for you, wait right here until the police find you. *Don't move.* Larry Morton, the guy I called, knows there's someone under the stage." He tucked the edges of the jacket around her. "I've put my jacket on you, it's dark, you should be camouflaged. Remember, no matter what, don't move until someone comes for you."

"Don't go," she whispered, head turned toward him. A lone tear tracked down the pale skin of her cheek. "*Please* don't go."

Kowalski closed his eyes in pain. Jesus, this was the hardest thing he'd ever done. "I have to, honey," he whispered back.

Midnight's shoulders were stiff. Anyone who didn't know John wouldn't have noticed anything, but Kowalski knew him like a brother. Whatever it was John was planning to do, he was going to do it *now.*

Kowalski bent to quickly kiss Allegra, his mouth catching the tear, tucking her arms into the protection of his jacket.

"Come back to me," she whispered urgently, her hands emerging from his jacket to cup his face.

"Yeah, count on it," he said in a rush, rolling away from her. Midnight was starting to slowly hyperventilate, pulling in oxygen needed for the burst of energy of battle. "You stay put now," he whispered again over his shoulder.

He rolled to the edge of the dais, starting to hyperventilate himself. The staging of an operation was always the most dangerous period. Once battle was engaged, he knew exactly what to do and how to do it. Here he was flying blind. He couldn't make a move first and sabotage a surprise attack, nor could he afford to be even a second late in making his move after Midnight and Bud made theirs. It had to be split-second precision timing. He breathed deeply and waited, tense and ready.

"Good luck." The sound was more a movement of air than a whisper. He nodded. She couldn't see it, but he didn't dare risk a sound. The thieves were nearing the end of their looting. They were pulling it off. They'd killed the security guards and neutralized the men in the great hall—or so they thought. The average age of most of the men in the hall must be about sixty—old, rich geezers, nearly every one. No threat.

The looters would have visions of half a billion dollars dancing in their heads. All the women, liquor or cocaine—or whatever would float their boat—they could ever want for the rest of their natural lives were contained in four canvas gym bags at their feet. They were already high on the idea.

Even the guy holding the women hostage had let his guard down, forgetting a prime rule of battle. It isn't over until it's over. You can be killed by the last bullet just as easily as by the first.

Kowalski would have to use this guy's weapon, because sure as anything, he would be the one John wasted first. Kowalski memorized the positions of the other jewel thieves. He ran through possible scenarios in his head, figuring out how to get to the weapon after the fucker holding the women hostage was dead. If John had a knife, he'd go for the throat and the guy would probably drop backwards to the ground. Kowalski hoped. His one chance was to grab the guy's weapon fast. If he had to kick a dead body onto its back to get to the weapon, he'd waste precious seconds.

Here it comes!

The big double doors at the back of the room burst open and Bud came through. Midnight surged up, sending blurs of steel flashing across the room. The man holding a gun to

Suzanne's head was bowled over backwards, feet flying up in the air as he frantically clutched the knife piercing his neck.

Kowalski ran crouching, rolled to reduce his target profile, and came up cradling the guy's AK-47, firing in short controlled bursts, blessing the hundreds of thousands of rounds he'd shot in combat training. No tame, target-practice shooting for SEALs. No careful sighting through the front sight, standing still, two-handedly. No, they trained for the real thing — running, rolling while shooting at a moving, hard-to-identify target, eight hours a day, several months a year.

He caught one thief in the head before the man even had time to lift his weapon, and another one — a clean double tap to the head — as he was dropping into a crouch. Both of them crumpled to the ground, lying there in the unmistakable stillness of death.

John had nailed two with knives before bolting to Suzanne. Bud caught a thief in the arm and the head, swayed, and dropped to the ground himself. With a cry, Claire rushed to him. Bud's shirtfront was bright red — he was wounded, and badly, judging from the blood. Midnight was holding Suzanne in a tight grip, head buried in her hair.

Shit! There were still the perimeter guards! Bud was out of commission and Midnight was out of his mind with fear for Suzanne.

Kowalski turned and lifted his weapon at the sound of the side doors bursting open with breaching explosives. His finger eased on the trigger when he recognized Larry Morton's tall wiry frame beneath the body armor.

Ten SWAT team members poured into the room, moving fast, moving precisely. They were well-trained. Within five seconds the team member had every inch of the room covered, in overlapping sectors of coverage. They kept their weapons up and trained, though it was clear the danger was over.

Kowalski walked over to Larry, letting the muzzle of the AK-47 point toward the ground. "What the fuck took you guys so long? We had to do it all ourselves."

"That right? I thought I told you to wait." Larry's words were directed at him, though his eyes, dark and sharp, were quartering the room. But there was no danger here. The only people standing with weapons were his team and Kowalski himself. The bad guys were all dead. At least those in the room.

"What about the perimeter guys?" Kowalski asked.

Larry shrugged. "Taken care of."

Kowalski nodded with his head to the back of the room. "Lieutenant Morrison is going to need medical care."

Larry's sharp sniper's eyes widened. "Bud? He's here?"

"Yeah, he took care of one of the guys, but he's wounded. He must have already been shot because none of the bad guys got off a round in here."

"Okay." Larry turned away and spoke in a quiet, urgent tone into his headset mike. He nodded grimly to Kowalski. "All right. Medics are right outside. They should be here any—ah."

A team of medics burst into the room. Larry directed two of them over to where Bud was lying on the ground, unconscious, watched over by Claire. The other medics were fanning out, touching the necks of each bad guy, then moving on. One checked the tuxedoed guest who'd been blown away. He shook his head and stood up. Two women had fainted and they were being revived by the medics.

Midnight walked up to Kowalski and Larry, his arm tightly around Suzanne's shoulders. She was shaking, which Kowalski expected, since she'd nearly had her head shot off. But Midnight was shaking too, which blew Kowalski's mind. He'd never seen John Huntington show any emotion after battle at all. And here he was, pale and shaking.

He addressed Larry directly. "I'm going home," Midnight announced. "I know you guys have to debrief me, and two of those," he turned to look at the thieves lying still and dead on the marble floor with eyes that were cold and flat, "are mine. Knife through the throat. You'll find my prints on the blades. I'll come downtown tomorrow if you need me, but right now I'm taking my wife home."

Larry nodded. "Okay. It all looks pretty straight to me. We'll want a statement but it can wait. The CSI guys will be here in a minute. We'll be busy for a while mopping up and identifying the dead guys. We'll be in contact with you." He looked over. "You too, Kowalski. Expect a call soon."

The medics had loaded Bud onto a stretcher and were carrying him out of the Foundation. Claire was by Bud's side, keeping a hand on the stretcher as she walked. Someone — probably one of the guests — had lent her a jacket and she held it tightly around herself. Larry went to check on Bud.

John's jaws bunched. He tightened his arm around Suzanne's shoulders. "Come on, sweetheart. Let's go home."

Suzanne had been crying, her makeup was smudged, there was a long rip in the skirt of her gown, yet she still looked beautiful. She murmured assent, then stopped and looked up. "John, what happened to Allegra? We can't leave without her. She came with us. How can she get home —"

"She's safe," Kowalski said. "I rolled her under the stage." He gave Midnight a hard look. "I'll take care of her. I'll make sure she gets home safely."

Midnight looked at him for a long moment, then nodded. "Okay. Let's go, love."

"No. No way. Allegra is our responsibility. She came with us and we have to take her home." Suzanne stood her ground. "I'm not leaving without her."

Kowalski was exasperated, but at the same time he had to admire Suzanne. She was white and shaking, she'd come *this* close to having her brains blown out of her head, she was probably longing for the safety and quiet of home, and her husband's arms, but she wasn't budging without her friend. "I said I'll take care of it, Suzanne," he said gently.

"Um...I don't know." She looked at her husband and then back to Kowalski. "I need to know that you'll see her to her door, Douglas. She's blind and she'll be scared. To tell you the truth, I'd feel better if we took her home."

Kowalski nodded once. "I understand completely, Suzanne. But you don't need to worry about Allegra. I'll take care of her."

"Poor Allegra..." she whispered. She watched Kowalski's eyes, looking for something, her chin wobbling. Her eyes grew wet. When a tear dropped over, Midnight reached to wipe it away. Stress was starting to break her defenses.

"You can trust Kowalski, sweetheart. He won't let anything happen to her," Midnight murmured in her ear. He gave Kowalski a sharp glance that clearly said, *If anything happens to my wife's friend, I'll have your hide.*

They'd spent a lot of time together under dangerous conditions and had perfected unspoken communication. Kowalski met his eyes—*Allegra's with me now and nothing bad will happen to her.* Midnight nodded and turned to his wife.

"Come on, sweetheart, it's okay, I promise. Allegra'll be fine. Kowalski knows what to do. Let's go, now." He turned Suzanne toward the door and she went without protest.

Kowalski thumbed the safety on the weapon, handed it to a SWAT team member and sprinted to the stage. He crouched to look underneath and saw her.

The actual takedown had been, as always, in the freaky slo-mo time soldiers knew as combat time. He and his men were so well-trained that what looked like a frightening blur of chaotic action to civilians was actually a series of moves practiced so often in training they could do them in their sleep. Though it felt as if hours had passed, he knew that not more than a quarter of an hour had elapsed since he'd left Allegra.

Still, a quarter of an hour alone and blind in the middle of violent action must have been terrifying.

She was lying on her back just as he'd left her, red hair shockingly bright against the white marble floor. One long-fingered hand was holding on to his jacket. Her face was turned toward the room, deathly pale and pinched. She looked so lost and so vulnerable, an angel fallen to earth, touched by tragedy. Kowalski's heart simply turned over in his chest.

"Allegra," he said softly.

Chapter Five

ଈଠ

Screams, blood, horror…that cruel face taunting her, eyes half-crazed, standing over her father's still body.

Blood, so much blood. Rivers of blood spreading out over the glass tabletop in streaming runnels. The white carpet and cream-colored walls were spattered wildly with bright red drops. The blood from her father's shattered head moved in a flood of red to the edge of the table, gathered trembling on the beveled edge of the table top, then spilled over, falling to the carpet in thick, slow drops. Drop, drop, drop…

Her father lay still, oh-so still, beloved face turned to her. His eternal smile was gone, gone was the humor in his eyes, gone the gentleness of his handsome Irish face.

He was gone. Her father was gone. Dead. No more.

And then that cruelly crushed head, impossibly, moved. Turned toward her. The eyelids opened and she saw her father's blue-green eyes. His dead mouth opened too and, horribly, he spoke in a deep, deep voice, shockingly unlike her father's light tenor.

"Allegra," he said.

Her father was speaking from beyond the grave. Oh God, he was dead and he was talking to her.

"Allegra," said the deep voice that wasn't her father's, coming from her father's dead mouth.

Her father never called her Allegra. "Allie," he called her, mainly. "Allie-me-darlin'" when he'd had a few too many. And his voice was Irish-light, not as deep as midnight.

His dead mouth opened wide, preternaturally wide, mouth and teeth stained with blood.

"Allegra," the deep voice repeated out of her father's mouth, and it was as if it came from the bowels of hell itself…

63

Allegra gasped in horror, bolting upright. She banged her head sharply against something hard, metallic, and dropped back down again, stunned.

"Jesus Christ!" that deep voice said, and a strong hand tugged her across the cold floor. She was lifted up and held tightly.

"Medic!" Someone bellowed high above her head. "Get me a fucking medic!"

Allegra jumped at the bellow. She blinked against the darkness, then remembered—with a wild cruel lurch to her heart—that blinking wouldn't help clear her vision. Nothing ever would.

She lost her foothold on reality, it slid right away from her, plunging her into a slithering, sliding nightmare world. She couldn't *see*! Where was she? What—there had been gunshots, screams...

"Move away," a new male voice said, then more sharply, "Listen, mister, let go of her. I need to examine her."

She'd been leaning against Douglas' strong body, massive arms holding her. She didn't want to leave this safe haven, ever. She snuggled more tightly against him.

"Let her go now, I need to see if she's concussed." The medic sounded exasperated.

The arms loosened and another male hand, smaller this time, carefully touched her forehead.

"Miss, are you seeing double?" a man asked.

"She doesn't see anything at all, she's blind," that deep voice said, and suddenly everything snapped into focus. Parks Foundation, opening night, jewel thieves...

"Douglas!" she gasped, swatting away the hand carefully touching her forehead. She leaned forward until she touched Douglas, hands moving over a huge chest, up to his broad shoulders, down his arms. "Are you all right? I heard shots. Oh, my God. Are you okay?"

"I'm fine," he rumbled. She was pulled back against his chest. Strong arms went around her. "What about you? That was some crack you took."

She burrowed her face against him, shaking her head. "Doesn't matter," she mumbled into his starched shirtfront. "I'm okay, it's just a little sore." Someone was trying to turn her around and she jerked her shoulders away. "I don't need any help. Make him go away."

"Miss, I think maybe we should take you into the hospital overnight for observation." That second voice again. "You've got a nasty bump—"

Allegra's heart lurched again with panic. "No!" she said sharply. "No hospital."

No hospital, not ever again. The very smell of hospitals made her stomach queasy to the point of pain. She'd spent months on a bed with those smells, blind and tied down by IV lines like some prisoner.

"I won't go to a hospital, not for anything. I just want to go home." She raised her head. She couldn't see Douglas but he could see her. She knew her desperation was showing on her face. "Please, I want to go home," she whispered, voice shaking. "Suzanne and John can drive me—"

"They've already left," Douglas said, and she knew her shock must be showing. She'd come with Suzanne. It never even occurred to her that Suzanne would leave her here, just forget about her. Allegra's grip on her control slipped just a bit further. "Oh, God, then how—"

"I told Suzanne I'd take you home," Douglas said swiftly. "She wanted to wait for you, but she was feeling shaky, so John took her home. Don't worry, Allegra. I'll drive you back. But don't you think a doctor should see you first? Maybe that medic's right. Maybe you should be checked into the hospital."

Allegra tried to sound rational and calm—*Oh no, I don't think that will be necessary*—when what she wanted to do was scream. Just the thought of a doctor at a hospital made her feel she was sliding into a black hole she could never get out of again. "No." Her voice was shaking. She waited a moment to be sure she had control over it. "I'm fine. I just bumped my head, nothing serious. I didn't black out or anything. I'll be fine."

She looked up anxiously, knowing she was in this man's hands, trying desperately to figure out what he was deciding. She had no other way to get home, save calling a taxi. She was absolutely certain he wouldn't allow it. If he thought she needed hospital care, he'd take her there. Her heart pounded at the thought. "Please," she whispered.

"Okay." Douglas sounded reluctant. "But promise to tell me if you get dizzy."

She was dizzy all the time. Morning, noon and night. She'd been dizzy since she lost her sight. "Promise," she said fervently.

"If she's not going to the hospital, make sure she doesn't feel faint," the medic said. "And she should come in if she has a headache, difficulty in concentration, depression or anxiety."

That more or less described how she felt every waking minute of every day. No blow to the head was going to change that.

"Do you—" Douglas began.

"Absolutely," she lied. "I promise."

"Well, if you're sure," the medic said reluctantly.

"I'll take care of it." Douglas' deep voice was so calm. It reassured even her, and it must have reassured the other man because she heard footsteps walking away. Douglas pulled her against him once more.

"Where's Claire? Is she okay?" Her voice was muffled against his chest, his big hand curved around the back of her head, holding her tightly. It was a shockingly intimate embrace, almost more intimate than the kiss under the stage had been, because it was out in the open. But she didn't care.

There was enormous confusion in the room. She remembered the big hall of the Parks Foundation from...from *before*. From when she could see. Claire had said that they were expecting around two hundred people to attend the opening. And it seemed as if all of them were talking at the top of their voices. Nearby, she could make out a few women sobbing and two sharp male voices raised in loud anger, voices echoing off the high ceiling. Radios crackled loudly in the background and every once in a while an official-sounding voice told someone to move along.

There was no focus to the sounds, it was one big wall of restless, confusing noise, the sounds bouncing around the walls until she almost couldn't tell up from down. Since her accident, she'd never been in a room with more than two or three people in it. She spent days and days on her own in her silent apartment, with only some background music for company. At no time since she'd lost her sight had she been unable to locate the source of a sound.

The utter chaos disoriented her, made her dizzy. The only safe and solid thing was Douglas Kowalski, tall and broad and strong, unmoving, the still center of her world. As she clung to him, the dizziness receded slowly until the noises became recognizable as individual voices. The mass of people was shuffling toward the exit. Her heart stopped beating the frantic tattoo of panic.

She took in a long, deep breath, then another.

"Better?" he asked quietly.

He knew. Somehow he knew.

Allegra swallowed. She lifted her head from his chest, suddenly ashamed of herself. The freak little flash of nightmare, the gunshots, the screams—they'd disoriented her badly, like falling into a deep hole you didn't know was there. She usually had better control over herself than this.

She frowned. "You didn't tell me where Claire is." A sudden fear made her clutch his arms. He hadn't forgotten to tell her where Claire was, he was holding something back. "Where is she? Is she okay? Oh, God, I hope nothing's happened to her." Allegra swiveled her head, as if she could see Claire in the room.

"I imagine she's at the hospital," Douglas said calmly, holding her as she jerked. "Claire's not hurt in any way, don't worry. But Bud took a round in the chest. The medics took him away and she went with him."

Oh, God, poor Claire... "Can we—can we find out if Bud's okay? Who do we ask?" Bud had to be all right, he simply *had* to be. The alternative—that Bud was dead, killed trying to save them—was something Allegra couldn't even think about. Claire was wildly in love with Bud. Claire had suffered so much already in her life. She'd had so much taken from her, ten years of her life sacrificed to leukemia. How could she take the loss of the love of her life only a few weeks after meeting him?

Before—in her previous incarnation as Allegra Ennis, happy singer and harpist—Allegra would have been absolutely certain that Bud would be okay. He'd have a mild flesh wound that served to patch things up between him and Claire. That was the way the world worked. Some bad things happened now and again—but not too bad. Just enough to make you appreciate what you had. And then they were put right again immediately.

But she knew better now. Big bad scary things happened all the time, things that could never be put right, ever again. The world was full of sorrow and pain, losses that would never be regained. Pain that was everlasting.

"Please find out if Bud's alive," she whispered to Douglas, shivering at the thought that Bud might be dead and that Claire's heart would be broken.

"Okay." Douglas released her and stepped back. "But first, put this on. They've got all the doors open, and it's cold. Then I'll go find out if anyone has word from the hospital."

A second later, his jacket was dropped around her shoulders. She recognized it by the smell and the size. It smelled faintly of mothballs and soap. No aftershave. Just as he wore no aftershave. And it was huge. It had covered her almost like a blanket while she'd been lying beneath the stage, waiting helplessly.

She put it on, grateful for the extra warmth. It hung past her knees, but it was warm. When she wrapped herself in it, the worst of her shivering went away. She waited for news, trembling, but not from cold.

Footsteps coming back. "Okay," Douglas said, touching her arm. "Here's what I know. He's been taken to Laurel Park Hospital and he's in surgery right now. I've got a number to call for more information."

"I've got Claire's cell phone number, too, if she's got it with her."

"Well, that's that, then. There's nothing more we can do here. I want to get you home and get something warm inside you." A large hand took her upper arm, swimming in his jacket sleeve. "Let's go, honey."

They hadn't taken more than ten steps when Allegra stopped, shocked that she could forget. "Oh my God! Dagda! I was about to leave Dagda behind!"

He stopped, too. "Who? Who's Dagda?"

"Not who, what." Though Dagda was as alive to her as any of her friends. "My harp. I can't leave him here. He's irreplaceable." The greatest harp maker in Ireland had crafted Dagda. Charlie McKerron had died two years ago of a heart attack while playing in a pub, drunk as a lord. He'd never craft another Dagda. "You'll need the carrying case. It's in the wardrobe room. Dagda's heavy with the case, though. About sixty pounds." Allegra thought she heard a little snort.

"Okay." Douglas pulled lightly on her arm to nudge her to one side. They must have been at the big open front doors because she could feel people jostling her as they streamed by. A gelid wind was blowing in from outside, and she could feel little needles of sleet against her face. In the distance, engines were starting up. The smell of car exhaust filled the chilly air. "This is what we're going to do. I'm going to take you to my car, turn on the heat, then I'll come back for Dagda."

"In his carrying case."

"In his carrying case."

She lifted her face to him, worried. "Dagda's very delicate. He needs to be covered carefully with a blanket. It's inside the case itself. The cold is bad for him, warps the wood."

"Right." There was a note of humor in the deep voice. He smoothed out the frown between her brows with his thumb. "Correction, then. I will take you to my car, then come back for Dagda and the case. I'll tuck Dagda up nice and warm in his blanket and put him in his case with a hot water bottle if necessary, then bring him back to the warm car. How does that sound?"

It was a feeble stab at humor but it made her smile. "Thanks so much."

"My pleasure," he said, and scooped her off her feet.

"Oh! What are you doing?"

He was carrying her as easily as most men could carry a child, walking down the big formal granite staircase to the gravel driveway. She could hear his shoes making a crunching sound on the gravel. When he spoke she could feel the vibrations of his deep voice against her side.

"There's snow on the ground and big ice patches. Your shoes are very pretty but they're not good for snow." She had on strappy, open-toed satin sandals.

"Well, boots don't go well with evening gowns."

"No, of course not. Not even green satin boots would do." He held her high in his arms. The only way to keep her balance was to put her arms around his neck. Her cheek was next to his and she could feel the muscles of his face move in a slight smile.

She'd never been carried as an adult. Now she realized why it figured so largely in novels and movies. Such a delicious feeling, romantic with the romance of another era. It was like being transported to another place, another time. He did a good job of it, too. He wasn't huffing or puffing or staggering. He breathed normally, walking with an even stride, as if out for an evening stroll. Those strong muscles she'd felt weren't just for show, they were real.

Douglas was strong and he was brave. If she lived to be a thousand years old she'd never forget him saying he was hoping he could stop a bullet for her. He'd been deathly serious. He'd covered as much of her as he possibly could, leaving her with no doubt that he was willing to take a bullet.

He'd left her only when he saw his friends were going to try to face the thieves on their own. He could have saved his own skin, easily. Just stayed under the stage with her, knowing help was on the way. But he'd chosen to stand by his friends, unarmed. She was sure of that, that he had had no weapons. She'd felt every inch of him, the front of him, at least. The memory of the only lethal weapon he had, his hot, hard, huge penis, made her blush.

He kissed like a dream. That was a pretty powerful weapon, too.

She'd actually forgotten the danger, forgotten everything, while he was kissing her. She'd been lost in a world of heat and vital power, holding on to that immensely strong body as if it held life itself. In a flash, the kiss had gone from a sweet meeting of lips to raw, pure sex. A steep descent into glittering passion. He'd been huge against her, pressing hard against her mound. She'd felt her body preparing itself for him, opening like a flower. At one point his penis had fit between the folds of her sex, rubbing against her, and she'd started shaking, lifting up against him to feel more of that vital power and heat. Every time she did that he swelled even bigger, so she could feel the ripples of his erection against the open folds of her sex. It had been the most exciting thing in the world.

When he'd rolled off her she'd been a minute away from climaxing.

What an extraordinary man. He'd made her smile, given her courage and protection, and turned her on like no other man ever had. And now he was carrying her, so she wouldn't get her feet wet.

They were at his car. Or SUV, judging from the height. She heard the "whump" of the doors unlocking remotely and he managed to open the passenger door and get her inside without jiggling her. A few seconds later, he was in the driver's seat, turning on the engine. His seat creaked as he reached behind him. A soft blanket was carefully tucked around her. The cab was already heating up.

"Here, if your harp rates a blanket, you should, too. It'll be warm in here in just a minute. I'll go get Dagda and then drive you home."

Allegra reached out, touched his forearm. He was wearing only his shirt in the bitter cold because he'd given his jacket to her. "Do you want your jacket back? I'll be fine with the blanket."

"No. You keep it. I'll be right back."

She reached into a tiny pocket sewn into the bodice of her gown. "Here's the key to Dagda's case, and my purse is inside the case."

"Okay."

Her hand was still on his arm. The arm was warm and hard, like the rest of him. When he moved, she tightened her grip. "Douglas?"

He stilled. "Yeah?"

"Thanks—for everything."

He cleared his throat. "No problem. Don't move now." A second later the door closed behind him.

True to his word, the cabin heated up quickly. The shivers slowly subsided as she waited patiently, huddled in his huge jacket, comforted by the softness of the blanket.

She heard the back door opening. "There you go, Dagda," Douglas said. "Nice and safe and snug in your case."

She turned around. "Did you—"

"Yes, I did. He's not feeling the cold, I promise you." The door closed and she smiled at the thought of Dagda safe and with her as she turned back around. The SUV dipped to take Douglas' weight. He reached over her and pulled her seatbelt down and across, fastening it. He placed her evening clutch on her lap and she curled her hand around it. "Now then. I need to know your address."

She could see him in her mind's eye, hands draped over the steering wheel, turned toward her. What she'd give to know what he looked like. Since she'd lost her sight, she'd only been with close friends, mostly Claire and Suzanne and Claire's father, and the Parks' housekeeper, Rosa, and Rosa's family. She wasn't used to having close dealings with someone whose face she couldn't picture.

"1046 Adams Drive. It's across town, close to—"

"I know where it is." The SUV started moving, big wheels rattling over the gravel driveway.

"I thought you were new to Portland? Just moved here."

"I am, but a good soldier always scouts the terrain. Are you comfortable? Do you want me to turn the heat up?"

"No, I'm fine, thanks. When we get to my house can we call the hospital? Or maybe I can try Claire's cell phone. I need to know what's happening." She couldn't bear the thought of Claire alone at the hospital, maybe mourning the death of her man. Allegra hadn't finished mourning the death of her father five months ago. It still seared her heart.

"We don't have to wait until we get to your house." She heard the electronic beeps of a cell phone number being punched in.

"Kowalski," a tinny voice said. The car had a speakerphone. "What's up?"

"Larry, do you know what's happened to Lieutenant Morrison?"

"Bud? Hang on a sec, I'll check." There were muffled noises, then the voice came back online. He sounded grim. "Negative, Kowalski, no news. Bud's still in surgery."

"Keep me posted, Larry."

"Will do."

Allegra huddled deeper in her swaddle of material. The shivers had started up again. Douglas switched on a button and a blast of hot air came from under the dashboard to warm her feet.

"That better?"

"Very much better, thanks. Next time I'll be sure to wear satin boots." She could feel the smile fade from her face. Next time...maybe the next time, Claire would have a shattered heart. "What do you think will happen to Bud?"

"If a gunshot wound isn't fatal immediately, there's a ninety percent chance of recovery. If Bud made it to surgery, he's going to make it the rest of the way." That deep voice sounded so matter-of-fact, so certain, Allegra could feel her muscles relax.

"Is that true or are you making it up to make me feel better?"

"I *would* make it up to make you feel better, but it just so happens to be true. I've never known a soldier to die if he managed to make it into the helicopter taking him back to base and to surgery. With each minute that passes, Bud's chances go up."

It was probably nonsense, but it did make her feel better.

They drove on in silence. At one point, Douglas turned on the windshield wipers. She could hear them swishing back and forth. "Is it snowing?"

"More like sleet. It won't stick. But the roads are icy."

Allegra couldn't see him in action, but she just knew that Douglas was a good driver. Even though the roads were slick with ice, the vehicle felt steady, the braking and curves were smooth. Two days before she'd had to take a taxi to the neurologist and the man had driven like a maniac, scaring her half to death. "Thanks for driving me. I'm glad I didn't have to take a taxi home."

"I'd never have let you take a taxi."

Allegra turned her head toward Douglas at that, but he didn't say anything else. It was warm now in the cab, and the aftermath of the violence was beginning to take its toll. It was a forty minute drive to her house. The silence, the feel of the big powerful machine rumbling beneath her, the regular swishing beat of the windshield wipers lulled her. Allegra was dozing off when the shrill ring of a phone jolted her awake.

"Yeah?" she heard Douglas say.

"Larry here, big guy. Listen, we just got word that Bud's out of surgery. He's gonna be royally pissed when he wakes up, he's got holes where he didn't used to, he's gonna hurt and he's gonna have tubes runnin' in and out for a while, but he'll make it."

She heard Douglas suck in air sharply. "That's great news. Just great. Thanks for calling, Larry."

"No prob. Listen, Detective Swanson says you gotta come in Monday morning. We need a deposition. From you and John Huntington. We'll wait for Bud's, for when he can talk, but you guys gotta come in."

"Right. See you Monday morning then."

Allegra let out a long shaky sigh of relief. "Oh, thank God! I'd been so worried. Claire would have been so devastated if something happened to Bud." She brought

75

trembling hands to her face, almost dazed with joy for Claire. Another loss would have been unbearable.

"Yeah, that's really good news." Her left hand was caught in his much larger one and he brought it to his mouth. He kissed the palm, closed her hand into a fist and returned her hand to her lap. "Listen, if you want to nap, go right ahead. The road's too icy for us to make good time. It'll be at least another three quarters of an hour before we get to your house."

Allegra turned to him. "Where do you live, Douglas?" She kept her voice steady, as if unaffected by the kiss. She wasn't. Her palm burned as she kept it curled in her lap, like a warm flower.

"I found an apartment on East Meadows."

She winced. "That's on the other side of town." The Parks Foundation, her house and his apartment made a huge triangle. "I'm really sorry to take you so far out of your way."

They turned a corner and she swayed toward him. "Don't even think about it. Rest now, I'll wake you up when we get there. I'll bet you're tired."

She was tired? She wasn't the one who'd gone into battle, rushing in to save the day like some superhero. Allegra opened her mouth indignantly to tell him so. "No, I'm not—" she began, but the word turned into a huge yawn, so sudden and uncontrollable she didn't even have a chance to cover her mouth. "Tired," she finished ruefully.

"Uh huh." He pressed something, and the back of the seat reclined several degrees. "Rest anyway."

"'Kay," she mumbled. The seat was very comfortable. She turned slightly toward him and closed her eyes. The blanket was tucked more carefully around her and she smiled... The car rolled to a stop and Douglas cut the engine.

Allegra sat up, blinking. "What's up? What's the matter?"

"We're here," Douglas said matter-of-factly.

"Here where?"

"Your place. I'm parked right out in front of your gate."

"*My place?* Oh, my gosh, I did fall asleep!" She pushed her hair out of her face as she sat up straight. "I'm really sorry."

"No apology necessary." He unbuckled her seatbelt and put a reassuring hand on her shoulder. "Okay, you know the drill now. The same as before. We'll get you in the house and then I'll come back for Dagda. Is that okay with you?"

"Fine."

"Right. Get out your house keys." In the time it took her to fish her keys out of her bag, he was at the passenger door. "Let me have the keys and then lean forward," he said, and she did, in utter faith that he would catch her. He swung her up in his arms, blanket and all, and started carrying her to her house. Again with that smooth, powerful stride, as if she weighed nothing at all.

It had turned incredibly cold and sleety. Snow struck every inch of her exposed skin. Douglas had wrapped her up, but her hands and cheeks were instantly numb with the cold. He still had on only his shirt but he didn't seem to mind the cold. Even swaddled in his jacket and the blanket, she started shivering, but he didn't. Maybe he didn't feel the cold. It was possible, considering the enormous amount of heat radiating from his big body. Her entire right side was warm where it came into contact with him.

It was thirty-five steps from the gate to her front door. She'd counted them. She'd *had* to count them, so she wouldn't smack her face on the gate or stumble over the front porch steps. The ones Douglas was walking up easily. He had probably taken only twenty steps to get there.

Somehow he managed to open the door without any trouble, even with her in his arms. He walked into the house and put her down gently. He didn't let go until he was sure she was stable on her feet. As he put her down she had to slide down against him and Allegra was struck all over again by how tall he was. At least a head taller than she was, probably more.

"Be right back with Dagda." The door closed quietly behind her and she was alone.

After the warmth of the SUV and his body heat, the house felt cold. Empty. Barren. Dark.

The way it always felt.

Panic and bile rose from her gut to her throat.

Allegra didn't know where she was in the living room. She hadn't been paying attention when Douglas walked into the house, too distracted by the feel of his hard muscles bunching against her as he carried her, by the intense heat he radiated, so that all she wanted to do was snuggle even more closely to him. Had he turned slightly to the left or the right while walking in?

Allegra froze, completely disoriented in her own home. Where had he put her down? If he'd put her down by the settee, she'd trip over the hassock if she moved to the right. If she was close by the window, on the other hand, moving left would mean running smack into the wrought iron floor lamp in the shape of petals with wicked cutting edges.

Suzanne had wanted to "blind-proof" her house, as she'd put it. Bless her, Suzanne had read up on architecture for the blind and had gotten all excited about putting tactile orienting strips on the floor, motion-sensitive acoustic cues in all the rooms, push-bars on all the doors.

Allegra had put her foot down at that. No, no way. She wasn't going to be blind forever. She believed that with every cell in her body. The doctors had said there was an operation. New, experimental stuff, even potentially dangerous, the doctors had said, but everybody knew how fast medicine advanced. If the technique had been experimental in September, it would be current practice by now. So damn it, she wasn't going to get used to being blind. She was *not*.

She wasn't going to learn Braille. She wasn't going to get a white cane. She wasn't going to get a seeing-eye dog. Above all, she wasn't going to rip up her home.

And now she was totally lost in her own living room, with nothing to guide her. The only thing she knew was up and down. Everything else was a black abyss.

The panic rolled in, the oppressive blind panic that roiled through her and devastated her several times a day, leaving her lost and shaken, in tears. She couldn't *see*.

She had nightmares, often. Scenes she barely remembered as she woke in a panic, heart pounding, tears drying on her cheeks. At times the dreams were of drowning, at times of being buried alive. At times of being beaten. Whatever it was, it was always, always, heart-stoppingly horrifying.

She'd had a waking nightmare this evening, when she'd seen her father, a first. Which meant she could count on having a particularly horrible nightmare tonight.

She faced it all alone. The oppressive silence and darkness of her house. The stumbling over objects she'd forgotten to put back in their habitual position. The fear of going out for a walk.

The terrifying nightmares, waking up in horror to an eternally bleak blackness, groping for a light that could never be turned on.

Allegra could feel the panic building as she stood there, rooted to the spot because she was afraid to move. Almost afraid to breathe, tight bands around her chest squeezing her heart. The heart that was thumping wildly in her chest, like a bird suddenly caged.

Tonight was going to be a bad night, she could feel it. The terror and violence at the Parks Foundation had eaten away at her reserves. That was why she'd had the waking nightmare and had seen her father. Dead and bloody.

Tonight would be terrifying.

79

Behind her, the door opened, letting in a swirl of cold. She could hear Douglas putting Dagda down. Instinctively, he was choosing Dagda's habitual spot—in the front right corner. Footsteps behind her, circling her. He moved quietly for such a big man, but her ears were attuned to silence.

She could hear his breathing, feel his heat.

She could almost read his mind. He'd accompanied her home, Dagda was safe. He had at least another half-hour drive ahead of him, probably more, in this bad weather. He'd want to be heading home.

In a flash, Allegra knew that she couldn't spend tonight, of all nights, alone. Simply couldn't. She'd rather die than wake up sweaty and shaking, a scream choking in her throat. Alone, in the darkness.

She twisted her hands together, gathering courage. She tried to keep her voice even, but it didn't work. She thought she might approach the subject in a roundabout way, but she couldn't do it. What she was feeling was too big, too scary to grope for words. It came out a stark plea.

She tried to feel where he was, but she couldn't. All she knew was that he was in the room with her.

The words came tumbling out, short and stark. "Douglas," she said, her voice shaking, speaking to thin air for all she knew, "please don't leave me alone tonight. I don't think I could stand it. *Please.*"

He was in front of her. A big hand touched her hair, then he pulled her into his arms. Her head was resting against him, ear pressed to his chest, so she felt the words vibrate in his chest as he spoke them.

"No, of course I won't leave." His arms tightened. "There isn't a force in the world strong enough to make me leave you tonight."

Chapter Six

ဢ

Please don't leave me alone tonight.

Allegra stood there in the center of her living room, forlorn and bedraggled, in his oversize jacket and his car blanket over that, one white hand emerging from the swathes of cloth to keep them around her.

She was deathly pale, the darkening bruise on her forehead standing out in shocking contrast. The glossy red hair he'd so admired was tangled, falling over her shoulders in rough red ringlets. The little makeup she'd been wearing was long gone. The unfocused green eyes had lost any mascara, the full lips were pale.

She was disheveled, frightened, lost.

She was so beautiful it hurt the eyes to look at her.

Kowalski held her even more tightly. He'd spoken the bald truth. There wasn't a power on earth strong enough to make him go away. All during the trip across town he'd been trying to figure out a way to stay with her and get her eventually back into his arms.

He was good at making strategic and tactical plans before action. He had his all mapped out in his head.

He'd make her some tea, taking his time, maybe even fix her something to eat. Say that he needed to stick around to see if she really was concussed. Say that he'd just bunk down on her couch.

See what happened tomorrow morning. See if he could wrangle a repeat of that amazing kiss and take it further.

It turned out that he didn't need to do any of that, and the reason was his own fucking stupidity. He'd scared the shit out of her. He'd just dumped her on her feet and left because he wanted to get the harp in and be back with her as quickly as possible.

Asshole blockhead that he was, he'd completely forgotten that she was blind. That she couldn't possibly know where he'd put her down. What was he thinking? He'd just dumped her and disappeared. When he came back in, he found her exactly where he'd put her. Looking so beautiful, and so lost.

Had he bothered to tell her where she was in her house? Nope. He'd been in too much of a rush. Result? She had no cues at all. What would it have taken to reassure her? Nothing. All he'd had to do was say—you're next to the couch, to your right is the hassock, in front of you is the coffeetable.

Shit, if she got it wrong, she'd have stumbled over the hassock and fallen onto the glass tabletop. Cut herself, maybe badly. His blood ran cold at the thought and his arms tightened even further around her.

Her arms emerged from his jacket and the blanket to embrace him. It was so mind-blowing, the way she responded to him. The way every movement of his was matched by one of hers.

"You're shaking," he said, and she nodded against his shirt. Short little tremors ran through her. It wasn't the cold. Her house was heated and she was covered in layers. "You're having a stress reaction."

"Is that what this is?" she murmured.

"Yeah. It'll pass. Not a whole lot of fun, though, while you're in it."

How often he'd seen it—the tremors that came after violent action. She'd been brave—amazingly brave considering her condition—and she hadn't broken down so far, but the delayed stress was finally getting to her. She was trembling. Tears were probably next.

That was cool. Physiology 101. Stress hormones are released via tear ducts.

His men didn't cry after the stress of battle—they usually drank themselves into oblivion, got into a fight, or fucked their way back to sanity if a woman was available. If not, it was the good old fist.

Kowalski had tried them all, every way he knew to bleed out stress, except for the tears. Fucking, drinking, fighting, jerking off. Once, after a particularly vicious firefight where he'd lost four men, none of the usual remedies had held even a remote appeal, so he'd donned sweats and ran all night. The base had a three-mile obstacle course and he ran around it over and over and over again for hours, until his legs turned to mush, until his breath seared his lungs, until his crotch burned with sweat. He ran until the sky turned pink with the coming dawn and then he finally ran back to his bunk, slipping between the sheets and staring at the cracked wooden ceiling until the military day started at oh-six-hundred.

Fighting, drinking, fucking...he knew which one he wanted right now, and if he didn't move, it would be prodding her right in the stomach.

He pulled away from her, and stepped to her side, keeping his arm around her small waist. To the left, a sideboard held a small but very nice collection of Irish whiskies. "Is that some of Ireland's finest I see there on yer sideboard?" he asked in his best Cork accent.

"The very same." Allegra gave a watery sniffle. "Would ye be wantin' a wee drop for yerself, then?"

"Oh, I surely would," Kowalski said fervently. A whiskey sounded just perfect right about now. Maybe it would numb his brain enough so he could keep his cock down.

She turned her head up to him and gave him a teary smile that weakened his knees. The blood rushed right back down and he nearly sighed.

"Here." With a hand to her back, he guided her to the couch and sat her down. "You'll be wanting some whiskey yourself, too."

"I will?" She looked startled at the idea.

"Oh, yeah. Trust me on this one."

Allegra settled down on the couch like a queen. Kowalski couldn't figure it out, how someone so mussed-looking could still look so regal. Tangled hair, makeup gone, tears drying on pale cheeks, his jacket which could have gone twice around her and his old blanket around that. Yet she sat down primly, white slender hands folded in her lap, as if she were dressed in satin and gold with a diamond tiara, looking for all the world like fucking Queen Allegra, preparing to greet her subjects.

He found glasses, poured a finger for her, filled his own glass three-quarters full and sat next to her, frowning. There was something wrong with the picture. He put the glasses on the coffee table.

"Come here," he murmured, lifting her up and settling her on his lap. Allegra turned into him, shifting until she was comfortable, ending up with her head on his right shoulder, soft hip right next to his hard cock. There. Perfect. "Give me your hand."

Like before, she held it out to him without question, and he curled her fingers around the crystal glass. "Here you go." He downed half his glass in one gulp, enjoying the fragrant peaty warmth as it slid down and settled in a warm ball in his stomach. Ah, nothing like Irish whiskey. Scotch whiskey couldn't hold a candle to it, in his opinion. Allegra sipped hers, too.

Kowalski waited. The drink would warm her up, start breaking down her defenses. She didn't want to cry in front of him, but the whiskey would shut down the part of her mind that wouldn't let her do what she needed to do—shed tears.

Allegra emptied the glass and held it out to him with a trembling hand. He took the glass and put it down next to his own and took her hand. It shook inside his. He brought it to his mouth and kissed the back of it, marveling at her smooth satiny skin, at the delicacy of it.

"It's okay to cry," he said quietly, and her head turned faintly at the sound of his voice. She hadn't quite figured out where his face was, but at those few words, her blind gaze honed in on him.

It occurred to him, in a flash of insight that penetrated even his thick skull, that she needed to hear his voice to orient herself. He hadn't talked to her nearly enough.

He wasn't a talker, with anyone, but especially not with women. The way he looked, he was never going to convince a woman to have sex with him by sweet talk. The women he bedded didn't need or want talk. They wanted to be fucked and more often than not they made that clear without too much input from him. He didn't need to talk them into it.

Beautiful women wouldn't even give him the time of day. Kowalski had never really tried talking to a beautiful woman, with the exception of Suzanne.

But Allegra needed for him to talk. She needed to be able to anchor herself in the darkness of her world by means of his voice. The tremors were increasing, despite the fact that she was visibly trying to hold them back.

"If you want to cry, it's probably the best thing for you." Kowalski shifted his arm slightly so that it created a cradle for her back. "Crying releases a lot of stress hormones. You'll feel better afterward."

She nodded jerkily. "I don't want to cry. Crying won't help anything."

Her voice was thick with tears. A little frown line appeared between her auburn eyebrows. Kowalski waited.

She suddenly buried her head in his shoulder. A shudder shook her entire body, and she broke into tears. Finally. It was what he had been waiting for. Allegra's long, slim arms wound around his neck, she pressed her face harder against his shoulder and sobbed her heart out. At first they were harsh little whimpers as she tried to repress the tears, then one great sob broke out, unleashing the flood. Her narrow rib cage shook with the force of her weeping.

Kowalski understood very well that she was weeping from not only the stress of the evening, but also the stress of the loss of her world. He didn't know what had happened to her—and now was no time to ask—but she'd lost a lot.

An accident, she'd said. Car accident? Had she slipped and fallen? Whatever, it must have been a bad accident to leave her blind. She must have been on her way to a fabulous career, with that voice, her skill with the harp and her incredible looks. He hadn't heard of her but then he'd spent most of the past ten years abroad. So this beautiful and incredibly talented woman, who'd already recorded, had already gone on tour, had had her career and her life stopped short by an accident, leaving her blind.

Crying was the least she could do.

He held her quietly through it all, giving her the animal comfort and heat of his body. At last, she stilled, exhausted. Kowalski glanced down. Even after a storm of tears, she was so beautiful. He pushed aside a lock of hair that had fallen over her eyes. Her shiny hair was so fiery red he was constantly surprised it felt cool to the touch.

Her eyes were closed, thick auburn lashes lying against the white skin of her cheeks. He dried the last of her tears away with his thumb.

"I was so scared," she whispered finally.

Of course she'd been scared. She'd heard flashbangs, machine gun fire, people screaming. All without being able to see what was going on. It must have been terrifying for her.

"I know, honey," he said. "I'm really sorry. But it's over. There isn't anything to be scared of now. Just put it behind you. You're safe."

"I was so scared something had happened to you," she continued, as if he hadn't spoken. Kowalski's jaw dropped in shock. "I couldn't believe you went out there barehanded. And

86

then I heard gunfire and—and screaming—" her voice wobbled and she stopped until it was back under control. "I thought you'd been shot and killed," she whispered finally, voice thick with tears. "There were all these shots...and noise...and no one was coming for me. I just knew that you would be coming back for me, but you didn't. It seemed like forever until I heard your voice. It was so horrible not knowing what was happening. I was imagining you lying in a pool of your own blood." A shudder ran through her and Kowalski tightened his arms.

Good God. How much time had actually gone by while he'd talked with Midnight and Suzanne and Larry? Maybe fifteen minutes? Not that long to him, but to her it must have seemed an eternity.

She'd been worried about *him*.

Kowalski couldn't remember a time someone had worried about him. Worrying about his men under fire was *his* job. Nobody worried about the Senior Chief. Everyone took it for granted that the Senior could look after himself.

"It was all under control," he said finally. "Bud gave me an opening and I took it."

"What happened?"

"There were five bad guys in the room. Bud took care of one of the thieves. John had knives and he threw them at two of the bad guys and they both went down. I grabbed a gun and took care of the other two. And Larry and the SWAT team took care of the outside guards. They never stood a chance—they didn't even manage to get off a shot."

She frowned. "What do you mean they didn't get off a shot? Bud was hit."

"That happened before he broke into the main hall. So you didn't have to worry about me."

"Of course I did." Her voice was soft, tentative. She loosened her hold on his neck, bringing one arm down. A long-fingered hand cupped his jaw. Thank God his scar was on the other side. It was as ugly to touch as it was to see. "I was praying you would make it."

Kowalski just looked down at her. Jesus, she was so fucking beautiful. It never occurred to him that he could ever hold such an incredibly beautiful woman in his arms. She was looking at him in admiration, too, which was even more mind-blowing. Well, not *looking* looking. But still.

A little dimple appeared by the right side of her mouth when she smiled. It appeared now. "You're very brave. I don't think I know anyone who would go after armed men while unarmed." A little line appeared between her eyebrows. "Well, maybe Suzanne's husband, John. You worked together, right?"

"For going on twenty years, yeah. And we weren't that brave."

Allegra gave a very unladylike snort. "Yeah, right."

"No, there was no question of the outcome."

It was true. He and John had faced much, *much* worse in their time in the Teams. And Bud had been a Marine. Much as SEALS made fun of jarheads, there was mutual respect there. Marines did hard, dirty and dangerous grunt work and they did it superbly well. The three of them had faced pros in their time—men who trained day and night to kill, just like they did. In comparison, the thieves they'd taken down were fucking amateurs, out for quick dough, thinking they were tough guys because they were armed. The thieves never stood a chance against him and Midnight and Bud.

What had terrified Midnight had been the guy holding the machine gun muzzle to Suzanne's head. That was the kind of potential goatfuck Murphy's Law was invented for. The guy could have squeezed the trigger by mistake, or tripped, or could have decided to celebrate his newfound wealth by blowing Suzanne's brains out of her head. All it would have taken was a four-pound pressure pull. The same amount of energy it took to open a beer can, and the heart of Midnight's world would have been ripped out.

That had been the only real danger, and it wasn't even to them.

"I thought you were pretty brave yourself, tonight."

"Me?" Her face went slack with surprise. "Good Lord, I didn't do anything but cower and quiver. That's not being brave."

"I don't know. There's bravery and then there's bravery. Going up on a stage and playing an instrument and singing in front of hundreds of people," he gave an exaggerated shudder she was bound to feel, pleased to see her smile, "I'd have been scared shit—er, spitless."

The smile widened. "You can say shit. I've heard the word before. Often."

"Have you?" His voice turned husky. "That's nice."

God, when she smiled, it was devastating. He forgot what they were talking about. He shifted her in his arms until she was more fully turned to him and reached out with the finger of his free hand. He had to touch her, touch all that softness.

Gently, barely brushing the skin, he ran his finger over her cheekbone, down, down, outlining her lips.

He had rough hands, full of calluses. He was scared to death he'd scratch that incredibly delicate skin. She stopped smiling as he ran the tip of his index finger around her lips, face intent as she concentrated on the feel of his hand on her. She moved slightly and her hip slid right over his hard-on. He caught his breath as his cock surged.

"Can I ask you a personal question?" That soft voice sounded breathless.

"Sure." The answer came out strangled. He hoped he could answer it. All the blood was draining from his head and he found it almost impossible to concentrate on anything other than the feel of her soft skin.

She shimmied a little over his hard-on and he bit his lips to keep from groaning.

"Is this," her hip rolled over him, making him even harder, "is this, um, a permanent condition with you?"

His breath exploded in a laugh. "It seems to be. Around you anyway. Doesn't seem to make any difference at all what else is going on—gunfire, danger...it just goes up when you're near. Though to tell the truth, usually, it pretty much does what I tell it to. Except with you."

"I'm...flattered." The dimple appeared. "I think."

"Um..."

Shit man, say something!

What wanted to come out of his mouth wasn't anything he could say to her. Jesus, how could he tell her he couldn't ever imagine his cock going down if she was in the same room? The same house. Hell, the same city. He clamped his lips closed because the words wanted to just come tumbling out.

He really needed to be able to talk to her normally, without sounding strangled and without her realizing there was no blood in his head at all. She had to know that he wasn't sex-crazed, though that was exactly what he felt like right now.

This was where Kowalski got to practice talking to a beautiful woman. He had tons of things to talk to her about. Her music, for one. He loved music, always had, but he'd never had the opportunity to actually speak with a musician. Certainly not with one as talented as she was. Or they could talk about the accident, how she'd become blind. What she liked to read, that was a good one. There were tons of books in the room, presumably from before the accident. All sorts of conversational gambits were possible.

This was probably his one shot in this lifetime at a conversation with someone like Allegra. Pity he couldn't think of one word to say. He could barely remember his own name.

He bent his head as the arm holding her lifted her up to him. As he slowly brought her face to his, her smile faded and her eyes fluttered closed. When his mouth touched hers, she was ready. She opened immediately for him and it was like before, under the stage. Like plunging into a warm, perfumed tropical pool. He wanted to stay there forever, tongue tangling with hers. Her left arm tightened around his neck and he deepened the kiss, lingering over her mouth, tongue deep inside her. Her taste was sweet and heady, totally intoxicating.

No bad guys with guns stealing jewels, no gunfire, no outside distractions at all, just the two of them in the quiet of the snowy night, the only sound in the room her sighs and his groans. The wet sounds of their mouths meeting, the rustle of clothes as she shifted in his arms.

He lifted his mouth for a moment to look down at her, amazed all over again that Allegra was in his arms. Watching her felt almost like voyeurism. He looked away from beautiful women, always. And yet, deep down inside, a part of him no one had ever seen, or even suspected existed, loved beauty. No one would credit him with an aesthetic sense since he looked like a knuckle-dragger and he spent his days training hard men to kill. Not much beauty in that. But the truth was, beauty moved him.

He was moved now. She was beautiful but she was more than that. Allegra was more than a pretty face. There was humor and character and intelligence in her. Courage, too, if she hadn't fallen apart over becoming blind.

He could look at her all he wanted, and his gaze roamed over the fine features, the delicate pearl-white skin, the grace of her. She must have sensed his rapt gaze because she smiled slightly and said, "What?"

"You are so fucking beautiful," Kowalski whispered, then winced. *Way to go,* he thought. *Very classy.* "Sorry."

Luckily, that smile didn't falter. "I've heard that word, too. I'm not made of spun sugar. I won't melt just because I hear a four-letter word."

Maybe not, but she *looked* like she was made of spun sugar. Her skin was so pale and so fine. He watched, fascinated, as a light flush rose up where he touched her. He ran his finger experimentally over her skin, from high cheekbone down to her chin, tapping the shallow little cleft there, then down over the long slim neck, across the delicate collarbones. It was all equally fascinating, pure pleasure wherever he touched her.

Kowalski had no idea whatsoever if what they were doing was going to lead to sex. Just the thought of it made his heart beat faster, but he had to get real here. What would someone like Allegra be doing in bed with him?

If she told him to stop, he would. He would, he would.

He hoped.

He had a hard-on that wouldn't quit, but it wouldn't quit even if they fucked. The way he was feeling, he could be in her for three days straight and still be hard.

And anyway, what he was doing now was almost as good as fucking.

Almost. Maybe.

Just the thought of being inside Allegra made his hard-on pulse and he shook, knowing he was weeping come in his pants. She nipped his bottom lip and his hips surged up against her in an uncontrollable movement.

She felt him and flushed.

He watched in fascination. The feelings tumbling through him were so intense it was almost like the slo-mo of battle. So many at once, all mind-blowing. The feel of her, the softest thing he'd ever touched. The colors, from the palest pearl of her shoulders and upper breasts to the faint pink of her cheeks and brighter pink of her lips. He bent to kiss her, biting her lips lightly, lifting his mouth for a better fit, then kissing her deeply again and again.

She fitted both arms around his neck, sighing softly. His right hand was clasping her waist. He opened his palm to run his open hand along her narrow rib cage, savoring the soft, delicate feel of her under the light cloth. She wasn't shying away from him. If anything, her arms tightened around him.

His hand cupped her breast. It was small, perfect, fitting neatly into the palm of his big hand. He could feel her swell under his hand just like his cock was swelling. Suddenly the feel of her breast under the soft gauzy material wasn't enough. He needed to feel her skin, needed to see what her nipples looked like. He was a real sucker for pale pink nipples, his favorite.

Kowalski reached around behind her and slowly unzipped the dress. The sound wasn't loud but Allegra must have felt what he was doing, must have felt her gown loosen and the cooler air of the room against the suddenly bare skin of her back. If she wanted to protest, now was the time for it.

But she wasn't protesting, not at all. She sighed, lifted her mouth away from his long enough to murmur, "Douglas," and then kissed him again.

She was kissing *him*. Kowalski was a good strategic thinker and in that electric moment, he realized that they *were* going to have sex — and soon.

Every muscle tightened as he warred with himself. Part of him wanted to rise up — *right now* — carry her into the bedroom, throw her on the bed and drop right on top of her. Now that it was completely unzipped, the pretty dress wouldn't have to be ripped off her, he'd just slide it off with a swipe of his hands. Whatever she was wearing underneath — well, that would have to go right away. Either he'd have to get her underwear off her the easy way or he'd rip it off. Either way, he wasn't about to wait more than two seconds to get her naked.

And a second after that, he'd be in her, fucking her hard. Full tilt, flat-out, pubis-grinding, bed-rocking fucking. Holding her legs high and wide as he pumped in her as hard as he could.

That image brought him up in horror. He actually jolted.

"What?" she whispered without opening her eyes. "What's wrong?"

"Nothing," he muttered, and bent to kiss her again.

Shit, he'd split her in two if he did that. He was big and as aroused as he'd ever been in his life. His cock felt like a baseball bat. Allegra was so delicately built, he just knew she'd be small and tight. Those two things together weren't going to work in bed without hurting her, unless he made sure she was ready.

Once in bed he was going to have to be very careful. Kowalski was used to rough fucking and probably subconsciously he'd chosen partners who wanted just that, because no one had ever complained. The women he'd been to bed with weren't looking for anything but a big cock that could stay hard long enough to please them. That was exactly what he had to offer. No more, no less.

This was something else entirely.

Allegra was a lady and needed to be treated like one.

And she was blind. Essentially helpless. *That* thought jolted him, too.

Kowalski had no illusions about how it was he'd ended up with this beauty in his arms. It wasn't his charm and it sure as hell wasn't his looks. Allegra had been through a traumatic experience tonight and was scared to be alone. It was very likely tonight was the only night he'd get with her. He had to do it right. He couldn't get out of control and forget she was blind.

The last thing he needed was to get too rough and spook her, make her scared.

Kowalski knew how to war-game. It was his specialty. Part of war-gaming is putting yourself in your enemy's head. In this case Allegra wasn't the enemy, of course, but for a second he could put himself in her head anyway. He could well imagine the feeling of being in bed with someone like him who got rough. He was two hundred-forty pounds of pure muscle. A man who'd trained in martial arts every day of his adult life. She couldn't control him in any case, no woman could. But a blind one—

Jesus. She'd be at his mercy. Completely. Not able to defend herself in any way. Not able to grab something to hit him with if she got scared. Unable to phone anyone.

He consciously gentled his hold on her, determined that she wouldn't have a second's hesitation about him, a moment's unease. Tonight had to be pure pleasure.

He lingered over her mouth for a long time, hand gently outlining her breast over the gauzy material. She shifted again and the dress gaped open.

Kowalski put his hand under the bodice of the dress, on the upper slope of her breast, and left it there, heavy and warm, while leaving her mouth to press soft kisses along her jaw. The corners of her mouth tilted upwards. He slid his hand lower, delighting in the feel of her silky skin on the palm of his hand and the silky material on the back of his hand.

Jesus, absolutely everything about this was pure delight. The feel of her, the sounds she was making, the smell of her.

He let his hand rest on her breast, the small, hard nipple stabbing into the cupped palm of his hand. Oh, yeah.

He rubbed her nipple and she purred. That was the only word for it. Fuck, she shouldn't do that. He was trying to take this slow but he was close to exploding. His balls were tight, close up to his groin.

His mouth drifted down, down, over all that smooth skin, holding her breast up for him. He opened his eyes long enough to look down for a moment, delighting in the sight. There she was and—yup—her nipple was pale, pale pink, his favorite.

She tasted pale pink, too, like some strawberry and vanilla ice cream cone. He suckled, trying to be gentle. When he lifted his head, she had turned a slightly deeper shade of pink, nipple and areola gleaming from his mouth. A lock of deep red hair had fallen over her shoulder and he shifted it away, kissing the skin beneath.

"Do we want to take this to the bedroom?" he asked, his voice quiet.

Allegra smiled. She cupped his head with both hands, thank God missing his scar again. She nuzzled his neck, feeling her way up to his ear. "Oh yes, Douglas. I want that very much," she whispered in his ear, raising the hairs on the back of his neck. Then she turned her head and kissed his ear and—bam!—he surged into orgasm.

Almost.

Damn! That was close! He was able to pull himself back at the last second, by tightening every muscle he had, but he hung there for long seconds, shaking.

He rose up off the couch with her in his arms and carried her into the bedroom.

Allegra felt set free from hated shackles when Douglas lifted her into his arms.

Every second of every day since she'd become blind required grinding effort, a second by second planning of every move she made, lest she fall down or bump into something or somehow hurt herself. She was exhausted by the time she made it to bed at night, only to stay awake for hours, tense and depressed, staring sightlessly at the ceiling.

When she did fall asleep, she had nightmares.

This was like having her life given back to her.

She was in Douglas' strong arms, content to let him take her where he wanted. Where both of them wanted to end up—in her bedroom.

She'd been as aroused as she had ever been on that couch, kissing him, feeling his huge, strong hand on her breast, as gentle as a feather. It was such a contrast—the deep power she felt in him, the oversized muscles, the big, long limbs and this gentleness, even tenderness, when he touched her.

Allegra relaxed completely in Douglas' arms. She didn't have to think, she didn't have to plan, she didn't have to worry—she could just *be*. Nothing bad was going to happen to her, not while she was being held by him. Not while he was with her. She trusted him deeply in that.

He was putting her down, so they must be in her bedroom. Allegra stood, hanging on to his arms.

"I'm not going to turn on the light," he said in that deep, gravelly voice that seemed to penetrate to her very bones.

"Thanks," she whispered. Allegra melted. Having the lights on would put her at a disadvantage, so he was depriving himself of light. It was such a thoughtful gesture tears sprang to her eyes.

"Hey," he rumbled. A large thumb wiped the skin under her eyes. "You want the lights after all? Is that what this is about?"

Allegra gave a watery half-laugh. "No, I don't want the lights on, silly. What I really want is for you to kiss me."

"Oh, yeah." His whisper was hot in the night. She reached up and met his mouth halfway. Oh, God, his mouth. He was a superb kisser, so skilled she felt the heat way down in her stomach and even lower. Each time his tongue touched hers, she could feel her stomach muscles tightening, her vagina clenching. She shuddered and clung to him even more closely.

This was so incredibly delicious, much more of a turn-on than even making love with another man had ever been. Such heat and power. She melted and would have fallen had he not been holding her up.

Allegra lost herself in Douglas' mouth, twisting to feel more of him, her arms reaching way up high to encircle his neck.

The heat coming off him was so great it took her a moment to realize that he had slipped her dress off her shoulders. It pooled around her hips, unable to fall to the floor because he was holding her so tightly against him. She pulled away for a second, just enough so that her dress could fall to the floor, then she leaned up against him as he kissed her and kissed her and kissed her. One long seamless kiss that lasted forever.

Her bare breasts were crushed against his dress shirt, but beneath the cloth she could feel the hard planes of his chest. God, such power. She wanted to feel his skin against hers and scrabbled to get him naked as quickly as possible. She unbuttoned his shirt and had to reach high and wide to try to slip it off his shoulders. The material stuck and she groaned impatiently.

There was a low rumbling sound, charming in its intensity. Douglas laughing.

"Hang on, honey. Let me do it." His voice was gravelly, heat in the tones. He set her away from him for a moment and she felt cold and abandoned. Whispers of cloth, the rustle of clothes falling to the ground and then he was back, completely naked, kissing her, and — oh yes! It was bare flesh to bare flesh and he felt just as delicious, just as powerful, as she had imagined.

Her arms stretched to hold him. The palms of her hands smoothed over the broad, deep shoulders, lifted to wind around his neck. She was on tiptoe, pressed against him. His erect penis was hot and hard against her stomach, like warm steel. All of him was like warm, hairy steel. He lifted his head a moment, holding her tightly against him. They stood there, her heart racing so quickly and so hard she thought it would pound its way out of her chest.

Her heart had pounded like this earlier, under the podium, from fear. Her heart was getting a real aerobic workout tonight, terror and sex instead of a five-mile run. Well, she'd take the sex any day, if it was going to be like this. She was so excited she could barely stand and they weren't even in bed together.

The feel of him was so luscious. Unlinking her hands from behind Douglas' neck, Allegra brought her hands down over his chest, lingering over the flat male nipples, so unlike her own. They were tiny and hard, like a bead of buckshot. As she moved her thumb over his nipple, wondering what color it was, she could feel his penis moving between them, swelling and rippling.

How delicious! She did this to him! Humming in delight, Allegra kept her finger on his right nipple so she could find it with her mouth and bent to kiss him there, a light licking, sucking kiss. From high above her head she heard a groan, his lungs bellowed and a light sheen of sweat covered his chest.

Oh, she wasn't poor, blind, helpless Allegra any more. No, no, she was big, powerful Allegra, reducing this enormous man to mush. She bit him lightly around the nipple and he cried out. She nearly laughed with delight. Biting him lightly on the hard chest muscles, she dropped a hand to his groin. His penis was huge, rock-hard, big veins standing out so far she could feel them. She ran her hand up its length, her fingers barely meeting around him, her thumb caressing the large bulbous head. He was weeping semen, a sign of uncontrollable male excitement, she knew.

Well, she was unmistakably excited, too, wet and hot, in a more private part of her body.

Douglas' hands were tight around her, one big hand cupping the back of her head, the other around her waist. He broke the silence of the night, walking her slowly backwards toward the bed. "Don't worry about anything, honey. I have protection."

Just moving with him was such a turn-on. Allegra was entranced at the feel of his muscles against hers as he moved. It took her dazzled brain a second to process his words. Protection? What—? Oh.

It was daring and probably risky, but the feel of him was so wonderful she didn't want to relinquish one inch of his body against hers. In hers. Just the *thought* of all that power, moving inside her...

She shivered in anticipation. One last brush of her body against his and she had decided. This man wasn't sick, in any way.

"You, um, you won't need condoms."

He stilled. He'd been kissing her neck but now he lifted his head. Her neck felt cold, and bereft.

"What?"

"I said, um, you won't need condoms. I was in the hospital...a long time, and they had to put me on the Pill."

A slow exhaling of breath. "I can come in you? Without a rubber?" His voice sounded hoarse, raw.

Well, that wasn't quite the way she'd put it, but... "Yes."

In a second, she was lifted, stripped of panties and stockings and laid gently on the bed by trembling hands and then he was on her, hard and heavy, kissing her deeply. These kisses were ferocious, taking, as if she had some secret elixir he desperately needed and could only get through her. He was holding her head tightly, tilting her head this way and that so he could kiss her from every possible angle.

Wonderful as his kisses were, Allegra was distracted by the feel of his naked body on hers. He'd been on top of her before, under the dais at the Foundation, but that had been different. They'd had layers and layers of clothing, and each second felt stolen. Now she felt as if she'd slipped into some different dimension, where time was like honey, golden and slow.

The feel of the man was so delicious she wanted to press tightly against him. Every time he moved, every time he *breathed*, he rubbed against her, his heavy, hard weight increasing the sensuality by a factor of ten. Sex had never been so...sensual before, where every sense besides sight woke up and smelled the roses.

One hand left her head and ran slowly down her side. He moved just enough so he could touch her breast and it was as exciting as before. More, because she knew they were going to have sex soon and each touch prepared her body for him.

It was so amazing. Her body had completely taken over. It was doing things without her having to direct it. She realized now that with previous lovers she'd had to turn herself on, in a way. She'd had to direct sexy feelings to her breasts and vagina all by herself because she hadn't been that turned on by the man. But not now. Oh God, not now. Now her body just melted wherever it touched Douglas' without her having anything to do with it.

His mouth left hers and traveled down her neck and to her breast. She shuddered as she felt his mouth open over her.

His light touch on her breast, his mouth on her nipple, excited her almost beyond bearing. She could feel how hard her nipples were, how his mouth seemed to touch her breast and between her thighs at the same time. Each tug of his mouth was met with a contraction deep inside her.

She could feel how wet she was, how soft she felt. She could feel how wet he was, too, lightly sweating, the tip of his penis wet with semen.

For her.

Douglas was being so very careful, touching her as if she were made of blown glass, capable of shattering at the lightest touch. She wasn't delicate and she was as turned on as she'd ever been in her life. He needed nudging along.

His hand was moving slowly, ever so slowly, toward her groin. At this rate it would take him all night. Allegra twisted against him, running her hands over that wide back.

"I'm ready, Douglas. Right now." The whispered words sounded loud, they seemed to echo in her head.

The big body stilled except for his chest, moving like bellows. She could hear his heavy breaths in the quiet of the night.

"I don't want to hurt you."

She could feel that. The way he touched her was as clear as words, the way he was obviously holding himself back, the way he never, ever used his strength against her...no, he didn't want to hurt her.

By way of an answer, she opened her legs under his, lifting them along his thighs. She was completely open to him, moist and swollen and ready. He had to feel that.

Oh, yes, he did. Douglas groaned, shifted slightly until he was at her entrance. He was absolutely enormous. She'd known that—she'd *felt* it—but somehow it was more real, now that he was preparing to enter her. He wasn't using his hand. Both his hands were now cupped around her head, his tongue stroking deep in her mouth, echoing what he wanted to do further down.

Several of the men she'd been to bed with had to use their hands to help themselves penetrate her because—she realized now—they hadn't been fully erect. That wasn't the case here. Douglas could just as easily have been made of warm steel. His penis was utterly rigid and perfectly capable of entering her on its own, without anyone's help.

She felt his back muscles move as he started pressing forward into her. Slowly. It didn't hurt because he was so careful, but it could have. He was entering her by degrees, the slow friction creating incredible heat, while kissing her deeply, and it was already the best sex she'd ever had. It was as if she were being penetrated for the first time, he touched so many parts of her that had never been touched before. When he finally stopped, he was so deeply inside her, she felt stretched.

Allegra ran a hand over his back again, feeling the ripple of deep muscle, until she came to the hard flesh of his butt. As she touched him there, he groaned again and circled his hips, grinding in her. His short, wiry pubic hairs felt stiff against her super-sensitized flesh.

The large base of his penis ground against the swollen lips of her sex and she felt pierced, completely taken. Her thighs quivered with the effort of keeping them open and with the orgasm she could feel coming.

Douglas' hands left her head and moved down to cup her hips, holding her tightly, moving even more completely into her and she held her breath, the slow free fall of climax moving closer. He wasn't moving but the weight of him, the fierceness of his grip, the depth of his penetration—it was almost too much. So when his lips left hers and he kissed his way along her jawline down to her neck, and nipped her there, right *there*, where stallions nipped their mares, it was like lighting a match to a fuse. With a wild cry, Allegra simply exploded, contracting sharply around him as he ground even more deeply into her.

Douglas moved his mouth to her ear. "Now it begins," he whispered darkly.

Kowalski thought he knew a lot about fucking. He had to. Ugly men had to know more if they wanted to get laid on a regular basis. He needed a lot of sex so he'd learned how to do it right. The good old fist worked when necessary, but women were better and he'd learned how to please them.

So he knew how to control his strokes, he knew how to read the signals a woman's body gave about how she wanted her fucking—slow and deep, hard and fast, a mix. He knew he did it right because they usually asked for seconds and thirds.

Pleasuring a woman meant using your head and not just your dick. Kowalski was used to keeping some consciousness alive in the back of his head while fucking, observing whoever he was with and adjusting his moves to suit her desires. There was always a little bit of him holding back, watching. He never lost it.

He knew how to keep his cool under fire, and in bed.

So nothing in his personal experience prepared him for the hot, raw pleasure of parting Allegra's soft tissues with his cock, pleasure he felt from his hair to his toes. Fierce, hot pleasure that had him shaking, a second from coming. Pleasure that wiped almost every single rational thought from his head and reduced him to an animal operating on raw instinct.

He'd never fucked bareback and when she'd told him he could, he'd been tempted to throw her on the bed and get his cock in her cunt as fast as he could. Both because it would be the first time ever for him and because it was *Allegra*, the most beautiful and desirable woman he'd ever laid eyes on.

He hadn't though. He'd held on to his self-control by his fingernails, even withstanding the initial jolt of entering her. It had been like sticking his cock in an electrical outlet, the shock was that great.

Some last vestige of thought, somewhere way back in his head, told him to go slowly because every instinct he had was screaming for him to slam into her and start doing her hard — wall-banging, violent fucking.

He couldn't do that with Allegra. The instant his cock entered her, even just the head, he realized he'd hurt her if he let himself go. She was aroused, she was wet — that wasn't a problem — but she was small and maybe a little unused. So he pressed forward slowly, sweat breaking out all over his body. He couldn't plow her with his cock, but he could ravage her mouth instead, and did. He wished he had a hundred tongues, a thousand cocks, all inside Allegra.

Inside Allegra was the most fabulous place in the universe to be. Warm, welcoming, the source of mind-blowing pleasure.

He bit her lips, then licked his tongue back into her mouth, angling her head for the best, closest fit. She tasted heavenly. He just bet her cunt tasted heavenly, too, but that was for later, when the excitement died down a little, when he'd had her a few…hundred times. Oh God, just the thought…

His tongue in her mouth was as exciting as his cock in her cunt and it was there, in her mouth, that he felt her climax first.

His cock was finally in her all the way, but he didn't dare move. He hardly dared breathe. He pressed forward, just a little, and felt her mouth soften, a little moan which he felt in his own mouth and she climaxed, just like that.

And, just like that, he did too.

It was unheard of. Kowalski could go for hours, but at the first contraction of her little vagina against the bare flesh of his cock he exploded. He ate at her mouth, holding her head with his hands because if he held her hips he'd hurt her. So they kissed and came and shook and moaned, both of them, for an eternity. At least that's what it felt like. Kowalski lost all sense of time while he was coming inside Allegra, the first time he'd ever come inside a woman and not a rubber.

It blew the top of his head off. He clung to her mouth, gasping and moaning, holding himself rigidly inside her while every drop of liquid in his body came spurting out of his cock. What little liquid didn't come shooting out of his cock came out his pores. At the end, he was wet all over, from her mouth, from his sweat, from his come — dripping with it.

It was the most intense climax of his life. He'd actually seen stars behind his eyelids, and he wasn't even close to being done with her, still hard as a rock and still so aroused he could hardly breathe.

"How are you doing?" he whispered against her lips. He felt her smile against his mouth, lifted his head and, with an effort, opened his heavy lids.

He'd let her choose whether to have the lights on or off to give her a semblance of control, but he had excellent night vision and saw just fine by the light of the streetlamps outside her window. She was still coming, he could feel the contractions of her pussy. In his experience, women got tense when they came, muscles rigid, faces strained, looking almost as if they were in pain. But not Allegra. Allegra's face was soft, dreamy, tender. Her mouth was swollen and wet from his. She was smiling, sightless eyes half-closed.

Her open palm was against his face, delicate fingers caressing him.

The contractions were dying down and her thighs fell open from where they'd been clinging to his hips.

"How am I doing?" she sighed. "Wow. That's how I'm doing." She lifted her head and kissed him, awkwardly, off center, hitting the side of his mouth. "Thank you," she said softly.

His chest felt tight, his muscles tense. The kiss had been tender, touching. He wasn't used to tenderness while fucking. It staggered him, made him uneasy. He wasn't recognizing anything that was happening as fucking-as-usual. It was all new and a little scary. "Don't thank me yet," he growled. "It's not over."

"Oh? Oh!" she cried out, startled, when he reversed their positions suddenly, rolling over with her in his arms until she was lying on top of him. A soft, fragrant curtain of red hair surrounded his head, fell over her shoulders onto his, like a warm, living blanket. He needed to start moving and if he was on top, he'd get rough.

That was the theory, anyway—putting her on top to give her a little control over what he was doing. In practice, he held her still, tightly against him, breasts to chest, mouth to mouth, hands on her hips holding her still for the thrusting he couldn't help now. It turned hard and fast because he was losing control. Putting her on top at least made sure he didn't have his heavy weight behind the thrusts.

She was warm and slick with her own juices and his come. His cock was probably making noises in her but he couldn't hear it above his grunts, the creaking of the bed and the thundering of his heart in his ears.

His big hands cupped her ass, pressing down and he settled into a driving rhythm, the hard, fast thrusts that usually came just before climaxing. He had no sense of time or even timing, he just moved straight into another orgasm with totally unstoppable and uncontrollable force, jetting into her and crying out at the same time.

Kowalski usually wore a watch but he didn't need to. He had an accurate clock in his head and could tell you the time to a minute, night or day, without checking his watch. The clock in his head always ran in the background and he could tell you how long anything had taken. Except now. Now he had no idea how long he spent in her, whether it was five minutes or five hours. He just lost himself inside her until he exploded.

Kowalski clung to her, shaking, as he came. He fucked her all the way through it, unable to stop, short hard jabs up into her, his cock on fire, coming so hard he almost blacked out. By the time the last drop of come had been wrung out of him, he was able to think, just a little.

She'd come again, too, thank God. When he stopped moving, he could feel her contractions, a gift of the universe because he hadn't done anything to merit that orgasm. He was behaving like an animal. He was lucky she wasn't sitting up in disgust, ordering him out of her bed, which is what he deserved.

She moaned and he stopped, panting, lifting her up a little so he could see her face. Her eyes were closed and she tried to smile.

"Douglas," she murmured. She was sweating too, not like a pig, as he was, but that was definitely the dew of sweat on her upper lip and forehead. She looked exhausted and wasn't responding to the exploratory little thrusts he was making with his cock. He wasn't done yet, not by a long shot, but she was.

Kowalski kissed her neck and her mouth, lightly—her mouth was a little honey trap—and lifted her off him as he pulled out of her. Her muscles were lax, pliant, unresisting.

Kowalski ran a hand down her side, marveling at how beautiful she was in this dim light, like a princess in a fairy tale. A very tired princess. He kissed her cheek, said, "Sleep now," and watched as she drifted off instantly.

He watched her for a long while as the sweat cooled on his skin. He'd sweated horribly, the sheets were wet with it and with his semen. He'd pumped what felt like several quarts of come into her and he wondered if he'd dehydrated himself.

Allegra was lying on her side, lower leg out, her thighs wet, pearly drops of come like little jewels in her pubic hair.

She looked so lovely lying there, long hair in silky ringlets over her shoulders and breasts, one strand lying across her mouth. The strand moved gently with her soft breaths. Kowalski shifted it with a finger, trying not to touch her skin. If he touched her, even gently, he'd want more, now that he had the feel of her in his hands. The temptation to bend down and take her mouth again was so great he nearly shook.

Kowalski wasn't used to holding back in bed. Once a woman was there, he took it as a given that he could have as much of her as he wanted and he hadn't been wrong yet. But Allegra was tired and stressed from the violence and the sex. However much he wanted her — more than he'd ever desired another woman — he wanted her to rest, too.

He looked down at himself, chest and pubic hair dark with dampness, his hard-on practically bursting out of its skin. It showed no sign whatsoever of going down. He hadn't even begun to get her out of his system. Well, there was only one remedy for a hard-on he couldn't use on a woman. With a sigh he headed for the shower, where he could take care of two problems at the same time.

Once in the shower, though, he had a shock, the latest in a whole goddamned series of them tonight. He lathered up with soap that smelled of Allegra while his hand reached reflexively for his cock. His fist had barely closed around his penis when he yanked it back, as if his cock were radioactive.

Kowalski had rough hands, the hands of someone who worked with them a lot outdoors. He made sure his nails were clean and cut short but that was it. The skin of his palms was calloused and he'd never thought twice about it until he clutched his cock and it practically howled its protest.

His cock did not want his rough hand around it. It wanted Allegra around it. It wanted her soft tissues, clasping warmly around him, it didn't want his fist.

And the damned thing was, it only wanted *her*, Allegra. Another woman wouldn't do.

Kowalski looked down at himself in bemusement, hot water sluicing over his body, running down in rivulets and circling around the drain. He stood there for a long time under the jets, feeling as if his life was circling that drain together with the shower water. He looked down at his red, inflamed cock that simply wouldn't go down. His tried-and-true remedy—jerking off—wasn't working. The only remedy in the world was Allegra, and that was scary as hell.

Gritting his teeth, Kowalski turned the water off, dried himself and padded back into the bedroom.

There she was, stretched out on the bed, slender and luscious and pale. Fairy princess and angel and magical musician, all rolled into one. She'd moved, to clasp her arms around herself. Maybe she was cold. The thought of Allegra even vaguely uncomfortable was unsettling.

He climbed into bed, rolled her into his arms and pulled the blanket up, tucking it around her shoulders. She sighed deeply and settled against him, a knee high up against his groin.

Jesus. Right against his inflamed cock.

He gently edged her knee back down and stared at the ceiling, left hand full of wondrous woman, right hand longing to drop down to his groin and do something, anything, to get rid of his hard-on. There wasn't anything he could do.

Finally, he cradled his head with his right hand and started counting sheep.

He stared at the ceiling, listening to Allegra breathe, until the sky turned pearl-gray.

Chapter Seven

** හ**

For the first time in five months, Allegra woke up happy. She usually woke up with tears drying on her cheeks. She had nightmares almost every night, judging from the heavy feeling of oppression every morning. Only the very bad ones woke her up in the night, the others were jagged, fleeting shards of horror and terror leaving a heavy residue in her mind, like lead dust. She never remembered the content of the nightmares, only the feeling of panic and terror. It often took her until midmorning to get a grip on her feelings.

Not this morning, though. This morning, she woke up on a hard, warm, hairy surface. Douglas' chest, to be precise. Her lips curled upwards in a smile as her hand moved across that broad hairy chest. The man was so big and so strong, she was constantly amazed.

He was awake. There was something about the quality of the air around him that told her that. Was she developing the extra-sensory abilities all the doctors had told her about? She shoved that thought away from her as soon as it formed.

"Hello," she whispered against the hard, warm skin of his biceps.

"Good morning." Oh God, she'd almost forgotten how lusciously deep his voice was. The voice vibrated in his chest.

"Yes," she said simply. She could feel the smile on her face. "It's a very good morning."

"Are you...all right? I got a little carried away there. I hope I didn't hurt you."

Allegra didn't even pretend that she didn't know what he was talking about. He *had* gotten carried away, pounding inside her until she'd finally been too exhausted to continue.

111

When he'd realized, he'd simply pulled out, still hard as a rock, draped her over him, anchoring her with a big, warm arm around her waist and kissed her on her sweaty cheek.

"Sleep," he'd ordered in a deep rumble, and she'd gone out like a light. And slept dreamlessly for the first time in five months.

Allegra stretched, and was caught unawares by all the sore muscles. She ached everywhere, particularly between her legs, where she seemed to still feel him. There she was sore and sticky. Her nipples were super-sensitized where he'd suckled her hard. Even her arms were sore from holding tightly to his broad shoulders.

Every sense she had—except for sight—was on sensory overload. She could smell him and—she sighed—herself. She could even distinguish between his smell, a mixture of male musk and something metallic—which she imagined was the cordite from the gun he'd fired, though there was an overlay of her soap so maybe he'd showered during the night—and her smell, cologne and sweat. Then there was the smell of sex, a combination of both their smells and the amazing amount of semen he'd pumped into her last night.

She could hear his heartbeat, slow and powerful in the deep chest. She could feel him against every inch of her body, warm and hard.

Douglas shook her lightly. "Allegra," he said, his deep voice worried, muscles suddenly tense. "Tell me I didn't hurt you. Tell me you're all right."

"Oh, yeah," she sighed, and turned her head so he could see her face. His tense shoulder muscles relaxed when he saw her smile. She was sore, but it felt distant, as if it belonged to another body. "I'm fine." She shifted on him a little and came up against his penis. Hugely erect, just like the night before. "And you seem to be fine, too. Once again."

"Not again." His big hand was caressing the back of her head. "Still."

"*Still?*" Allegra lifted her head at that, mouth falling open. He'd been erect *all night?* "Is that—is that normal? Are you on something?"

There was a deep rustling noise in his broad chest. It took her a moment to realize he was laughing. She smiled. Never in her wildest dreams would she have imagined waking up to this. To this big, strong man in her bed. Last night he'd burned away her usual nighttime anguish. Grief, sadness, fear, panic—it all burned away in the heat of passion.

"On something? On what? You mean like—Viagra?"

"Well, something like that. I didn't know it was possible for men to stay, um, erect for so long."

Another deep chuckle. "No, I'm not on Viagra. I'm not on anything. In fact, technically speaking, you're on me."

Allegra smiled. "So I am." She rubbed her toe against his hairy shin and cupped his huge, hard shoulders.

"So I guess the question this morning is, what are you going to do about it?"

"Do?" Allegra lifted her head at that. "What do you mean—"

As if she were a doll, Douglas lifted her torso up and, opening her legs with his own, shifted her until she was sitting on him, straddling him.

"Oh." That's what he meant.

She wiggled experimentally. He'd placed her—quite by design she was sure—so that her sex was over his penis. All it took was a small movement and the lips of her sex opened up over him. It was electrifying. He managed to swell even larger—she could actually feel the ripples of his penis against the sensitive flesh of her sex.

She flushed deeply. She had very pale skin and even the slightest flush was visible. She must be beet red. His hands spanned her waist and she leaned forward to brace her own hands against his chest. When his penis had moved, there'd been an instantaneous reaction in her own sex.

113

She was melting, hot all over, but still sore.

Douglas lifted his hips, moving back and forth so that he was stroking her. She could feel every inch of him, the ridges and heavy veins. It excited her, but...

"Douglas," she murmured as his hands tensed on her waist. He was about to lift her again, position her for penetration. She couldn't do it. "I'm so sorry, but I don't think I can. Not right now." She was too sore. The thought of having him inside her again, moving hard and fast, was enticing in theory but she couldn't take it. Not yet.

Douglas stilled immediately. He was immense and hard between the lips of her sex, his hands tight at her waist. She could feel the tension in the hard striated muscles of his chest. It was like sitting on a massive powerful engine, revving, ready to take off.

For just a second, a fraction of a second, Allegra was afraid. She'd said *no*. Not just to anyone, but to a very powerful man, massively aroused, muscles tight with need.

She hadn't meant to say no, it had just come out, her deepest feelings. Right at this exact moment, though she was aroused, she didn't want him to enter her.

A wisp of memory drifted across her mind, a ghost of a thought, gone almost before she could grasp it. Only a fleeting emotion remained, but it was enough.

You don't say no. You can't change your mind. You don't tease. Otherwise...

She shivered, suddenly cold. "Sorry," she whispered tensely, "I didn't mean—if you want, of course you can—um..."

He was immobile, an immense, warm, hairy, marble statue. "That's okay." Her hands were over his pectorals and she could feel the vibration of his deep voice.

"No, no, sorry," she said hastily. She took his penis in her hand, shifting to her knees so she could rise up above it. It was so stiff she almost couldn't lift it away from his stomach. This man was seriously aroused. Maybe he would be in pain if he couldn't have sex. "It's okay, I don't mind. Honest." She braced herself over him, trying to ready herself for penetration, though she wasn't aroused enough. She hoped it wouldn't hurt.

"Stop," he said quietly. All the muscles in his body relaxed, except for the big one between his thighs. That stayed incredibly hard. His hands gentled. He wasn't holding her so much as he was touching her. He slid his hands up and down her back, softly, more to reassure than to arouse. "There's no problem, honey. We don't have to fu — make love now."

"No, really, I don't mind."

"This is just fine." His hands whispered up her back, rubbed her shoulders, traced down the curve of her spine to her waist again. "More than fine. Has a little magic all its own." She couldn't see him, but there was a bit of a smile in his voice.

"Sorry," she whispered, miserable. Allegra bit her lower lip. "I don't mean to be a tease. It's just that I'm a little — "

"Sore? I thought you might be." He shook her, just a little. "I asked, too. Remember?"

This was so complicated. She hadn't realized precisely how sore she was until she'd sat up, until they were halfway toward making love.

He kneaded her shoulders gently.

"Oh." Allegra's head tilted as she leaned back into those big hands. It was really hard not to melt into a spineless ball of wax. "That's nice."

"Mmm. Oh yeah." He purred. That was the only way to describe the extraordinary sound. Like a lion in the savannah, lying in the sun. Those large, rough, warm hands were gliding over her back, somehow drawing the tension out of her muscles. "This is really great. I love touching you."

He made no effort to make it sexual. He didn't try to rub her breasts, or touch her sex. Though it wasn't sexual, it was deeply sensual, a feast of simple warm human contact in the quiet of the morning.

"I don't ever want you to do something you don't want to with me, honey. I want you to promise me that." The deep voice was so steady, so sure.

Allegra closed her eyes. Not to shut out the world—the world was shut out for her permanently. She simply wanted to savor this moment of utter trust and human warmth.

"Allegra...answer me." His hard abdominal muscles tightened as he prepared to lift his torso. "I want your promise."

"Okay," she murmured on a sigh. "I promise."

"That's my girl. You don't need to feel you have to do anything with me. Don't ever pretend. I don't want that, don't need it. Just being with you like this is an incredible pleasure. Now relax for me."

That last was said almost as an order. Well, he was probably used to giving orders, having been in the Navy. He must have been instantly obeyed, too, because Allegra could actually feel all her muscles relaxing even further, one by one.

This was so delicious.

He wasn't asking her to perform, to become turned on, to do anything but sit there on him, enjoying the feel of him between her thighs, enjoying his hands on her.

The simple human contact was so wonderful. She hadn't really touched anyone since...the accident. Not really. Oh, she'd taken Claire and Suzanne's arms when they were out, but just to negotiate obstacles. She never went for long walks with them. She couldn't orient herself and was too scared that they'd forget to tell her about a curb or a hole in the sidewalk. So what she'd had was a hand in the crook of a coat-covered elbow. A kiss on a cheek. A quick hug. That was it.

Only now could Allegra face the fact that she'd been so *lonely*, so starved for human contact.

116

She was making up for it big-time now. There was a lot of Douglas Kowalski to touch.

Lightly, hoping he wouldn't mistake it for a sexual advance, Allegra ran her hands over his shoulders. She'd touched him all night last night, but this was different. This wasn't clinging to him in the throes of wild passion. She wanted — *needed* – to touch him, to get to know him.

The muscles over his shoulder bones were deep and hard. There was no way to perceive the bone underneath. How on earth did a human being develop muscles like this? He must lift weights for hours every day.

Every single aspect of his body was so utterly unlike her own.

Long, powerful, striated muscles with no give to them at all. The sculpted, delineated contours of a hard male body. The textures of smooth skin and hair-roughened skin.

It was fashionable nowadays for men to shave their chest hair but Kowalski obviously hadn't heard that, because there was a thick mat of rough curly hair covering his chest from the top of his pectorals down past his stomach. She followed the line of hair, dreamily, until her hand brushed against his penis just below the belly button. She jerked her hands away in the instant she heard his breath leave his chest in a whoosh.

"Sorry," she whispered, as she heard him swallow.

"Touch whatever you want, honey. However you want to." His voice was low, steady. So incredibly reassuring.

Allegra's hands returned to his chest, outspread fingers reaching up to his shoulders.

She hadn't been to bed with many men and they'd all been musicians, like herself. She remembered untoned bodies, definitely not ripped. Her last lover, Steve, had been rail-thin. She couldn't remember what he felt like. She could hardly recall what he looked like.

He had a pointy face, she remembered suddenly, with a wispy little beard.

What did Douglas look like?

Her doctor had told her that blind people learned how to build up a mental image of a person by touching them. She'd seen that in movies, too. How did they do it? Maybe she should have practiced on Suzanne and Claire, whose faces were as familiar to her as her own. Touching noses and foreheads, outlining mouths—would that let her learn how to "see" a face?

She had to try now. She desperately wanted a mental image of Douglas in her head. In only a few short hours, he meant more to her than any other man she'd ever met, yet she had no idea what he looked like.

Allegra suddenly *had* to know what Douglas looked like.

She knew what his body must look like. She knew he was tall and incredibly broad-shouldered. He had very long limbs. His arms seemed to be twice the length of hers. She knew firsthand the strength in the deep muscles. She knew his hands had rough, calloused skin but were incredibly gentle in their touch.

And his face?

Allegra ran her fingers gently over his collarbones and up his neck. He had stubble. It started halfway up his neck, leaving only a short space of smooth skin between his chest and facial hair. The pads of her fingers moved upwards...

Douglas caught her hands in his, his fingers closing around her wrists, like warm, living manacles. He wasn't hurting her, but she couldn't move.

"Douglas?" she whispered and tugged lightly. There was no give at all to his hold. "I want to know what you look like. Let me touch your face."

That swishing sound must be his hair rasping across the pillowcase as he shook his head. She didn't need to see to know what it meant—*no*.

"Douglas?" She pushed a little against the implacable hold on her wrists.

He made a strangled sound deep in his chest.

"No." The word lingered in the air, stark and hard.

"Why?" she asked softly.

"I'm...ugly." The words came out low and harsh, guttural. As if between clenched teeth. As if from a terrible place inside him.

"You're *ugly*?"

"Very."

The idea shocked her. How could Douglas be ugly? He seemed the very epitome of attraction, a true alpha male.

He had the physique of a god. He was almost over-endowed—in every way, she thought with an inward smile as she wiggled over him.

In response, he surged up against her, hot, hard and huge. He subsided immediately.

Of course. She'd said no and he was honoring that. He was an honorable man. Now *that* was attractive.

He loved music and was knowledgeable about it, too.

He had a sort of old-fashioned chivalry, choosing to carry her to his car rather than letting her get her feet wet.

He'd been willing to die for her. And for his friends. Thanks to his courage, there hadn't been a bloodbath at the Parks Foundation. Bud and Claire and John and Suzanne were alive because he'd been brave enough to face armed men unarmed.

He had the most delicious male voice she'd ever heard. After a two-minute conversation, she'd been halfway to falling in love with him on the basis of his voice alone.

And he was *ugly?*

"Let me touch you, Douglas," she whispered. "You can't possibly be ugly. Not to me."

He was silent, fingers around her wrists, preternaturally still. It seemed as if he'd even stopped breathing.

"Please, Douglas," she pleaded. "I need to touch your face. I don't know what you look like. We've made love. We're on this bed together, naked and...and *I can't picture you in my mind.*"

There was no way on this earth Allegra could force Douglas to do something he didn't want to do. All she could do was ask and wait.

His fingers around her wrist tightened, briefly, then he let her go, arms coming down to his sides to rest his big hands on her thighs.

"Okay. Touch me if you want." The deep voice was flat, emotionless. "Go ahead."

Hesitantly, Allegra bent to him, hair falling forward over her shoulders.

What were people's faces made of, anyway? The basics were all the same, for everyone on earth, unless they were disfigured. Two eyes, two ears, one nose, one mouth. Eyebrows and lashes. Beard and moustache, sometimes, if they were men. Or sometimes even if they weren't men.

Allegra thought of Rosa Mancino, the Parks' housekeeper. Rosa's sister Elena did pretty well in the beard and moustache department.

How do you *feel* what someone looks like?

Her hands drifted, gently, building up sensory impressions.

She feathered her fingers over his neck, corded with muscle and tendons, tense. Then she ran a finger lightly over a raised vein, following it up to the underside of his jaw and back down again. He had raised veins everywhere, the kind Olympic athletes had. Something about carrying more oxygen to the muscles, she'd read somewhere.

She could feel his life's blood pulsing through the vein, in time with the steady, slow heartbeat under her right hand, which had come to rest on his chest.

Now she brought both hands up, to feel his jawline.

Her wrists were caught again in that gentle, unbreakable hold. She didn't try to break it or push against him, but simply waited.

"I have...a scar." He bit the words out.

"Do you, Douglas?" she asked softly. It made sense. He'd been a soldier, of course he'd have scars. "You know what? I don't care."

She had her own, by God. It's just that hers didn't show.

She waited patiently, hands encircled by his. He was the one who had to allow her this intimacy. They'd made love — had sex, she corrected herself. There wasn't a part of her body he hadn't touched, fondled, caressed. And yet he was upset at the thought of her touching his face.

There was nothing she could do but wait while he battled whatever demons he had inside him.

Allegra knew all about battling demons. It's what she did, all day, every day.

There was utter silence in the room, save for the faint sound of her own breathing. Douglas was so still, so silent, he could have been dead. If it weren't for the fact that she could feel his chest expanding between her thighs with every breath he took, she couldn't even be sure he was alive.

"Go ahead." He released her with a small exhalation of breath and her hands landed gently back onto his neck, to continue their journey of discovery.

He did indeed have a scar, on the left side of his jaw, a big, ugly one. It was like a road map of pain, wide and long, running the length of his jawline, hairless, very thick and smooth, a large raised welt. Irregular lines crossed it. Sutures? If so, the surgeon had been a clumsy one.

"This must have been very painful."

He didn't answer, but gave only a small shrug.

Allegra knew that she herself had been given the best possible medical care. She'd spent the better part of three months with her jaws wired shut and yet she was told that nothing showed on her face.

This scar must be very visible on Douglas' face.

"Do you care? About the scar?"

"No." His voice was curt, leached of all emotion.

Allegra ran her finger over that deep scar, backwards and forwards, while he lay utterly still beneath her. It was as if she were trying to draw the memory of the pain it must have caused away from him, absorbing it through her fingertips.

Finally, Allegra bent to the task of figuring out her lover's face. How to do this? She lightly circled the contours. It was broad, square-jawed, the lower half bristly with the new growth of beard.

She ran her fingers into his hair. It was short, but not military-short, a razor-cut.

"What color is your hair?"

"Dirty blond."

"And your eyes?"

"Light brown."

The coloring probably came from his Slav ancestry, as did the high, broad cheekbones she could feel. He had a high, large forehead with a few deep wrinkles. There were deep wrinkles at the corners of his eyes, too.

"How old are you?"

"Thirty-eight."

Then the deep wrinkles she felt were those of a man who'd been out in the sun and wind too much, not those of a man edging toward old age.

Allegra continued touching, lightly following the lines of his features, feeling the textures of his skin, tracing his eyebrows, his lips. His nose was big, broad, the cartilage crooked.

"Your nose has been broken," she said.

"Couple times, yeah."

She couldn't seem to put all the sensations together to form a picture in her head. But one thing was clear to her, and it went way beyond the actual shape and form of his face. What was clear was that he had a face that matched his body — hard, unadorned, purely male.

She sat up, acutely aware of her nakedness and his. Aware that somehow the light touches of his face had become caresses. Though he hadn't moved under her ministrations, she'd felt his penis swell impossibly larger between the lips of her sex when she touched his mouth. The friction aroused her, too, made her wet and soft.

Somewhere deep inside, she was preparing herself for him. Maybe in a little while she could...

But first, there was something she had to do.

"Douglas?"

His fingers tightened on her thighs when she ran the tip of her index finger over his upper lip. "Yeah?"

Allegra bent forward completely so that her breasts rested against his chest, his penis a hard cylinder between their bellies. She lowered her face until her nose bumped against his. Her curved hands framed his face. She could feel the hard knobs of his cheekbones, the deep wrinkles fanning from his eyes, the bristly beard. She could feel his breath washing over her face, his utter and complete stillness.

How she wished she could *see* him.

"For the record, Douglas, I don't think you're ugly," Allegra said softly. "As a matter of fact, I think you're beautiful."

He bucked, once, powerfully. Suddenly he was kissing her wildly, without any finesse at all, holding her head as he ate at her mouth, teeth grinding against hers, tongue thrusting deep. Between their bellies, his penis rippled and swelled. He moaned deeply, harshly into her mouth as he surged into orgasm. She could feel the wetness as he jetted semen over her stomach and his, and with an excited cry, she climaxed, too.

Chapter Eight

ဢ

Allegra was singing something in the shower. Something complex, yet oddly simple too, heartbreakingly beautiful. Haunting. As enticing as a siren's song, luring him in.

No way. Shit, no.

Kowalski didn't want to go anywhere near the bathroom. He didn't want to go anywhere near *her*. As a matter of fact, if he had even the smallest shred of sense, he'd walk right out of this house. Hell, he should quit Alpha Security now and move across the country because even being in the same city with the woman was dangerous to his mental health.

He should stay far, far away from this woman.

Kowalski had had well over five thousand orgasms in his life, yet nothing — *nothing!* — could have prepared him for the explosive, totally out-of-control fireball of emotion in his chest when he'd come. And he hadn't even been fucking her. Didn't make any difference at all that he hadn't even been in her. It had been devastatingly powerful, and for a second there it felt as if he'd died.

He'd been unbearably moved, watching her try to feel her way over his face. So absorbed, so intent, trying to learn to see through her fingers. It was clear she'd never done that before. His was the first face she'd tried to see by feeling with her fingertips since she'd been blinded.

With any other woman, he'd have stopped it right away, no reason for anyone to be messing with his face. But how could he say no to Allegra? She was perfectly right — they'd had sex and she had a right to try to figure out what he looked like.

She'd leaned down, bumping noses with him, awkwardly, endearingly.

He'd been trying his best to ignore the fact that they were both naked and that he'd had a hard-on for half the night that showed no signs of going down.

Not grabbing her, rolling over with her and entering that smooth little body was one of the hardest things he'd ever done.

Then she'd cupped his face, delicate hands gripping him, huge sightless eyes so intense he couldn't possibly look away—and told him he was beautiful.

He'd come so hard and so long it was a miracle he had any liquid left in his body.

It was only long moments later, when he had his breath back, when his heart had stopped trying to hammer its way out of his chest, when he could see again, that he felt shame. Their stomachs were smeared with his semen and he felt like a teenager who'd come in his pants. He hadn't done that since he was a horny fifteen-year-old with a perpetual hard-on.

That shamed him. But it was the dazed, lost feeling of skidding out of control that scared him.

He was thirty-eight years old and he'd fucked his way through a battalion of women and he'd never had this feeling of being on the edge of a precipice, about to fall into an abyss. It scared the holy shit out of him.

With the excuse that he needed to clean up, he'd gotten out of bed as soon as he humanly could, showered up and changed into sweats. From the safety of the doorway, well beyond touching distance, he told her he would cook breakfast while she had her own shower, and had fled to the kitchen.

Kowalski thought longingly of his apartment. It was big and empty, with a functioning kitchen, an oversized bed, a couch and a state-of-the-art home entertainment system, all he needed. Whenever he made a noise in it, there was an echo. But it and every thing in it was completely under his control.

Just listen to her, he thought, edging closer to the door leading into the bathroom. Just listen to that. It was fucking magic. She was trying scales now, up and down, as pure as a waterfall. After a while, she went back to the original melody, a little more complex now, since she was a little more sure of it.

The shower water stopped and Kowalski headed back into the kitchen. Making breakfast hadn't been hard at all. She had an amazingly well-stocked fridge and a freezer filled with plastic containers of home-cooked meals, just ripe for the nuking. The cardboard tops had been scored with the letters B, L and D. Breakfast, Lunch and Dinner, he found, when he opened a B filled with homemade blueberry muffins. There was another B container with a cheese omelet right next to it. He'd nuke that, too.

He'd eat breakfast and get out of here, get out of pretty, talented Allegra Ennis' life. Not for her sake, but for his. This was scary shit and he could be cut off at the knees at any moment. He was tall and strong and tough, had been so all his life. There wasn't a man alive on the face of the earth that he feared.

Allegra terrified him.

The coffee filtered down from the coffeemaker, the microwave dinged and the short hairs on Kowalski's neck rose.

She was here.

He could feel her, he could smell her, that faint scent of spring.

"Hi," she said softly.

"Hi." Kowalski slowly turned around. She'd changed into faded jeans and a bright green sweater. Her hair was loose around her shoulders and she was barefoot.

She was so fucking beautiful. This wasn't fair. Why did she have to be so beautiful?

She was looking in his general direction, hesitating on the threshold, one pretty bare foot folded over the other.

Kowalski walked over to her slowly, making sure she could hear his footsteps. He could move silently when he had to, but he wanted her to hear him coming.

The way he'd simply rolled out of bed and escaped to the shower without even a kiss—well, if she spat in his eye, he had it coming.

When he was so close to her that spring-like scent filled his nostrils, she straightened. "Douglas," she said and smiled, holding her hand out. His heart gave a sharp kick and he rubbed his chest absently before reaching out to her.

Kowalski placed her hand on his forearm and he could feel the almost audible *click!* as everything in the universe fell into alignment, like tumblers in a slot machine. His arm was made for her hand. Her hand belonged there. This was the way it was meant to be.

Allegra Ennis was going to break his fucking heart, and there was damn all he could do about it.

"Breakfast is ready. I hope you're hungry because I made a lot."

"Good." She drew in a deep breath, delicate nostrils flaring. Though Kowalski couldn't seem to smell anything but her, he knew she was smelling coffee and muffins and omelet and toast. "I'm starving."

He walked her over to the kitchen table and pulled out a chair for her with his free hand. "Here, honey."

"Wait a minute." She stood a moment, frowning. Her fingers plucked at his sleeve. "This isn't a tuxedo. What on earth are you wearing? Nothing of mine could possibly fit you."

He sat her in the chair and placed a warm muffin on a plate in front of her, gently guiding her hand to the plate. She felt awkwardly for the knife. Once she had it, she cut the muffin neatly in quarters and ate a quarter daintily.

Kowalski sat next to her so he could help, if she needed it. "I keep a gym bag in the car with two changes of clothes and a toothbrush and razor in case I want to take off for a weekend without going home. I've got on sweats. If you don't mind, later on I might take off for a run. I'm used to a lot of exercise."

"Fine. I need some time too, on the harp, practicing." She smiled as she popped another bite of muffin into her mouth. "I guess we have that in common—we're both pretty disciplined."

The idea startled him. So far, he'd been completely and utterly blown away by the differences between them. Her beauty, her delicate physique, her incredible voice and musical talent. Her charming smile and easy way with people. She was his polar opposite. But look beyond that, he saw now, and they were in many ways alike.

The women Kowalski had dated so far—well, fucked more than dated—weren't real big on discipline and hard work and steadfastness. They'd been the kind of women to hang out in bars, hoping to snare a SEAL—for some goddamned reason SEALs seemed to be flavor of the month for the groupies—or at least have themselves a hot time between the sheets. They were women who weren't that good at holding down a job, who looked at other women as competition, who couldn't see much beyond tonight's beer party.

Allegra was completely different. Everything about her showed discipline and hard work, a sober lifestyle. Her house was filled with books—from when she could read—and CDs. Everything in the house was neat and showed good taste. Her friendships with Suzanne and Claire were real. He could never forget her not wanting to bother either of them when she desperately needed help getting up on the stage. After a near-death experience, Suzanne's first thought had been for Allegra.

"How many hours a day do you practice?" he asked.

"Depends." She daintily picked up another quarter muffin. Kowalski had already had four muffins himself. "If

I'm close to a concert or a recording, I can go up to eight hours a day." She turned her head toward him. "If we lived together I'd drive you crazy. Guaranteed."

Kowalski's heart gave another huge kick in his chest at the idea of living with this woman. At this rate, he was going to have a heart attack.

"Look." She held her hand out to him, and he took it. "Look at my calluses. I'm surprised you didn't say anything when I was touching your face."

Kowalski held her hand, delicate and long-fingered, trying to figure out what she was talking about. Then he saw them — tiny little circular calluses on the pads of her fingertips. They were incredibly cute — harp calluses.

"My skin's pretty weather-beaten, honey. You'd have to have tougher calluses than those for me to feel them. Here, feel mine." He brought her hand to the web between the thumb and index finger of his right hand, to the thick scarred skin there.

"Oh, my." Allegra looked startled as she felt gingerly. "Whatever caused that?"

"When we start training on short guns — mainly .45s — that's what we get. They carry a big kick. When we shoot, the hand absorbs the kinetic energy. A big blister forms where the gun impacts the hand most. It bleeds and breaks open every night because we're firing hundreds of rounds a day. Thousands a week. Finally, the blister just heals over into a big callus. Sort of like a shooter's badge of honor. See?" He held out his left hand, touching her lightly to let her know his hand was there. She felt carefully over that hand, too.

"You've got the same scars on this hand. Are you left-handed or right-handed?"

"As it happens, I'm right-handed but it doesn't make any difference. You shouldn't favor either hand when you shoot. What happens if you're in a gunfight and your good hand is out of commission? We need to be able to fight with both and we practice with both."

Allegra rubbed the webbing of his hands. "That must have hurt."

Like a bitch, he thought. "A little, in the beginning," he allowed.

She smiled to herself. "Something else we have in common. Matching calluses." She dropped his hands and he instantly missed her touch, as if a current had been switched off. "Can you please tell me where the milk is?"

It was scary that her touch could affect him so deeply. He was thinking about how much he'd like to just stay here forever, by her side in the quiet morning light, sipping coffee and talking. And he was thinking at the same time that if he had any brains in his head at all, he'd get into his SUV and just drive away, double-quick time. What had she asked? Oh, yeah. Where the milk was.

"Bravo red, eleven o'clock," he said absently.

"I beg your pardon?" Allegra whipped her head around to him so quickly, soft thick strands of fiery hair caught in the zipper of his sweat-parka. Her lush mouth formed an O.

"Sorry." What an asshole he was. He'd spoken without thinking. "Sorry, honey. That's spotter's language. The milk is—"

Wait a minute, he thought, as he gently disentangled the lock of hair from the zipper before it could hurt her. He needed to think this through.

Kowalski's job in the Navy had been to break strong, hard men, beat them down to a pulp, rob them of their self-confidence until their characters were down to bedrock. What was left couldn't be intimidated and if it could, they were out. Kowalski had been the recruits' worst nightmares because he knew full well that they would face horrible things in battle, worse even than the worst things he could throw at them.

Working men till they bled on the training ground so they wouldn't bleed in battle wasn't pretty. He'd had three death threats from men who'd desperately wanted to make the Teams but had crumpled under his brutal, unrelenting pressure.

Kowalski had seen good men, strong men, finally give up their highest ambition, their most cherished dream, because he'd asked the almost impossible of them and they couldn't do it. Kowalski wasn't particularly proud of it, but that was what he did. He was a master at breaking men down until they touched bottom. Whether they came up again was their business, and if they came up, they were unbreakable.

Now was his chance here to do the opposite — to give this wonderful woman some self-confidence, teach her how to negotiate her world of darkness a little better. She wasn't dealing well with her blindness. He could help.

"Listen, honey." He edged his chair closer to her. "When soldiers observe something in the field through their scopes, they need a language to tell the others what they see. The info has to be given fast and it has to be right. So we've built up a code that lets a fellow soldier know exactly where something is. So here's the deal. Imagine a building, any building. Picture it in your head."

"Okay." Allegra's eyes were closed as she concentrated. She was smiling. "Great-grandma's house in Ireland."

"How high is it?"

"Three stories. My great-grandparents had eleven kids. My second cousin Moira turned it into a hugely successful bed-and-breakfast last year. I spent a lot of time there when I was a child. We had family reunions all the time. Big, noisy, singing-and-dancing reunions."

Kowalski tried to imagine a big, noisy, singing-and-dancing family reunion and failed. He'd grown up with a sad, drunken father and a mom who'd lit out when he was eight.

"Did you have your own room?"

"No. I always slept with Moira's two eldest daughters, Kathleen and Sinaid."

"Where was their room?"

"On the third floor. Front right-hand corner window."

"Okay. So the first thing you need is a system of reference points for a building. We call it the color clock. Each side of the building has a color code. The façade is white, the back is black, the left-hand side is red and the right-hand side is green. Can you repeat that?"

"Front white, back black, left red and right green," she said promptly.

"Good girl," Kowalski said, and she beamed at him, pleased.

Shit, his heart did that huge thump again. Oh, Christ.

"Now, from the ground up. Each floor has a letter and we use military designations. Alpha, Bravo, Charlie…"

"So I would have been sleeping in Charlie green?"

"Hey, so you know this stuff already. You were in the Navy, then, and didn't tell me. No fair," Kowalski said in a heavily exaggerated suspicious tone, and Allegra laughed out loud.

"I don't think I could be in the Navy. Can you be in the Navy if you can't swim?"

"Be a little hard." He took her hand and lifted it to his lips. "But you're smart and brave. If anyone can do it, I'd bet on you."

"Ah, Douglas Kowalski, of the County Cork Kowalskis, ye've kissed the Blarney Stone one time too often, ye have." She lay her hand on his arm, which he was beginning to recognize as her way of orienting herself. Grounding herself through him. "But bless you for it, me lad."

"No, no, you're a natural." Kowalski loved everything about this. The gentle flirting, the feeling that he could help her gain self-confidence. The feeling that she depended on him for something he could give her. "Okay, pay attention, now. Let's say we're talking about a surface, like this table. Under the table is Alpha. The table itself is Bravo, above the table is Charlie. Now we go by another clock, this time a real one. Imagine the table surface as a clock face. So straight ahead of you on the table is six o'clock, across the table is noon, to your right is three o'clock and to your left is—"

"Nine o'clock." Her head wobbled gently as she took all of it in. "So, tell me. Where is the milk again?"

"Bravo red eleven o'clock," he said, and her hand reached out and unerringly found the milk carton.

"Oh! Oh my God!" Allegra's face lit up as she grasped the carton. There was no other description for it, she simply glowed, with pride and delighted surprise. "Again! Tell me to find something else!"

"Coffee pot at Bravo green three o'clock."

She reached for the coffee pot and he managed just in time to turn the handle toward her so she wouldn't burn herself, cursing himself for not thinking. Damn it, he always thought things through, several moves ahead, but Allegra simply ate up huge portions of his hard disk.

"Bingo," she said, and hefted it.

"Here, honey, let me pour." There were limits to what he'd let her do. Pouring boiling coffee in her lap was not in the program. She sipped and he watched the thoughts going through her head as she realized new possibilities. She felt for the saucer, placed the cup delicately in it, and turned to him with huge gleaming eyes.

"Again," she breathed.

"Muffins. Bravo noon."

Muffins, check. Sugar, check. The omelet plate, check. His fork, check. Her fork, check. They covered every object on the table.

Finally, Allegra sat back, a brilliant smile on her face. "That's really great," she said. "Let's try you." Her left hand tapped its way up his right arm and stopped, cupping his right shoulder, delicately kneading. "Charlie red."

Kowalski placed his hand over hers. "That's right," he said huskily.

Her right hand slowly felt its way to his other shoulder. "Charlie green."

She was holding him in her arms, awkwardly, leaning forward from her chair. Kowalski lifted her up and over him, straddling him.

They sat quietly a moment, adjusting to the feel of her on him, Kowalski's hands resting loosely on her small waist. Her hair spilled over his arms in a shiny fall. He looked down, watching her face intently. She was staring straight ahead, at chin level. Her breath washed over his neck. She was caressing his shoulders, slowly, learning him all over again through touch.

Allegra slowly leaned forward until her forehead touched his chin, rolling her head back and forth, as if she could get to know him through her skin. Then she turned her head slightly to kiss his jaw. Exactly where his ugly scar was. She lifted her head to look sightlessly at him.

Kowalski's chest grew tight. There was no mistaking Allegra's expression, a mixture of admiration and affection. He didn't even try to lie to himself about it because it was the first time he'd ever had a woman look at him like that.

Women had two expressions with him—repulsion or lust. No in between, certainly never anything like what he was seeing on Allegra's face right now.

She brought her right hand down slowly over his chest until it rested over his heart. The heart she could clearly feel beating rapidly, like someone in fibrillation, on the verge of a heart attack.

Kowalski was an athlete, had been all his life. He had a resting pulse of sixty-five, but not now. Now his heart was beating triple time, the beats thundering through his body, completely out of his control.

He was a man whose heart rate actually slowed down in danger, like a cobra's. His heart didn't beat like this even under enemy fire.

"Your heart." She rubbed lightly. "Charlie white," she said, her voice low. The corners of her soft mouth were slightly upturned. She had to be feeling exactly how she affected him. She looked up and the smile widened, filling his horizon, until he couldn't see anything else. Couldn't think of anything else but her lovely face.

"Oh, Douglas," she whispered, hand over his heart.

It was too much for Kowalski, simply over the top. He didn't have a name for what was going on inside him and he didn't know how to react to Allegra. How could he deal with that soft expression on her face, that smile just for him, the palpable tenderness in her voice?

He could feel himself start to shake and it terrified him. He had to bring this back to something he recognized and he had to do it *now*, otherwise he'd fly into pieces. He had to reduce this to something he could deal with.

Lust. He could do lust.

He just couldn't do what he saw on her face.

He tightened his hands on her, making his touch deliberately not gentle. Fisting his hand in her hair, pulling her hard against him with his other arm, he kissed her. He ate desperately at her mouth, tongue deep inside, slanting for the tightest, deepest fit possible, though he knew his beard-roughened skin was scratching hers.

He didn't care. He just wanted to be *inside* her.

He lifted his mouth and looked at her, head pulled back by his own hand, a vein beating visibly in that long white neck. Her lips were wet and swollen, eyes wide and unfocused, red streaks of arousal along those high cheekbones. Kowalski pulled her sweater over her head, roughly, in a move calculated to get her naked as fast as he could, not to arouse her. She wasn't wearing a bra. Good. Kowalski lifted her off him, making her stand just long enough to rip open her jeans and slide them down her long legs together with her panties.

Allegra simply stood there, like a little doll, sightless gaze fixed over his left shoulder. Getting himself naked was no problem because he hadn't bothered to put on underwear. All he had to do was yank at the zipper of his sweat-parka and lift just long enough to lose the sweat pants. He worked one-handed, because his other hand was sliding between her legs, separating the soft folds of flesh, probing.

If she wasn't wet, this wasn't going to work. But— *yesss!!!* —she was. Not as much as he would have liked, but it would have to do because if he didn't get into her right now, first his head would explode and then his cock and maybe he'd even spontaneously combust with the heat that suddenly filled him like a wildfire.

Getting himself naked only took a few seconds and then he was lifting her bodily over him with one arm. With the other hand, he was holding his cock away from his stomach as he positioned her over him. He groaned when, in one smooth motion, his swollen Bravo white slid hard and fast into her soft, wet Bravo white.

Douglas was panting, sweating, his heart racing. Almost out of control. Allegra should have been scared—something deep and black lying in wait for her at the farthest edges of her consciousness had the color and shape of an out of control man—but somehow she wasn't.

There was nothing painful in his grip, she had no sense of danger, just of red-hot desire, incredibly sexy in its own right. She'd never been wanted like this before. He'd kissed her as if he would die if he didn't. His hands were shaking. Allegra didn't imagine that the hands of an experienced gunman, a warrior, shook too often.

She did that to him. She, Allegra Ennis, perfectly staid harpist and singer, made this incredibly strong, tough man shake and shudder.

Allega was used to affecting people. Back when she could see, there'd always be a few people in the audience reduced to tears by her music. Women mostly, at the slow ballads of love found and love lost, but some men, too. Probably men of Irish heritage, haunted by the pain and the tragedy of the Irish people filtered through the haunting beauty of Celtic music. Still, it was the music that moved them, not her.

Douglas was affected by *her*, as a woman. It was heady and thrilling. For the first time since her accident she felt powerful, able to take the strongest man she'd ever known and reduce him to a sweaty, shaky being.

They were naked, and he was embedded in her. It hurt just a little. She'd become excited, touching him. It was so thrilling, having the freedom to roam all over that huge, strong body. He couldn't have made it clearer that she could do what she wanted with him. That had been its own excitement.

Still, he was so large and he'd entered her so quickly she was just a little uncomfortable. Douglas seemed to understand, because he wasn't moving. They sat there like a little sex *tableau vivant*, she thought.

"God, you're tight," he murmured, that deep voice rumbling, scratchy, a little hoarse. "I don't dare move. I don't want to hurt you."

Allegra shifted on him, sort of uncomfortable, sort of...not. He was holding her tightly and her arms were looped around his neck, her hands dangling down over his back. Slowly, carefully, she felt the muscles in his back, excited all over again at his size and strength. She let her hands run up the deep indent of his spine, over the shoulder blades, up the back of his neck and into his hair.

Hesitantly, cursing herself for her clumsiness, Allegra felt for Douglas' mouth with her own. When she found it, she slumped forward into him, mindless with pleasure as he took the kiss over, his tongue stroking deep into her mouth. God this was so exciting. She clutched the back of his head as he lifted his mouth, slanted it, and kissed her again, so deeply she felt as if she were falling into some endless, honeyed bower of pleasure.

Allegra was so taken with his kiss that it took her a moment to realize that he was moving inside her in short, rhythmic strokes. It didn't hurt at all. Maybe he'd waited until he felt her growing wetter, knowing her almost better than she knew herself. This was working – very well, in fact.

Though she was technically on top, she didn't have to do anything, just hold onto him with her arms as he kissed her and made love to her.

The strokes slowly deepened, grew harder. Douglas' hands were on her hips as he held her still for him. When he surged upwards, it felt as if he were delving into the deepest reaches of her body, where there were pleasure points she'd never suspected. Oh, God, it was electric, the pleasure. He held her tightly and moved upwards in the strongest, hardest stroke yet. Allegra moaned softly into his mouth, unable to speak, unable to move, unable to think.

She was so wet now they were actually making noises, embarrassing slapping noises when their hips met. She made a little grunting sound at every upstroke, as if she were being jolted. It was in counterpoint to his low growls. This was raw sex, at its most basic, most animal.

It was hard now to keep her mouth against his. His strokes were moving her strongly up and down. Though she was very wet, there must have been friction because she felt immense heat where they were joined.

Douglas removed one hand from her hip and slid it to where she was stretched around him, moving a rough, callused finger forward until he touched her...*there.*

Allegra cried out, her entire body clenching around him. When the sharp contractions began, he simply moved in her harder, deeper, keeping her on some delicate balance between pleasure and pain. The climax lasted forever as the entire world fell away. Allegra was aware only of Douglas moving in her, hard and fast, his fingers digging into her hips, his mouth eating at hers.

When she thought she couldn't take any more, when she was limp with exhaustion, he swelled inside her and with a shout, erupted into orgasm, jetting fiercely into her depths.

Impossibly, Allegra felt the sharp contractions of another climax start. The feeling was so intense she burst into tears, burrowing her face into his neck as her body took over. Douglas continued moving in her even as he was climaxing himself, the semen making her slick and smooth.

It took them both a long time to settle down. When she could finally breathe again, think again, she found herself slumped against Douglas, sticky and wet. Tears were drying on her cheeks, she was covered in sweat—whether his or hers she couldn't tell since she was plastered against him—and her groin and sex were wet with arousal and semen.

Allegra gave a half-laugh, wiped her eyes on his naked shoulder and eased herself away.

"I hope to God those are tears of joy," he rumbled above her.

"Yes." Allegra sniffled inelegantly. "That was, um, pretty powerful."

"Yeah, it was." Amazingly, Douglas was still hard inside her. Not steel-hard like before but definitely erect. She wriggled around him and felt the surge of blood run through his penis.

She took in a deep breath. "And I hope this doesn't mean you're ready for round three, because I'm sure not."

Silence. She looked up. "Douglas?"

It was so horrible not being able to see someone's expression.

His arms tightened around her briefly, he dropped a kiss on the top of her head and sighed as he lifted her off him. "I can wait. Whoa, easy now."

Her legs wobbled as she tried to stand. She would have fallen if he hadn't steadied her. A second later, Allegra was in his arms and he was carrying her into the bathroom.

Douglas kept one arm around her as he turned on the hot water in the sink. She could feel the warmth and the steam rise in her small bathroom. A moment later, Douglas was running a warm washcloth over her front, between her legs.

She'd been washed before, in the hospital, but this was entirely different. It wasn't impersonal, a job someone had to do. He would bend, from time to time, to kiss her on the cheek, her ear, the tip of her nose. It was much, much nicer than being washed by a nurse. He wrapped her in a warm towel he must have put on the radiator and rubbed gently.

"Just a second, honey," he said, and let her go. The door to the bathroom opened and closed, letting in a swirl of colder air. In a second he was back with her clothes and helped her dress.

He rinsed out the washcloth and then she could hear him briskly washing himself and the rustle of cloth as he got dressed. He pulled her in his arms and she rested against him, completely content. She could stay this way forever. There were no demons anywhere in the house or in her head, just the warm glow of happiness.

She gathered her courage in both hands. The sex had been hot and raw, but this was so nice, too. Did he like it like this, too, sweet and quiet, or was he here just for the sex? Only one way to find out. She tilted her head back even though she couldn't see him. "Can you—can you stay the day?"

"Oh, yeah." His deep voice was low and soft. "Just try kicking me out. But I need to go for that run now. Do you have a set of keys you can give me so you don't have to walk to the door when I come back?"

"There's a set in a crystal bowl on the sideboard to the right of the entrance. I'll practice while you're gone."

"Right. I'll walk you to Dagda, then go for my run. Be back in an hour or two."

Allegra smiled. A Sunday with Dagda and Douglas. As the song went—who could ask for anything more?

Chapter Nine

∞

Kowalski ran and ran and ran. He ran until he was bathed in sweat, until his lungs burned, until he couldn't hear the cars swishing by in the snow over the drumbeat of his own heart.

Portland was a pretty little city, circular and contained. The forest began right at the outskirts. Kowalski could have run to the edge of the city, easy, and just continued on out. Maybe that's what he should do—just run right out of town.

But however hard and fast he ran, there was no getting away from Allegra. She was in his head, in his nostrils, in his very cells.

Running always cleared his mind and by the end of the run, whatever it was that bothered him had flattened out and disappeared. He'd either solved the problem or decided it wasn't a problem, after all.

Allegra was a problem he couldn't solve, in any way. Problems were things outside you, things or situations that could be reasoned about. Kowalski had always been good with things and situations, able to manipulate them until they did his bidding.

He never had problems with himself. He knew who he was, he knew what he could do and what he couldn't do. He knew what he could have in this life and what he couldn't have and he'd never confused the two. He always gotten what he wanted and what he didn't have he didn't want. It kept things simple.

This problem here wasn't simple or easy. It wasn't anything that could be solved by strength or smarts. He had no way to cope with his slippery-sliding feelings when he thought of Allegra.

This was way more than the excitement of a new sex mate, though the sex was more intense than any he'd ever had. New bedmates become old bedmates pretty fast, but that wasn't going to happen with Allegra.

There was a sudden snow flurry and Kowalski stopped, running in place so he wouldn't cool down. Unconsciously, he'd been heading toward his place as if to a refuge or a sanctuary. He could picture it in his head—large, cool and empty. No strong feelings there he didn't know how to handle. No feelings there at all.

But he didn't want to go back to his place. He wanted to be in Allegra's pretty house with her in it, hearing her soft Irish-tinged voice talking and singing, listening to her play the harp. No, he had to be honest with himself. He didn't just want it—he craved it.

It suddenly occurred to him, as he hopped from one booted foot to another, breath clouding the air in front of him, that he'd never be content alone in his apartment ever again. The old way, the way he'd lived his entire life up to now, was suddenly gone. A new life—one where he needed Allegra in it like he needed to draw his next breath—had taken its place.

This was serious shit. Not even as a child had he been dependent on anyone, and now this slip of a woman had suddenly become essential to his wellbeing. It was frightening as hell, but it was what it was. Kowalski wasn't someone to hide from reality. The reality of his life now was that he needed Allegra in it for however long she cared to stay.

With a mixture of doom and anticipation, he turned right around and headed back the way he came. If he hurried, he could be with Allegra again in half an hour. He picked up the pace.

He could hear it from half a block away. At first, it was a disembodied heavenly sound coming from the swirling depths of the snow, so muffled it had no origin except seemingly from the snowflakes themselves. As if the snow was bearing music, snowflake by snowflake, note by note. It was only when he saw the lighted windows of the living room that he recognized the music as that of Allegra playing her harp.

Kowalski stopped a moment on her covered porch to catch his breath. He was panting and sweaty and he wanted to cool off a little before walking in.

The sound of her music was more distinct now, coming through the door and the windowpanes. He recognized the air she'd been humming in the shower, only now it wasn't tentative, hesitant. Now it was a full-blown melody, haunting and lovely, complex yet heartbreakingly simple, the kind that sinks into the bones and sinews. She was singing along to the melody, though he couldn't hear the words.

He could see her through the window—he frowned. Shit. The very first thing he'd do once he was inside would be to draw the curtains. She was so absorbed, he didn't want to interrupt her. But he wanted to hear that song.

Using the key she'd given him, Kowalski quietly opened the front door, just a crack. She was in the far corner, she shouldn't feel the cold air.

As he opened the door, the words of the song hit him like a hammer to the chest.

"*New love,*" she was singing, words repeated over and over again in a hauntingly beautiful refrain. "*I've found a new love, to fill the holes in my empty heart. New love...*"

Every hair on Kowalski's body stood up.

"New love." That song was about *him. He* was the new love.

On suddenly weak knees, Kowalski quietly closed the door, tottered to the edge of the porch and sank to the steps, sitting there, stunned, watching the snow falling from the sky, barely hearing the music over his hammering heart.

That song was so beautiful. He knew enough about music to realize that it would become an instant classic. Beautiful music was forever. It never died. A hundred years from now, a thousand years from now, people would be singing "New Love" and something of him would be living on when his bleached bones rotted in the cold, cold earth.

Never in his wildest dreams could he imagine a woman like Allegra writing a song about loving him. Or—his mind balked at the thought—that a woman like Allegra could actually love him.

Kowalski sat listening to her as she practiced the song, as it became truer with each singing, until in the end, to him it was as perfect as a Mozart sonata or a Picasso or a sunrise over the sea.

When he trusted his legs to carry him and his voice not to quaver, he stood up and made a point of making noise on the steps. He stopped outside the front door, knocked twice and used the key.

The music had stopped. Allegra sat back in her little chair, hands resting in her lap, face turned to the door. "Douglas?"

"Yeah—" his voice was hoarse. He cleared his throat. "Yeah, I'm back from my run."

She'd done that wobbling thing with her head again, until she got a bearing on his voice. She smiled brightly, and he stepped back at the welcome and warmth on her face. No one in his entire life had looked at him like that. "I'm glad you're back. I missed you."

He stood, jaw clenched tight, fists clenched tight, chest tight, until she said, "Douglas?"

He had to will his boots to move. "Good thing you had Dagda to keep you company." He walked to her and reached out to touch her face. He ran the back of his forefinger down her cheek, marveling at the velvety smoothness. "What was that you were playing?"

She blushed lightly and thrummed a scale with her left hand. "Nothing really. I had an idea for a song and I was fooling around with it. It's a messy process, I'm glad you weren't around to hear it."

He cupped her neck and bent to place a quick kiss on her lips. "When it's written, when you're happy with it, you'll let me listen?"

"Sure." Allegra's hand clung to his wrist. "How was the run? You feel wet, is it snowing?"

"Yeah, but it's letting up. There are about three inches of snow on the ground."

She sighed and rose, holding on to his arm. "I love the snow," she said wistfully. "I loved that about Portland when we moved here. Ireland doesn't really get much snow, just rain. I wish I could go out. Besides not being able to read, it's the thing I miss most since the—the accident. Not going for walks."

"No problem." Kowalski sat her down on the couch, went to the windows to pull the drapes, then walked back to her. He picked up her hand and lifted it to his mouth. "I'll take you out for a walk whenever you want, honey. All you have to do is ask."

"Thanks." She gave a sad smile. "But it—it's hard. Sometimes people don't know enough to tell me when there's a curb or a hole and I trip. Or they tell me too late or too early and I trip. I fell a lot in the beginning and now I think I'm just too—too scared to go for walks."

"You won't fall down with me, guaranteed," he said. "I won't let you trip or fall."

"No," she replied softly, hand kneading his forearm. "Maybe not."

It hurt him to think of all that she'd been deprived of. Five months without going for a walk. He shuddered at the thought.

Kowalski scooted closer, wondering how to say it, trying to choose his words carefully. "You know, honey, one of my men lost his sight in Afghanistan. Land mine." Scotty'd lost

147

more than his sight. He'd lost an arm and a spleen. Still, since then he'd married and had found a job at a radio station. Life after catastrophe was possible. "At the Vet's hospital, they had rehabilitation courses. They taught him to read Braille and use a cane—"

"No!" Allegra stood up abruptly. "I don't need to—" she stopped, biting her lip.

Kowalski was silent. Yes, she did, of course she did. She definitely needed to learn to read Braille and to use a cane. She needed a seeing-eye dog. She needed to change her house around. From what he could tell, the house didn't make any concessions to a blind person at all. There were thousands of ways she could hurt herself.

Like now, for instance. She was shaking with distress, clearly wanting to pace her nerves away, but she didn't have her bearings. One wrong move and she'd crash into the glass coffee table. A glass coffee table wasn't a smart thing for a blind person to have in the home.

"Sit down." Kowalski tugged at the sleeve of her sweater. She pulled away.

"Don't you need to take a shower after your run?" This was said pugnaciously, that cute little chin thrust out.

"Sure do," Kowalski said equably. "I stink like a goat. Now sit down."

"Heavens." A quick intake of breath. "Sorry." She shook her head, biting her lip. "Oh, Douglas, I wasn't thinking—I didn't mean—"

Kowalski laughed. He couldn't help it. Allegra thought she'd hurt his feelings. She'd clearly mentioned the shower to get him off a touchy subject.

Well, time for a reality check. It took more than the suggestion of a shower to offend him, when he'd spent twenty years in the Navy being called every insulting and blasphemous name imaginative and angry recruits could think up. By the same token, however, it would take more than a change of subject to deflect him when he wanted information.

"No, you're right, I need a shower, but I need to cool off first," he lied. "Now sit down. Right now." That was said in his command voice and she dropped abruptly to the sofa, blinking at her instant obedience.

"We were talking about learning how to get around when you're blind."

"No we weren't." Allegra's pretty bottom lip stuck out slightly. She had a mouth just made for pouting. "*You* were talking about it."

"Uh uh." He took her hand. "*We* were talking about it. As I was saying, I can talk to this guy I know at the Vet's hospital and see if he knows some good rehabilitation people in this area. We can—"

"No." Allegra withdrew her hand and stared straight ahead, not making any attempt to follow his voice. She was closing him out. This was not something she wanted to talk about.

She was saying no to him.

No. To *him*.

Kowalski's jaws clenched so hard it was a surprise shards of enamel weren't shooting out his ears.

Kowalski had very definite ideas on the way things should be, and he'd spent most of his life getting what he wanted. More to the point, he'd spent the past twenty years being instantly obeyed.

The navy was full of hard-headed men who knew what they wanted, too, which would be a recipe for disaster if it weren't for the magic word that made it all work, that made the whole system hum smoothly—hierarchy. Kowalski gave orders to the men under him and in turn accepted the orders of his commanding officers. For the past twelve years, his commanding officer had been John Huntington, which was great because he and Midnight saw eye-to-eye on most things.

Kowalski had literally no tools to deal with a *no*.

Allegra wasn't a recruit he could order about. She wasn't even his official girlfriend or — *God!* — his fiancée, though if it were up to him she'd be his in the eyes of all the world. Still, she wasn't. Yet. He had no right to tell her what to do and above all, she didn't have to obey him. Even if, the way she was going about things, she was bound to get hurt sooner or later, and the very idea drove him crazy. He couldn't do anything to protect her from herself.

Kowalski wasn't used to putting reasonableness into his voice, but he gave it a shot. "Listen, honey, you really need to—"

She turned to him, her chin another notch up. "Speaking of need, I wish you'd hurry up with that shower because I'm getting hungry." She flashed a dimple. "If you're lucky, I'll let you cook for me while I finish practicing, how's that for learning how to be disabled?"

Kowalski's jaws clenched again. She'd turned the tables on him.

"Okay," he got out, rising reluctantly. This was going to have to be an act of persuasion, but it wasn't going to be easy. He wasn't used to persuading anyone. Looked like he was going to get a crash course in the art with Allegra. "I'll go grab a shower then rummage in your freezer."

She'd made her way back to the harp and plucked "From the Halls of Montezuma" from the strings with a devilish smile. "You do that."

Chapter Ten

I'm developing that sixth sense they all talk about, Allegra thought, as she practiced scales. She could practically *feel* Douglas' will beating down on her. He was a very forceful man, but then she was a stubborn woman. She'd even exasperated her father, at times.

"Allie, me love," her father had said once, throwing up his hands, "you could give stubborn lessons to a mountain goat."

She blinked back tears at the memory, taking a hand off Dagda to swipe at her face.

Douglas wanted her to blind-proof her house, walk with a cane, learn Braille. She'd heard it all a hundred times before, from the doctors, from the nurses, in gentle tones from Suzanne and Claire and Claire's father, not to mention from the assorted Mancinos who were taking turns looking after her.

It was a total waste of time because she wasn't going there. No way.

Allegra wouldn't be blind forever. She believed that with every cell of her body. She had a deeply superstitious fear that giving in and adapting would lock her into blindness forever. She couldn't bear the thought.

The doctors in Boston had been clear about the dangers of the operation, but Allegra didn't care. Medicine was advancing rapidly and soon the surgical procedure would be perfected and life would return to what it had been before...before.

Something dark and jagged winged by in her mind, unsettling her.

151

She shook her head, as if to loosen the sensation, and bent to Dagda. She limbered up with a scale or two, then cleared her mind to focus on her playing. She'd start with "The Cliffs of Moher," she decided.

The spell came, as always, without any notice, slamming into her, dropping her instantly into the blackest of black holes.

...you stupid little bitch! I'll teach you to talk about breaking contracts!

...you can't talk to my daughter that way!

No Pops!

Blood. Oh God, the blood! So much of it, streaming out of his head in a dark black lake... Pop's legs kicking, then suddenly going still...

She turned around, backing up, but there was no stopping him. He was coming for her...

She tried to run, but he caught her by a hank of hair, pulling so hard tears streamed down her face. A vicious yank and she slammed against the wall, blood drops spattering, oh God, she was going to die, too, just like Pops...

Allegra sat, stunned, overwhelmed by the sudden burst of images in her mind, coming up from some dark, dank hell. It was as if her head had been taken over by a monster.

There was a dark, satanic new edge to the waking nightmare—smell. She could smell the coppery metallic scent of blood and the fetid smell of death. It was in her nostrils still, even as the images faded, receding back into the hellhole they came from, like some dark hellish tidal wave leaving broken bits of horror on the shore in its wake.

Allegra stood up suddenly and then froze, paralyzed, heart pounding with panic but no way to work it off. She'd completely lost her bearings, with no sense of anything but up or down.

Sounds to her right, which must be where the kitchen was. She turned gratefully, suddenly remembering she wasn't alone. She instinctively reached out a hand to touch him, though he was in the next room. "Douglas?"

Her voice came out scratchy and thin, her throat closed with terror still from the panic attack.

How could he hear her? She took in a shuddery breath to try to call him again when suddenly he was there, and her hand was touching the very solid muscles of his forearm. How could he have heard her, when she could barely hear herself? But there he was, and the panic started loosening its hold on her chest. A large warm hand covered hers.

"I'm here, honey," that deep voice said quietly, "you're okay."

No, she wasn't okay, but at least that horrible feeling that a step in any direction would plunge her into a deep, dark abyss was gone. If he hadn't been there, she'd have stood rooted to the spot until the panic subsided and she could make short, shuffling steps before bumping into the first obstacle to ground herself. Instead she was grounded on Douglas' strong forearm.

Allegra leaned forward, arms open, and was immediately engulfed in his embrace. She huddled in a panic, pressing as hard as she could against him. He was so warm and solid, when everything around her was so cold and slithery.

"Douglas," she whispered, voice shaking. "Oh, God, Douglas, the blood."

"It's okay," he repeated, tightening his hold. His hand covered the back of her head. "What blood, honey?"

She burrowed deeper, trying to catch her breath, trying to stop the deep tremors racking her body.

"Honey?" Douglas' deep voice was in her ear. "What blood? You're not bleeding, I promise."

Not where it could be seen, no. Allegra wiped her eyes on the soft material of his track suit, still in the grip of terror.

It was like the nightmares she had at night, only she was awake. There would be the immediate plunge into some horror, triggered by God knows what, leaving her trembling and crying and lost. And whether asleep or awake, she was unable to remember what the nightmare had been about. The spells came from nowhere and she was powerless while in their grip. They left in a slithering tide leaving her broken and stranded on some desolate shore.

This time wasn't so bad because she was clinging to Douglas. He was so steady, like a rock. It helped, a little, to be able to push against him, push away, because it gave her a feeling of being in control.

She probably looked like a wild woman. She felt like a wild woman, eyes swollen with tears, babbling. Her hair, never tame at the best of times, was probably flying around her face.

Allegra pushed harder against Douglas' broad chest. When he released her she wiped her face with the heels of her hands.

"Sorry," she gasped, gulping in a huge breath of air. It felt like she hadn't breathed for an hour.

This was so horrible. If she could see, she could quietly excuse herself, rush to the bathroom and splash cold water on her face and wrists. Apply makeup and comb her hair, all those things women do to restore themselves, make themselves able to face the world after something devastating. Right now, if she made a dash for the bathroom, she'd run smack into a wall and break her nose.

So she was, as always, trapped.

"Allegra?" That calm voice again, with a small note of worry in it.

"Sorry," she gasped. There were no words, really, to describe what had happened, not without making her sound like a total lunatic. "I had, um, a panic attack. They come, um, at times. I never know when. Sorry."

"Don't apologize. You can't control panic attacks." Oh God, just the sound of his voice made her feel better. It was so calm, so deep, so powerful. She wished she could catch his voice and hold onto it like she held onto his arm. For dear life. Nothing bad could happen to her while she was listening to that voice, holding onto that arm.

"Come with me." Douglas' arm was there and, as if it were iron and her hand a magnet, she found it unerringly. He walked them into the kitchen. "Sit down and I'll make you a cup of tea. How does that sound?"

It sounded wonderful.

"Great. Whoa." She sniffled. "I'm sorry, but I need a—" Before she could even finish the sentence, a paper napkin was pressed into her hand. Allegra wiped her eyes, blew her nose and felt a little better. Though she probably looked like a witch, he didn't seem to be running away in horror. That was good.

Something dinged—the microwave—and she heard the sound of something being set on the table in front of her. Vanilla tea, she could smell it. Her favorite.

Allegra gave a half laugh. "You nuked my tea?"

"Always do, it's easier and quicker. Less mess to clean up. Good God." A pause and she could almost hear the gears grinding in his head, together with possibly his teeth. Allegra thought she could hear him frown. The man had an incredibly forceful personality if his disapproval could be felt across a table. "Please, *please* don't tell me you heat up the water for your tea on your stove."

"Well, um...yes. Yes I do." What did he think—that she blew on it to heat it up? Waved a magic tea wand?

"You have a *gas stove*." He breathed it more than said it, in exactly the same horrified tones in which he'd say—*you eat children for breakfast?*

"Yes, yes I do. I have a gas stove. Always have. Food cooks better with gas," Allegra said, mystified. She felt for the handle of the cup and brought it to her mouth. It was a little ritual with her. First she'd breathe in the heavenly vanilla and tea smell, letting it seep into her bones, then start sipping. Vanilla tea was perhaps the only thing in her life that had improved since she'd become blind. "Is that a crime?"

"It is if you're blind," he said, his deep voice harsh and disapproving.

Allegra stiffened. "Look, being blind doesn't mean being spastic or stupid. I'll have you know —"

His deep voice rode right over hers. "One miscalculation and your fu—freakin' sleeve can catch on fire. Or if you forget to turn the gas off you can burn your hand, badly. A gas stove is a disaster just waiting to happen to you. You need to get yourself one of those ceramic-top stoves. At least you would cut down the chances of burning yourself alive. Cooking with an open flame when you can't see is insane."

Well, that was pretty clear. Allegra hated being criticized, it brought out the worst in her and the words were out of her mouth before she could stop them. In her anger, she said what she hadn't said to anyone, not even to Suzanne and Claire.

The words came tumbling out, rising in tone until she was shouting at the end. "You listen to me. I don't want to get a ceramic-top stove, I don't want to learn Braille, I don't want a seeing-eye dog. I don't want to walk with a white cane, I don't want to rearrange my house. I don't want to take lessons in being blind because you better believe I won't be blind forever."

Allegra raised a hand to her mouth, but it was too late. The words had escaped and were now out there, stark and real.

Can you *feel* stillness? Douglas was an unusually calm man, he never seemed to fidget or make any untoward noises, but now he was utterly and completely still. She had no sense of him at all. It was as if he'd vanished from the room.

The moment stretched on, Allegra with her hand over her mouth and Douglas seemingly disappeared. There was no noise at all in the kitchen, not even the usual sounds of traffic seeping in from the road outside. The only sound she could hear was her heart, beating triple time.

Finally, Douglas stirred. His chair scraped over her kitchen tiles as he reached out and took her hand in his. As always, touching him grounded her, made her feel connected to the rest of the world through him.

"Is that so? You're going to regain your sight?"

Allegra nodded, throat too tight to talk.

"You know that for a fact? Is that what the doctors told you?"

Not really, but Allegra nodded anyway.

"Tell me about it," he said, his deep voice gentle.

She waited a moment for the bands around her chest to loosen a little and to gather her wits about her. This was going to be hard and she was going to have to skirt around a few things and hope he didn't notice.

"You know I had—had an accident. Head trauma. I was in a coma for a while. The reason I lost my sight is that I have a micro-hematoma pressing down on the main optic nerve. A hematoma is a swelling—"

"I know what a hematoma is. Go on."

"Okay." She drew in a deep breath. This is the part that was so scary to tell because it was so tenuous. Based on hope and prayers. "The hematoma is stable. It's not growing but by the same token it's not getting smaller. The CAT scan taken when I was first hospitalized shows the exact same shape and size as the last CAT scan I had about three weeks ago. So there's good news and bad news and bad news. The good news is that it isn't life-threatening. I could live forever with this—this *thing* in my head." Allegra tried to keep the loathing out of her voice, tried to make this a mere medical report—*there's a clot of blood pressing down on the nerves I need to be able to see, but hey, no big deal, I'm not going to die from that*—when what she wanted to do was scream. "The bad news is that it isn't going down, either. I will be—be blind for as long as the clot is in there. The *other* bad news is that the clot is in an almost inaccessible place in terms of surgical removal. The doctors have explained it all to me in technical terms I can't possibly repeat, but the gist is that to get to where it is, they'd have to cut through so much tissue I'd essentially end up a vegetable with excellent eyesight."

Douglas' hand tightened so much it almost crushed hers.

"But? There's a 'but' in there somewhere, I can tell."

"Yes, there is. There's a surgical technique. It's, ah, experi—" she stopped. "It's—it's new," she faltered. "But they think they can get close enough to the swelling itself surgically to use a new instrument that eliminates only special types of tissues. Blood clots are one. The doctors snowed me with science, but essentially it's a new type of focused microwave beam that will burn the hematoma without affecting the tissue the beam goes through. And then—*voilà!*" she finished brightly. "Goodbye blood clot and I can—" Her voice shook and she swallowed convulsively, though there was no moisture whatsoever in her mouth. "I can see again."

Please, please, God.

Every time Allegra thought about recovering her sight, she trembled. It was such a huge, scary idea. She wanted it so much she sometimes thought her head would explode from the force of it. The yearning ate into her until it hollowed her out, leaving her a thin shell surrounding an empty hole of want.

Tears sprang to her eyes and she shifted her face away from him. From where she thought he was. A blind person could never hide, wasn't ever granted the dignity of sighted people who could turn away, run away. She felt stripped of everything, all her emotions raw and on display.

Her fear, her wild hopes, her vulnerability—all were right out there, for Douglas to see.

"They're going to *nuke* your brain?" There was incredulity and disapproval in his voice. It got her dander up.

"Microwaves are used in medicine. So is radiation. When controlled, they can be beneficial."

"Uh-huh." The chair scraped as he moved even closer to her. "So just how new is this operation? How many people have had it?"

Allegra was silent.

"Honey?" A large, heavy hand cupped her shoulder. "*How* new is it?"

"New. I told you that." She shrugged his hand away.

"Okay, it's new. So...how many people have had this operation?"

Allegra turned her head away from him and bit her lips closed. Silence. Total, complete silence, except for the sound of her own breathing. She couldn't hear him breathe. But she could hear him think.

"O-*kay*. I'm going to take a wild guess here. I'll just run a little scenario by you and if I'm wrong, you tell me where I'm wrong. How does that sound?"

Allegra shrugged her shoulders. She didn't want to be having this conversation. There was absolutely nothing he could do or say that would make her change her mind.

"What I'm guessing right now is that this operation you're talking about isn't just new, it's still in the experimental stage. Now, I'm not a doctor, but I've had training as a medic and medicine interests me. We get serious injuries in the Teams and I always follow what's happened to my men after they've been wounded. We get pretty good medical care, some of the best available. I think I know a lot about leading-edge medical treatment, but I've never heard of a microwave beam that can target specific tissue and spare intermediate tissue. So what I'm thinking is that they've done some animal studies and they're trolling for human volunteers. Which, as you know, is insane for elective surgery."

Allegra closed her eyes and bowed her head.

His voice was steady, even, reasonable. "You know that, don't you, honey? You don't have a life-threatening disease-"

"Not true!" she said suddenly. "This *is* life-threatening! I don't have a life anymore, not in any sense of the word! I might as well be dead!"

"No, that's where you're wrong." He took both her hands in his and continued in that slow, deep voice of his. "You have a wonderful life. You're healthy, you're incredibly talented, you're beautiful, you have friends who love you, you have—" He stopped, as if biting back a thought. "You have everything to live for. And in a few years' time, when they've perfected the technique, when it's routine, then you can think of having the operation."

Douglas had That Tone in his voice. How many times had she heard it?

Ms. Ennis, I don't want you to get your hopes up too much. Maybe you should start preparing yourself to live with your condition. And then in a few years' time, when the technique has been perfected, we can talk again.

She didn't want to listen to the voice of reason. She knew exactly what she wanted, and it was to see again—*now!* She wanted that so fiercely that not even the thought of dying under the surgeon's scalpel put her off.

It was no one's decision but hers to make. She didn't want to discuss it and she didn't want any interference.

"You know what? I'm really hungry now," she said brightly. "Really, really hungry, and since you don't want me to cook, I guess that makes you Chef in Chief. A Senior Chief Chef in Chief." She smiled, her brilliant fake stage smile, the one she could put on at any time of the day or night. Performers learn the trick early and well. "So get cracking, Senior Chief."

Silence, then an exhalation of air, which in a lesser man would have been a sigh. "Okay. Lunch it is." She could hear him rising, the freezer door opening. A little swirl of frozen air curled across the room.

"You've got an amazing amount of food in here," he rumbled. "You could keep a SEAL team well-fed for a month with what's here, and that's saying a lot. Let's see," the sound of plastic containers scraping across the ice, "we have, hmmm, looks like minestrone. And here—wow, one of my favorites—eggplant parmesan. Frozen sourdough bread, apple pie. This is amazing stuff. I hope it tastes as good as it looks. Do you have a secret fairy who sneaks great food in during the night or something?"

Better than a secret fairy. "The Mancinos," Allegra smiled.

"The what?"

"Claire's housekeeper's name is Rosa Mancino and she comes from this huge, wonderful family. For years, I've sung at their weddings and funerals and christenings and graduation parties." Not to mention the wild, women-only divorce party Rosa's niece had thrown after getting rid of "the bum", as she'd called her ex. "Since, um, the accident, I've had to beat them off with a stick. The women come in turns to clean for me and they always leave cooked food in the freezer. Francesca, Rosa's sister, is coming in on Monday, as a matter of fact. All the Mancino women are great cooks, I'm really lucky. And the men look after me, too, helping with repairs and things. As soon as the snow stops, a Mancino will come around to shovel my sidewalk, you just wait and see."

"I'll shovel your sidewalk and take care of repairs for you from now on, you don't need them," Douglas said. "Let the Mancino men know I'm around now."

"Oh. Right."

Allegra had no idea if she would actually do that. Would she? The Mancino men made her feel safe, one or another stopping by every two or three days to see if she needed something. And she always did. It seemed that when she became blind, her house decided to fall down around her ears.

There was always something that needed fixing. Telling the Mancinos to stay away when she didn't know how long Douglas would be around was crazy.

He was here now. They'd had wonderful sex, and maybe he wanted to stick around for some more. But in the long run—what would such a vital man want with someone like her?

The microwave dinged and two seconds later a bowl was set in front of her. She didn't need to see to know what it was. It practically announced itself. "Mmm." She breathed the fragrance in deeply. "Rosa's minestrone. Heaven. Did you get yourself some?"

"About double what I gave you." Douglas' voice sounded amused. "Plus I heated up the eggplant parmesan, maybe I'll even leave some for you if you ask nicely. By the way, I opened a beer for myself, what will you have to drink?"

"I save alcohol for the evenings. Water is fine, thanks." Luckily, alcohol wasn't a temptation. If she were a drinker, if she'd inherited the Ennis drinking gene instead of her mom's temperate nature, she'd have disappeared into a bottle after the accident and never emerged. A glass of wine in the evening was more than enough. "If you look carefully you'll find a bowl of tiramisu—the real kind, not the faux-Italian restaurant pap—and some homemade ice cream in there somewhere."

"Yeah, I went on a little scouting expedition, found those items and more. You've got an interesting selection in there. You eat better than anyone I know."

"The Mancinos are really sweet people."

"They seem to be. They seem to care for you a lot. They're going out of their way for you. I'll bet they'd love to do more than etch a B, L or D into the tops. If you learned to read Braille, I'll bet they'd take the trouble to get a machine that can punch the contents of the containers on the tops in Braille, so you know what you're picking to eat for dinner, instead of guessing."

He'd turned that right around on her. Well, two could play at that game.

Allegra angled her chin upwards. "Were you blowing smoke when you said you'd take me for a walk? Or are you too tired after your run? What's the weather like outside?"

Another exhalation of breath. A slow drumming of fingernails on the tabletop. Tension she could actually feel.

She was exasperating him. Well, she exasperated a lot of people. Tough. He was a big boy—a really big boy—he could take it.

There was silence again in the kitchen as Douglas' gears worked in his head.

Suddenly, the skin on her right side felt different. She turned and felt light on her face. It was an unmistakable feeling. "The sun's come out," she said.

He finally spoke. "That's right. The snow has stopped and there's some sun now. If you want to go for a walk, now would be the time for it. It'll probably start snowing again in the evening when the temperature drops. Do you have cold-weather clothes? And rubber-soled boots?"

"Yes. To everything. And just because I wore inappropriate footwear last night doesn't mean I'm a ditz, Senior Chief Kowalski. I'll have you know—"

"Okay, okay." Allegra didn't have to see him to know he had his big hands up, palms out.

The quality of the air around her changed, became dense, and she realized he was standing beside her. As if it were the most natural thing in the world, Allegra held out her hand and was unsurprised to find it resting on his strong forearm.

"I'll walk you to your room and we'll get those boots and your cold-weather gear."

"Whah thank you, Senior Chief," she said, in her best honeyed Scarlett-O'Hara-in-Tara imitation of a Southern belle. She fluttered both her lashes and an imaginary crinoline skirt. "That's raht kahnd of you. Ah can tell you're a gentleman of the old school."

There was a little snort high above her head, either laughter or exasperation. Either one, it didn't matter. This was so exciting. She was going to go out for a walk for the first time in what felt like forever.

Chapter Eleven

ℰꙮ

It had never happened to him before, but Kowalski was no dummy. He recognized it for what it was. He was falling in love with Allegra Ennis. Hell, belay that. He was in love with her already and had been since the instant he heard her sing that first note. It was easy at first to mistake it for lust because his body had been in lust before, many times. His head was only now catching up with what was really going on.

What a joke. Here he'd spent thirty-eight years without any serious emotional involvement, not even close, and now he'd fallen for a woman who had trouble written all over her beautiful face.

What they had here wasn't exactly a match made in heaven. Any self-respecting dating service would freak at the thought of them together — their files would be cancelled on the spot.

They had exactly zero in common.

Allegra was ten years younger than he was in human years, and about a zillion years younger in SEAL years. He'd seen and done things she couldn't ever know about without running away screaming.

She was so stunningly beautiful heads turned when she walked by.

Heads turned when he walked by, too, only the other way.

She came from a happy family and had an easy way with people. She had a gift for friendship and her life seemed filled with people who cared about her.

Kowalski had just about the worst family background you can have and still function. His interpersonal skills were negligible. He had colleagues, not friends, with perhaps the solitary exception of Midnight.

On top of it all, gorgeous, talented Allegra Ennis, who had the power to massively fuck with his head, had a stubborn streak a mile wide—and Kowalski was powerless to deal with it.

Kowalski was a brave man. He'd faced death many times. There wasn't much that scared him, but he was shit-scared now. When she'd put her cute little chin in the air to say that she was contemplating risky, experimental surgery—some Frankenstein operation that had probably only ever been tried on cocker spaniels and rhesus monkeys—he had to use every single ounce of self-control not to scream and shout and forbid her to even think about it.

Unfortunately, he had no right to forbid her to do anything. He would, though. Oh, yes. He'd stick around until she realized she belonged to him, and then he'd have that right.

As if the surgery wasn't enough, she was flat-out refusing to deal with her blindness, putting her at risk every fucking second of every day.

He thought he would have a heart attack right there in her kitchen when he realized that she cooked with gas. Someone blind, cooking with gas, was a crispy critter in waiting.

So now he had a nice choice of nightmares—imagining her dead under the knife so some scientist could add her data to his statistics for a paper or—even better—burned to a crisp.

He was feeling shaky and stressed when she came out of her room dressed for the cold, looking happy and beautiful and smiling right up at him. He rubbed his chest, where it hurt.

"Well, Senior Chief?" She twirled like a fashion model. "Do I pass muster?"

Oh, yeah. She had on a long, dark green eiderdown coat with a fur-lined hood framing her heart-shaped face, thick gloves, thermal pants and lined, waterproof boots.

She lifted her face to his, slightly off-kilter. He had to say something so she could orient herself, but the words stuck in his throat.

"Douglas?" she frowned, holding her hand out. When her hand touched his arm, it was as if a switch was thrown, releasing him from a spell.

"Yeah, here I am." She found the source of his voice, so she turned slightly, face still upturned to his, beaming. He tucked a stray red curl back into her hood, then kissed the tip of her nose. "You look like a gorgeous Eskimo. We ready to roll here?"

"Absolutely. Oh, Douglas, I can't wait." She was quivering with excitement. "Is the sun still out?"

He looked out the window at the blue sky. The pale yellow disk of the sun was just beginning its downward journey toward night. There were a few clouds on the horizon, but they wouldn't gather until after dark. They had several hours of light and decent weather ahead. "Yep. It's a good day for a walk, but it'll be chilly. You sure you'll be warm enough?"

"Yes. God, yes." She was practically hopping with repressed energy. "Come on, come on, I can't wait, let's *go*."

Out on the porch, Allegra lifted her face to the sky. Her eyes were closed, delicate nostrils flared to take in the fresh clean scent of snow. She looked so happy it made him happy. He put his right arm around her, wishing he were touching her skin instead of a gazillion duck feathers.

She fingered his parka. "So you had a cold-weather jacket in your truck, too. I'm impressed. You seem to plan for all contingencies. What else do you have in there? Beach balls and suntan lotion? A business suit?"

Well, let's see. In his SUV he had his MP-5 9 mm submachine gun with six thirty-round magazines, M24 sniper rifle and ammo, M9 pistol with five magazines, body armor with PASGT helmet, two weeks' worth of MREs, five gallons of water, GPS receiver, night-vision goggles and a laptop hooked up to SATCOM transmitters.

He had a quarter-pound of perfectly illegal C4 in the false bottom of his tool kit. If there was one thing he knew how to do well, it was blow things up. He subscribed to the SEAL philosophy — there were few problems that couldn't be solved by judicious application of a properly sized, shaped, timed and detonated explosive.

He had an emergency trauma kit, extra-thin leather shooting gloves, cold weather survival gear, mountaineering equipment, his diving suit, scuba tank and fins.

And four boxes of condoms.

"Nothing much," he said. "This and that. Stuff. You never know what you're going to need and I like to be prepared. Okay now, listen up. This is how we're going to work it. When you're close to a barrier or a step, I'll give you a light squeeze, like this," he tightened his arm briefly, "so you'll know what's coming. And when I say step up or step down, that's what you'll do, right when I say it."

There was a little frown between the wings of her eyebrows. Allegra hadn't had good experiences with people gauging distances for her.

She couldn't know that he was an expert at range-finding. He used laser range-finders in the field, to position shots, but he could do it without equipment, out of a natural eye for terrain and distance and endless training. Maybe he couldn't set up a sniper shot at a grand out without his range-finder, but he could certainly help her negotiate obstacles.

"Trust me," he said, "I won't let you fall or bang into anything."

"No." Her lips tilted up, the small frown disappeared. He saw utter trust on her face. "You won't. You told me that, and I believe you. So now let's go." She hopped in place. "Now. Right *now*."

"Okay." He tightened his arm, counted, then said, "Three steps down...now. One, two, three."

Allegra walked down the steps as easily as if she were staring at her boots. A minute later they were out the gate and walking along the sidewalk. Kowalski kept the pace slow, fitting his long stride to her much shorter one, letting her gain confidence.

Her head was swiveling left and right, like an eager puppy let out to play after being confined in the house for too long. She wasn't seeing, but she was absorbing sensations through every square inch of exposed skin. Kowalski let her set the pace.

His job was to make sure she didn't get hurt. Her job was to enjoy it.

Soon, they found a rhythm that allowed her to start gradually moving a little faster. It was clearly what she wanted. She must have spent the past months walking slowly, hesitantly. Now that she wasn't afraid of tripping or finding a lamppost with her face, she started walking with a more confident stride, head up.

Inside of ten minutes, her cheeks were bright pink with the cold. She chattered, high on excitement, in her musical voice. Kowalski gave appropriate responses, listening while scouting the terrain for obstacles. It was hard keeping his eye on the road, though. Allegra was coming alive, like a flower unfurling, the most incredible thing he'd ever seen and it was all thanks to him.

He'd done this. He'd given her the gift of freedom of movement. It was almost unbearably moving, watching her taste her re-found freedom.

After they'd negotiated several curbs and steps, Allegra completely lost her shuffling gait and started walking normally. Her excitement level was way up. She was humming with energy and vibrancy.

The weather was cold but dry, sunny, perfect for a walk. There was just enough snow to make a satisfactory crunch under their feet without slowing them down.

"Are we past the blue house, yet?" Allegra asked. "It should be on the right."

Yep, there it was, a Cape Cod in several shades of blue. All the curtains were drawn, no cars in the driveway, it looked deserted. "Yeah, we're coming up to it now. Looks like no one's home, though."

"No, there wouldn't be. It's owned by this great gay couple, Tom and Jerry. Can you believe those names? Tom Edelman and Jerry Solarian. Jerry's company had an IPO. He had a gazillion options that vested and he made a killing, he'll never have to work again, the lucky sod. The two of them are on a year-long trip around the world. I should imagine they'd be in Tahiti by now. They're going to have a cow when they come back to find that disgusting McMansion next door. The owner has a chain of restaurants and organizes Republican fundraisers. He's incredibly smarmy and brags about his money all the time. Tom and Jerry are going to hate him. I'll bet you anything that they'll sell after they get back and find out who their new neighbor is, and that he's built this monstrosity next door. Isn't it awful?"

Sure enough, the house next to the blue one seemed almost bigger than the plot of land it was on. It had the same lines as the other houses on the street only blown up by a factor of ten. A Cape Cod on steroids.

"It's pretty awful, yeah," Kowalski said mildly. "But I don't think Republicans have a lock on ugly houses."

She laughed. "Maybe not, maybe it just seems that way. The house next to the McMansion belongs to a really nice couple. He teaches American history at Portland State and she's a lawyer. He plays a mean bluegrass guitar. He's been nagging me for two years to jam with him. Can you see it— bluegrass on a Celtic harp?"

Kowalski thought about it. "Might work. You might have fun."

"Maybe. One of these days I just might take him up on the offer. Are we at the corner of McPherson yet? Because I want to turn right and go toward Lawrence Square. Sometimes there's a group of madrigal singers on Sunday afternoons."

"We're coming up to the corner...right now." Kowalski tightened his arm. "One step down." They crossed to the right, walking down another street. She seemed to know everyone on this street, too.

How did she do it? How did she know all this stuff? Even if he lived in his new apartment for twenty years, he'd never know anything about the private lives of his neighbors.

She told him the history of the street—it was once a deeply-rutted dirt track for horse-drawn carriages carrying lumber from the forest to a mill, which had once stood two miles from here. All of it was fascinating for a man who'd never had neighbors before and had never lived anywhere long enough to know local history, unless it was the military history of a base.

Even more fascinating was Allegra, bright-eyed and vivacious. It struck him with the force of a blow that *this* was Allegra. This gorgeous laughing woman. He hadn't recognized the melancholy shrouding her like a somber veil until it was lifted. If he thought she was beautiful before, now she was stunning, a magnet for the eye.

He wasn't the only one who thought so, either. The few people they passed did double takes. You could almost hear the wheels grinding in their heads as they stared at her, looked at him, shuddered, then looked back at her. What was someone like *her* doing with someone like *him*? Kowalski had his war face on and had a lot of fun giving his Death Glare and watching them turn away, eyes down.

They'd been walking for half an hour and were now approaching some kind of outdoor mall far down a long block. The sidewalk was getting crowded.

Everyone was staring at the *Beauty and the Beast* thing they had going. Kowalski supposed if he and Allegra had simply been walking side by side, not touching, they wouldn't have attracted all this attention. He could be her chauffeur or her butler or her bodyguard. Bodyguard. Yeah, now that was a scenario people could go with. Young, beautiful woman with thug—he had to be the bodyguard, right? What else could he be?

But with his arm around her, and her face adoringly turned up to his, they were lovers. You couldn't miss it and that bothered some. People reacted to them like he was Frankenstein's older brother hitting on Princess Leia.

He had the Death Glare on permanently now and people simply skittered away. He hadn't kidnapped Allegra, he wasn't forcing her to be with him, and she was obviously enjoying his company. If anyone had a problem with that— fuck 'em.

"Are we close to the mall?"

Down the long sidewalk Kowalski could see a little landscaped plaza. "Yeah, we'll be there soon."

"What time is it?"

Jesus, time. Something else to think of. How did blind people tell the time? He just bet there was some kind of open-faced watch he could buy her if only she weren't so hell-bent on *not* being blind. "Three o'clock."

172

"Wouldn't that be oh-three-hundred?"

"Actually, it'd be fifteen hundred hours. The military runs on a twenty-four-hour clock."

She slowed, then stopped. Kowalski stopped too.

Allegra tilted her head to him. "It's all sidewalk now, isn't it? No curbs, no steps?"

"No curbs, no steps," he agreed. "Straight on into the square."

"Then I want to walk arm in arm with you like any normal couple. Can we? And if there's something I need to know, you'll tell me?"

Like a couple.

Shit, what did he know about being a couple? A *normal* couple at that? Zilch. Still, it was worth a shot. He'd always been a fast learner.

Allegra stood there, looking up at him, mouth slightly upturned in a smile, the most beautiful thing he'd ever seen, beaming right up at him.

Kowalski crooked his arm, tucked Allegra's small, gloved hand into his elbow and leaned down. She must have sensed his movement because her eyes closed as he bent down to her. He touched his mouth to hers. Her lips were warm, the tip of her nose cold. She opened her mouth immediately to him, warm and welcoming. He couldn't allow himself more than a minute kissing her. Any more and he wouldn't be able to stop.

He lifted his mouth. She was smiling up at him.

"Like a couple," he agreed, his voice husky. "Let's go."

Chapter Twelve

Walking with Douglas was like…like flying.

Allegra used to love going for long walks. Like everything else, it seemed, even this simple pleasure had been taken from her. Who could go for a walk when you risked smacking your face or tripping over a rock at any minute? The few times she'd tried going for a walk with friends, it had been a disaster. They'd tell her to turn or to step up and step down too early or too late. The last time she'd gone for a walk with one of Rosa's sisters, she'd come back black and blue.

Douglas had given this back to her. When she realized that she could trust Douglas to warn her about steps and obstacles, and that his strong arm would keep her from falling in any case, it was as if he'd smashed hateful chains shackling her in place.

It was so great to feel free again.

If—*when!*—she regained her sight, she wasn't going to take anything for granted again, ever. She'd be grateful for everything. For being able to take a walk in the park, for reading, for cooking—she'd been too proud to tell Douglas since he'd made such a fuss, but the gas stove terrified her—for a rainbow or a sunset.

For Douglas.

She was grateful right now for him and everything he'd so generously given her. Without Douglas, she'd have spent a nightmare-haunted night followed by a hollow, empty day.

Suzanne was with her husband, and Claire was with Bud at the hospital.

Allegra had lots of friends, but none she'd want to call up and ask to spend the day with her. And no one would have been the company Douglas had been.

Allegra blushed as she remembered the feverish night in his arms. No nightmares, no falling into black holes of terror, no agonizing loneliness, just hot, powerful sex.

That had been like flying, too.

"There are a lot of people around," she said. She could not only hear them, she could...*feel* them.

There were voices, lots of them, laughter rising in the chilly air, a mother admonishing a child, a couple arguing, kids playing. Some were moving fast—she could feel the displacement of air as they went by. Lawrence Square wasn't big and on Sundays it was always crowded.

Yet no one jostled her. She felt as if she were walking in a protective bubble. Well, she was. It was called Douglas.

"Yeah. Everyone seems to be having a good time. It's a nice place."

Allegra smiled. "Yes, it is. It's fabulous in the summer, too."

Would Douglas be around next summer? She lifted her face to his and was instantly rewarded with a warm kiss.

Maybe he would.

Silver notes sounded in the air and Allegra turned eagerly toward the sound. "They're here!" She hopped, hanging on to Douglas' arm. "Oh, let's go, the group is usually in the corner right in front of the coffee shop. You're going to love them!"

They made a beeline toward the music, which became louder and purer with each step. No one bothered them, they didn't have to side-step anyone. It was as if they were completely alone in the square. How did Douglas do it? No one even swished by her.

Douglas gently pulled her to a halt. By the quality of the sound, they were right in front of the singers, in a ringside seat, only standing.

Allegra settled in happily to listen to the group. They were so good. It was a young group, she remembered, three men and four women, with an unusual purity of sound. They were singing "Take Time While Time Doth Last," light and delicate, one of her favorites. She'd sung that once with her cousins, only they'd been drunk. It hadn't affected the harmony, however, she remembered fondly. There wasn't anything an Ennis could do sober that he couldn't do better in his cups.

"Wonderful soprano," Douglas rumbled, "great breath control." Allegra nodded. She remembered the woman. Tall and geeky-looking with wild corkscrew black hair. Yes, she was a great soprano and yes, she did have great breath control. What a pleasure it was to listen to her, to them all. And the pleasure was doubled because she was listening with Douglas, who loved music, too.

Now they were singing extracts from *The Fairy Queen*, her favorite opera.

Douglas had positioned himself behind her, arms loosely clasped around her waist, a wall of warm strength.

Allegra closed her eyes, swaying gently to the music, leaning back into Douglas, feeling his strong arms tighten around her. This was so perfect—the man and the music and the day. If she kept her eyes closed, she could almost imagine her life intact again. More than intact. With a new love in it. She smiled at the thought of the song she'd been composing, "New Love." It fit her feelings exactly, that delicious tingling excitement of someone new. That thrill of connection, the zing of anticipation. The feeling that maybe this time was going to be It.

There was that with Douglas, yet there was something else, as well. Something more powerful than novelty. She'd had lots of flirts, though not many lovers, and the men had all had one thing in common—they'd been fun and, she understood now, shallow. Allegra tried to imagine Billy Trudloe or Davis Cleaver spending a day with her after she'd been blinded. She failed completely.

She wasn't fun now, she knew that. It took a lot of patience and attention to detail to be with her. The men she'd known would have shied away from her and her problems, running away like rats from the proverbial sinking ship. She needed help every second of every day and that sucked.

She couldn't go to the movies or the ballet or the theater, or at least not with any degree of enjoyment. Restaurants were a nightmare because she could so easily make a mess. Now she would go to a restaurant only with Claire or Suzanne, who loved her.

Look at today—going for a walk in the snow was a big, big deal. It required planning and time and attention. What kind of man wanted that grief?

What kind of man wanted to start a relationship with a handicapped woman, a woman who couldn't *see*? Who had nightmares at night and demons in her head? Who cried more often than she laughed?

No, she wasn't dating material. She was a burden. Though apparently—by some miracle—not for Douglas.

Somehow, Douglas didn't seem to notice what a raw deal she was. Not once had he expressed impatience or annoyance or anything but a red-hot desire for her coupled with a drive to help her. There was something rock-like about him, even beyond his massive size and strength. Something immensely reassuring and patient. Reliable. He was here, with her, and from what she could tell, he intended to stay.

Muscles which had been tense for months started slowly relaxing. She shut off the worry lobe in her head and let it all go—her despair and grief. It felt like lancing a black, putrid boil. Joy slowly filtered its way back into her soul, and she welcomed it back like a beloved friend who had been away for much too long. *This* was happiness, right here, right now. She could feel sunshine on her face for the first time in months, she was listening to beautiful music, and she had Douglas to lean back on.

The future all of a sudden took on a new glow. She'd been living strictly day-to-day. Thinking of the future was too painful, so she just plodded through her days, one by one. Now there was something to look forward to. Maybe Douglas would take her to the Bach concert on Thursday night. Maybe he'd take her for another walk during the week if it didn't snow too hard. Maybe next Sunday they could come back to Lawrence Square again.

"If love's a sweet passion, why does it torment?" the musicians sang.

Allegra smiled and, eyes still closed, turned to kiss Douglas on the shoulder. Instead of warm hard muscle, she kissed the nylon of his parka. Worked for her.

The singers were winding up. As the last glorious note lingered in the air, the people around them burst into applause. What kind of hat did the group have to take donations? Last summer it had been a top hat.

She tilted her head up and sideways. "I don't have any money with me, can you give them something? They're students and they're probably poor."

"Sure thing, honey," he answered. "A twenty okay?"

"Oh, yeah." A twenty would cover hot dogs and coffee for all. "Thanks, Douglas. That's really generous."

"Be right back." He left her for a moment, to drop the money into the hat.

"That was very inferior work my dear, but then you never could recognize quality," Corey Sanderson's snide tenor said, right in her ear. Her mind blanked with shock and her knees buckled.

Kowalski placed a twenty-dollar bill in the felt bowler hat at the feet of the singers. They deserved it. They weren't in Allegra's class, but then few singers were. Still, it felt good to encourage young talent.

He hardly recognized that thought as coming from his own head—and yet this seemed to be his new mode in civilian life. He snorted at this new image of himself—Senior Chief Kowalski, gentle, tender mentor of the young.

The lead singer met his eyes in thank you as the banknote drifted into the hat. This new and kinder version of Senior Chief Kowalski nodded his head back. *Nice feeling*, he was thinking as he turned—just in time to see Allegra start to fall.

One long stride and he was there, holding her tightly.

"Douglas! Oh my God!"

She was shaking, face completely bloodless.

"Easy honey, it's okay, I've got you. What's wrong? Did you trip?"

"I—" she gasped, unable to continue. She was going to break a bone if she shook any harder. He wrapped his arms around her to comfort her and try to dampen down some of the trembling. She burrowed deep as if to hide from something.

Allegra grabbed his jacket and tugged downward, wanting to talk into his ear. She couldn't get the words out and had to swallow to talk. "Douglas, quick! Do you see an elegant middle-aged man, not too tall, slender, shoulder-length blond hair?"

Kowalski lifted his head. He was taller than anyone here and could see the entire square and everyone in it. He scanned the crowd as he would a combat area, in quadrants. He looked hard at one quadrant, blinked to black, then scanned the next. He was fast but thorough. If the guy Allegra described was here, he'd see him.

First quadrant. Couple in jeans and parkas with baby in stroller. Young couple in designer duds, arguing. Old man with cane and cashmere overcoat. Tall, lanky redheaded guy, leather jacket and high-tops. Two young punks, both with green hair and enough metal in their faces to set off a metal detector.

Next quadrant. Two families with about a dozen kids between them. Three sharp dudes on the prowl for women. Black couple dressed for end-of-the-world winter weather. Three elderly ladies walking gingerly over an icy patch. Blink to black. Third quadrant. Every variety and race and gender except medium-height, middle-aged, blond elegant male. Fourth quadrant ditto.

Kowalski scanned the entire square again, fast. Nada. Zip.

Allegra's head was tilted up to his, her face anxious and white. The tremors had died down a little but she was still shaking. Whoever she thought was here scared the shit out of her.

Kowalski normally lived his life in Condition Orange. He was ready for anything at all times. More than one woman had called him paranoid. He wasn't paranoid, just very alert and ready for trouble. What was happening right now pushed his buttons, every single one. Allegra frightened of someone edged him right up to Condition Red.

Whoever the motherfucker was, he going to die if he so much as touched Allegra.

"Do you see him?" Her voice was breathless with fear.

He wiped everything from his voice but gentleness. She didn't need to hear the red alert in his voice. She was scared enough as it was. "No, honey. No one of that description. Who is this guy?" Whoever he was, Kowalski was going to nail his hide to the wall.

She simply stood there, breathing fast.

Allegra was terrified. Unless you've trained and trained hard for it, fear slows the mind, makes you stupid. Fear makes civilians easy prey. Kowalski shook Allegra a little, to nudge her out of the stupor of terror.

"Honey? Who am I looking for? Did he threaten you? What's his name?"

"Name? Oh, ah—" A little color had come back into her face when he told her no one matching her description was in the square. She shook her head sharply. "Oh, God, Douglas, I'm so sorry." She leaned into him. "I thought—" She shook her head again, clutching him around the waist. "Never mind, it can't possibly be the person I thought it was."

"Tell me who—" Kowalski said, at the exact same moment she said, "I want to—"

"What, honey?" Good thing she couldn't see his face. He kept his voice gentle but he had on his War Face and people were backing away. "You want what?"

She was looking up at him, still pale, eyes glossy with unshed tears. "To go home," she whispered. "Take me home now, please, Douglas."

Chapter Thirteen

ಖ

"Here we go." Kowalski held the door open for Allegra and ushered her over the threshold with a gentle hand to her back. It was already dark. It had taken them twice the time to come back from Lawrence Square than it had taken to walk there. She'd lost that confident, quick stride, and shuffled back hesitant and slow. Kowalski hadn't tried to hurry her up. He'd simply kept pace with her, patient and worried.

Allegra entered the house silent and pale, head bowed. The laughing, confident woman who'd walked at an almost normal pace to Lawrence Square with him was gone and this white, hesitant wraith had taken her place.

Whoever she thought she'd seen had jolted her back into the frightened, faltering woman of before. This was shock. Kowalski didn't know what had caused it, but by God he recognized it. Her senses were dulled. It took her several seconds to answer questions, almost as if a question had to sink in first. Shock.

Classic.

With new recruits, he had to bully them out of it fast. A soldier has to train himself to resist the paralysis of shock and Kowalski was the one who had to drum it into his head. Kowalski's methods were brutal, deliberately so, and if the soldier couldn't take it, he was out.

The idea of browbeating Allegra made Kowalski physically sick. He was going to have to pamper and love her out of her shock, definitely a new one for him.

Kowalski stripped her of her gloves, hat and eiderdown coat. Allegra stood still and silent, like a little doll, as he got rid of her outerwear. She shivered, wrapping her arms around her middle. It wasn't cold in the house. Kowalski had kept the heat on. She was suffering from the cold of exhaustion—her first long walk in months had tired her out—and shock.

"You know what you need, honey?" It was a symptom of how she was feeling that it took her two beats to respond. She lifted her head.

"No. What do I need?" Her voice was low, almost a whisper. She sounded beaten. Jesus, but it hurt to hear her like this.

"You need to take a warm bath, then you need something to eat." Heat and nourishment, the eternal healers.

She stood stock-still in the little living room. "I do?"

"Uh-huh." Kowalski ushered her into the bathroom. He started running hot water for the bath, rummaging among her toiletries, fingers lighting on a little bottle of lavender oil. He'd read somewhere that lavender oil was relaxing, so he poured half of it into the tub. Soon the bathroom smelled like a friggin' lavender field.

As the steam filled the room, he carefully stripped her. If she resisted, he'd stop immediately, but Allegra stood completely still, obediently raising her arms as he pulled the sweater up over her head.

The semi-hard-on he always had around her graduated to a full-fledged one as he gently unhooked her bra and slid her panties down her long legs. He bent and she fitted a hand to his shoulder for balance, lifting one foot, then another. "That's my girl," he murmured.

He remembered, vividly, touching every inch of her. He remembered that she shuddered with pleasure when he lightly bit the side of her neck. He remembered the taste of her breasts, creamy and salty at once, heaven. He remembered that her stomach muscles clenched when he sucked her nipples and that she panted when he sucked hard. He remembered that when he got her wet, little droplets formed in the cloud of soft red hair covering her mound, and that his come looked exactly like little pearls there.

Kowalski straightened, wincing at the boner pressing against his pants. She was so lovely, standing naked here in the scented bathroom. Her skin glowed like alabaster, delicate and smooth, the only colors her rosy nipples and the fiery red hair between her thighs.

He wanted her even more than he had last night. Usually a night of fucking got a woman out of his head, but with Allegra the hunger just kept on growing.

If she hadn't been so shocked, looked so unhappy and lost, he'd have carried her right into the bedroom, laid her on the bed, climbed on top and slid right in. The way he was feeling right now, he probably wouldn't even have the patience for foreplay.

That was the last thing she needed now. Her face had the pale pinched look he hated to see, the look of fear and anguish. She wouldn't want sex right now, no way.

So Kowalski tucked his lust away in his mind, putting it in that place where he put fear and hunger and thirst when in the field. It was okay. He was used to ignoring the demands of his body.

He shut the water off and tested it. It was just warm enough to heat her up nicely, not so warm it would burn that delicate skin of hers. "Water's ready now, honey." He frowned as he lifted her long hair away from her shoulders. It slid like silk between his fingers. "What do we do about your hair? I don't want to get it wet."

Allegra lifted her head. "On the shelf above the sink there should be two picks. One ivory, one ebony."

Picks? For an instant, Kowalski had a vision of a miner's pick. Did she want to hack off her hair? His head swiveled and he stared at the shelf above the sink. The only things on it were two funny looking sticks, one black and one white.

Oh.

The sticks were picks? Apparently. Though what she could do with two sticks was beyond him, he pressed them into her hand. "Are these what you mean? What are you going to do with them?"

A little smiled creased her face for the first time since they'd walked home from Lawrence Square.

"Watch, O Great Warrior, and learn," she said. Two swipes of her hand and all that hair—enough for eight women—was swept up and tied into some kind of elegant knot at the top of her head, as smooth as if she'd just spent the day at the beauty parlor.

Kowalski was dumbfounded. "How did you *do* that?"

"Practice. Is the water ready?" She turned to the tub, sniffing delicately. "I think you dumped the whole bottle of lavender oil in. Just a few drops are enough."

"Sorry," Kowalski rumbled.

"No, no, please don't apologize." Allegra held out her hand, waiting until he fit his forearm to it. She clutched his arm. "I was just teasing you, Douglas. I don't have words to say how grateful I am to you. For helping me. For being here. You can dump a ton of lavender oil in my bath if you want."

Jesus. She was standing there naked, all that smooth white skin gleaming in the steamy bathroom. Douglas had a stab of lust that nearly brought him to his knees, electricity running through his cock. He waited for a moment to guide her to the tub because his hands were shaking.

As he helped her into the tub, he caught a glimpse of himself in the mirror and nearly recoiled with shock.

Who was that monster in the mirror?

He'd forgotten how butt-ugly he was. Now he was even uglier than usual, his face contorted with lust, sallow cheeks and lips suffused with blood. That horribly disfiguring scar was white against his sun-darkened skin. His nose was smashed against his face, as ugly and brutal as a boxer's—he'd broken it enough times he could qualify for the heavyweight championship. Acne scars from long ago pocked his cheeks. His eyes were small slits in tough bone and weather-beaten skin.

He looked like your worst nightmare.

This time alone with Allegra was like a gift life had thrown at him—a bone, maybe, for all those years spent alone, fighting for his country. He was being allowed time with the most beautiful woman in the world, but only because she was blind.

This was his time out of time—she was going to kick him out soon enough. Hell any woman would, let alone one as desirable as Allegra. Might as well stock up on memories.

"Come on, into the tub." He picked Allegra up, clenching his jaws against the feel of her in his arms, and stood her in the tub. The water came almost to her knees. Allegra held onto him as she sank gracefully down. Kowalski gritted his teeth as he grabbed a sponge, soaped it and started washing that smooth, smooth skin. Even the fucking soap smelled of flowers. He was suffering from sensory overload. Every single atom in the room reeked of woman and sex. If he stayed any longer, looking at her, smelling her, his head was going to explode.

He kept the sponge between his hand and her skin because otherwise he'd be too tempted to start touching her. He knew exactly how she liked it. And where. She liked it when he stroked her thighs, slowly, running his rough fingertips up the smooth skin of her inner thigh. She liked it when he entered her with his finger, circling her clit with his thumb. She liked it when he cupped her ass in both hands, lifting her into his strokes.

Kowalski sat on the edge of the tub, clutching the sponge, and let his head fall forward. Maybe his harsh breathing worried her, because she said, "Douglas?" hesitantly. She was probably wondering if something was wrong.

Well, it was. Keeping his hands off her was torture.

"Douglas?" Her voice was sharper now and she tried to sit up in the water.

Way to go Kowalski, get her worried and upset because you've got a boner that won't quit.

"Just sit back, honey. Let your muscles soak in the warm water, they're stiff from the cold."

"Oh." Satisfied when she heard his normal tone of voice, Allegra settled back down.

Kowalski took a deep, silent breath, then another, then settled himself down to doing the hard thing. No problem. He'd been doing the hard thing all his life.

He soaped her up, then gently helped her settle deeper into the water. Only her head was out, resting against the rim of the tub. "Stay there," he said quietly. "I'll go get you a cup of tea."

She was leaning with her head back, eyes closed. There was a faint undertone of rose to her skin now. She nodded. "That would be nice."

"Be right back."

Kowalski found a packet of Earl Grey bags, nuked a cup, then put an ice cube in the cup to cool it down. She was in the exact position he'd left her in.

"Here, honey." He took her hand, curling it around the cup. His hand supported hers as she lifted it to her mouth. She sipped, gingerly at first. When she realized that he hadn't given her boiling hot tea and that she wouldn't burn herself, she drank deeply.

"Mmm." She drained the tea, handing the cup back to him. "That was really nice. Thanks. I think I'll get out now." The water made silvery rippling noises as she held onto his hands to pull herself up.

She was so quiet, with a sad, poignant smile, brave and beautiful. She held onto his arms, lovely face upturned to his. Her hands rested lightly on his arms but there was the full weight of her utter trust in him. He knew, with every beat of his heart, with every cell of his being, that he would do whatever it took to keep this woman safe and happy.

Grabbing a big bath towel he'd put on the radiator to heat up, he gave her a light kiss then dried her and dressed her in a warm nightgown. She stood still and quiet under his ministrations, making sure she always touched him in some way.

After he slipped the nightgown over her head, she moved in close, unexpectedly, to hug him tightly. "Thanks." The word was muffled against his chest, but he heard.

They stood for a moment, Allegra's cheek against his shoulder, her hand over his heart. His fast-beating heart. It was a moment out of time, completely unlike any other moment in his life. He couldn't begin to put a name to what was churning around inside him, all he knew was that he wouldn't have traded places in this exact moment with anyone in the world, and that he would remember this moment for the rest of his life.

Kowalski dropped a kiss on the top of her head and nudged her toward the door and into the kitchen. He wanted to know who or what had spooked her, but first he had to feed her.

The cornucopia in Allegra's freezer yielded up lentil soup and frozen slices of rosemary focaccia—perfect. While two bowls were heating up in the microwave, he put four slices of focaccia in the toaster oven. He was hungry, too.

They ate quietly in the dark kitchen. It would have helped if she'd drunk more wine, but she couldn't get down more than a third of a glass. He topped his own three times. He had three full bowls of soup to her half-full one. Even downing that much taxed her. She swallowed the delicious, fragrant lentil soup as if she were being force-fed castor oil.

Finally, Allegra put the spoon back in the bowl with a clatter and sat back, staring blankly ahead.

Kowalski was puzzled. Something tickled the edges of his consciousness. Something...familiar? Allegra was subdued, senses dulled. But there was something about her reaction...

Kowalski tucked it away for consideration later. His first priority now was finding out what had happened in Lawrence Square.

"So." He picked up her hand, marveling again at the delicacy of it, the fragile bones and tendons, the long fingers that could pluck magic from strings. "Do you want to tell me who you think was there this afternoon? Who was this guy? Medium height, elegant, middle-aged blond, you said. Who is that?"

Kowalski kept his voice calm and even. No big deal. Guy asking his girlfriend some casual questions.

Yes, love. Who is this fucker who scared you so much you practically became catatonic? Let me know, honey, because I will fucking tear him limb from limb. I will cut his heart out and eat it for fucking breakfast.

"I—it doesn't matter." Pale, lifeless, Allegra's weak voice contrasted with the tight grip she held on his hand. "It wasn't the person I thought it was. Couldn't be. He's—not here."

Patience, Kowalski told himself. Patience was a hallmark of his. He could—and had had to—lie in ambush for days. He could set up a sniper shot and hold it for hours. Patience was his old friend. But now his old friend deserted him. Patience slipped right through his fingers. He was burning to go out, find this guy and rip his freakin' head off.

He tightened his hold on her hands. "Well, maybe it was and maybe it wasn't. But who did you think you—" *Saw.* Kowalski nearly said saw. He closed his mouth with an audible click. "Who was it you think you heard?"

Damned if that pretty chin of hers didn't go up a fraction. Damned if Irish stubbornness didn't settle in.

"No one." Her mouth tightened. "No one—I was mistaken."

Kowalski's jaw tightened in return. "Okay, so you were wrong. But who did you *think* was there?"

The stubbornness fell from her like a veil. Allegra looked young and vulnerable and lost as she pulled her hand from his. She dropped her head down, frowning, and rubbed her forehead.

"I don't know, Douglas. It doesn't make any sense at all. How could he possibly be here? I don't—Oh, God, it *hurts*." Pale and stricken, she clutched her head with both hands. "My head hurts. I'm sorry—I can't think straight. This happens to me when I—oh, God, it hurts so *much*." Her voice dropped to a whimper as she rubbed her temples. She blinked hard but a tear rolled down her cheek.

Jesus. The hairs on the back of his neck stood up.

If Kowalski could reach his own butt, he'd kick it. Allegra had head trauma, had been in a coma. She had a blood clot in her brain, this little time bomb just waiting for some asshole to push her and stress her so it could pop and—no more Allegra.

Her hands trembled. His nearly did, too.

"Okay, baby, that's okay." He tried to put soothing tones in his voice but it came out a croak. "That's fine, don't worry about it. It'll come to you." He patted her hand, his touch awkward, terrified he might jar her, hurt her. "We can talk about it some other time."

Allegra planted her hands against his cheeks and leaned forward to kiss him. She missed slightly, the kiss catching him on the corner of his mouth, but when she lifted her mouth to kiss him again, he took control.

The kiss was long, luscious, heated, pulsing with desire, as hot as sex.

She came up for air, leaning her forehead against his. "Take me to bed, Douglas. Take me to bed and make love with me," she pleaded. "Take me away from the here and the now. I can't remember and I can't forget."

He rose with her in his arms.

Douglas put her down somewhere in the bedroom. She recognized her bedroom by the smell. Her special potpourri from Florence, Italy, fabric softener and now the overwhelming smell of lavender oil from the bathroom made an unmistakable mix.

She knew where she was. She didn't know *who* she was anymore, but she knew where she was.

Didn't matter. If there was anything in the world guaranteed to take her mind off her troubles, it was sex with Douglas. He simply swept her away from this world and—most importantly—from herself.

He'd dressed her, so now she let him undress her. She stood quietly while he gathered the folds of her nightgown and pulled it up over her head. She was naked underneath. Though she hadn't heard the click of the lights, there was light coming in from the streetlamp outside her window. He could see her.

What was he seeing?

"You're so beautiful." His voice was raw and low as he stripped. She could hear his clothes dropping to the floor.

Oh. That's what he was seeing. She was pretty, she knew that. She had a nice enough body. It was healthy. She wasn't fat and she wasn't thin, not large in the breast department.

But the men she'd been to bed with before Douglas certainly hadn't been overwhelmed. They'd been cool and laid-back, happy to bed her but perfectly capable of living without her. Their hands didn't shake when they touched her, they weren't in a constant state of semi-arousal, they couldn't go all night.

Douglas seemed to think she was so beautiful, so she felt beautiful.

So was he. Allegra stretched her arms up to run them over his shoulders. Her body wasn't anything spectacular, but his sure was.

It still surprised her, the power she felt in him. There'd never been anyone like him before in her life. Her father had been small and slender, with Irish-handsome features and a light voice. Her cousins all had the Ennis frame, too. Her boyfriends and lovers had all been…well, musicians. Cute and funny and klutzy in real life, outside music. Not at all like Douglas, powerful and masterful and capable in so many ways.

This time with him was special. Who knew when she would ever have a chance to be with someone like Douglas again?

"You're beautiful yourself," she murmured, running her hands down the contours of his body, over hard, bulging biceps, down over large forearms, linking briefly with rough, calloused hands. "You feel wonderful."

She ran her hands over his stomach and came across his penis. Amazing. It nearly reached his belly button. She ran her hand over it, lightly, and it quivered in response. Allegra smiled. There was no faking this, no way he could be pretending because he felt sorry for her. Men were at such a disadvantage. She'd faked arousal and she'd faked orgasms in her life and there was no way they could. Men were so…*binary*. Turned on or turned off.

Women had the option of being on a spectrum running from boredom to pleasure, though right now she was way over on the excitement side of that spectrum.

She kissed his chest while her hand fondled him. Nuzzling against the chest hairs, feeling the heavy pectorals against her cheeks, her hand ran up and down along the broad length of his penis. It was alive in her hand, the blood running in hot spurts beneath the skin. She felt every pulse of blood, she could feel his heartbeat, she could feel his desire.

He was breathing heavily and she smiled against his chest. Oh, wow. It was so delightful to hear his breath bellowing in and out and know that she'd reduced him to this. As if she were a four-mile race.

Turning her head, she bit his right nipple, a tiny rock-hard bead. He gasped.

"You like that." It wasn't a question.

"Oh, yeah," he breathed. She could feel the vibrations of his deep voice against her mouth. "Don't stop, please." He gasped when she bent down to lick him, delicately, like a cat. "Please," he repeated, the deep voice a low whisper, as if he desperately needed something only she could give him.

Maybe only she could.

It was his gift to her—the power she wielded over him.

Allegra slowly kneeled, kissing her way down his chest and stomach, feeling his muscles contract where she touched him with her lips.

Had she ever met another man as powerful as Douglas? He was not only physically overwhelming, she had the impression that he had a very strong character, as well. She wasn't his equal in any way, not physically, probably not emotionally. And of course she was at such a huge disadvantage in being blind. Any other man would have taken advantage, but not Douglas.

Actually, she felt incredibly powerful in his presence. The power was all hers, at all times. It was there, in the way his hands sometimes trembled when they touched her, in the way he gentled his hold, in the way he seemed to hesitate before making a move, as if to make sure it was pleasing to her.

It was. It was all pleasing. Like now, touching him. She was on her knees but she was still all-powerful. Every time she touched him with her mouth, she could feel the reaction in his penis. It moved strongly in her hand as she nuzzled his groin, her nose in the dense, rough, curly hair there.

He smelled strongly of Douglas' male musk—a smell that would forever be associated with amazing sex in the primitive recesses of her brain—and, incongruously, of her French triple-milled rose-scented soap.

Douglas' large hands came down lightly on her head as she inched her face closer to his penis.

"Please," he said again. "Please." He was begging.

Allegra had her hand around him so she knew how to angle her face to lick him, even if she couldn't see him. She could feel him, though, and that was enough. She lay a hand on his massive thigh and cupped his testicles while running her tongue along his length. Slowly, taking her time. When she made it to his broad tip, she licked the dense wetness there. He was weeping semen. She licked it all off, slowly.

Douglas was making delicious moaning sounds and his hands clenched briefly in her hair, then he immediately opened his fists, clearly afraid he might hurt her.

Allegra didn't need to see. She had all the sensory input she needed. The feel of him, the taste of him, the smell of him, the helpless sounds of pleasure he was making—it was all imprinted in her mind. Even if she *could* see, her eyes would be closed in concentration as she tasted him, licking her way back down to the thick base of his penis. And back up again, slowly.

She didn't even try to take him in her mouth. He was too enormous for that and she'd gag. This was much better, nibbling her way up the column of his sex, feeling the blood course through him just beneath the skin.

She sat back on her heels for a second, one hand tight around him, slowly pumping up and down, the other exploring his groin, feeling her way around to the hard muscles of his butt. She dug her nails in, briefly, and felt the answering surge of blood in his penis.

This was so delicious!

"You're killing me, you know that, don't you?" he rumbled way above her head.

"Yes?" The thought was wonderful. She was reducing him to weakness. "I thought you were such a tough guy." She leaned forward and bit him, lightly. He jerked.

"That's it." The deep voice sounded strangled as he lifted her and placed her on the bed so her legs dangled over the edge. "Now it's my turn."

"Your...? Oh." Hard hands opening her legs, soft kisses along her thighs, his thumbs opening her up and — "*Oh!*"

He was kissing her there exactly as he kissed her mouth, with finesse, angling his head for the best possible fit, tongue deep inside her, moving gently. In seconds she was trembling, starting the free fall...

"Douglas," she whispered. He shifted, his tongue moving more deeply, faster...

"Oh, God." She shook and when he licked her clitoris, she exploded.

Douglas shifted her further up the bed and entered her as she was coming. He moved in her in short, hard strokes. He seemed to know exactly how to move in her to keep her coming. Her contractions went on and on, her heart hammering as her whole body throbbed.

He was above her, his heavy weight resting on his forearms next to her head. She could feel it as he lowered his head to her ear.

"That's it, honey. Keep going." His chest was against her breasts and she could feel the vibration of his deep voice echoing the hot whisper in her ear. The contractions were finally dying down, his strokes sharp, hard. "No, don't stop. I want you to keep coming for me." The tempo of his strokes increased, moving hard and fast in her and Allegra moved right into another climax, the first time she'd ever had two in a row. He was relentless, gripping her hips so that they tilted up, so that somehow his penis touched her way deep inside, touching her...*there*.

This time her entire body seemed to go haywire as her body arched under his. A low keening sound echoed in the room and it took her a second to realize that she was the one making that animal sound.

"More." His voice was so close to her ear it raised goose bumps along the flesh of her neck. "More, give me more."

There wasn't anything more to give him, yet somehow he seemed to wring another climax out of her, his strokes becoming longer, even faster. Every hair on her body stood up as her orgasm went on and on...

She could barely breathe. "Again," he growled, and it was as if the mere sound of his voice, more than the rough pumping in and out of her, was causing her to climax, over and over again. Who knew she had this in her, this wild passionate response? Her lower body had turned into this sex machine. It was her arms and legs that finally gave out. She simply couldn't hold him with her arms and legs any more. Her arms fell to the mattress, her legs fell from his hips. She had no more strength left.

Douglas stopped when he felt her lose the tight grip she'd had on him and stilled inside her, steel-hard. They both waited, panting, while the contractions of her sheath died down.

"That was amazing." She felt his finger run down her cheek. What she wouldn't give to see his face right now. Did he have a tender expression? Was his face distorted by lust? Maybe she should touch his face to see whether he was smiling, but her arm wouldn't obey her. Douglas kissed her, briefly. "Just amazing."

"Yes," she whispered. There was no strength left in her at all, all her muscles felt like water. "It was wonder—" A huge yawn overtook her, impossible to suppress.

Douglas bent to kiss her, thoroughly, deeply. While he was kissing her, he slowly withdrew from her. She wanted to protest, but couldn't. A second later, she was asleep.

Evil—slick and cold as ice—hung in the air. Blood gleamed red on the white marble floor, red gleaming rivulets merging into streams. The coppery smell of blood filled her nostrils, making her sick. *They were high up, floating above the city whose lights were spread out below like a jeweled carpet, bright and heartless as diamonds. Up here was madness and death, reflected in the gleaming windows, reflected a thousand times off the silver and crystal.*

The face was pure malice, cold eyes and calculation, as it turned to her. She had nowhere to run, nowhere to hide. A tide of blood was rising in the white elegant room, covering the cream carpet, lapping at the table legs, staining the cream couches. The smell was unbearable, the putrid stench of death. Red and white, red red red...

He moved through the blood. It didn't touch him. Ever the dandy, he was wearing a light-gray designer suit. When he walked toward her, the movement made little wavelets in the river of red, but he walked through it as if across an empty room. He looked down briefly, and distaste crossed his face at the sight of the blood.

His eyes, a chilly ice blue, rose to meet hers. It was as if there was no person behind those eyes. Just malice and calculation.

She had to get away because her blood would soon join the sea in the room. She knew that like she knew her name, like she knew music. She turned to run away but the blood turned viscous, like mud. She couldn't move her feet. Her heart pumped madly, she had to run now! But she couldn't move. She opened her mouth to call for help but no sound came out.

Closer, closer, with a shard of ice in his hand. No, not ice, steel. A razor-sharp dagger flashing silver in the light, raised to slash down, coming closer... The panicked scream in her chest couldn't make it past her throat. She tried to run but couldn't move!

Oh God, he was so close, eyes so icy cold. The dagger had disappeared and in its place was a club, swinging down...

"Hey, hey honey, wake up."

Allegra screamed and scrambled to escape, but she was entangled in soft folds, a nightmare of cloth. She was wound tight in sheets and blankets, no defense against a swinging club. That blinding white light was gone. She was in the stifling dark, defenseless against a murderer.

Don't kill me, please! The words were in her head but couldn't make it past her tight throat, trapped inside. She desperately pressed her back against the headboard of the bed, wrapped in a sweaty cocoon of sheets and blankets impeding her movements. There was nowhere to run. She was trapped in the dark.

A big hand touched her and she screamed again, flailing desperately, uselessly.

"Whoa. Bad one."

She was pulled against a body, a big one. Strong arms went around her, not crushing, just holding.

Fighting him made no impression at all. She wore herself out quickly, trying to fight against the strength holding her. It was like fighting a wall. She struggled, twisting and squirming. She beat her fists against his chest, but he didn't move. Didn't even make a sound. Finally she stopped, panting.

She didn't stop because she was tired. She'd fight for her life with her last breath if she had to. She stopped because the pervasive sense of horrible menace—something close and evil and out for *her*—was gone. All she felt now was…quiet strength, encasing her in the darkness.

"It's okay, honey. You had a nightmare." Quiet words. Deep voice.

Douglas.

Safety.

She was sobbing, breath coming in hitches. She tried to control her breathing to get the panic down and was finally able to draw a deep breath, then two. The bright panic was gone, replaced by confusion, a sinking feeling of loss and desolation.

And darkness. She hated the dark, always had, even as a little girl.

A kiss on her hair, then that deep reassuring voice. "That was a doozie. Do you want some water?"

She rested her forehead for a second against his chest, panting, trying to gather her scattered self together.

Water? She shook her head. No, right now she wanted light.

She lifted her head. It was so damned *dark*. It made the fast-fading memory of the nightmare worse. You get rid of nightmares with light. Everyone knew that.

"Switch on the light, Douglas." She rubbed her eyes. Her eyes were wet, though she didn't remember crying. "God," she gasped. "That was awful. I need some light."

His arms tightened around her.

Darkness, still.

Why wasn't he listening to her? She raised her voice. "Douglas, please turn on the light. I hate being in the dark."

"Allegra—"

The darkness made her panic. She struggled vainly against the soft blanket and his hard arms. Dammit, she couldn't *see!*

"Douglas, what's the matter with you, are you deaf? *Turn on the damned light!*"

Light…light…light…

The word echoed around the little room. Allegra stopped breathing.

Two heartbeats later, he spoke. "The light is on, honey."

The light is on.

She was blind.

The realization was just as horrible as the first time—waking up in the hospital bed with sharp sickening smells, tethered to the IV. She'd screamed then for help. Now she had to clasp her hands over her mouth to keep from screaming again. She was blind, and screaming wouldn't help.

There was utter silence. Tears rose from that deep inexhaustible well she'd discovered in herself five months ago.

The first tear to make it down her face and over the back of her hand made a faint *plop* noise on the sheet. Then the second tear, and the third.

There was a silent scream in her throat she wouldn't let out. Couldn't. If she started screaming she'd never stop.

It was hard to breathe, to think.

Douglas left her. She wanted to call him back, but her throat wasn't working. She felt empty and lost without that strength and warmth surrounding her. The cold seeped into her bones immediately. He'd left her. Where had he —

Then it struck her with the force of a blow — *of course*. Of course he left the bed. He was leaving more than the bed, he was leaving her.

She could imagine him getting dressed now, repacking his bag. Of course he was going. Who wanted to stay with a crazy woman with monsters in her head that came tumbling out at night, fanged and ravening?

She steeled herself for the stilted apology, the awkward leave-taking. The cold, empty silence once he'd gone.

She would not cry, she would not cry, she would not cry. She wouldn't beg him to stay. Douglas leaving her was perfectly natural. He'd have to be insane to stay, and he'd struck her as a very sane, balanced man.

Allegra lifted her head, turning it, trying to locate Douglas by sound. He moved so quietly for such a big man. Maybe — maybe he was dressing in the next room. She hoped he'd at least come to say goodbye before —

"Here." The bed dipped and a glass of cold water was put in her hand. His hand cupped hers as he lifted the glass to her mouth. "Drink."

Allegra's hand trembled. How could she drink when her throat was closed so tightly she could hardly breathe?

"Come on now, honey. Drink this, you need it."

That was a voice to obey. She drank, and to her surprise the ice water went down.

"All the way, that's a good girl."

She finished the glass. Somehow she found herself sitting back against a wall of hairy man. Douglas' arms were around her, crossed at her waist. She tilted her head back against his shoulder and closed her eyes. "I thought you'd gone away," she said wearily.

"Now why would I leave?" He sounded genuinely puzzled.

Because I'm blind. Because I think I'm going crazy. Because I rarely sleep without waking up screaming from nightmares I can never, ever remember. Because my life is gone.

"Thought I'd scared you away," she mumbled.

His arms tightened briefly. "Can you talk about it? What was the nightmare about?"

Good question. She never remembered. It washed away immediately, a great sucking tidal wave of jumbled images, leaving a detritus of horror. She'd wake up in a sweaty panic, the sense of imminent menace making her heart pound, and a second after waking, she could never remember what the nightmare was about.

It was an added touch of horror. At least if she could remember what she'd dreamed, these nightmares that had her panicked and sweaty, she could rationalize them away. But there was nothing to be done—the nightmare disappeared like smoke in the wind. The harder she tried to catch meaning, the worse her head hurt.

"I can't remember," she said dully. *I never do.* "I—" She shrugged, shards of jagged memories jumbling and dissipating. "It's gone."

"Does your head hurt now?"

How did he know that? "Yes," she whispered.

"Don't think of anything, anything at all. Make your mind a blank."

She tried. Some of the images and words whirling in her head slowed, disappeared.

"Now think of something calm. The ocean—think of the ocean. Waves rolling in one after another, the foam rising up like lace."

"The sea at Dingle," she breathed.

"Yeah, I've been there, I know that beach. Long and white, big cliffs at the back, right?"

"Oh, yes." She'd played on that beach endlessly as a child with all the Ennis cousins. Just thinking of the beach calmed her.

"It's always chilly along the beach, but the air is clean and pure and has a special light to it. You can walk for hours and all you see is sea and sky and gulls. It's like living at the dawn of time, isn't it, honey?"

Yes, that was exactly what it was like.

A click. The light going off.

Douglas slid down in bed, taking her with him. She was on her side, Douglas spooned behind her. He was deliberately surrounding her with warmth and human contact.

It felt just as good as the sex that had gone before.

Her heart rate was slowing down. She could hear his heartbeat against her back, slow and steady. She tried to breathe calmly, tried to order her scattered self.

It was hard because she was coming to a chilling realization. She thought the very worst that could happen to her in life was the loss of her sight.

She'd been wrong.

Losing her mind was infinitely more terrifying than losing her sight.

Chapter Fourteen

∽

"Honey, wake up. Allegra, come on, open those gorgeous eyes of yours." Kowalski shook her shoulder gently. He didn't want to leave while she was still asleep.

Allegra nestled deeper into the blankets. One slender hand pulled out from under the blanket and her forefinger waved back and forth. *No.*

Kowalski grabbed her hand and kissed it. "Time to get up."

"What will you give me if I do?" Her voice was muffled by the pillow.

He smiled. "Well, coffee and what looks like the world's finest croissant."

She turned her head on the pillow but didn't open her eyes. "The Mancinos call them 'cornetti'. Okay, cornetti. That's good, but not good enough. What else?"

"Whole-wheat bread, butter and homemade jam. Don't know what kind it is, but it sure smells good."

"Color?"

"Ahh..." Kowalski was stumped. "Purple?"

"Blueberry." Allegra finally opened her eyes. "You drive a hard bargain, Senior Chief, but blueberry jam it is."

"Uh huh, tough guy, that's me." Kowalski bent to kiss the tip of her nose. He kept his tone light but watched her carefully.

She'd slept the rest of the night after the nightmare, thank God. Fuck, but she'd scared him. The terrified mewling sounds she'd made while in the grip of the nightmare had made his hair stand on end. She'd been clammy and shaking when he'd roused her from whatever horror she'd been living in her head.

He made sure she slept surrounded by him for the rest of the night. He was going to nip any other nightmares right in the bud from now on. But luckily, she seemed to have slept easy the rest of the night.

He hadn't. He'd slept in a state of combat readiness. It was a shallow-sleeping technique SF soldiers used to give their bodies necessary downtime but allow them to be ready to fight in a split second.

He hadn't had to fight, he'd just had to worry.

Allegra this morning looked just fine, though, he thought, as he helped her to the bathroom. Rosy and rested.

They were getting a rhythm. She'd hold out her hand, waiting for his arm. Once she had a hold on him, she relaxed and was able to follow his lead. He left her in the bathroom and finished preparing breakfast.

It was going to be a busy day, so he fixed a big breakfast for himself. He had a lot to do today and wanted to get back to Allegra as soon as possible, so that meant skipping lunch.

The bread popped out of the toaster as she walked into the room. She stopped at the threshold, waiting, slender hand out. It pleased him beyond measure that she wanted him, needed him. She smiled when she felt his arm.

"Wow, smells wonderful," she said, once she was sitting down.

"You know, you could make a fortune by selling to restaurants what's in your freezer. Butter?" She nodded. Kowalski poured her coffee and buttered her toast for her. "Bless the Mancinos, whoever they are. This stuff is great."

"Oh, yes." Allegra smiled.

"What are you doing today?" Kowalski asked, polishing off his third piece of toast and picking up the next.

"Well, Rosa's sister-in-law Francesca is coming to clean house for me, so there will be a whole new layer of food, in case that interests you. Francesca's specialty is homemade pasta, so expect pans and pans of lasagna and ziti, and this funny ear-shaped pasta called orecchiette. I usually practice the harp while she's cleaning. She says she loves to hear me play and sing, so it suits both of us. And anyway, I'm practicing for her son's christening. I promised I'd play at the reception next month. So I'll practice all morning. Then I'm meeting Suzanne for lunch at The Garden. We made the date last week. She hasn't called to cancel, so I guess it's still on. Suzanne's very reliable that way. Claire was supposed to come, too, but she'll probably still be at the hospital with Bud."

Kowalski put down his fourth slice of toast with a frown. Lunch...hell, it was going to be tricky and tight. He had to run downtown to Portland Police HQ for a debriefing, and then he had an 11:30 appointment with a former FBI Hostage Rescue Team member, Jack Thompson. Thompson had a great résumé, and both Midnight and Kowalski thought he'd bring deep skills to the company. But the interview would take time. *Shit.*

"When's your appointment?"

"Noon." Allegra serenely finished her toast. "Where's the milk?"

"Bravo, red, two o'clock." She found it immediately and smiled, pleased. "Listen, honey, I don't know if I can make it here in time. I've got a really heavy morning."

"In time for what?" she frowned, as her head swiveled to his voice.

"To drive you to The Garden. Do you think you could call Suzanne and ask her if she could put lunch off until one?"

"You don't need to drive me anywhere, Douglas. Suzanne will be stopping by to pick me up and anyway, if she can't, I'll just call a cab. I have the number of the cab company memorized."

"No." Kowalski kept his tone even, though the thought of Allegra calling a taxi, being alone in a cab with a stranger, made him want to punch his fist through the wall. "Don't call a cab. Call me if Suzanne can't make it. If I'm not free, I'll send one of my men." Jacko was free this morning, Kowalski would see to it.

Jacko was even a worse nightmare to look at than he was. At least Kowalski dressed normally. Jacko dressed in ancient sweatshirts with the sleeves cut off, raggedy torn jeans and scuffed boots, no coat, no matter what the weather, even in the snow. That put people off almost as much as the viper tats, shaved head, and nose and brow rings.

People looked away when Kowalski entered a room. People crossed to the other side of the street when Jacko walked down the sidewalk.

Didn't matter. Jacko might look like something out of a horror movie, but Kowalski trusted him with his life. Had trusted him with his life several times. More importantly, he trusted Jacko with Allegra's life.

Allegra was frowning as she sipped her coffee.

"Promise me you'll call." Kowalski covered her hand with his and waited. The one thing he didn't want was for that lovely chin to go up, for her to get into a pissing contest with him.

He already knew that he was weak where Allegra was concerned. He'd never backed down from anything in his life, but he would with her. However long she wanted to stay with him, they'd do what she wanted. Eat what she wanted to eat, go where she wanted to go, do what she wanted to do. She could wrap him around her little finger. That was simply the way it was and the way it would be. He accepted it.

Except for one thing. Her personal safety. And there Kowalski was a rock—he wouldn't give an inch. She was *not* going to take a cab, and that was that.

"Promise me," he said, and watched her carefully.

That chin went up as she contemplated Irish rebellion, then trembled. She clearly knew he was right. Maybe she'd had a bad experience or two in a taxi. "Promise." His grip on her hand tightened slightly.

He watched Allegra teeter on the edge, then give up.

"Okay. I promise."

Nail it down, he thought. "You promise what?"

She heaved a sigh. "I promise, I *swear*, I won't call a taxi."

"Not today, not ever."

"Not today, not ever," she repeated obediently, and blinked. "Wow, that's going to be hard."

"Nope, easiest thing in the world. You need a ride, you call me. Simple as that. Memorize my cell phone number." He gave it to her and made her repeat it until he was satisfied she'd remember it. "If I can't drive you, one of my men will. I'll see to it." Kowalski was going to find himself a trusted man—a retired cop, say—and keep him on retainer to act as Allegra's driver. It would save his sanity.

"And you?" Allegra's small hand flexed under his. "Will you—will you be back tonight?"

Her eyes were huge as she turned to him. She couldn't see him but she was listening with every cell of her body.

Was she unsure about him? Unsure that he'd come back? That was crazy. He'd walk barefoot over live coals to be with her.

"Oh yeah." He breathed the words, and his tone must have reassured her because she relaxed slightly. "I'll be back, count on it. I'll try to make it back—" *Home.* He almost said 'home'. "I think I'll be back by around 5:00."

"I'll be back by then, too. You can explore what Francesca left for me, have fun sifting through the pans. She's a fabulous cook." She smiled at him. "So—what's your day like? Will you be busy?"

"Yeah. I have to go down to Portland PDHQ. Police Headquarters," he added, when she looked puzzled. "I'll have to be debriefed about what went down Saturday night." Jesus, it felt like a century ago. A lifetime ago, when his heart had been whole, when his life had been his to decide. B.A. Before Allegra. "I have to make it back to the office by 11:30, though. I'm interviewing a guy for an executive position with the company. He's got good credentials, looks fabulous on paper, former HRT."

"That's nice," Allegra said absently, delicately picking up a slice of toast. She froze, the toast an inch from her mouth. She put the slice down slowly and turned to him with a furrow between her brows, looking baffled. "Douglas?"

Kowalski drained his cup and stood. He ran the back of a forefinger down the smooth curve of her cheek. "Yeah, honey?"

"Why on earth do you need a man who used to be on Hormone Replacement Therapy?"

Little bitch would be off balance today. That was good, that would make her weak, vulnerable. Ready for the end game. She wasn't made for the big time, that was clear. She was soft, easy to scare. It took balls to become a star.

Yesterday she'd freaked. Alvin watched her turn white and collapse after he played Mr. Sanderson's recording. She'd simply folded. She was with a guy—big ugly bruiser, and he'd caught her before she fell to the ground. Alvin wasn't worried about the bruiser. He couldn't know who Alvin was and the next time Alvin got near the little bitch, she'd be alone. He'd make sure of that.

Bitch was dangerous to Mr. Sanderson. She could put him behind bars forever and then how was Alvin supposed to make it?

Mr. Sanderson needed her dead and he needed it to look like a suicide. Easy enough. Have her think she was hearing ghosts, drive her crazy, then walk into her house when the big guy was gone and put her head in the oven.

She cooked with gas. Alvin knew because he'd been in the house while she was out. It was going to be a piece of cake.

Drive her nuts, wait for the boyfriend to leave, then walk in. Hold her by the hair so bruises wouldn't show, then shove her head in the oven.

And then he'd be the new Eminem. No more changing bedpans and washing down freaks. No more shit work. Just music and babes and snow, forever. There was just one thing standing between him and his destiny — Allegra Ennis.

She was going down.

"Oh sweetie," Suzanne said, "are you okay? I was so worried about you. I tried calling but the phone was always busy."

Allegra tried not to blush. Douglas had taken the phone off the hook so they wouldn't be disturbed.

They were in The Garden, waiting for their orders to arrive. Claire had phoned to say she'd be late and to go ahead and order for her. Her usual — soup of the day and a small salad.

Allegra knew Suzanne so well, it was as if she could see her. She'd have on one of her form-hugging, pale pastel, killer designer numbers that would never, ever show sweat or dirt or even wrinkles. Suzanne seemed to have an endless variety of them, bought from some secret source. Her dark blonde hair would be perfectly coiffed, discreet expensive jewels glinting from ears and hands. The only non-discreet thing was the humongous wedding ring on the ring finger of her left hand. Allegra had touched it once and it felt like a faceted pigeon's egg. Very non-Suzanne, but then her husband struck her as a non-Suzanne husband. Still, she seemed happy with him, which was what counted.

She'd be leaning forward now, tucking a stray lock of shiny hair behind her ear. When she talked to you, she focused and listened. Allegra loved that about her.

"I'm okay." Allegra smiled, to take the worry out of Suzanne's voice. She deliberately injected some Ireland into her own. "Quite a time we had at the Foundation, eh? Nothin' like a little ruckus to keep the blood up."

"Horrible." Suzanne's voice was quiet. "That such a violent thing should happen at the Parks Foundation. The next jewelry show will be bristling with guns and guards and will be one further step down into barbarity." Allegra could feel the air displacement as Suzanne shivered with disgust. Suzanne's hand covered hers for a brief moment. "It must have been so awful for you. I wanted to wait for you, but Douglas insisted he'd take you home. Did he see you to your door all right?"

"Ah, yes, yes he did." *And beyond.*

Allegra blushed beet-red. She could feel it, feel the rush of blood to her face and throat, and cursed her pale Irish skin.

"Oh." Suzanne blinked when she was surprised or taken aback, which wasn't often. She was such a cool customer. But right now she was probably blinking up a frenzy. "*Oh!*" Quick intake of breath. "You mean you and—you and *Douglas?* I never would have—oh my gosh."

Allegra knew what Suzanne was thinking.

After the accident, when she'd woken up from the coma to find herself blind, it was as if she'd entered some no-sex, no-pleasure zone. She wasn't an attractive woman any more, one who could expect a degree of constant male interest in her, one who liked being young and pretty and female. No, now she was this damaged and neutered...thing. She'd been robbed of her femininity. Pretty clothes, daring makeup, the mild flirting any pretty young woman carries on with the men she meets— they'd all been taken from her. She lived in a dark, grim world where just getting through the day—keeping herself clean and fed and free of bruises—drained her of all energy. Boyfriends, lovers, flirting, sex—they were all beyond her, disappeared into the great yawning chasm of darkness that had engulfed her life.

But now she had someone in her life and it astonished her, too. She wouldn't have talked about it, out of fear of jinxing it. She wanted to wait and see if Douglas was going to stick around for a while before letting Suzanne or Claire know about it. Damn her skin and her tendency to blush. Well, the secret was out now, no sense denying it.

"Yes, um, Douglas stayed. And he's, um, coming back tonight." She frowned. "Or at least he said he was. I hope his word is good."

"Oh, his *word* is good." Suzanne's voice held something. What? Some odd inflection as if she was trying to tell Allegra something without saying the words. "There's no doubt about that. Douglas is a thousand percent a man of his word. If he said he's coming back, count on it—he'll be back. I don't think grenades or machine-gun fire could stop him. It's just that..."

"What?" Allegra leaned forward, suddenly anxious and scared. Had she missed out on something? Not recognized something? What if Douglas wasn't as wonderful as she thought? What if he was hiding something, like—

"Heavens! He isn't married is he? He said he wasn't. Or rather," she frowned, "he implied he was single. It would be just too awful if he was married with a dozen kids." She clapped her hands to her still-red cheeks in horror. Oh God, she simply couldn't stand it if her time with Douglas had been a lie. He seemed so steady and—

"No, sweetie, Douglas is definitely not married, never has been. There are no kids anywhere, I can assure you of that."

Allegra sat back in her chair, relieved. Wow. Maybe she should stop thinking in such catastrophic terms all the time. Not everything was destined to turn out for the worst. Maybe.

211

"Well, this is a real surprise." Suzanne touched the back of her hand lightly, letting her know she was there, listening. "I want you to tell me everything. What happened? He accompanied you home and then just walked right in?"

"Mmm, not quite. We had a little...interlude at the Foundation."

"What?" This was actually fun. Allegra was enjoying the shock and surprise in Suzanne's voice. Not much knocked Suzanne off course. "At the *Foundation?* Between the concert and the bad guys? No wait, you were singing when they broke in! Just when did you have time to carry on a romance? This is incredible."

It was so romantic, Allegra wanted to tell the tale. For just a second, she allowed herself a flash of thought of the future. And since it was in the privacy of her own head, she could think what she wanted. She imagined telling her grandchildren the story. And since it was her head and her daydream, there were lot of kids listening.

Ah, me darlings, gather 'round and listen to when your grandfather started seducing yer grandmother under the podium while bad guys were shootin' their guns.

"Well, you and Claire weren't around, so Douglas accompanied me up onto the podium." She shushed Suzanne, who'd groaned. "And don't you dare apologize for not being there because if you had, I wouldn't have had a chance to connect with Douglas. Anyway, he walked me to Dagda and said he'd wait for me to finish, so he was close by. I was halfway through the set when I heard noises from the audience. It was only later that I found out the lights went out. And then—and then there was a huge explosion. Only just as the noise of the explosion hit me, something else hit me— Douglas, flying off the podium with me in his arms. Amazing. He rolled us right under the concert podium. He was on top of me. And we, um, stayed there...for a while."

Long enough to almost have an orgasm, she thought, and blushed bright red again.

"It was so wonderful, Suzanne," she said dreamily. "I just can't tell you how—how wonderful and exciting and thrilling it's been. Just amazing. I mean, I know perfectly well that there are huge differences between us. Don't think I don't realize that."

"Well," Suzanne said, her voice kind. "What does that matter? After all, looks aren't every—"

"I mean," Allegra interrupted, "I'll just bet you anything he's a Republican."

Suzanne laughed.

"What?"

"Oh, yes, I think you can safely say that Douglas is a Republican. And definitely John and probably Bud, too. It's okay, your vote can cancel his out. Who cares about politics? There are more important things. Are you—are you happy with him?"

"Absolutely." With all her doubts about herself and what she could offer, that was a question Allegra could answer without hesitation. "It's been wonderful—so far, at least. I feel incredibly *safe*, with him, you know?"

"Yes," Suzanne said softly, putting her hand over Allegra's and squeezing lightly. "I can imagine. I know how I feel with John, like nothing bad can happen as long as he's around. I'm only sorry that on Saturday night I insisted that he and Douglas be unarmed. I was wrong. *How* wrong was, uh," Suzanne's voice turned wry, "pointed out to me very forcefully all day yesterday."

"Exactly." There was something about Douglas that made her feel safe, just having him in the room made her feel better. She'd never seen John, Suzanne's husband. She'd only had dinner with him and Suzanne once, and they'd spoken briefly at the Foundation, but something told her he was in many ways similar to Douglas. Tall and with a deep voice, though not as deep as Douglas', steady and calm.

You could almost feel the glow coming off Suzanne whenever she talked about her husband.

"That's the way I feel about Douglas. Like he knows exactly what he's doing. And, boy, does he." Blood rushed back to her face. She felt like a stoplight. "Whoa, did that come out wrong."

Suzanne laughed again. "Uh huh. If he's anything like John, um, in intimacy, I'll just bet he knows what he's doing."

"Who knows what he's doing? Hi Allegra, hi Suzanne." Before Allegra could answer, there was a flurry of air, soft lips kissed her cheek, and Claire's voice said, "I made it! I left Mr. Impossibly Grumpy for two whole hours and got here! It's so good to be out of the hospital and," Claire breathed in deeply, "smelling something besides rubbing alcohol and formaldehyde! It wouldn't be so bad if it weren't for the fact that Bud keeps trying to get out of bed, though he's attached to machinery by a thousand tubes. If I hadn't stopped him, he would have pulled out his IV this morning. I swear, that man survived surgery only to get murdered by his nurses."

"Hi, Claire." Allegra smiled. Claire was so sweet. She could just see her with Bud, patient and gentle with a grouchy male. Men could be so impossible. She remembered her father when he'd had gallstone surgery and had morphed right into a cranky old bear who—

A sharp pain flared deep in her head then spread, pounding. Allegra gasped and held her head.

"Hey, sweetie." Suzanne's cool hand touched her forehead. "Is something the matter? Do you need something?"

Another head. That's what she needed. And while she was at it, another life. This happened to her often when she thought of her father, another cruel blow of fate.

"No, no, nothing's wrong," Allegra lied. She brought her hand down, forced a smile on her face. "I'm fine. Sorry. So Bud is okay? We were so worried, Douglas and I. But Douglas told me that if a gunshot wound doesn't kill you immediately, there's an excellent chance of survival and recovery. And I suppose he should know."

"Yes, he'll be fine. I think it's a sign of recovery that Bud's threatening to pull his gun on the doctors unless they tell him when he can go home. Preferably yesterday, to his way of thinking. Why, right after surgery..." Claire's voice trailed off and Allegra could practically *hear* her head swivel. "Douglas? You've got a guy named Douglas? Who's Doug—*heavens*! Not your husband's partner?" This to Suzanne. She sounded shocked.

"The same." Suzanne's voice was dry. "Senior Chief Douglas Kowalski."

Silence. More silence.

"Wow," Claire said finally.

"Yeah," Allegra said, feeling the blood rise to her face again. "Wow. You can say that again. It's been great. Just great. I've never had such an exciting time with a man before. I mean—oh God." That came out all wrong, all over again. She must be radiating heat from her blush.

Suzanne and Claire laughed.

"Ladies? Your meals will be here shortly. May I take your drink orders?" Allegra wondered if it was the tall waiter who had the demeanor of an undertaker or the short, hairy one who looked like Robin Williams. They each ordered a glass of wine—a Merlot for her, Riesling for Claire and Zinfandel for Suzanne. The waiter disappeared in a cloud of scent. He'd obviously rolled out of bed this morning straight into a vat of aftershave.

"So," they said all at once, and laughed.

"So." Allegra turned toward Claire. "I want to hear all about Bud."

"I don't," Suzanne said promptly.

"Me neither." Claire tapped Allegra's hand. "I'm sick of thinking of Bud. I've done nothing but care for him for the past thirty-six hours and I'm going back to him when lunch is over,

215

so I'm all Bud-ed out right now. I want to hear about…Douglas." There it was again, that tone. Suzanne had it too, when she said his name. What was that about? "Come on, Allegra. Tell all. And I mean everything. Every little detail."

There was a scraping sound as the two minxes actually brought their chairs closer to her, so as not to miss anything.

"Not talking," Allegra said primly, miming a zip across her mouth. Claire made a shocked sound.

"Not at all?" Suzanne's fingers tapped impatiently on the wooden tabletop.

Allegra shook her head. Not a peep.

"Nothing? Not the tiniest detail? Ah, come on," Claire whined. "I told you all about Bud and when we met."

Allegra shook her head, vigorously, enjoying the suspense. Claire had indeed talked, in shocking, red-hot detail. Well, she had her own red-hot story to tell. Putting on a smug smile, she waited. Let them suffer for it if they wanted dish.

"Nothing for it but to bribe her," Claire told Suzanne. "But with what? Chocolate mousse?"

Allegra hesitated a moment—chocolate mousse was tempting—then shook her head. She had chocolate mousse, Francesca's tiramisù and Sacher torte in her freezer. They'd have to do better than that.

"I know what will get her to talk," Suzanne said slyly. "A secret. A big, *big* secret. Big, fat, juicy secret."

"What?" Allegra and Claire said together.

"Wouldn't be a secret if I told, would it?" Suzanne sounded incredibly smug. "And yet, I'm willing to talk if Allegra is."

The sound of the serving trolley, then the sounds of the waiter placing their plates on the table. Allegra leaned forward to take in the scent of her order—gnocchi in gorgonzola sauce, a specialty of the house. Her favorite dish at The Garden was onion soup, but soup was too messy for her to eat in public, even with understanding friends like Claire and Suzanne.

Claire dinged her water glass with the spoon. "Okay now, we've struck our deal, so who goes first? I vote Allegra."

"Nope." Allegra brought one of the gnocchi to her mouth and savored it. The Garden's chef was fabulous. "I'm not talking until I know that Suzanne's news is worthy of my news. On a scale of one to ten, mine is a hundred." She had the upper hand and she knew it. New loves were the atom bombs of gossip. They blew everything else right out of the water.

"How do we know you won't cheat? Suzanne tells her secret and then you zip up again?"

Allegra sipped her Merlot. "You'll have to take it on faith." She smiled and sipped again, waiting. "Take it or leave it."

"We'll take it," Claire said.

"Absolutely."

"You first, Suzanne." Allegra smiled. She loved besting Suzanne in negotiation. Suzanne in a previous life must have worked in the Casbah in Casablanca, buying and selling carpets. Getting the upper hand with her ranked right up there with winning the Pulitzer Prize.

"Okay. Well, this is my news." Suzanne took a deep breath, let it out shakily. "I'm...pregnant."

Claire and Allegra squealed at the same time, cutlery clattering to the table. Allegra reached over to clasp Suzanne's hand. "Ohmygodohmygod!"

"This is great! Oh, wow! I can't wait to tell Bud!" Claire laughed. "He'll have a cow. Gosh, this is all so sudden!"

The three friends hugged and Allegra heard Suzanne sniffle. Well, that's why she kept pocket handkerchiefs in her purse, for friends. Suzanne took the proffered handkerchief with a muffled, "Thanks," and blew her nose. Hormones, Allegra thought. Had to be hormones. Suzanne never cried.

"Whoa, sorry, I don't know why I'm crying. I mean I'm happy and everything, it's just—" Suzanne honked in an unladylike and very un-Suzanne-like way into the handkerchief. "It's all so overwhelming. Everything's happened so *fast*."

And it had. Suzanne only met her husband for the first time a month ago. She'd had wild sex with him the evening they met—Allegra and Claire had dragged that out of her—and the next day she was running for her life, after John shot and killed two men gunning for her.

Then she and John holed up in some cabin in the mountains, which she said was very dingily furnished. Man, woman, alone in shabby mountain cabin—well, you have some baby-making ingredients right there.

Then the FBI had taken her away for four days until the bad guy had providentially ended up dead. The next day she and John were married.

And now she was expecting. Talk about the pace of modern life.

"I was on the Pill," Suzanne said, and honked again into the handkerchief. "I know how to take care of myself. But things got so muddled there. I must have skipped a day or two. And then John and I—" She stopped abruptly and Allegra wished she could see her, see whether Suzanne could blush. She had a very good idea of what she and John had been doing. "It's really early, I'm only a few days late but somehow I just *knew* I was pregnant. So I bought the kit and took the test this morning. I was a little shell-shocked. I still haven't told John."

"Do you want a child?" Claire asked gently.

"Yes." Suzanne's voice was clear. She sounded like her old self. There was a rustle of clothes as Allegra imagined her sitting up straighter in her chair. "Absolutely. I wouldn't have chosen to get married and get pregnant quite so quickly, but there it is. Now I just have to screw up the courage to tell John."

"You don't think he'll want a child?" Allegra asked. How sad. This had happened to several of her girlfriends. The husbands or boyfriends hadn't wanted children, hadn't wanted the burden or distraction. It was a shame because Allegra couldn't imagine anything more wonderful than bearing a child to love. She herself wanted a big family. She'd always suffered from the fact that she was an only child.

"No, he wants it. He was saying just the other day he thought we should start a family. I just didn't think it would be so...*soon.*" Her voice wobbled at the end. She drew in a long breath and her voice steadied. "The truth is, I wanted to come up with a sure-fire John Management Technique before having a child. I still haven't figured out how to keep John on the other side of the line as far as arranging my life is concerned, and this is going to send him over the top. John tends to go wildly overboard in the protection department."

"Tell me about it," Allegra and Claire said at the same time, then laughed.

"Well, you see? Maybe they all studied at the same School for Overprotective Men. I swear, it was a struggle to be able to drive here today. I mean, there's maybe a quarter inch of snow on the sidewalks, the streets are clear as anything, but John kept insisting that he have one of his men drive me here. His men are not what you'd call great company. They sit at the wheel like great lumps of protoplasm and scowl at each passing car and pedestrian as if they were terrorists just waiting to whip out a gun or a bomb. It's so totally annoying. And of course his men are supposed to be working, and I don't want to keep them away from it for too long, which means I have to calculate when I'll leave and when I come back. That's really annoying, too. I won today because I really put my foot down, but once John knows I'm pregnant, well I can kiss my steering wheel good-bye."

Allegra had a sudden vision of Alpha Security International, John and Douglas' company, turned into a glorified chauffeur service.

"I'm going to have to fight now to get to the big Home Decoration Exhibit in Savannah in March. I so look forward to it every year. I love meeting colleagues from all over, catching up on new trends, and now I'll bet you anything John's going to insist on coming with me. He'll stick by me like glue. Can you imagine chatting with Willard Sykes of Textiles Ink about the new damasks out of China with John there, glowering?"

Wow. Allegra tried to imagine it—Suzanne and a colleague talking textile shop with a very large, bored, armed man sitting right next to them. It would put a damper on things, that was for sure. Not too good for business, either.

"And afterwards," Suzanne continued, and Allegra could practically hear her roll her eyes. "Can you imagine how protective he's going to be with a child? And I'm expecting a girl, I just know it, I can feel it in my bones. She'll be lucky if he'll let her out of the house before college."

Silence as all three mulled over Suzanne's little girl trying to date when she reached her teens with John running interference.

"Well," Allegra ventured softly, "he'll love her, that's for sure. Like he loves you. That counts for a lot."

Suzanne heaved a great sigh. "I know. I know how lucky I am. John's a wonderful husband and he'll be a loving father. I'm delighted about the child. I just wish I felt a little less…off balance about it."

"Give yourself a break, Suzanne," Claire said. "Of course you're off balance. You almost had your head blown off Saturday. That would make anyone a little uncertain, even Suzanne La Cool."

"What?" Allegra straightened as if an electric prod had stung her. "What's this about Suzanne's head being blown off? What are you talking about?"

"Oh." Allegra could hear the gears grinding in Claire's head. She clearly wished she hadn't spoken, but now she had. "Well, at the Foundation, Saturday…um, Suzanne was taken hostage by one of the robbers."

"Together with a number of other women," Suzanne intervened hastily, as if that made it somehow better.

"Yeah, but the creep didn't have that huge black bazillion-round submachine gun against *their* head," Claire objected heatedly. "Just yours."

"And Douglas didn't say a thing, the *rat*." Allegra was going to strangle Douglas when she got home. If she'd had any inkling Suzanne's life had been threatened, that she'd undergone such a traumatic event—well, more traumatic for Suzanne than for anyone else—she'd have called yesterday, to find out how she was.

"He didn't want you to worry." Claire placed a hand over hers. "I guess all three of our guys went to that same school. It's like they want to protect you from—life, I guess."

"Well, enough about me," Suzanne said briskly, sounding like her old self. It had been so weird hearing her sound a little lost and uncertain. It was so totally unlike her. "I've paid up, so now it's your turn, Allegra, and it better be good. We want to know *everything*."

"Oh yeah." Claire turned on a dime. "Time to put out."

Claire had been very forthcoming about the hot weekend she'd had with Bud, when she lost her virginity to a man she thought was a lumberjack, but who was, instead, a homicide detective. But Claire had been new to sex and was overwhelmed with the power of it. Allegra wasn't new to sex—though she was very definitely new to the type of sex she'd had with Douglas. Still, it felt too…fragile, yet, to tell the details. She could tell the heart of it, though.

"Well…" Allegra could feel the waves of rapt attention coming off her two best friends. "You know how when you first meet a man and you're on your best behavior and you want it all to be perfect and somehow it never is? No matter how hard you work at it? Well, I didn't work at anything with Douglas. Our first kiss was under the podium at the Foundation while I was cowering in fear at the sound of gunshots. He's the first man I've been with since...since." Her voice cracked and Suzanne's fingers touched her face, smoothing back a lock of hair.

"We know, sweetie." Her voice was soft with acceptance and understanding. Another thing she loved about Suzanne, and about Claire, too. They always understood.

"Anyway," Allegra continued, when the tightness in her throat eased up, "I think what's so incredible is that at all times I've been completely myself with him. I feel total freedom. I never once worry about the effect I'm having on him or how I look or...or anything."

She twisted the linen tablecloth, searching for the words to tell her friends the deepest secrets of her heart.

"I thought my life was over, when I woke up blind," she said finally, quietly. "I honestly thought I might just as well be dead. I couldn't imagine falling in love, ever again. More to the point, I couldn't imagine anyone falling in love with me. Who would want me? I can't do anything for myself, I'm no fun at all." Allegra toyed, briefly, with the idea of telling her two best friends about the nightmares, waking and sleeping, but that felt too raw, too scary. "So you can imagine my surprise when this big strong man, who can do anything or have anything he wants, apparently wanted—wants—*me*. Not only does he want me, but he wants the unvarnished, damaged me. He doesn't seem to find me lacking in any way." She wiped away a tear. "It still feels like a miracle and I'm waiting for him to tell me that I'm too much trouble, but so far..." *Knock on wood.* "So far, he seems to be sticking. It's only been two days—less than two days, and I don't know what the future holds, but even this little bit of time has helped me find myself again. I can let myself be *me* with him. I thought I'd never be happy again, but Douglas has given me happiness back. It's such a big, scary risk for me, opening my heart to him, but I feel safe with my heart in his hands." She turned to her left. "You know, Suzanne? Like you feel with John?"

There was utter silence.

"Yes, I know." Suzanne honked into her handkerchief again. Allegra wondered if she had any mascara left.

To her right, Claire sniffled. "That's wonderful," she said in a watery voice, then she exclaimed, "Oh my gosh! Look at the time! I have to get back to the hospital before the afternoon rounds. If I'm not there, Bud's capable of pulling all his tubes out and staggering away. Or punching out the doctors' lights. Suzanne, can you settle my bill and I'll pay you back later? Allegra, I'm so happy for you... Oh, God, I've got to *run!*"

With a flurry of kisses, Claire left.

Suzanne settled the bill, refusing Allegra's credit card. "Put it back, sweetie. And I won't accept Claire's money, either. Think of it as my little celebration lunch, to announce my pregnancy. Come on, now, the sky's darkening. I want to get you home and then drive back before John sends out the Marines—or the SEALs—to find me."

Allegra stood shivering outside the door of The Garden, waiting for Suzanne to bring the car around. A tiny snowflake fell on her cheek and she lifted her face to the cold air, breathing deeply, feeling peace settle in her heart.

She was so lucky to have Suzanne and Claire in her life. Not everybody had such good friends.

Not everybody had a Douglas.

To her shame, she found herself counting her blessings for the very first time since she'd lost her sight, something she should have done earlier. There were plenty of them. She had no money problems. She was in extremely good health. People cared for her. All of that was worth celebrating.

For the first horrible, black week in the hospital, Allegra had seriously considered suicide. Just ending it all, any way she could. She missed her father fiercely and she simply could not contemplate life in an endless black abyss. But she'd been wrong. There were things to look forward to. Bud and Claire were definitely going to get married and they'd want her to sing at the wedding. One part of her brain, the music lobe, was already putting together the selection of songs, if she could keep from crying with happiness. And Suzanne's child. If it was a little girl, the three of them would keep her knee-deep in dresses while John drove them all crazy, hovering. A little girl to love. Douglas in her life, in her bed. Maybe, just maybe, life was good, after all.

Allegra smiled.

"You little bitch. You're going to get what's coming to you. I'm going to see you dead and then you'll roast in hell." Corey Sanderson's voice was in her ear and his hand grabbed her arm in a painful vise.

Allegra screamed at the top of her voice.

Chapter Fifteen

∞

Hormone replacement therapy.

Kowalski was still chuckling over that one back in his office. Jack Thompson was about five-foot-eight, two-hundred-and-ten pounds, a real ace with a rifle, hairy as a bear and looked like a wrestling champ.

Not a likely candidate for HRT anytime soon.

Hormone replacement therapy, indeed.

"We've got to get on top of the Robertson account." Midnight walked in, frowning over a clipboard. "Fuck, he wants two bodyguards, asap. So I guess we—" he looked up, stopped in his tracks and stared, jaw open.

Kowalski had already deputized two men to protect the publisher who'd published the tell-all memoirs of a former Aryan supremacist and had received death threats from no less than three militia movements.

Midnight was still standing there, catching flies with his mouth. "Well, what the hell you staring at?" Kowalski waved his pen impatiently.

"You're...smiling." John hitched a hip on the corner of his desk. "Threw me for a loop there."

Kowalski immediately frowned. "Am not smiling," he growled.

"Are too."

"Am not." Kowalski's jaws clenched at how childish they sounded.

Midnight's grin split his face. "You sure as hell are— were. I haven't seen you smile since 1999, and that was only because that sadistic fuckhead Gannon fractured his leg on a

HALO." Midnight shook his head. "Had a smile over that one myself." He looked at Kowalski, eyes narrowed. "But I have never seen that particular expression on your face before. You look like a sap, my friend. Like a fish with a hook in its mouth, happy to have been landed."

John easily evaded the book Kowalski threw at his head and laughed. He tilted his head. "Hook looks good in your mouth, though, Senior Chief. I wonder if it has anything to do with a certain gorgeous redhead with a fabulous voice?"

Kowalski bent his head over the report, pretending to read with rapt interest a cost breakdown of a new computer system, when he wasn't taking in a word. He willed Midnight to get up off his desk and walk away, but Midnight was as strong-willed as he was and looked so settled in he could sit there for days.

This was completely new for Kowalski—being teased about his love life. He'd never had a love life before, just a sex life that no one ever teased him about, for the excellent reason that it wasn't public. He'd never gone to a party with a woman on his arm, never introduced a woman to his teammates. He'd never been part of a couple.

It occurred to him, for the first time, that now he was. He'd been so overwhelmed with everything that it hadn't had time to penetrate his thick skull, but all of a sudden there it was—Douglas Kowalski had a mate. Someone to share things with, someone to look after, someone to care about.

It was so odd, that thought. He turned it over in his mind.

A couple. He was part of a couple. Maybe even…an engaged couple. Oh yeah, he could get behind that.

"Come on, Kowalski. I know what you're going through. I have that hook in my mouth myself. Threw me for a loop, I'll tell you, and I've been out of my head ever since. I'm really happy for you, Senior. Allegra seems like a nice kid. Suzanne loves her so that puts her real high up in my book. Pity about that fucker who beat her up and got away with it. Killed her dad. Blinded her. Personally, I'd have cut his balls off, but what do I know? I'm just a sailor."

Kowalski put his pen down slowly. There was a loud buzzing in his ears.

"What did you say?" He enunciated each word carefully. His tongue felt big and awkward in his mouth. Someone had beaten Allegra up? *Beaten her up?* He couldn't move, could hardly breathe.

Midnight's eyes bored into his. "Fuck," he said quietly. "You didn't know. No one told you."

"Told. Me. What." Kowalski wasn't screaming. He thought that showed enormous self-control. Midnight held his hands up, palms out—*okay now, keep calm.* Kowalski wondered if what was in his eyes scared Midnight.

"Right, this is what I have, and it's all from Suzanne, you understand."

Kowalski nodded, his throat too tight to talk. Every cell of his body was screaming to go out and kill whoever the motherfucker was who'd hurt Allegra, but he was a soldier. He had discipline. Discipline was what had made him what he was.

Midnight raised troubled eyes to his. "The story is this. Allegra was barreling right along in her career, a sort of Irish Norah Jones—that's straight from Suzanne, what the fuck do I know about music? So anyway, Allegra was very successful and this guy, this, this manager or producer or something who was Mr. Big in the '80s. Guy named Corey Sanderson—you ever heard of him?"

Kowalski had. Anyone who followed music had. Sanderson was a big-time producer-turned-manager, had helped create a number of the sounds of the '80s and '90s and ruled the music world of the Pacific Northwest. Hip-hop, skat, grunge, world music, you name it, Corey Sanderson somehow was behind it or close to it or managing it or making money off it. Corey Sanderson was The Man.

Kowalski nodded and Midnight continued. "Anyway, Allegra signed with this guy who was supposed to help her make this leap right up into superstardom, but he fumbled the ball, lost his mojo. From what I gather, this Sanderson guy started pushing Allegra to go in directions she wasn't musically suited for. Now that's a direct quote from Suzanne, I wouldn't know musical directions if they hit me upside the head. Allegra was increasingly unhappy, her career was tanking because this guy was forcing her to sing and play things that weren't her style. Allegra was on a big tour last summer, and they were selling fewer and fewer tickets, lots of cancellations, the whole enchilada was sinking fast. Allegra confessed her unhappiness to Suzanne and Suzanne took a look at her contract. And I gotta say that as a businesswoman, Suzanne is sharp as a tack. She's given me excellent business advice. You really want my girl on your side, and not as your enemy. Sanderson was her enemy. She hated the guy's guts and found a way for Allegra to get out of her contract with him."

Kowalski had goose pimples. A sudden flash of what was coming made his skin crawl.

"At the end of the summer tour, Suzanne had Allegra make an appointment with Sanderson to discuss terminating the business relationship. Allegra took her dad with her. According to Suzanne, Allegra's dad was this really sweet professor of music, but not the most forceful guy in the world, you know what I mean?"

Kowalski glared at Midnight. "Cut to the chase."

Midnight rolled his eyes. "Okay—bottom line. A week after the end of the disastrous summer tour, on the 9th of September, Allegra and her father went to Sanderson with a letter of termination of contract drawn up by Suzanne. At midnight, Suzanne was called in by the police because they'd found her number in Allegra's purse. The father was dead— blunt instrument trauma to the head—and Allegra was in a coma. She'd been severely beaten around the head and her jaw was broken. Now sit down and listen to the rest." Midnight put a hand on his shoulder. Kowalski had risen, murder in his heart. "So this fucker Sanderson wriggles out of it. He lawyers up fast and good, hires one of the best mouthpieces around. Allegra stayed in a coma for six weeks and when she finally came out of it she was blind, her jaw was broken and she had amnesia. No way could she testify. Sanderson's lawyer pushed for a speedy trial, his story was they had a disagreement, Allegra's father and Allegra herself became violent and he defended himself."

"Bullshit." Every muscle Kowalski had was taut, fighting ready. He was literally seeing red, veins popping in his eyes from rage. He was vaguely aware of a crackling sound and looked down at the pen he'd snapped in his fist, wishing it was this Sanderson fucker's neck.

"Yeah. You know it, I know it, Suzanne knew it and probably the judge and lawyers knew it, too. He gets a reduced sentence of manslaughter for killing the dad, self-defense for beating Allegra up. He's not even in jail, the fucker, he's in some fancy psychiatric institution to learn something called 'impulse control'." Midnight snorted his disgust. "Shithead got away with murder and a brutal assault. But the only eyewitnesses were a dead man and a woman in a coma with her jaw wired shut and—later—a woman who has total amnesia regarding the event. Allegra apparently can't remember anything past a week before the night of the attack, when she'd just come back from the tour. She doesn't even remember wanting to get out of the contract. Doctors say that with the amount of head trauma she'd sustained, amnesia regarding the event is not uncommon. And no one can say when she'll regain her memory."

"Soon. It'll come back soon." Kowalski looked up at Midnight. "She's having flashbacks."

"She's having what?"

"Flashbacks. It's coming back to her, faster and faster, I'd say. And she's suffering from PTSD." *That* was what he'd seen in her, though he hadn't recognized it. The other cases of PTSD he'd witnessed had been in soldiers, so he hadn't recognized it in Allegra.

One of his men who'd suffered head trauma in an attack had had partial amnesia. Two months gone from his life, starting from a month before the attack. His memory of the firefight had come back in vicious little spurts—like sudden glimpses of hell, he'd said—that had scared him shitless. That was what was happening with Allegra. "What's this guy Sanderson look like?"

"I've never seen him, just saw the photos in the papers. Medium height, long blond hair. Dandy, real fancy dresser."

"Uh huh." Exactly who Allegra thought she'd seen in Lawrence Square. "She's definitely having flashbacks, she's getting her memory back. Yesterday—"

Midnight's cell rang and he held a hand up, glancing at the display with a frown. "It's Suzanne, I wonder if something's wrong." He opened the cell phone. "Yeah honey, you okay? Uh huh. *What?*" Midnight's gaze shot to Kowalski. "Allegra? She hurt? Uh huh. I'm on my way."

Midnight was closest to the door but Kowalski beat him to it.

Kowalski drove. Midnight didn't even press the issue, and he didn't say a word when Kowalski broke three state laws and a couple of federal ones on the way to The Garden.

Kowalski got there as fast as a land vehicle could make it and was out of the SUV while it was still rocking to a stop.

While rocketing toward the restaurant, Midnight had told him what he'd heard from Suzanne. Allegra had heard Corey Sanderson's voice—and his hand touching her—and had panicked.

Kowalksi burst into The Garden. He had tunnel vision, just like in combat, and all he saw was her, Allegra, sitting on a chair, stricken and shaking, rocking back and forth with her arms wrapped around her waist in an attempt to comfort herself. Her face was bloodless. Suzanne was sitting next to her, a hand on her shoulder.

"Allegra?" he croaked, and she looked up, head wobbling, beautiful blind eyes dark with distress.

"Douglas?" She sounded lost and helpless. "Oh God, Douglas, you came!"

She was up and running into his arms. He met her halfway, folding her tightly in his embrace and simply hanging on. He didn't know who was clinging more tightly or who needed comfort more. He knew he sure as hell needed the contact to make sure she was physically okay, safe.

Hearing his voice, her face had changed. 'Til his dying day, he would never forget the look on her face when she knew he'd come for her. Through her fear and despair, there had been a sudden surge of hope and joy and—yes—love. For him. He would never forget that moment as long as he lived.

And through his own terror and panic, the love and joy he felt for her filled his heart. This was his woman. He would pay any price to keep her safe and happy.

But first he had to calm her down.

Allegra was shaking in his arms, terrified and panicked. She was mumbling something in a high-pitched keening wail. It took him a minute to decipher the words, she was trembling so hard her voice shook.

"He was here, Douglas, he was here, he was here," she chanted, breathless. A violent shudder. "Oh God, he *touched* me. He was here! Keep him *away* from me!"

She was talking about Sanderson. Somehow Corey Sanderson had escaped from prison and had come after her. The fucker had touched her, terrified her. If he had come after her, it was to finish the job he'd begun five months earlier. Corey Sanderson was a dead man walking.

"He was here, I heard him, right here." Allegra's voice rose with the rough notes of hysteria. Her arms squeezed desperately around him, seeking shelter. "Keep him away from me! Oh, God, I'm so scared."

Behind her, Suzanne watched somberly. When Kowalski looked at her, she shook her head in a slow negation. "Corey Sanderson wasn't there." She kept her voice low, but Allegra heard.

"Yes he was, yes he was! Why won't anyone believe me?"

Allegra was in full-blown hysteria now, a freakish mix of present fear and flashback. Kowalski wrapped one arm around her waist and covered the back of her head with his hand. Symbolically, he was offering her what soldiers went into battle with—Kevlar body armor and helmet. The soft viscera and the head were the most vulnerable points of the human body. The human animal knows this at a level almost deeper than instinct. It is in the DNA. Holding her like this, protecting her vital organs and head, was the only thing that could calm her down, penetrate the fog of hysteria.

She was so scared she couldn't think. Right now it was pointless trying to coax her down from the ledge of utter terror she teetered on.

At a level deeper than words, deeper even than rational thought, his body was telling hers that no harm could come to her as long as he was alive and holding her.

Kowalski needed to climb down from utter panic, too, freakish as that sounded. He was known for his calm under fire. But in those first moments, clinging to Allegra, his heart had pounded and his brain had gone blank with panic. Under his winter clothes, he was sweating like a pig, the smelly sweat of fear. A slithery hollow terror he'd never felt before.

Finally, they both started calming down. Allegra's keening stopped, her tight hold eased slightly. The trip-hammer heartbeat visible in her temples slowed, as did his. His tunnel vision dissipated and he was able to take in his surroundings. Lifting his head, he looked around and saw Midnight with an arm around Suzanne.

She was coatless and for the first time, Kowalski noticed that Allegra had on her own coat and what must be Suzanne's, as well. Smart Suzanne had instinctively known that the first treatment for shock is warmth.

Seeing that Allegra was calming down, Suzanne approached, John by her side, an arm around her shoulders.

"What happened?" Kowalski asked quietly.

Suzanne looked troubled and pale. "We were outside. I left Allegra just outside the entrance to the restaurant and went to get my car. I came back to find her —" She bit her lip not to say "hysterical". "I found her badly upset. She said that Corey Sanderson spoke to her and —"

"He touched me." Kowalski looked down at Allegra, their position mirroring that of Midnight and Suzanne's, his arm around her shoulders. She was leaning heavily into him. Her voice had quieted, sounding dull and lifeless. Her eyes were dry but her cheeks were still wet with tears of fright. "I know you don't believe me, Suzanne, but I heard Corey. His voice is unmistakable. And he *touched* me." She shivered, pulling Suzanne's coat more tightly around her.

Suzanne reached out to gently touch her shoulder, looking troubled. "Oh honey. I don't know what happened, but it wasn't Corey. He simply wasn't there. I would have seen him. Someone might have almost tripped and grabbed onto you by mistake. But I swear to you, it wasn't Corey Sanderson who touched you. I would have seen him." Suzanne's eyes welled as she had to say the words, the harsh, cruel words. Allegra was the one who was mistaken because she couldn't see, and Suzanne could.

Suzanne looked up at Kowalski. "Corey Sanderson is in a psychiatric institute for felons. He hasn't been released. I know that for a fact. I made one of the police officers following the case promise that he would call me the minute there was any change in status." Her jaws clenched. On her it looked pretty. "That man is never getting within a mile of Allegra ever again, I'll make sure of it."

At that moment, Kowalski loved Suzanne and if Midnight weren't around, he'd have kissed her right on the mouth, a big fat thank-you smack. She cared deeply for Allegra, was willing to take measures to protect her. Kowalski loved Suzanne for that.

He nodded. Under his arm, Allegra straightened. "I know you all think I'm crazy," she said, her lovely voice clear and distinct. "But I know what I heard and what I heard was Corey Sanderson's voice saying, *'You little bitch. You're going to get what's coming to you. I'm going to see you dead and then you'll roast in hell'.*"

Her voice changed pitch. Kowalski assumed she was imitating this Sanderson. It was eerie and scary, as if she were channeling someone else. For a second he believed her, then glanced at Suzanne. Tears in her eyes, she was shaking her head no.

"Allegra was out of my sight for just a moment. The car was just around the corner. There were people on the sidewalk, coming in and going out from The Garden, but not many and none of them was Corey Sanderson. Believe me, I'd have recognized him. Corey Sanderson wasn't here today. I can assure you of that."

Flashbacks. It was the only explanation. Still, Kowalski wasn't going to take any chances. He knew what he had to do.

"Come on, honey." Kowalski tightened his arm around Allegra's shoulders. "I think I know what's happening. I want to get you home. Suzanne, Midnight, we'll call you later, okay?"

Suzanne opened her mouth, then closed it when she saw his face, and the grim expression on Midnight's. She sighed, leaning forward to give Allegra a gentle kiss on the cheek. "We'll talk later, sweetie, okay?"

"It was him. It was Corey. I know you don't believe me, but it was him. I'd recognize his voice anywhere." Allegra's voice was low and sad. She didn't protest when Kowalski took her arm to guide her outside, moving slowly in a defeated shuffle.

Midnight opened the passenger door of Suzanne's car, settling his wife in. Kowalski met his eyes over the roof of her car. Midnight looked as troubled as Suzanne as he climbed into the driver's seat.

Kowalski settled his own woman into his SUV. As he'd done on Saturday night, he covered Allegra with the blanket he kept in the backseat. "There you go. The heat will be on in just a second." He called Jacko on his cell while circling the SUV, then climbed in.

Kowalski drove for ten minutes in silence. Allegra's face was slightly averted. She looked hollowed out by sadness and misery. Kowalski's heart ached for her. It was bad enough having flashbacks—sensory ones that felt real to her. Added to that was the horror of feeling that no one believed her.

Kowalski wasn't good at beating around the bush, so he just leaped in. "I just found out today how you lost your sight, Allegra. It wasn't an accident, like you told me. This Sanderson fuck beat you up and killed your father. Why didn't you tell me? Why did you let me think you'd lost your sight in an accident?"

Allegra sat quietly without answering.

"Honey?"

Allegra stared down, sightlessly, at her hands, twisting and turning in her lap in a physical manifestation of the misery she felt inside. When she spoke her voice was quiet, without inflection. "I didn't tell you because—because I don't remember anything. It isn't real to me in any way. The last thing I remember was the day after my summer tour ended. The tour lasted ten weeks, I'd played in twenty-five cities and it had been just awful. I was so exhausted and depressed. Everything about the tour was painful—from the music Corey chose for me to play, to the interviews I had to give, to the increasingly empty concert halls. Apart from everything else, I also found out I hated touring. I hated bouncing from one city and one hotel room to another, I hated the stress and the lack of privacy. I hated the huge stadiums and concert halls, which aren't suited to my voice or my music. Whatever happens to me in the future as a musician, I know that I don't want to tour. I want to do some studio recording and play in small events in the Portland area and—and have a life. Corey was already planning another big tour for the spring and I just knew I'd hate it. I was continually arguing with Corey about everything—about the type of music he was scheduling, about the photo ops he planned—he'd actually promised a gossip magazine a series of photographs of me topless with Dagda, can you imagine? We had a big fight over that one when I said no, because he'd already hired this expensive fashion photographer for the shoot. That was in Chicago, just at the end of the summer tour."

Kowalski's hands tightened on the wheel. Good thing he hadn't known Allegra then. He'd have smashed Sanderson's face in for even suggesting it.

"What kind of fights were you having? Knock-down, drag-out?" He kept his voice even. No sense overwhelming her with his own emotions.

"No, no, not at all. Just strong differences of opinion. I mean, he couldn't very well force me to pose in the nude, could he?"

Not and live, Kowalski thought. "So what happened at the end of the tour?"

She lifted her hands from her lap and let them drop. "I don't have the faintest idea. I remember absolutely nothing. The last thing I remember was unpacking my bags the evening I got back from the last concert. That was the 2nd of September. The next thing I remember, I woke up in the hospital almost two months later, on the 24th of October. My father was long dead and buried. I was blind, I couldn't speak and I was in constant pain."

Oh, honey, Kowalski thought. He could just imagine what it had been like to wake up to darkness and grief.

"You know what happened the night you went to get out of your contract with Sanderson?" Kowalski asked, his voice harsh.

"Yes, of course." She frowned. "I mean, I was told what happened, first by the nurses, then by Suzanne and Claire. But it's abstract. I don't remember anything at all. It's as if they were telling me the plot of a movie or a novel. Suzanne says I told her I wanted to break my contract and she found a clause I could use, but I don't even remember that. I don't *feel* it, you know what I mean? All I know is I woke up and my father was dead and I was blind, with a broken jaw." She turned to him, her lovely face earnest. "You know, Douglas, I still have problems believing it. I mean, okay, Corey's a bit of a megalomaniac and a control freak, but—violence? He's such a...a fop, you know? He won't even go to scary movies because the violence bothers him. Suzanne is absolutely convinced he killed my father and beat me up, but somehow, it just doesn't...doesn't compute. I believe it in my head because it happened, but not in my heart."

Kowalski didn't find it hard to believe at all. Now that he thought about it, Corey Sanderson hadn't been in the news since around—what? 1998? So this guy, who was used to being treated like the Sun King, complete with millions and groupies and absolute power in the glittering music world, was on the slippery slope toward being a has-been. The music business was brutal, full of sharks who can scent blood ten miles away. This Sanderson fuck had obviously latched onto Allegra to make his comeback, but she wasn't cooperating and he'd flipped. Allegra might think he was a dandy, some soft guy who wasn't prone to violence, but to get as far as he did in the competitive world of popular music there had to be a core of steel in Sanderson.

Kowalski knew what had gone down—Allegra and her father had wanted to break her contract with Sanderson, a contract Sanderson clearly saw as his lifeline to a comeback, and he'd lost control.

The flashbacks Allegra was having were of the real Corey Sanderson—cruel and violent. She'd been terrified when she thought she'd heard his voice. Her body knew exactly how dangerous Sanderson was, even if her head had lost that knowledge.

Well, Sanderson wasn't ever going to touch Allegra again, that was for sure.

"You thought you heard Sanderson yesterday, too, didn't you? In Lawrence Square."

Allegra nodded. "Yes. I was so sure...and yet you didn't see anyone who matched his description."

Kowalski didn't answer. The truth was there between them, stark and leaden. He hadn't seen Sanderson or anyone who remotely looked like him, unless this Sanderson was a master of disguise. He turned onto Allegra's street.

"We're here, honey." Kowalski brought his SUV to a halt right in front of Allegra's house. Jacko was already parked across the street, and was out of his car and crossing the street by the time Kowalski opened the driver's door.

Good man.

For the first time, Kowalski was glad Allegra was blind. She would have flipped at the sight of Jacko. He looked like a lethal street punk, with his shaved head, grungy clothes and piercings. At least he'd put on a parka over the torn sweatshirt, though Kowalski knew it wasn't because of the cold. Jacko never felt the cold. He'd put it on to cover the shoulder holster and its lethal cargo.

Kowalski helped Allegra down and turned her slightly. "Honey, I want you to meet—" For just a second Kowalski pulled a blank. What the *hell* was Jacko's real name? Something totally incongruous, that he knew. Jacko had once had a fight with a jarhead who'd called him by it.

"Morton," Jacko said, in his deep drawl. He'd moved around a lot but his early years had been spent in a trailer park in the Texas panhandle, and he'd never gotten the Texas out of his voice. "Morton Jackman. Pleased to meet you, ma'am."

Allegra looked puzzled, but held out her hand. Kowalski wondered what she would have thought, seeing her hand engulfed in Jacko's paw, with its barbed wire tattoos and big silver skull ring. Jacko held her hand for a second, then dropped it.

"Pleased to meet you too, Mr. Jackman." She shivered with the cold. "Ahm, if you'll excuse us now, we have to get inside."

"He's coming with us, honey." Kowalski put his arm around her waist and walked her up the porch stairs into the house. Jacko followed.

If Jacko was curious about the fact that Kowalski had the key to the front door, or about Allegra's house with the harp in the corner of the living room, he didn't show it. He simply stood, in a modified parade rest, and awaited orders. Good man, Kowalski thought again.

Kowalski helped Allegra get her coat off, then sat her down on the couch. He sat next to her, holding her hand. "Listen to me, honey. I'm going to be gone for a couple of hours. I really need to find out where this Sanderson guy is."

Her hand jumped in his.

"Oh my God, Douglas!" her expression was stricken. "Be careful!"

Not violent my eye, he thought. This was Allegra's gut instinct, that Sanderson was dangerous. He wasn't half as dangerous as Kowalski, who was going to bring the sick fuck down.

"I'll be careful, don't worry about that. I know how to handle myself. Listen to me, though." She was focused on him, hand tightly holding on to his. "If you heard Sanderson this afternoon, that must mean he's somehow gotten out of prison.

I need to track him down, but I can't do anything if I'm worried about your safety. So Morton here—we call him Jacko—is staying with you until I get back. You'll be safe with him, honey."

Kowalski glanced sharply at Jacko. Jacko understood perfectly well that if anything happened to Allegra on his watch, he was a dead man.

You carrying? Kowalski mouthed, just to be on the safe side. Jacko gave him a *get real* look and shifted the parka so Kowalski could see the big butt of his weapon. He'd have a backup weapon in an ankle holster and his big folder knife in his jeans pocket.

Yeah, Allegra would be okay. Jacko was as careful as he was. No one would get past him.

"I don't know…" Allegra sounded worried.

Jacko walked silently until he was in front of her. He hunkered down so that she wouldn't hear his voice above her head. "Don't worry about me, ma'am," he drawled. "You just go ahead and do whatever you'd normally do and pretend I'm not here. I'll just sit here until the Senior gets back. I won't bother you at all."

"Okay, Mr. Jackman."

"Just Jacko is fine, ma'am."

"Okay…Jacko. Would you mind if I play my harp? It always settles my nerves."

"No ma'am, that's fine."

Jacko—whose idea of classical music was ZZ Top—rolled his eyes. Kowalski grinned and slapped Jacko on the back on his way out.

Chapter Sixteen

∽

"What do you know about Corey Sanderson, and where's the fucker right now?" Kowalski grabbed the only chair in the hospital room, turned it around and straddled it.

He'd met Claire just outside the door and had sent her out for coffee. She'd looked harassed and grateful to be leaving Bud to someone else. Bud had tubes with fluids running in and out of him, and was wearing one of those awful hospitals gowns and a scowl.

Kowalski didn't even want to think about what the tubes were for or where they went. Doctors and hospitals gave him a queasy feeling.

Though Bud was pale beneath his tan and had deep grooves running down his cheeks, he looked alert, which was good. Kowalski needed info from Bud and he needed it yesterday.

"Hello, Senior Chief, and I'm doing just fine, thanks so much for asking. It's nice to know that people care." Bud's voice was weak and scratchy but he managed to inject sarcasm into it.

Kowalski waved his hand impatiently. Bud was alive. That was all he needed. "Talk, man. Did you hear what happened this afternoon? Allegra heard Corey Sanderson's voice. And she heard him yesterday, too." He frowned. "Personally, I think she's having flashbacks, but I need to be sure Sanderson is under lock and key, so talk. What do you know about where he is?"

Bud coughed, a deep hacking cough that had him wincing with pain. He'd probably just had the tube removed from his esophagus. Bud leaned his head back, visibly exhausted. "God, Kowalski, take my advice and never get shot."

Too late. Kowalski had been shot four times.

Kowalski edged the chair closer, making sure he kept it away from the IV tree. "Sanderson," he prodded.

Bud's eyes focused sharply. "This is about Allegra, right?"

Kowalski nodded. "I need to know if that son of a bitch is out. She's heard his voice twice in two days. Where the fuck is he?"

Bud sighed. "Listen, when Claire told me her story, I had the guy checked out. I was as mad as you that he got away with murder and the brutal assault on Allegra. It was her bad luck she wasn't in a condition to testify. Believe me, if I'd been investigating it, I wouldn't have given up so easily. But I only found out about it a couple of weeks ago." He closed his eyes briefly, then opened them, his gaze alert and fierce. "Trust me on this one. I really, really hate it when the bad guys win."

Kowalski's feeling exactly, not to mention the fact that Sanderson had assaulted Allegra. That was motive enough for hanging—and drawing and quartering—as far as he was concerned.

"Yeah." His jaws clenched. "So where is the fucker now?"

"Sanderson? He's—" Bud choked and coughed spasmodically, then groaned. His stitches were probably pulling.

"Here." There was a glass of water with a straw on the bedside table. Kowalski held it steady for Bud with one hand while holding Bud's head up off the pillow with the other. Bud drank half the glass, then eased his head back. Kowalski sat patiently on the chair, eyes glued to Bud's face. "Whenever you're ready to talk," he prodded.

Bud nodded. "Okay, okay. So what's the story? Allegra's heard Sanderson's voice?"

"Twice in two days. I need to know whether she actually heard his voice—she says he was talking to her and was close enough to touch her—or whether she's having flashbacks."

Bud was still. "Flashbacks." He nodded slowly. "Her memory's starting to come back, then. She's starting to remember the fucker killing her father and beating her up. That's not good news for Sanderson, even though he can't be tried twice—double jeopardy—more's the pity. He got really good lawyering. I can't believe what a light sentence he got away with. Basically, he was given a minimum sentence for manslaughter, three years. And his lawyer argued that he suffered from 'impulse control,' so he's now in some Club Fed for rich assholes who think they can get away with murder, instead of in a maximum security jail with a three-hundred-pound biker who wants him for a girlfriend. So the shithead got away with murder and will never get the needle because Allegra couldn't testify."

"Not even now, if her memory's coming back? She's an eyewitness, after all—" Kowalski stopped abruptly.

"A blind eyewitness," Bud said, his voice dry. "Who's suffered amnesia. Any decent lawyer would eat her up in cross-examination and Sanderson had the best lawyers money can buy. The DA made a decision to go for manslaughter and not murder one because Allegra couldn't testify and even if she could have, it wouldn't be considered valid enough testimony to convict a man for murder. So there you have it— no matter what happens with Allegra, even if she gets her memory and her sight back, Sanderson's been tried for that crime and can't be tried again."

"Double jeopardy." Kowalski's fists clenched.

"You got it, big guy."

"So she's not a threat to him anymore. He wouldn't have a motive for coming after her."

Bud was silent a moment, his face looking even more drawn as he thought it through, cheekbones standing out in harsh relief.

"Well," he said finally, "that's not quite true. If Allegra wants to, and has time and money to spare, she can sue Sanderson in civil court for wrongful death. Try him for damages. Oh yeah, she could do that." Bud was visibly warming to the idea. "A jury in civil court wouldn't be bound by the rules of procedure and discovery that apply in criminal court. Pretty young talented singer deprived of her father and her sight and her career, man—they'd convict the fucker in a heartbeat, make him pay damages up the wazoo. Serve the bastard right. Strip him of his millions, if nothing else. It won't bring her father or her sight back but by God, he'd be hurting." He smiled happily at the thought. "But coming back to Allegra—she can't have heard Sanderson's voice. He's in a psychiatric institution for felons that's vetted yearly on its security arrangements. No one's getting out of there. Sanderson sure hasn't. My partner just stopped by an hour ago to bring me up to speed. He would have told me if Sanderson's escaped. He knows I'm interested in the case. So Sanderson's still there."

Kowalski wasn't too sure. There were few buildings on Earth he or Midnight or any other SEAL couldn't get out of. It was also true that, generally speaking, music producers didn't go through SEAL training. Still, he wasn't taking any chances.

"Where is this place? What's the name?"

"The Spring Harbor Psychiatric Institute and Correctional Facility. They get big grants for research. It's about thirty-five miles out of town, toward Mt. Hood."

Kowalski calculated. With the traffic, it would take him about an hour to get there, and back, calculate another hour while there. Whatever it took, though, he wasn't going back to Allegra without some solid answers. Jacko would stay and guard her for however long it took. "Okay, I'm going now to check it out and see if Sanderson could leave long enough to terrorize Allegra and sneak back in." Bud was shaking his head. "What?"

"I guess you didn't hear me the first time around." Bud brought his left hand with the IV needle taped to the back up to tick off the points. "First—he's in a psychiatric institution. They don't 'let' guys waltz in and out of there, otherwise they'll lose their contract with the government and would be hauled before the Prison Board. Second—whatever's going on out there, they're not going to tell you, a civilian, squat. You'd need a warrant, or at least you'd need to go with a cop and I'm not going anywhere at the moment. Three—*what the fuck are you doing?*"

Bud's weak voice registered shock as Kowalski calmly reached into the top drawer of the hospital bedside table and pulled out Bud's badge. He hung the badge over his belt as Bud struggled to sit up. "Listen, don't even think of it," Bud said, breathing heavily as he made it to a semi-sitting position, wincing as he leaned on one elbow.

The two of them locked gazes like two old moose locking antlers. But Bud's antlers had been clipped. He gave up. "Ah, shit." His head hit the pillow again. "Don't kill anyone while flashing my badge."

"Try not to." Kowalski headed for the door.

Bud raised his voice. "And I want that badge back tomorrow, you hear!"

Kowalski closed the door quietly behind him and headed for the stairs, moving fast.

It was a place for the rich. The crazy rich, Kowalski thought, as he walked the perimeter of Spring Harbor Institute. His SUV was parked a mile down the road at a roadside dive. He'd smeared some mud on the fenders and sidewalls to make his vehicle fit in. No one was going to notice his vehicle among the thirty others parked there outside the shabby building with loud music leaking from every joint.

Kowalski had fast-walked to the Institute, staying just off the two-lane blacktop, about ten feet into the old-growth forest, ready to leap away at the first hint of a car, but there had been no cars along the way. Just the fading day, the tall, ancient trees looking ever more ghostly in the twilight, and silence.

He hit the walled perimeter about two hundred feet from the gates, visible—along with the road—to his left. Instead of moving there, he walked around the entire wall counterclockwise, checking security arrangements.

They weren't top-of-the-line, but they weren't bad. He and Midnight might actually have a little trouble getting in and out. Not much, but some. There were unobtrusive security cameras on stanchions rising every twenty feet from the stone wall. Every five minutes, the cameras made a full revolution. Kowalski recognized the make, and they had a deep security flaw—they only had a narrow angle of vision, which meant that if you timed it right, you could waltz right by through the dead zones. He didn't even have to time it right because the cameras weren't equipped with infra-red detectors, so all he had to do was stay in the gloom of the trees and observe.

He finally came full circle to the gates, observing them through his spotting scope. Very discreet brass plaque with the words *Spring Harbor Psychiatric Institute and Correctional Facility* engraved in fancy script. The security cameras trained on the entrance were heavy-duty and very visible. The gate was big and thick, the lock ten inches high. A steel plate running the width of the road would, at the push of a button, rise and present spikes to any incoming or outgoing vehicle. All in all, a very impressive-looking security system, and perfectly useless. It obviously hadn't occurred to the administration that anyone seeking illegal entry or looking to escape wasn't going to use the front gates.

It would, however, impress visiting physicians and politicians.

The perimeter walls had a twenty-foot clearing so the cameras could observe anyone attempting to climb them. Doubtless there was another twenty-foot clearing on the other side. That was asinine. If Kowalski were to design a secure site, there would be no vegetation of any sort for at least a thousand yards around the perimeter, only raked earth designed to show any footprints, not grass.

Kowalski climbed a nearby tree and found a perfect perching spot. Through the scope he saw a large, three-story, turn of the century mansion that had been retrofitted for the 21st century. Bars on the lovely corniced windows, which had been fitted with bulletproof glass. A security door, which had replaced what had doubtless been a carved wooden front door on the big white porch. Clear lawn with no shrubs or trees. Security cameras mounted under the eaves.

He collapsed the scope. He'd seen all he needed to see.

Half an hour later, he drove up to that big security gate and pressed the brass button.

"Yes?" a disembodied voice said.

"I'd like to speak to the Director." Window down, glaring up at the camera.

"May I ask what this concerns?"

"You may." He held Bud's badge up.

Silence, then a loud *click!* And the big gates slowly started to part.

Kowalski drove through, up the large graveled drive. Yep, his first impression was right. This was for rich crazy fucks. No way would some poor redneck who'd offed someone's dad and beat a woman land up here, with its manicured lawns, discreet bars on the windows and—he heard as he walked up the white marble steps—Mozart playing on the loudspeakers. The "Sonata No. 4 in E-flat major." Good choice.

No, your average schmo with "impulse control" problems would definitely not be here. But Corey Sanderson had money to burn and no eyewitnesses.

Kowalski looked up impassively at the two security cameras just under the torchére lights and waited. A squat man in pristine whites opened the door. Kowalski pegged him for an orderly. Without a word, the man accompanied Kowalski down a long corridor with a gleaming hardwood floor and into an office that looked as if it could belong to a multinational. It was pristine white—white couch, white carpet, white walls, white laminated bookshelves, platinum blonde secretary in a tight white suit typing on a white computer keyboard.

She looked up. "Yes?" No smile, no frown, just polite disinterest.

"Who's the director here?"

"That would be Dr. Childers."

"I need to talk to him. Now."

"Her." The temperature in the room dropped several degrees. "And I am sorry, but I'm afraid you can't speak with Dr. Childers at the moment. She's busy." Ms. Frigid Receptionist pretended to leaf through a white leather agenda. "Dr. Childers will be free next Tuesday at 10:00 a.m. if you'd like to make an appointment."

"Dr. Childers better get unbusy real fast." Kowalski opened his jacket enough to show the badge and the shoulder holster. He knew how to look threatening, and baring his teeth in what was a technical smile only added to the menace.

Pink-tipped fingers reached under the desk and two minutes later another cool blonde in a white coat stepped into the room, looking annoyed. Dr. Childers, he presumed. "Amanda, I thought I told you to use that bell only in emergencies."

Amanda's eyes slid over to Kowalski. He bared his teeth, his badge and his gun all over again.

The cool blonde's lips tightened. "Follow me."

She led him into a big, airy room just off the lobby. White, cool and orderly. She sat down behind her elegant oak desk and folded her hands. "How may I help you, Mr.—" her voice dropped off delicately.

"Lieutenant," Kowalski said. "Lieutenant Tyler Morrison of Portland PD. Homicide."

Her eyes opened slightly, but she kept her cool. "Yes, Lieutenant. How may I help you?"

"You've got a prisoner here, a Corey Sanderson. Beat a man to death, mutilated a young girl."

Dr. Childers' lips primmed. "We have a patient here by that name, yes. Mr. Sanderson. He is responding very well to treatment. He is a very cultivated man, very knowledgeable about music. A gifted piano player. He played for a visiting delegation just the other evening." A faint smile creased her face. "Mozart and Schuman. Lovely."

Fucker knew how to play more than just the piano, Kowalski thought. He played Dr. Childers very well.

"Yes, ma'am," he replied. "We're wondering whether besides playing the piano, he can walk through walls."

She stilled. "I beg your pardon?"

"We have a reliable eyewitness who put Corey Sanderson in Lawrence Square yesterday around 4:00 p.m.," Kowalski lied without compunction. "And today just outside The Garden, a restaurant on Stillwell. Around 1:30 p.m."

Dr. Childers stared blankly, then gathered herself together. "I'm afraid your eyewitness is quite mistaken, Lieutenant. Mr. Sanderson has not left these premises in three months. Since his trial, as a matter of fact."

"And conviction." Kowalski nodded, just to see that slight flush rise over her pale, severe features. "That may well be, Doctor, but I'd like to see Mr. Sanderson for myself."

"I'm afraid that's not possible," the good doctor replied, not without satisfaction. "There are rules. You'd need a warrant."

He lifted his cell phone. "Yes, Doctor, that's no problem at all. I have the judge right here on speed dial." Kowalski looked her straight in the eye. He was capable of reducing the toughest recruit to tears through eye contact alone. She wouldn't be able to stand more than ten seconds of it, he'd wager. One, two, three…

"Oh, all right." Irritated, Dr. Childers rose, meticulously straightening her white coat. "Follow me. You'll see for yourself how impossible it would be for Mr. Sanderson to leave the premises."

The security was better than he'd imagined. Not great, not impossible to get through, but still definitely not a cakewalk. Dr. Childers' sharp, annoyed voice echoed in the large corridor. "Though it seems excessive to me, in my professional opinion, Mr. Sanderson has been confined to Wing C. The patients in Wing C are kept in lockdown. That's—"

"I am aware of the concept of lockdown, Doctor. I just need to know how good your lockdown is." She shot him a look of pure venom as they came to the end of the corridor. Once, the door must have been an elegant wood-paneled door like the others in the corridor, but it had been replaced by a white steel slab. Dr. Childers held her forefinger up to a green screen and waited as it counted ridges in a flash of green light, comparing the ridges with the fingerprints of cleared personnel in the database.

They had biometric security. Biometric security was a bitch to get through. Doable, but a bitch. You'd probably have to cut someone's finger off to get through.

The door slid open soundlessly and they walked in. The soundproofing was stronger here. There was no noise whatsoever in this section, though there were nurses and orderlies coming and going, pushing crash carts and IV trees, transferring inmates in wheelchairs.

Kowalski looked around curiously. The décor was spare but elegant, the security discreet. He would bet anything that the food was tasty and nutritious. It was much more like a cross between a private clinic and a posh hotel than a prison. Nothing but the best for the man who'd murdered Allegra's father and beaten her up, put her in a coma and blinded her.

The doctor stopped at the third door down, glancing through the mesh wire window set in the upper part of the door. The door had an alphanumeric keypad on the wall next to it.

Dr. Childers signaled to a passing nurse, quietly asked for the chart for the patient in room three and stepped aside so Kowalski could get a look inside.

The room was nicely appointed, with a high hospital bed, a couch, a designer wooden table with two chairs, a bookcase full of books, a small state-of-the-art hi-fi set—a very expensive Swedish make—and an extensive collection of CDs. On the left hand wall was a door, which he presumed led into the bathroom. No mirrors, no pictures.

Rich crazy murderers got good treatment here.

A man was lying on his back on the bed with an IV running. The shoulder-length blond hair had been cut, he wasn't dressed elegantly and lying down it was hard to judge height, but it was him, the man Allegra had described. Corey Sanderson.

Kowalski stared hard at the man who'd beaten Allegra up, feeling the blood pound through his body. Killing the fucker wouldn't solve anything, but still he yearned. He schooled his face and voice to impassivity before turning around.

"I assume you're willing to swear that he hasn't been out of this institute and that it wasn't him yesterday and today."

The doctor's voice was cool and calm. "I would be willing to swear that not only has Mr. Sanderson not been out of the institute, but that he hasn't been out of this room. He had," she looked pained for a moment, "an...an episode Saturday evening. A psychotic episode. He broke all the furniture in his room. I had to have almost everything replaced. And he'd been doing so well, his parameters—well, never mind. The point is, we were forced to administer a sedative Saturday, yesterday and again this morning. Believe me, even if every single door in the institute had been open, Mr. Sanderson would have been quite incapable of walking out of here. Quite incapable of walking, actually. We had to use a heavy dosage to sedate him."

"Uh huh." Kowalski watched the man lying still on the bed, hating every cell, every molecule of him. "What dosage and what drug?"

He turned his head at her silence. Finally Dr. Childers spoke. "Is this information necessary?"

Kowalski stuck his hand briefly in his pocket, deliberately exposing Bud's badge. "Yes, Doctor, it is."

"Oh, all right." With bad grace, the doctor checked the clipboard a nurse had handed her. Her eyes scanned the sheet of paper. "Let's see now...the patient was administered 120 mg of Thorazine Saturday evening at 9:30 p.m. subsequent to a violent psychotic attack. The usual dosage is 100 mg but Mr. Sanderson was very...agitated. And continued to be agitated as soon as the dosage wore off. He has since received two injections of 120 mg. In technical terms, Lieutenant Morrison, it's enough to fell a horse."

Kowalski thought it through. *Be thorough. Don't leave any loopholes.* "How do I know he was actually administered the sedative?"

Faint pink flags rose in her cheeks. She stabbed the clipboard with a manicured nail. "It says so right here!"

"Uh huh." His gaze was unwavering. He repeated stolidly, "How do I know he was actually administered the sedative? How do I know that someone didn't just mark it down on that sheet of paper? How do I know Corey Sanderson didn't just waltz out of here, secure in the knowledge that he had an alibi because someone scribbled something on a sheet of paper?"

Dr. Childers' cheeks were red now. "I've never heard of anything so impertinent in my life! Are you suggesting that our records are falsified?"

"I'm not suggesting anything. All I'm saying is that we have reason to believe that Corey Sanderson was outside this institute both yesterday and today and I have only your word that he wasn't."

"My word and the medical register."

"Uh huh." Kowalski made himself into a wall. He stared at the doctor for a couple of minutes. She stared back. No doubt she thought her stare intimidating. Well, she didn't know who she was trying to intimidate. He sure as hell wasn't going to back down because a snooty doctor who was snowed by a murderer narrowed her eyes at him. "Would you swear to that in court?"

She stared back, obviously secure. "Yes, I would, Lieutenant."

Kowalski made a split-second decision. He could force her to take a blood sample and have it analyzed, but it was illegal and he knew it. Above all, she knew it. And he'd get Bud into no end of trouble, because Dr. Childers would be calling in a complaint to Portland PD the instant the door of the clinic closed behind him. Kowalski was impersonating an officer and had no ground to stand on.

If Allegra's safety depended on it, he'd walk in and take a blood sample himself—and he wouldn't be too careful about sticking in the syringe, either. But all in all, weighing the pros and cons, Kowalski would lose more than gain from it.

"I want a copy of Mr. Sanderson's clinical chart." He was on safer ground here. Dr. Childers would fight it on principle, but he had a right to ask.

"*What?*" For a second, Dr. Childers' mask of professional hauteur slipped. Her mouth dropped in astonishment. She sucked in her breath. "You want what?"

"You heard me." Kowalski's gaze was hard and unblinking. "I want a copy of his records for the past three days."

"There's no question of that, Lieutenant." Dr. Childers glared at him. "It would be an unconscionable violation of Mr. Sanderson's privacy. The only way I would acquiesce would be with a warrant, so you go to your judge, get one and then we'll talk." For emphasis, she crossed her arms over her scrawny bosom.

Kowalski moved in close, invading her private space, going toe-to-toe. In alarm, Dr. Childers took a step back, then stopped herself from taking another one. She was a psychiatrist, she knew body language. Physical retreat echoed psychological retreat.

Kowalski kept his voice low and deadly. "I will get my warrant, make no mistake about it, doctor. The only thing is, it will take me a while to do it and whatever it is you say has been pumped into that fu—that guy's veins might just have had a chance to be absorbed into the system, so I'll never know, will I? And if that happens, if I have to wait for the results until the whatever finally comes back is inconclusive," he stepped even closer, his face hard and set, "then I will be royally pissed. To my way of thinking, doctor, that would be obstruction of justice and I don't take kindly to that. My colleagues don't take kindly to obstruction of justice, either. So we might just suppose that you're hiding something here, hmmm? And we would be forced to dig pretty deep to find out just what that something is. And I can guarantee you, doctor," he took another step forward, satisfied that she stepped back involuntarily, "that we will turn this institute inside out. We will camp out here for days on end, going through every single scrap of paper on file here. And if we find anything, anything at all, and I'm talking about a misplaced aspirin, *doctor*, you're going to pay."

It was a bluff. The drugs would be gone by the time a warrant could be issued. But Kowalski knew how to put menace into his voice and face. He took a surreptitious step forward, straightening his shoulders, presenting a large outline. Basic psychology. He was an imminent menace and all she wanted now was to get rid of him.

Dr. Childers had gone white. Kowalski wondered what she was afraid of, though he really didn't give a shit. He was intensely mission-oriented. His mission right now was to find out whether or not that fucker Sanderson had been out and about yesterday and today, terrifying Allegra.

Kowalski and Dr. Childers stood there in a staring match, and he won. White-faced, she went to the nurses' station and came back with a folder. She held it out between two fingers, careful not to touch him, as if he were a leper.

"I hope you're satisfied now, Lieutenant," she said icily.

"Depends," he replied, and walked away.

It was late when Kowalski pulled up outside Allegra's house. He'd dropped by a lab his company had used a few times, and got a lab tech to assess the medical information. The lab rat had used more or less the same language Dr. Childers had used. "Guy's been essentially meat since Saturday," he'd said cheerfully.

Sanderson hadn't been anywhere but flat on his back in bed.

Which meant that Allegra was having flashbacks to the night Sanderson had killed her father and beaten her up. Though Kowalski doubted she was in any real danger, he'd still taken precautions, including the necklace he fingered in his pocket.

Allegra was playing and singing up a storm, the notes lingering in the nighttime air as he walked up to her porch.

He'd called ahead to Jacko to let him know his ETA. You don't walk in unannounced on an armed, alert man bodyguarding, especially when he's a sharpshooter with fast reflexes.

He knocked, shouted "Hoo-ah!" and let himself in with the key. Allegra was at her harp, Jacko in an armchair turned so he could watch her and the door, his gun on his knee, finger inside the trigger guard.

The music stopped.

"Douglas?" Allegra stood and stepped back from the harp. Kowalski crossed the room quickly, pulling her into his arms. "I'm glad you're back," she mumbled into his coat.

"Yeah." Kowalski rested his cheek on the top of her head briefly, kissed her and led her to the kitchen. "I'll make you some tea in just a minute."

She understood he had business with Jacko. "Okay," she said quietly as she sat down, folding her hands in her lap.

Jacko was still sitting in his armchair. When Kowalski approached, he looked up, eyes glazed. Oh, God. Had he been *that* bored?

"Thanks, man." Kowalski let his hand drop onto Jacko's shoulder. "I really appreciate this. It probably wasn't necessary, but it made me feel better."

Jacko blinked and seemed to come back into himself. "That music." He sounded stunned.

"Yeah, it's an acquired taste. And it's not at a hundred decibels, like your favorite garage bands. Some of us like our music with notes in it." Jacko's taste in music was legendary. Kowalski had once accompanied Jacko to a concert of his favorite band and it had taken him three days to get his hearing back.

"Beautiful," Jacko murmured. "So beautiful."

Kowalski looked at him sharply and sniffed. No, Jacko hadn't been drinking Allegra's excellent whiskey. Kowalski felt ashamed of himself. Jacko would *never* drink on the job. "Uh-huh." He held Jacko's parka up, anxious to be rid of him and get back to Allegra. "Thanks again. You were a real big help. I owe you one. Count on me for a big favor, okay?"

Jacko turned his head slowly to look at Kowalski and blinked. God*damn! Had* he been drinking?

"That music," Jacko whispered. "So sad. So beautiful. *She's* so beautiful."

Oh. Jacko'd fallen under Allegra's spell.

"Yep. That she is. Pretty girl, pretty music. You might try them both sometime." Jacko's sex partners usually had more tattoos and piercings than he did.

Kowalski slipped Jacko's gun back into his shoulder holster for him, held the parka up so he could slip his arms in. When Jacko just stood there, Kowalski herded him to the front door, gave him a helpful slap on the back to get him over the threshold, said, "Thanks again," and closed the door behind him.

Next time, he'd get someone gay to bodyguard Allegra. Not, unfortunately, a SEAL. There weren't any gay SEALs.

Allegra was where he left her, sitting sad and subdued on a kitchen chair. He touched her shoulder, bending to kiss the top of her head. Three minutes later, vanilla tea—her favorite, he'd discovered—was steaming in front of her. She cupped her hands around the mug as if she needed the warmth, but didn't sip. "So. What did you find out?" she asked finally.

Kowalski sat down next to her, his hand on her knee so she could feel his presence. He picked up Allegra's hand and held it firmly sandwiched between his.

"Okay, I went to the psychiatric institute where Corey Sanderson is being held. Spring Harbor Psychiatric." She jerked slightly when she heard Sanderson's name. "I checked very carefully, honey. The guy's in lockdown, which means you can't get in and you can't get out of the place. It's as secure as a prison. It *is* a prison. Not only that, apparently Sanderson had some kind of psychotic episode Saturday night and they've been pumping him full of psychotropic drugs. Sanderson's been in a chemical straitjacket since Saturday. He's not going anywhere drugged to the eyeballs, so it couldn't have been him today. And it couldn't have been him yesterday, either."

Allegra listened, her head slightly averted, making no attempt to hone in on his voice. She sat breathing quietly. Had she absorbed what he'd said?

"Honey?" She was pale, her skin felt cold. He frowned, lifting her hand to his lips. "Do you understand? You're not in any danger. Corey Sanderson isn't on the loose. He's locked up. He can't hurt you in any way. You're in no danger."

She wasn't reacting and he was starting to get scared. "Allegra?"

"I guess that means I'm going crazy," she whispered finally, her voice raw. She turned her head now toward his voice, eyes wide and scared. "Douglas, I swear to you I heard Corey's voice. I swear. Nobody believes me. Why won't anyone believe me?"

His heart clenched in his chest at the misery on her face. "Yes, you heard his voice, only it wasn't his voice from today or yesterday. You heard him from five months ago. It's a perfectly normal phenomenon." He closed his eyes. What a dumbass thing to say. Being blind and an amnesiac was anything but normal. "What I mean to say is, you have temporary amnesia due to severe concussion. Your memory is coming back. Your brain is sending you messages from five months ago, that's all, like—like an undelivered email finally being delivered. What you heard happened, only just not now. You are definitely not going crazy."

Was she even listening? Her pale face was still, remote.

"You should leave now." Her lips trembled. It was as if the words were being dragged out of her. "Just go away."

What?

She sat back, withdrawing her hand from his, breaking the physical connection between them. "Just go now, Douglas. Go right now, get out of here. What are you doing here with me? What could you possibly want with me? I'm just a drag on you. Get out while you can."

"You're talking nonsense, Allegra."

"No, I'm not," she whispered, eyes glassy. "I'm finally facing reality. Oh God, Douglas, I'm...blind. I tell myself I'll get better, I'll have this operation but...chances are I will stay blind for the rest of my life. And I hear," her voice was shaking, "I hear voices. I have nightmares. My head hurts whenever I think too hard about things. I'm like this long slow train wreck. You should get away while you can, I'm nothing but a burden to you."

Oh honey, he thought, his heart turning over in his chest. He couldn't bear to listen to her for another second.

"No, no. Listen to me." He kept his voice quiet, clasped her hands. She tried to tug her hands out of his, but he tightened his grasp. "Listen to me carefully. I can't believe what you're saying. You're not a burden, you're a joy. You're beautiful and talented and smart. I never thought I'd ever be with a woman like you. You're the best thing that's ever happened to me, bar none. I've never felt this way about anyone before, Allegra. I—"

He swallowed heavily, aware that he was about to say words he'd never said to anyone in his life. Aware that he was crossing a divide. Aware that his life would never be the same again.

"I love you," he said quietly. "So much it scares me. I've only known you for a couple of days and yet I feel like I've loved you all my life. I know I'll love you for the rest of my life."

This was crazy talk and it was profoundly true. Nothing he felt for her had any precedent in his life. He'd had on-again off-again sex with an on-base secretary for two full years a while back and he could barely remember her face. Everything about Allegra was burned into his neurons. He would swear that his last thought in this life would be of her.

"Oh, Douglas." A single, solitary tear gleamed on her cheek, rolled down that ivory skin. She leaned forward, catching his face between her hands and holding his head still, palm right over his ugly scar, so she wouldn't miss his mouth with hers.

They kissed tentatively at first. It felt odd, and scary and exhilarating, too. Kowalski's first kiss of love. A slight touching of lips, soft and heated. Gliding, tentative, as if they were two teenagers making out for the first time. Exploring.

He let his lips curve over her jaw, drift up over her high, delicate cheekbone. His long fingers spread out in her thick hair, curving over the skull, holding her in place for the exploration of her face with his mouth. He feathered light kisses over her closed eyelids, past her temple, along the jawline, burying his face in her neck. He licked the skin of her neck, running his tongue over the long tendons. She tilted her head to one side so he could have better access. He opened his heavy lids long enough to see that she had a slight smile on her face, then closed his eyes again. He didn't need sight. It was enough to smell her and feel her and taste her. Heaven.

He could stay in this place forever, this special world that smelled of springtime, made of gentle touches and soft sighs. His lips drifted slowly back up to hers. There was no sense of time here, in this enchanted place. He lost track of where they were, his entire world reduced to her mouth and long slender hands cupping his face.

Kowalski had never really paid much attention to kissing. Women liked it, so he learned over the years how to kiss well. The way he looked, he needed all the ammo he could use to get women into his bed. So he could kiss with the best of them, all the while figuring how long it would be before he could get horizontal and naked with the woman he was locking lips with.

This was something else entirely. This was learning the shape of Allegra's mouth, her face, all over again, finding out what she liked by the minute changes in her breathing. When his tongue touched hers for the first time, the shock was so electric he saw lights behind his eyes. It was so intense he went back to the soft, tentative kisses of before, light and fleeting.

This was completely new for him. When the kisses heated up, Kowalski wanted to move straight ahead to sex, it was all he could think about. He often kissed while fondling the woman, stroking her breasts and her sex. He'd learned to kiss by feeling with his hand what made a woman wet enough to fuck. When he could get his sex partner wet enough for his cock was when he stopped kissing.

He was hard, primed for sex, but though burning desire was there, it was distant, remote. He could even do without sex right now—just stay here forever, in the glorious Land of Allegra, lips meeting and lifting and meeting again.

It was Allegra herself who bumped it up to the next level. She moaned and moved in close, opening her mouth under his, greedy for more contact. She slanted her head, breathed in deeply and dived into a long, gliding kiss, endless and heated. She fought to get as close to him as she could, arms twined around his neck.

Kowalksi lifted her onto his lap and she pressed herself against him, tight and warm, starting to breathe fast. Clinging to him as if he were about to leave and she was desperately trying to make him stay.

Her cheeks were wet.

"Hey, hey," he murmured, lifting his head. She buried her face in his neck, hanging on for dear life. He kissed her forehead for comfort, her lips for pleasure.

"I'm not going anywhere, you know. I'm right here, just as long as you want me." He shifted uneasily, aware that her hip was about half an inch from his hard-on. He tried to make his hold non-sexual, wondering how to do that while holding in his arms the most desirable woman in the universe. Her rich hair fell over his arms, the delicate smell of her rose to his nostrils. He was so hot he thought he'd burn up.

He should cool things down, for her sake. Maybe she didn't want sex now, maybe she wanted comfort. With a wrench, Kowalski tried to get his mind off his swollen cock, away from the fact that her small breasts were pressed against his chest, not thinking *at all* about her lips so close to his neck he could feel the small puffs of her breath.

She was traumatized. This was no time for sex.

Allegra gave a small, sensual sigh and turned her face to bite him, delicately, on the neck. She shifted her hips, rolling over his hard-on, biting harder when she felt him swell even more. The feel of her small teeth on the tendon of his neck, her hip on his cock, electrified him.

Then again, maybe it *was* time for sex. He rose with her in his arms, debated letting her walk into the bedroom with him and decided against it. *Take too long*, he thought. He needed to get them into the bedroom, get them naked and into bed *now*.

He moved as fast as he could, operating by instinct alone, and in a moment, they were by her bedside and he was sliding her down his body. She kept her arms around his neck, kissing him wildly. She moved against his cock, laughing when she felt him swell even more through her clothes and his.

"Now now *now!*" she chanted into his mouth, removing one hand from around his neck to run it over his chest and down to his cock. She gripped him through his pants and pumped him, one long stroke to the tip, then back down.

He had to be in her or he would die. There wasn't even time to strip.

Kissing her deeply, he reached up under her skirt to pull down her panties, then with one hand opened his pants and briefs just enough for his straining cock to spring out, while easing her down onto the bed with his other arm. Was she ready? He slid his fingers over her sex, stroking the folds and yes, she was wet, but not enough, not nearly enough.

He eased a finger into her. She was as responsive here as she was with her mouth. He could feel how her muscles responded to the strokes of his tongue and when he slanted his mouth for a deeper drink of her, her little cunt contracted around his finger. She was easing already into orgasm, almost before she was aroused enough to take him.

That pushed him over the top. He spread her, fitted himself to her opening and started pushing.

The kisses were wild now, an eating of lips, clashing of teeth, tangling of tongues. She was getting wetter by the second and he moved steadily forward into her until he stopped, halfway in, breathing heavily. It was so mind-blowingly hot inside her, tight and soft. Allegra lifted her knees along his legs, opening hers wide for him and he was able to slide all the way home, completely inside her.

They both stilled, panting. Kowalski lifted his head to look down at Allegra. She hadn't wanted the light on that first night—a million years ago—but there was enough light from the streetlamp outside for him to see her features. Her skin was so pale, it was like having his own moon right under him, up close and personal. Her lips were swollen and wet, just like her cunt. Wet for him. From him.

Those glorious green eyes were shut, long luscious lashes dark against her pale cheeks.

Their clothes were bunched around them. He wanted to feel her naked skin against his when they started fucking—whoa, he corrected himself immediately, inside his own head—when they made love. Kowalski was trying to figure out how to get them naked, planning his moves, starting to toe his shoes off before tugging his pants down, when she blew him away.

Kowalski was wrestling with his shoes when Allegra took his face between her hands, turned it gently, and placed her lips against his ear. She kissed him softly on the ear and whispered, "I love you, too, Douglas."

Kowalski exploded. There was no other word for it. He bucked once, hard, feeling the rush of electricity race along his spine and started coming in endless jets, digging his shoes into the mattress to push as hard into her as he could. He broke out in sweat and his eyes started leaking tears. He was helpless to stop his reactions and could only hold on to Allegra in desperation as he went up in a conflagration, every cell of his body destroyed in the fireball.

Senior Chief Kowalski, the tough, lonely warrior, died in a burst of blinding heat and light and was replaced later, much later, by Douglas, beloved man.

* * * * *

Allegra woke to Douglas curled around her back, mantling her. They'd made love last night and afterward she'd fallen into a dreamless sleep like a stone sinking deeply into the ocean. She dimly remembered falling asleep with him on top of her, inside her.

They were both naked now. Somehow, during the night, Douglas had managed to take all her clothes off without waking her. His clothes, too.

She could feel every glorious, hard, hairy inch of the front of him all along her back. He was heavily aroused. She could feel his erect penis in the small of her back. Something—some muscle memory—told her he'd been that way for a long time.

Ouch. Did it hurt men when they were erect and didn't make love?

She stirred slightly and he tightened his arms around her.

"Good morning, love," he rumbled in her ear and nuzzled. Allegra broke out in goose bumps. How could she wake up ready for sex after last night? And yet she was, there was no mistaking it. Douglas' large hand was sliding over her stomach, his palm resting over her mound, and she knew what he would find once his hand slid lower. She was wet already. Or still? Maybe she'd had the equivalent of an erect penis all night herself, her body primed for sex with Douglas. Maybe even in the unconciousness of sleep, all it took was Douglas' presence, which she registered at the primal level, at the level of smell and touch, and her body prepared itself for him.

Even before his callused palm caressed her breast, her nipples were hard, so sensitive it almost—but not quite—hurt, when he cupped her breast, circling the nipple with his finger.

She was ready, totally ready for him.

This had never happened to her before. With her other lovers, she'd always been slow to warm up, so slow a couple of men had complained. She'd even been resigned to thinking of herself as a cool lover. Not frigid—she'd had her share of orgasms—but definitely cool.

Not now. Not with Douglas. Now she felt as if she were burning up, and all it took was his presence.

Allegra opened her mouth to wish him good morning too, but all that came out was a moan. He'd lifted her leg up with a hard thigh, opening her up to his touch, and slid a long finger inside her.

He stiffened. "You're wet," he growled into her ear. "You're ready."

She couldn't talk, she couldn't breathe. Oh God, how could he know exactly how to touch her? Where to touch her?

She writhed against his finger, trying to get his hand...*there*. She stilled, her mind going into that wild free fall just prior to orgasm.

"Turn over." Douglas' voice was low, guttural.

"What?" She was dazed, barely able to take his words in.

Douglas grabbed the two pillows and placed them against her belly. "Turn over on your stomach." Without waiting for her to obey, he shifted her until she was lying with her belly over the pillows, which had the effect of lifting her butt in the air. "Grab the mattress." He placed her hands over the edge of the mattress and curled his big hands over hers. "Hold on tight."

His voice had a completely new tone, one she'd never heard before. By contrast with his guttural tones now, she realized he's always spoken to her tenderly, gently. Not now. Now his voice was harsh with command, as if there was no question that he held absolute power over her.

It was pure male command and to be resisted, out of principle, but that voice overrode entirely her usually healthy ego. That utter male dominance called up something wild and purely female in her, two animals obeying their deepest instincts.

By contrast, Allegra realized how Douglas moderated his touch with her, his hands always gentle. His touch, now, was no longer soft and gentle. Now he was using the strength of his hands to grip her hips, position her for him, a stallion readying his mare.

Every cell in her body woke up and opened to him. She felt as if she were at the bottom of some deep ocean, far from land. The air was thick and hot, with a weight of its own.

He mounted her. There was no other word for it as he covered her. His hard, rough hands pulled her hips up higher, powerful hairy thighs parted her legs and he entered her with a thrust that jolted her, and started moving immediately in her. He usually hesitated slightly before entering her, testing to see if she was ready. He was very large and she'd appreciated his thoughtfulness, aware at all times that he treated her with delicacy and tenderness. He always entered her slowly and usually stopped for a moment after entering fully, allowing her time to adjust. Always the perfect gentleman.

Not now.

Douglas clearly wasn't thinking about his size or her readiness. Now he was a pure male in rut, his thrusts so hard they lifted her and propelled her forward. She needed her outstretched hands to brace herself against the bedstead. Low, harsh sounds came from him, from deep in his chest, in time with the squeaking of the bedsprings, as he worked her mercilessly, hard and fast.

It didn't hurt, not even a little. Douglas' transformation from gentle lover to out-of-control male excited her on a deep level, in a way she'd never felt before. She had no idea this was in her — this intense excitement at being...taken. It was pure animal lust — Douglas grunting over her body, pistoning in and out of her in long, hard thrusts, the smell of sweat and sex surrounding them like a fog.

Prickles of heat raced over her spine, she felt her face burn, droplets of sweat fell off her face onto the sheets. Douglas' fingers tightened and he positioned her even higher, moving so close she could feel the wiry short pubic hairs rasping against her smooth inner thighs. He began a series of short, hard thrusts that stretched her inside, reaching around her, touching her...*there.*

Oh God!

With a wild cry, Allegra erupted, her whole body exploding in a flash of heat. She shook with the force of her contractions, feeling herself tighten around Douglas' penis so strongly it was a miracle he could still move. His thrusts speeded up, wild, almost out of control, low moans torn from his throat as he loved her through her orgasm. And the next. Impossibly, as soon as her contractions started dying down, Douglas did something, changed the angle of his entry, and she climaxed all over again, in sharp, almost painful pulses of her vagina.

That one set him off. He started thrusting even harder, even faster, a low animal growl coming from him. She felt him swell inside her until he exploded with a huge shout, shooting jets of semen in her so hard she could feel every pulse. He was no longer pumping in her, but grinding, buried in her as far as he could go. They froze for a moment, Douglas deep inside her, while she lost contact with her senses, every circuit on overload.

With a groan, Douglas toppled forward, his heavy body crushing her to the mattress. They lay there panting for long minutes.

Allegra slowly regained her senses. Douglas was so heavy on her she had to work to expand her lungs enough to breathe. She couldn't ask him to move because she could feel him still shuddering above her, breathing heavily. She could feel his hard chest muscles bellowing as he caught his breath. If he felt anything like her, his muscles were like water. He was still inside her, his penis still hard, though not steel-hard like before, his hands covering hers, head next to hers on the bed.

They were covered in sweat, his and hers, plastering them together. Her entire groin area was wet with semen, as was the sheet below her. Crazily, it wasn't unpleasant. Sex was an animal pleasure as well, she now realized. She liked the tenderness, but there was something wild and real and primitive about the kind of sex they'd just had, too.

Her breathing slowed and she drifted...

"Oh, *God*," Douglas moaned. "I think I just died."

She would have reassured him that he was still very much alive, but who had the energy?

Douglas groaned heavily and rolled off her, allowing her to pull in a deep breath now that her lungs could expand. His hand touched her back, his touch now gentle again, almost tentative.

He was back.

"Are you okay?"

She didn't have the energy to respond.

"Allegra?" The deep voice sounded worried. He shook her gently. "Allegra, did I hurt you? Are you all right?"

She wriggled her toes and fingers. They worked, so she was probably still alive. Talking required too much energy, so she nodded her head once and murmured, "Mmm-hmm." Saying *I'm okay* would have taken too much effort.

"Wow, that was *intense*. I thought I was going to have a heart attack."

"Mmm-pphhh." Now that breathing was easier, she did some more of it, drifting lightly…

"Wow." Douglas sat up in bed, the springs protesting, jolting her awake. He clapped his hands once. "I feel great. Boy, am I *hungry*. I think we'll have some more of those cornetti the Mancinos made. And that whole-wheat bread. Maybe make a few pancakes."

Food? He was thinking about *food?* Allegra found breathing to be about the extent her abilities. "Mmm."

He slapped her lightly on the butt. "Get up lazybones. I'm taking a quick shower now and I'll fix breakfast while you have your own shower. Come on now, I've got to get to work."

He wanted her to get *up?* No way. She shook her head on the pillow, using up the last of her energy reserves.

He kissed her shoulder. "I want to have breakfast with you and I want to tell you what I'm going to do during the day and I want you to walk me to the door and I want to kiss you goodbye."

Well, that was clear. Without shifting her head on the pillow, she said, "I'll do that if you shout out 'Honey, I'm home' when you come back."

"Deal."

Allegra smiled and didn't move.

"Come on, honey." The beast simply lifted her up until she was sitting with her back against the headboard, forcing her to come completely awake. He lifted her hand to his lips. "I want us to have breakfast together. Don't make me eat alone, okay?"

This was unfair. She sighed and opened her eyes. "You're cooking?"

"Absolutely." He sounded insanely cheerful. "It'll all be ready by the time you get out of your shower."

And it was.

When she stopped at the entrance to the kitchen, hand out, she smiled when she touched his arm. The smells were delicious and she suddenly found she was voracious. Sex as an appetite stimulant. Now there was a new thought.

"Everything smells wonderful."

"Wait until you taste it."

"So you've already started without me?"

"Couldn't wait." He sounded sheepish. "I was starving. You're going to have to work to catch up with me."

Douglas walked her to the table, sat her down. She could hear him pouring liquid. "Coffee at eleven o'clock bravo red."

She found it immediately and sipped. Wonderful.

He touched her knee and she turned to him. "I'm going to work through the day and see if I can come home early. Maybe we could go for another walk this afternoon if it's not too cold, what do you say?"

Oh yeah. What could be better than looking forward to a walk? "I'd love that. Thanks."

He held her hand. "And then…I was thinking maybe I could get tickets for the Bach concert on Thursday, would you like that? They say this new pianist, what's his name? Orloff— is great. And then maybe we could go for a bite to eat afterwards. There's that new French restaurant near the concert hall. Maybe you'd like to go there?"

"I think I'd prefer Italian. And I'd love to go to the concert. I've been wanting to go ever since I heard about it."

"Italian it is. I'll ask around for a nice restaurant and I'll order the concert tickets today." She felt him coming closer, and he kissed her on the cheek. "See how nice it is to have breakfast together? I wouldn't want to miss this."

Suddenly, it was clear to Allegra why he'd insisted that they have breakfast together. He was setting up a routine for them, habits they could forge together. He was creating a life for them. Well, wild monkey sex followed by a wonderful breakfast and plans for a walk and a concert was certainly a routine she could get used to.

She breathed in deeply. This was just so *wonderful*. Before Douglas, mornings had been sad and difficult. She usually slept badly and woke up tired, feeling dull and lonely. When she finally managed breakfast, her morning coffee sat acidly in her stomach without waking her up. She knew she had the whole day to get through, in darkness and silence, until night fell, with only another restless night to look forward to.

Nothing like now, with the prospect of a walk with Douglas in the afternoon, dinner together, sleeping with him, waking up with him. Today she just knew she'd finish writing her song, "New Love," and get in some good practice sessions. She actually looked forward to today.

She held her hand out and smiled as he fitted his arm to it. "Thank you," she said softly.

"For what?" He sounded genuinely puzzled.

"For...for breakfast. For wanting to take me for a walk and to a concert. For being here." She leaned forward, hoping she was hitting his face, and planted a soft kiss on his jaw, right on his scar. "For being you."

He cleared his throat. "My pleasure, honey, believe me." He lifted her hand to his lips and sighed. "I have to go now, if I want to get—oh!"

"What?"

"Almost forgot." He left her and came back immediately. He slipped something over her head, lifting her hair so it could rest around her neck. She touched it. A necklace with a long, cylindrical pendant, only it felt somehow different from most necklaces.

"What's this?"

"I got it yesterday. It's a signaling device. Look." Douglas fitted her hand to the tip of the pendant. It was concave, warm to the touch. "It's connected to a receiving device. If you press this," he pressed down lightly on her finger and placed her other hand on something that felt like a cell phone or a remote control, "this vibrates. Or emits a whistle, depending on the setting. This is what receives the signal. It's got a display connected to a GPS unit, so I always know where the signal comes from."

He sounded excited, and Allegra realized one more thing about her Douglas. He loved gadgets. He was such a...a *guy*.

Allegra fingered it, wondering what it looked like. "It's...nice. Thank you."

Douglas chuckled. "Well, it's not a gold necklace or a piece of jewelry. I'll get you something like that some other time. This is something different. It's to call me if you need help. Here, I'll show you. Press this—" He took her hand, fitting her fingertip against the tip of the pendant. He pressed hard on her finger until she felt a click and Allegra jumped as a sharp whistling sound filled the air. "That's for when I'm in the car. If I'm at work or in a meeting, it does this," the device that felt like a remote control hummed and vibrated. "If you need anything, anything at all, if you hear something that scares you, if you need me in any way, I want you to press this pendant and call me."

Allegra fingered the necklace, touched that he'd thought of this.

"Honey?" She turned to him. "Do you understand me? I want you to use this if you need me in any way at all. Will you promise me that?"

Tears rose to her eyes and she bit her lip.

"Talk to me." He shook her shoulders gently. "I'm not leaving unless you promise me that you will press that button if you need me. I'll come as quickly as I can. Now promise me."

She swallowed. "I promise."

"Good girl." He kissed her swiftly, a warm peck on the cheek. "I gotta run now. So what do you do?"

Allegra smiled. "I walk you to the door and say have a nice day, come home soon."

"That's my girl. And what do you do if you need me?"

"Press the button."

"Very good."

They were at the door. She heard the rustle of clothing as he put on his coat. Instinctively, she reached out to him and he folded her hands in his, lifting her fingers to his lips.

She hated to have him leave. But he'd be back this evening. She knew this like she knew the sun would rise in the east tomorrow morning.

"Have a nice day," she said softly.

"Better believe it," Douglas said cheerfully. "I'll come home as soon as I can and we'll go for that walk if the weather holds, okay?"

Allegra smiled. "Okay."

Another kiss and he was gone, whistling off-tune.

Allegra closed the door behind him, smiling.

Douglas left a presence behind in the house. It didn't feel as empty or as cold as it usually did in the mornings. Maybe it had something to do with the fact that she knew he'd be coming back in the evening. And the evening after that. And the evening after that…

There'd be long walks, and dinners together, and concerts and…well, fantastic sex.

Oh, yeah.

Humming, she moved toward Dagda.

What a wonderful thing a new love was, she reflected. This secret excitement, this bright anticipation. *That* was what was missing from her new song. That sense of excitement and brightness. "New Love" was too slow. She'd speed up the beat, add a few riffs to the refrain, maybe the notes at the end could simulate a heartbeat...

What was that?

It sounded like the kitchen door closing. But she hadn't opened it. Had Douglas left the door open? It wasn't like him. She turned to the kitchen and froze when she heard a man's voice.

"A bitch like you needs to be punished. I'll see to that."

It was Corey Sanderson's voice. But Corey was in prison. She needed to get a grip.

"You're not real, Corey." Allegra whispered, as she turned in a circle, heart pounding. "You're not here. You're nothing. You're a figment of my imagination."

She gasped then screamed as a hand fisted in her hair and pulled so hard tears sprang in her eyes.

"You're right, pretty girl, Corey's not here," a male voice she'd never heard before growled, "but I am. And I'm going to kill you."

Kowalski was arranging his day in his head as he drove to the office. If he skipped lunch and got his paperwork out of the way by 2:00, he could spend a couple of hours on the McBain contract and then get home by maybe 4:30. Plenty of time to—

Kowalski's heart nearly stopped at the sharp noise coming from his coat pocket. Not the cell phone. It was a shrill whistle, coming from Allegra's signaling device, and it could only mean one thing—Allegra was in trouble.

Kowalski had bought the system in a medical supplies shop and it was intended for invalids and the elderly. It was designed so it couldn't go off by mistake. If it went off, Allegra was calling him for help. And if she wasn't phoning him, but pressing the signaling device, it meant she had an emergency.

There were lots of emergencies for a blind woman. Horrible ones. She could be burning, bleeding, dying…

Kowalski lost it, totally.

He was a hard man trained to deal with hard situations. He never panicked and he always thought situations through. But now he simply lost it. All his training, all his experience was totally forgotten as he rammed his way through an illegal U-turn in the middle of a busy highway and broke speed records racing back toward Allegra's house.

He could barely see to drive. Visions of Allegra catching fire, of Allegra pouring boiling water over herself, of Allegra falling onto the glass coffee table, a sharp shard cutting an artery, bleeding out…these images and others even more gruesome filled his head, lit it up with panic, so that at the end he was driving hunched over the steering wheel, as if he could actually will his vehicle to go faster. He was topping a hundred as it was, leaving behind a wake of angry, honking vehicles.

He didn't even notice.

He didn't pay attention to anyone else on the road, to the traffic lights or to the ice-slicked streets. He used every ounce of driving knowledge he possessed to keep the heavy vehicle steady, playing the brakes and the accelerator, going at maximum speed.

And when he braked in front of Allegra's house, Kowalski forgot twenty years of training in his terror and panic. He'd drilled into his men's heads over and over that you scout out terrain before moving, and he forgot his own training.

Running up the little sidewalk, he jumped the porch steps in one leap and made a dynamic entry, going in blind. He'd have had the ass of the lowliest recruit who did something boneheaded like that, but Kowalski wasn't thinking—he was running on pure, wrenching terror.

Allegra burning, Allegra bleeding, Allegra dying...he couldn't think past those images and when he burst through the front door without even bothering to use the keys and saw Allegra in the brutal grasp of a tall, redheaded man with a gun to her head, he had a sudden sunburst of clarity lighting his own head, and realized he'd just sacrificed his own life and Allegra's in his panic.

A thousand thoughts ran through him, in the freaky timeless zone of a man about to die.

He thought—

Fuck! Allegra was right, she was being stalked, only not by Corey Sanderson, but by this guy.

That's the guy I saw in Lawrence Square. If only I'd believed her...

Fucker's holding a .38. He can't miss at short range. He'll take me down and then kill Allegra. She can't defend herself.

This is a stupid way to die.

I didn't keep Allegra safe.

He watched as the man brought the short snub nose of the revolver up, tracking him, and had time for one last burst of regret that he'd been so panicked over Allegra that he'd forgotten his own weapon, a Beretta that would trump the revolver any day. Shit, if he had his weapon, he could take the guy out easy, oh yeah, in a single three-shot burst. But no, the Beretta was back in the SUV, snugly and uselessly fitted into its holster, tossed onto the backseat of his vehicle.

So much regret.

The man let Allegra go. He was bringing the revolver up in a two-handed grip, dropping into a professional gunman's crouch, trigger finger tightening. The only thing Kowalski could do was feint to the right at the last split second, so the bullet took him high in the chest instead of in the heart.

He was so hyped on adrenalin he didn't hear the shot, but he felt it, a massive punch that slammed him against the wall. He slid down, legs no longer capable of holding him, his shoulder a fiery mass of pain. He breathed in deeply, his lungs filling with air. The bullet hadn't penetrated the lung, which was the good news. The bad news was he was losing blood fast and his vision was blurring.

The man took a step forward, gun still aimed at his chest. He was looking for a place to finish him off. Kowalski knew he'd go for a head shot now. Head shots in battle were hard and you always aimed for the torso. But Kowalski was a sitting duck at short range and if the guy was smart and knew what he was doing, he'd go for the killer shot—aiming for the bridge of the nose and taking out the cortex.

Kowalski scrabbled uselessly for purchase, his numb legs slipping in his own blood. He pushed his back against the wall, trying to brace himself...

Jesus — what was Allegra doing?

Kowalski met the guy's eyes, staring hard, willing the fucker to look at *him*. He didn't dare glance away, even by an inch.

Allegra felt around until her hand had encountered the wrought iron lamp next to the couch. She silently pulled the plug and hefted it, waiting for the man to make a noise. She was going to try to take the man down with a lamp base! Kowalski groaned at her courage. If she missed, the guy would simply turn around, nail her, then turn back to Kowalski.

Kowalski realized that they had this one chance at taking the intruder down. Kowalski might not survive his wound, but Allegra would. She had to.

Kowalski would do whatever it took to help her. He glared at the man, holding his gaze, watching Allegra with his peripheral vision. She hefted the lamp, gliding forward. There was utter silence as the man lifted his gun. Allegra couldn't hear where he was, she was going to swing the lamp and miss him. She drew her arms back...

Kowalski stared down the barrel of the revolver as the man's trigger finger tightened...

"Charlie, green, three o'clock!" Kowalski shouted.

Allegra swiveled, swung and connected, catching the guy full in the head. He went down like a rock, spouting blood.

"Douglas!" Allegra slid on her knees to him, crying and shaking. "Douglas, oh my God. Oh my darling, tell me you're alive." Her hands reached out to him, crying even harder when her right hand touched blood.

Kowalski touched her face, leaving bloody prints, memorizing those lovely features. He was fading fast. He wanted her face to be the last thing he saw in this life.

"Allegra," he rasped, then coughed. "God, I—I love you."

"Yes, me darlin'," she whispered back, Ireland in her voice. "I love you, too. So don't you dare die on me, Douglas Kowalski, or I swear I will haunt your grave! Do you hear me, man? You live, you hear? Live for me!"

He smiled and coughed. How could he deny her anything?

"Yes, ma'am. Do my best."

Epilogue
Six months later
Boston Eye Clinic

She was so still, her face as white as the hospital sheets, her bald skull wrapped in bandages, a plastic oxygen mask over mouth and nose.

Breathing. Alive.

Allegra was alive, and that was what mattered to Kowalski. She'd survived the operation. Now he hoped, desperately, for her sake, that it had been successful. Allegra so wanted to see again.

Allegra couldn't get it into her head that Kowalski didn't mind her being blind, didn't mind caring for her. How could he? He loved her. Caring for her, making sure she had what she needed, was a privilege.

He gently smoothed a finger down her soft cheek, watching her eyelids flutter. Soon she'd be coming out of the anesthesia.

His heavy, broad wedding band caught and reflected the harsh neon hospital light. He pulled Allegra's wedding band out of his pocket and slipped it onto the ring finger of her left hand.

She hadn't said a word when they'd cut all her glorious hair off and shaved her head, but she'd balked at taking her wedding band off. All her Irish temper had come to the fore as Allegra and the doctors butted heads. No jewelry was allowed in an operating theater. And Allegra had taken a solemn vow never to remove her ring.

It had taken all Kowalski's diplomatic skills to head off disaster. He'd promised Allegra that when she woke, her ring would be back on her hand.

Allegra's eyelids fluttered again and she sighed softly into the mask.

Kowalski had finally broken down and agreed to the operation, not that he had any choice—Allegra was hell-bent on it. She wanted children, and refused to be a blind mother, unable to see her child's face. That was what secretly tipped Kowalski. A child. His child and Allegra's. Once he had a vision in his head of a little girl, a tiny redheaded replica of Allegra, it was impossible to shake it. And so he'd reluctantly agreed to accompany her cross-country to the clinic that had pioneered the operation to rid her of the blood clot and restore her sight. It had taken a lot to convince him, but the operation so far had worked in 100 percent of the cases and he'd researched the surgical team thoroughly. They knew what they were doing.

Allegra moaned lightly and her eyes opened for just a moment, then closed again.

Kowalski leaned in toward her, wincing at the sudden stab of pain. His shoulder still wasn't healed completely. He ignored the pain and watched Allegra's beloved face.

He'd nearly lost her six months ago and he counted each second with her a little miracle.

It had been easy enough to piece together the story. The redheaded man's name was Alvin Mitchell, a rock star wannabe who'd fallen under Corey Sanderson's spell. Sanderson had promised him wealth and fame if he'd drive Allegra crazy and then fake her suicide.

Kowalski had gotten word to Mitchell in prison that if he so much as ever came within ten miles of Allegra again, he would regret it. The warning had teeth, too. Corey Sanderson hadn't lived long enough for another trial for conspiracy to murder. He'd been shuttled right back into the prison system and two days later, a felon stabbed him to death with a shiv made from a sharpened spoon.

Kowalski smiled coldly. It was the best fifty thousand he'd ever spent. No one would ever threaten Allegra again.

She stirred again, moving her legs restlessly, coming up from the anesthesia.

Kowalski bent over her, holding the hand that wasn't connected to the IV tube.

The next few moments were crucial. If the operation wasn't successful, if she couldn't see, she'd be grief-stricken. No matter what, Kowalski would be there to comfort her.

If it *was* successful, then she'd see…him.

What would she see?

He'd taken a good look at himself in the shaving mirror this morning and had groaned. He was even uglier than before. His wound and worry for Allegra had carved deeper lines in his face then ever. Nothing had changed, except for the worse. He still looked like a thug—an ugly thug with misshapen features.

"Doug…" Allegra's voice was a croak, muffled by the sheer plastic oxygen mask. She licked her dry lips, breathing rapidly.

"I'm here, honey." He leaned closer.

"Douglas." The word came out more clearly.

"Yeah."

Her breathing calmed. He was wondering how long it would take her to become fully conscious, when suddenly her eyes opened wide.

She had such beautiful eyes. Luminous, long-lashed. Beautiful, green Irish eyes.

Focused eyes.

She could *see.*

Oh, God.

Kowalski didn't even have time to panic. Allegra reached out and cupped his face lovingly. Her fingers touched his weather-beaten skin, ran over the scar, traced his lips, touched his battered nose. Her eyes examined every inch of his face, her expressions solemn.

Suddenly, she smiled.

"Oh Douglas," she murmured. "I knew it. I just knew you'd be a beautiful man."

The End

Enjoy an excerpt from:
Midnight Man

Chapter One
December 21st
Portland, Oregon

&

She's scared of me, he thought.

Damn right.

Seven hours ago, he'd killed two men and wounded four others. Death and violence clung to him like a shroud. He was still wired from the kill, blood pumping.

Which might be why ever since crossing the threshold of Suzanne Barron's office, he couldn't think of anything but bedding the damned woman.

John Huntington eyed Suzanne Barron across her very stylish desk in her very stylish office. She was stylish herself: classy, elegant, stunningly beautiful. Smooth, creamy ivory skin, dark blonde hair, gray eyes like a pool of still mountain water, watching him warily.

"So, Mr. Huntington, you didn't say in your email exactly what your business is."

The way she was looking at him, if he'd said 'bear hunting and cannibalism' she just might believe him.

In the corporate world he was a wolf carefully dressed in the sheep's clothing of pencil pushers—Brioni and Armani. It took a while to see the kind of man he was and some people never managed until it was too late.

But right now, just in from Venezuela, he looked like the wolf he was. In black leather jacket, black turtleneck sweater, black jeans and combat boots, adrenaline still coursing through his system, he wasn't anyone pretty Ms. Barron would or should want in her building. Especially since–he'd seen the signs–she lived alone.

She was already leery of him and she didn't even know about the Sig-Sauer in the shoulder holster, the K-bar knife in the scabbard between his shoulder blades or the .22 in the ankle holster, otherwise she would have probably ordered him out of the building.

She watched him, anxiety clouding luminous eyes.

He was coming down off an adrenaline high. The consulting job teaching soft oil executives in Venezuela how to deal with a hard world had gone very bad very fast. A small army of Frente de la Libertad terrorists had come down from the hills and tried to kidnap the entire top management of Western Oil Corporation there on a junket.

Luckily he'd been on the spot and had routed them, taking down three tangos and wounding four. The rest had been mopped up by the local police.

John had been flown back up Stateside in the grateful CEO's private Learjet, with a contract to provide security for Western Oil worldwide until the end of time and a $300,000 bonus check in his pocket, just in time for his appointment with the gorgeous Ms. Suzanne Barron.

Time to convince her that he wasn't dangerous. He was, but not to her.

"I own and run my own company, Alpha Security International, Ms. Barron. I have an office just off Pioneer Square, but my company is expanding quickly and I need new premises. There's plenty of space here."

John looked around her office. He hadn't been expecting anything like this. The ad in The Oregonian had simply stated the footage and the location, in Pearl, a rough part of town slowly gentrifying. Outside was a wasteland. Walking through the front door of the two-story brick building had been like walking into a little slice of heaven.

And the four interconnected rooms she'd showed him–it was as if they'd been fashioned for him. Large, spacious, high ceilinged. The smell of new wood and old brick, so completely different from the modern crapola suite he'd rented in an expensive high rise off Pioneer Square.

Inside, the building felt like an exquisite jewel with its brass fittings, light hardwood floors and soft pastel furniture. She'd put up some discreet lights to mark the holiday season and the air was spiced with the evergreen boughs on the heavy mantelpiece and what smelled like oranges and cinnamon.

Harp music that sounded as if it was being beamed down directly from heaven played softly from hidden speakers.

He'd had an instant sense of homecoming, strange in a man who'd never had a home. His nerves, still jangled from the takedown, started calming. This was exactly what he'd been looking for, without knowing he was looking for it.

Add to that the cool, luscious blonde who'd met him at the door, offering her soft, slim hand. His body, already primed for battle, had immediately become primed for sex.

Hell, since when had he become so easily distractible? In the normal course of events, gunfire couldn't distract him from a mission. Of course, gunfire wasn't a wildly attractive blonde, but his mission here was to find a new office and now that he'd seen this place, he was determined to have it. And the landlady. But first, he had to get his hormones under control; otherwise he'd come up empty-handed on both counts.

Down boy, he ordered himself.

He must be pumping hormones into the air by the ton, because she was sitting way back in her chair in an unconscious attempt to put distance between them – the thought that a desk and some air could stop him if he really wanted to jump her was so ludicrous he wanted to snort – and her eyes were so wide he could see the milky whites around the pupils.

Time to get her to climb down from that emotional ledge and reassure her that he wouldn't gobble her up.

Not yet anyway.

He studied the room, deliberately not looking at her. He kept his face bland, giving her time to study him, and heard her breathing start to slow down.

Pretending to study the room was a ploy but he soon found himself distracted by its beauty. He didn't have the tools to analyze how she did it, but he could appreciate the end result. Stunning, soft pastel colors. Comfortable furniture that managed to be both modern and feminine. She'd kept the architectural details of the period – early '20s he'd guess. Everything – every detail, every nook and cranny, every object – was gorgeous.

She'd had enough time to calm down so he turned back to her.

"Did you do the restoration work, Ms. Barron?"

The question relaxed her. She looked around, a smile curving soft pale pink lips. It was raining outside. The dim water-washed light coming in through the tall windows turned her skin the color of the mother of pearl bowl holding some kind of fragrant plant on the windowsill.

"Yes. I inherited the building from my grandparents. It used to be a shoe factory but the company went bankrupt 20 years ago and has stood empty ever since. I'm a designer and I decided to restore it myself instead of selling it."

"You did a wonderful job."

Her eyes rose to meet his. She stared at him and her breath came out in a little huff. "Thank you."

She toyed for a moment with a pen, tapping it lightly against the highly polished surface of the desk. Realizing she was betraying nerves, she put it down again. Her hands were as lovely as the rest of her, slim and white. She had two expensive-looking rings on her right hand, no rings on the left.

Good. No other man had her and now that he'd spotted her, no other man was going to get her. Not until he'd finished with her and that was going to take a long, long time.

Her hands were trembling slightly.

Suzanne Barron might be one of the loveliest women he'd ever seen but reduced to essentials she was an animal—a human animal—and she could sense, probably smell, the danger in him, especially acute now.

He'd always had this effect on civilians. Well, he reminded himself, he was a civilian now, too. He wasn't in the service anymore where he could be instantly recognized for what he was.

All his life he'd lived in a fraternity of like-minded men, friend or foe. Fellow warriors knew who he was and usually treaded lightly around him.

Civilians never knew how to cope, like lambs sensing a tiger had infiltrated the flock. Uneasy without knowing why.

Moving slowly so as not to alarm her, he reached across and handed her a folder. His hand briefly touched hers. It was like touching silk. Gray eyes widened at the touch and he withdrew.

She rested her hand on the cover sheet. A small furrow developed between curved ash eyebrows.

"What's this, Mr. Huntington?"

"References, Ms. Barron. My CV, service record, credit rating from my bank, three letters of recommendation, and a list of the major clients of my company." He smiled. "I'm honest, pay my taxes, I'm solvent and practice good hygiene."

"I don't doubt any of that, Mr. Huntington."

A thin line appeared between her brows as she leafed through the folder. He kept still, moving only his lungs, a trick he'd learned on the battlefield.

"What do you mean by service—Oh." She looked up. Something moved in her eyes. "You're a Commander. An officer in the Army." He could see her relaxing faintly. An officer seemed safe to her. She couldn't know what he'd done in the service; otherwise she sure as hell wouldn't be relaxing.

"Was an officer. My discharge papers are in there, too. And I was in the Navy." He tried to keep the scorn out of his voice and barely restrained himself from snorting. Army indeed. Candy-ass soldiers, all of them. "It's not the same thing."

Her smile deepened. She was softening. Good. John was good at reading body language. The lease was a done deal. She relaxed as she read his service record.

The record mentioned some of his medals, enough to impress a civilian. The rest–for missions no one would ever know about–were in his shadowbox.

The list of clients didn't hurt, either. He had more than a few Fortune 500 companies in there.

She now knew he wasn't going to get drunk and disorderly. He wasn't going to skip town without paying the rent. He wasn't going to make off with her silver. Which was something, since she had a lot of it in here, mostly in the form of antique silver frames and a collection of tea services. Everything in his file said he was a sober highly respected citizen.

What the file didn't mention was that before becoming an officer he'd been a trained sniper-scout, with a certified kill at 2500 yards. That he knew 45 different ways of killing a man with his bare hands. That he could blow up her building with what was under her kitchen sink, and that by this time tomorrow night he'd be in her bed, in her.

"Navy. Navy officer. Sorry. Should I call you Commander Huntington or Mister Huntington?"

"John would do nicely, ma'am. I'm retired."

"John. I'm Suzanne." A lull in the rain outside created a little oasis of quiet in the room.

All his senses were keen. He could hear the breath soughing in and out of her lungs, the slick sound of nylon as she recrossed her legs under the desk.

He had a view only of the delicate ankles but he knew they were attached to long, slender legs. He could just feel her thighs around his waist, calves hugging his hips hips…

"I beg your pardon?" She'd said something and he'd been so busy fantasizing getting her into bed he'd missed it.

John shifted, uncomfortably aware that it had been over six months since he'd last had sex. He'd just been too damned busy with getting his company up and running. Their gazes met and held.

"You'll want to call the people on that list." He kept his voice low, calm, unthreatening.

"I will, yes." She drew in a deep breath. "Well, um..." She turned a ring nervously around her finger. "So. I guess - I guess you'll be my new tenant. My first. You can do whatever you want in the rental. Though I'd rather you didn't knock down any walls."

"I could never in a million years do as good a job as you did decorating your office. I might just hire you to do mine."

"Actually, um..." Her pale skin turned the most delicate, delightful pink. She reached behind her for a file. She opened it and turned it around so he could see it. "While designing this office, I fiddled with a few ideas for the rental. I used a different color scheme, made it more..." She looked up at him through thick lashes - "more masculine." John moved his chair forward. His senses were so heightened that he could smell her skin. Some mixture of lotion and perfume and warm woman. She was blushing furiously now under his intense scrutiny.

John wrenched his gaze back to the drawings she had fanned out on the desktop, and then he focused in on what he was seeing.

Amazing.

"This is wonderful," he breathed. He studied each sheet carefully. She'd used unusual tones—dark gray and cream and a funny blue—to create a sleek, modern environment. Practical, comfortable, refined. It was as if she had walked around inside his head to pull out exactly what he wanted without him knowing he wanted it. "Elegant, but understated. I really like the beige ceiling with the blue thingies."

"Ecru." She smiled.

"I beg your pardon?"

"I'm sure you have technical terms in your business, Commander Huntington—John. Just as I have them in mine. The colors are slate, ecru and teal, not gray, beige and blue. And the blue thingies are stencils." She pushed the drawings across the desk to him. "Keep these. You're welcome to them. And if you need any help in getting the furnishings, let me know. Nothing in my design is custom-made. You could buy everything immediately. I'd be happy to help. I get a professional discount at all the major retailers. "

"That's very generous of you. Would you be willing to design living quarters for me, too? For a fee, of course."

She drew in a quick breath. "Living quarters? You want – you want to live here, too?"

"Mm. There's plenty of space. Those three big back rooms would be more than enough for me. I keep odd hours in my business and I need to be close to the office. This would suit me fine. Now I want you to call some of the people on the list on page two."

"I beg your pardon?" When she shifted in her chair, some floral scent wafted his way. His nostrils flared to take it in.

"I've provided five people as character references. Call them. Call them before we sign the lease. We can do that tomorrow."

"I'm sure that won't be necessary, Comm – John."

"It's absolutely necessary, Suzanne." He looked around then brought his gaze back to her. "This is a beautiful space and you've done a great job renovating the building, but we're in a rough neighborhood."

It was one of the reasons he wanted his corporate headquarters here. He sometimes hired people who had looked wildly out of place in the prissy downtown building. Like Jacko, with his pierced nostrils and the viper tats.

"If you're going to be alone in a building with a man, you need to know who he is and that you're safe with him." His eyes bored into hers. "You'll be safe with me."

But not from me, he thought.

"I guess you're the expert." She blew out a little breath.

"Yes, ma'am. You'll call?"

Her eyes dropped to the paper. "Of course, if you want me to. You have an impressive list of references. Wait. Lieutenant Tyler Morrison, Portland Police Department. You know him?"

"Bud? Sure. We were in the service together. Then he quit and became a cop. Call him. And one more thing before I sign. What's your security system?"

"Security system? You mean like the alarm system? Let me check." She opened a Filofax and started poring over the pages with a tapered, pink-tipped finger. "I don't remember off-hand, but I know it was expensive. Ah, here we are. Interlock. Do you know them? Oh, how stupid of me. Of course you do, security is your business."

"I deal in personal security, not building security, but I know them." Interlock was a crappy outfit. They'd have snowed her with fancy alarms and 7 digit codes and their equipment could have come out of a cereal box. No freakin' way was he going to live and work in a building secured by Interlock. He stood up. "I'd appreciate it if you were to secure the alarms after I leave."

"I - okay." She stood up too; looking puzzled, and walked around the desk. "If you really want me to. I tend to just have the door locked during the day because it's so fussy putting on the alarm system then switching it off when I want to go out. So...I guess we have a deal?"

"You bet."

He stuck out his hand. After a second's hesitation, she offered hers. It was almost half the size of his, slim and fine-boned. He carefully applied a little pressure and ordered himself to let go. It was damned hard to do. What he wanted to do was pull her into his arms and take her down to the floor.

Some of that must have been coming through because her eyes widened in alarm. He stepped back.

"I'll start moving my stuff in tomorrow. And I'll definitely be taking you up on your offer to help me decorate. Of course I'd like to pay for the design of my office. I can see that a lot of work went into it."

She waved that away. "No, don't worry. I was just doodling. Consider the design a welcome present." She turned into the hallway and he followed, trying not to ogle her backside and trying not to be obvious about smelling the air in her wake. His men said he had the sense of smell of a bloodhound. He could smell cigarette smoke on a man's clothes a day after he'd smoked. Suzanne Barron's smell nearly brought him to his knees.

Her scent was perfume, something light and floral, mixed in with an apple-scented shampoo, the smell of freshly washed clothing and some indefinable something that he just knew was her skin. Soon, very soon, he'd be smelling her skin close up. Just a matter of time.

The sooner the better. Christ, the view from the back was as enticing as the one from the front — sleek curves, dark-honey hair bouncing with every step she took.

He'd never seen a woman as curvy yet as delicately made as Suzanne Barron. Everything about her was dainty, fine-boned. He was going to have to be careful. No rough sex when he took her to bed. He'd have to enter her slowly, let her get used to him before...

She turned and smiled at him. "That's all right, then."

All right! His eyes narrowed and his body quickened until he stopped himself just short of reaching for her. She's talking about the lease, you idiot, he told himself.

"I'll get a contract drawn up and have a copy of the keys made for you. When do you want to start moving in?"

Now! His body clamored. Right this second. But he had things to take care of. "I'll probably move some of my gear in tomorrow morning. I don't have much. Mostly filing cabinets and computer equipment. Lots of that." He smiled into her eyes. "You're going to order the rest of the furnishings for me, right? Spend whatever you have to, I'll be good for it."

She was looking up at him, breathing slowly.

"Right, Suzanne?"

She blinked and seemed to come out of a daze. "Oh, yes, um, that's right. And I'll have a copy of the keys made for you."

He opened the door. The contrast between what was behind him–a delicate lady in a jewel of a building–and what was in front of him–bleak burned out storefronts, liquor stores and empty lots–made him turn back to her. Little Miss Muffet had to know that there were spiders out there. Big bad ones.

"Check me out, Suzanne. Make sure you know whom you're putting in your house. Call Bud. Call him now."

Pale pink lips slightly parted, gray eyes wide, she stared at him. "Okay, I…" She swallowed. "I will."

"And set the security system when I leave."

She nodded, her eyes never leaving his face.

"Do you know the seven digit code by heart?"

"How do you –? All right, no I don't."

"Start getting used to keeping the building secure. Learn the code by heart. I'll bet you keep the code on a piece of paper taped to the underside of your desk. You're right-handed so it's probably taped to the right side."

She blew out a little breath and nodded. Bingo.

"That's not good. From now on keep the code in a safe and memorize it. You've got a security system, so use it. I want this building locked down after I leave."

"Yessir, Commander, sir." A dimple twinkled then disappeared. "Or would that be aye aye?"

"The correct answer is – yes, I'll do exactly as you say."

She was so close he could have seen the pores in her skin if she'd had any. Instead, her skin was as smooth and perfect as marble, except soft and warm, he'd bet. He had one foot out the door, stepping from one world into another. He had to force himself to move.

"Lock the door, Suzanne," he said again as he crossed the threshold, pulling on the handle.

He waited patiently on the steps until he heard the distinctive whump-ding of the Interlock security alarm going on then walked down the steps into the rainy morning...

Why an electronic book?

We live in the Information Age—an exciting time in the history of human civilization, in which technology rules supreme and continues to progress in leaps and bounds every minute of every day. For a multitude of reasons, more and more avid literary fans are opting to purchase e-books instead of paper books. The question from those not yet initiated into the world of electronic reading is simply: *Why?*

1. *Price.* An electronic title at Ellora's Cave Publishing and Cerridwen Press runs anywhere from 40% to 75% less than the cover price of the exact same title in paperback format. Why? Basic mathematics and cost. It is less expensive to publish an e-book (no paper and printing, no warehousing and shipping) than it is to publish a paperback, so the savings are passed along to the consumer.

2. *Space.* Running out of room in your house for your books? That is one worry you will never have with electronic books. For a low one-time cost, you can purchase a handheld device specifically designed for e-reading. Many e-readers have large, convenient screens for viewing. Better yet, hundreds of titles can

be stored within your new library—on a single microchip. There are a variety of e-readers from different manufacturers. You can also read e-books on your PC or laptop computer. (Please note that Ellora's Cave does not endorse any specific brands. You can check our websites at www.ellorascave.com or www.cerridwenpress.com for information we make available to new consumers.)

3. *Mobility.* Because your new e-library consists of only a microchip within a small, easily transportable e-reader, your entire cache of books can be taken with you wherever you go.

4. *Personal Viewing Preferences.* Are the words you are currently reading too small? Too large? Too... ANNOYING? Paperback books cannot be modified according to personal preferences, but e-books can.

5. *Instant Gratification.* Is it the middle of the night and all the bookstores near you are closed? Are you tired of waiting days, sometimes weeks, for bookstores to ship the novels you bought? Ellora's Cave Publishing sells instantaneous downloads twenty-four hours a day, seven days a week, every day of the year. Our webstore is never closed. Our e-book delivery system is 100% automated, meaning your order is filled as soon as you pay for it.

Those are a few of the top reasons why electronic books are replacing paperbacks for many avid readers.

As always, Ellora's Cave and Cerridwen Press welcome your questions and comments. We invite you to email us at Comments@ellorascave.com or write to us directly at Ellora's Cave Publishing Inc., 1056 Home Avenue, Akron, OH 44310-3502.

erridwen, the Celtic Goddess of wisdom, was the muse who brought inspiration to storytellers and those in the creative arts. Cerridwen Press encompasses the best and most innovative stories in all genres of today's fiction. Visit our site and discover the newest titles by talented authors who still get inspired - much like the ancient storytellers did, once upon a time.

Cerridwen Press

www.cerridwenpress.com

LaVergne, TN USA
01 October 2010
199258LV00002B/77/P